CARRONADE

Carronade

A Jaco Jacinto Age of Sail Novel

by

Marc Liebman

www.penmorepress.com

Carronade by Marc Liebman

This is a work of historical fiction. While based upon historical events, any similarity to any person, circumstance or event is purely coincidental and related to the efforts of the author to portray the characters in historically accurate representations.

ISBN-978-1-950586-89-9(Paperback)
ISBN 978-1-950586-90-5(e-book)

BISAC Subject Headings:
FIC014000FICTION / Historical
FIC032000FICTION / War & Military
FIC047000FICTION / Sea Stories

Editor: Chris Wozney
The Book Cover Whisperer:
ProfessionalBookCoverDesign.com
Address all correspondence to:

Penmore Press,
920 N Javelina Pl,
Tucson, AZ 85737

or visit our website at:
www.penmorepress.com

Other Books by Marc Liebman

The Josh Haman Series

Cherubs 2

Big Mother 40

Render Harmless

Forgotten

Inner Look

Moscow Airlift

The Simushir Island Incident

The Jaco Jacinto Age of Sail Series

Raider of the Scottish Coast

Carronade

The Derek Almer Series

Flight of the Pawnee

TABLE OF CONTENTS

CARRONADE

A carronade is a short-barreled muzzle loading cannon designed to shoot a heavy cannon ball. The gun was initially designed as a smaller and lighter weapon than a conventional cannon with the same bore size. In tests, the Royal Navy determined that if the bore (and ball size) was enlarged, the large, heavy, relatively slow-moving ball would splinter bulwarks. Carronades became known as "smashers." After testing, the Royal Navy saw the value and began to equip merchant ships and its own vessels with carronades during the American Revolution. Carronades, thanks to their lighter weight, were mounted on the main or even the quarterdeck, replacing the smaller 6-pounders and swivel guns.

HISTORICAL BACKDROP

In June of 1778, the War for Independence by Thirteen Colonies had been raging for three years and three months and the outcome was still very much in doubt. However, the French King, Louis XVI, and his Foreign Minister, Charles Grazier, concluded the Continental Army had won enough victories to have a chance of winning independence, and saw an opportunity to recoup France's losses from the Seven Years War. France signed the Treaty of Alliance on February 6th, 1778. The British declared war on France on March 17th, 1778 right after they learned of the treaty.

At the same time, King Carlos III of Spain was deliberating whether to shift from simply assisting the rebelling colonies with arms, ammunition and safe havens for their ships to declaring outright war on England. The Dutch continued to supply the Continental Army and Navy with munitions and allowed their islands in the Caribbean to be used by American privateers and Continental Navy ships. They also loaned the Continental Congress money.

The American Revolution was also a civil war. A sizable minority of the population preferred to stay loyal to King George III and many joined the British Army. The rebellion split many families, pitting brother against brother, father against son.

In Florida, most of the citizens were pro-British. Despite both formal and informal invitations, Floridians elected not to join the rebellion. St. Augustine and Amelia Island became bases for the British Army to support their Indian allies and launch attacks in Georgia and South Carolina. Many battles were fought in the panhandle of Florida as the rebels tried to gain control of the colony.

To disrupt the economies of Georgia, North and South Carolina, and Virginia, early in the war on November 7th, 1775, John Murray, the 4th Earl or Dunmore and the Royal Governor of Virginia, declared martial law in Virginia. His proclamation promised freedom and English citizenship for slaves who joined the British Army. Dunmore's Proclamation caused many slaves to flee the plantations, which affected loyalists and rebel owners alike. On June 30th, 1779, General Clinton issued the Phillipsburg Proclamation which reinforced Murray's offer. Slaves who fled plantations were formed into units known as Black Loyalists.

In Philadelphia, the Continental Congress was struggling with managing the war while at the same time working through a governing document, which became known as the Articles of Confederation. Because the Congress couldn't levy taxes, the majority of the money to pay for the war for independence came from donations and loans from its citizens who supported the rebellion, the government's share of prize money, and loans from foreign governments.

In England, the war was becoming more and more unpopular. The British population understood war with France, but fighting Englishmen who wanted the same rights as they enjoyed was harder to understand. By 1780, the pro-war British prime minister Lord North still lead a majority in Parliament but was facing a growing opposition led by Lords Rockingham and Shelburne.

Despite a mix of wins and losses, Washington kept the Continental Army together; so the British, to use a modern term, had to honor the threat. American privateers and the fledgling Continental Navy constituted another threat.

General Clinton's strategy to quell the rebellion by crushing resistance in the northern colonies died in the fall of 1777 when Burgoyne surrendered at Saratoga. Encouraged by Loyalists in the south and reinforced with mercenaries from German duchies, Clinton decided to use Florida as a base to conquer Georgia and then South Carolina.

Slang

Throughout this novel there are common 18th century words and expressions not used today. The context of their usage should be evident in the story, but if not, here's an excellent (and my) source: *Partridge's Dictionary of Unconventional Slang, 1954 Edition,* printed by The McMillan and Company, New York.

The historical basis for Miriam Hildesheim

During the American Revolution, a woman by the name of **Abigail Minis** of Savannah, Georgia, played a significant role in keeping the guerrilla units as well as the Continental Army fed, clothed and sometimes housed. She arrived from Prussia on July 11th, 1733. After her husband died, she was left to find a way to support eight children. When the American Revolution began, Minis was in her 70s. She was arrested and jailed twice for her anti-British actives and then released. Much has been written about this woman, who lived into her mid-90s. Here are the sites of two articles to learn more about this remarkable woman.

https://georgiahistoryfestival.org/a-legacy-of-leadership-abigail-minis-family-leader-and-businesswoman/

https://jwa.org/encyclopedia/article/minis-abigail

Historical note about Curaçao and Congregation Mikvé Israel Emanuel

When *Scorpion* visits Curaçao in April of 1779, there were over 2,000 Jews on the island. Most were descendants of Spanish and Portuguese Jews who fled the Inquisition and came either from Spanish and Portuguese colonies in South America or The Netherlands. Samuel Cohen arrived in 1634. By the time Jaco Jacinto and *Scorpion* visit in 1779, about 40% of the island's population were Jews.

In 2021 the population has dwindled to about 600 individuals, but there is still a vibrant Jewish community on the island. Congregation Mikvé Israel-Emanuel is the oldest synagogue in the Americas that has been in continual existence since it was founded. The Torah, brought to the island in the mid-1650s, is still there in Curaçao and on exhibit in the museum next to the original synagogue.

Enjoy *Carronade,* another sail, errr, tale of a turbulent time when iron men manned wooden ships.

Marc Liebman

August 2021

The Frigate Scorpion

In the late 18th century, warship design was still evolving, even though the construction material—wood—and the propulsion method—wind—had not changed since the Age of Sail began at the Battle of Lepanto in 1571. When the American Revolution began, ship designers experimented with hull configurations that could give newly built ships distinct advantages over their counterparts.

In the late 1770s, two American ship designers—Joshua Humphreys and James Hackett—were coming into their own. Humphreys designed the conversion of the merchant ship *Black Prince* into the Continental Navy frigate *Alfred.* Hackett created and built *Ranger*, the frigate that John Paul Jones used to raid Scotland and capture *H.M.S. Drake.* Both men were testing ideas that were ultimately incorporated into the designs of the first generation of frigates built for the modern U.S. Navy after the American Revolution.

In 1794, Humphreys designed the frigate *Constitution. Constitution* and her sisters—*Constellation, Congress, President, United States,* and *Chesapeake*—were faster, more maneuverable, and carried heavier armament than any other comparable ship in any navy. Ton for ton, they were the best frigates ever built. Any one of these frigates was an ugly surprise to any ship that met them in battle.

Back to the fictitious *Scorpion.* Conceptually, *Scorpion* incorporates design elements that would be used by Humphreys a decade later. The 600-ton *Scorpion* is small compared to the typical fifth- and sixth-rate Royal Navy frigates, which displaced 700 tons or more. If *Scorpion* had been in the Royal Navy, based on her number of guns, the frigate would have been a sixth-rate ship-of-the-line.

There is not one factor that makes *Scorpion* unique and a formidable adversary, but five. What follows are the five elements that give *Scorpion's* captain tactical advantages in any fight with a fifth- or six-rated Royal Navy frigate.

1. Hull design

Around the time of the American Revolution, ship designers were learning how the flow around a hull affects a ship's speed. The French were the first to note that if the shipbuilder tapered the hull beginning in the middle of the vessel to a stern slightly narrower than the bow, the ship would go faster.

Other designers rightly concluded that a narrower hull was faster than a wider one. Hence *Scorpion's* beam is 28 feet, *vice* the 35 common on Royal Navy frigates of the time, and tapered slightly after the middle of the ship.

The third element is the frigate's bow. Instead of a "bluff, rounded bow" common at the time, *Scorpion* has a more pointed bow, which early in the 19th century became known as the "clipper bow."

The mythical *Scorpion* has a longer, narrower, tapered hull with a pointed bow that reduces hydrodynamic drag. The result is a hull speed—the fastest the ship can possibly go through the water—of 15 knots *vice* the 10-11 of a comparable Royal Navy fifth- or sixth-rater. While the difference between 10 and 12 knots doesn't appear to be much, the difference of two knots means *Scorpion* is 20% faster!

2. Hull construction

During the Age of Sail, most battle casualties were caused by "splinters", not by the cannon balls themselves. Balls hitting the side of the ship caused the wood to shatter into deadly shards—what we now call spall—that ripped men apart. Crews hung their rolled up hammocks in nettings inside the bulwarks to reduce the spall. This worked until the hammocks were shredded by splinters.

Shipbuilders experimented with layering wood to reduce splintering. But adding layers added complexity, weight and cost. More weight required more sail area to reach desired hull speeds and caused another problem called hogging. Unless the shipwright took specific measures to reinforce the ship's skeleton, over time the ship would sag in the middle, i.e., hog.

To prevent hogging, Humphreys used diagonal bow-to-stern stringers to strengthen the hull and resist twisting when the ship sailed at angle through the waves. Instead of using three layers of oak, Humphreys used pine in the middle to reduce weight. This is why *Constitution* and her sister ships could carry 18- and 24-pounders.

Experiments in the 18th Century, similar to those described in *Raider of the Scottish Coast,* empirically showed that the softer pine compressed when the outer layer of oak was hit. The force of impact on the outer layer of oak was dissipated over a larger area, thus absorbing the energy of the ball. The inside or third layer of oak added resistance and prevented the ball from sending splinters throughout the gun deck. The layered planking as envisioned on *Scorpion* was designed to be effective against 9- and 12-pound balls. In a fight with a ship with larger cannon firing 18-, 24-, or 32-pound balls, the planking on *Scorpion* would resist but ultimately give way from the impact of the heavier shot.

3. Weighted keel

Every ship of the 18th century carried ballast in the form of large boulders placed in the hold along the sides of the keel. Netting kept them in place so they wouldn't shift in heavy seas. This was a practical, effective, and cheap solution to keep a ship from capsizing.

The depth of most harbors make large keels on sailing warships impractical. However, if one extended the existing keel just two feet for the length of the ship and filled the void between the sides with lead, iron ingots or stones, the ship could carry much more sail on a beam reach and reduce leeway. *Scorpion* has just such a keel extension.

4. Copper bottom

Until copper sheathing was attached to wooden ship bottoms, sea worms ate the wood and vegetation hung from the bottom, reducing speed and maneuverability. Ships had to be hauled out of the water regularly and cleaned to eliminate the source of 'drag' and repair damage from sea worms.

In 1761, the Royal Navy built its first copper-bottomed ship, *H.M.S. Alarm*. Due to a lack of copper in Great Britain and the expense, the Royal Navy was slow to apply copper to the bottom of its ships even though the value—ships could remain at sea longer and retain their sailing qualities—was understood.

Copper mining began in Colonial America in the late 17th Century in Connecticut, Rhode Island, Massachusetts and Pennsylvania. By the time the American Revolution broke out, there were coppersmiths throughout the colonies. American shipbuilders and their suppliers were quick to figure out how to roll copper plates and attach them to a ship.

5. The long 12-pounder

Gun designers were aware that barrel length increased accuracy by minimizing the oscillations of the ball going down the barrel and the velocity of the projectile. By the time the American Revolution broke out, the "long nine," a 9-

pounder with a barrel approximately two feet longer than the standard 9-pounder, was already in wide use as a "bow chaser," i.e., a gun mounted in the bow for firing forward.

In researching *Raider of the Scottish Coast,* the author came across references to "long twelves." After the Revolution, cannon-makers created the long 18- and 24-pounders that equipped the *Constitution* and its sisters. So, why not, as an evolution of the long 9-pounder, lengthen the barrel of the 12-pounder and install of them as the main battery on *Scorpion*?

Doing this is not without design challenges for the ship designer. The long 12-pounder forces the ship designer to deal with six significant issues. The first is weight. Cast iron is heavy and the additional two feet of barrel adds between 500-800 pounds to the weight of each cannon. If a ship has 20 or 22 long twelves, that's 10-11 tons more weight.

The solution for *Scorpion* was to reduce the main armament from 24 traditional 12-pounders to 20 long 12s. Later, in a refit during this novel, the main battery is increased to 22 long twelves. The traditional 6-pounders on the quarterdeck are replaced with lighter swivel guns, two on each masthead and two in the forecastle.

Gun crew size is issue two. The added weight of the cannon has to be hauled back in battery by the crew after reloading. This requires more men, i.e., 10 men vs. six or eight for an ordinary 12-pounder.

The long 12-pounder has a third disadvantage caused by the longer barrel. The cannon has to be pulled farther back into the ship so the crew has the space to ram the powder charge and then the ball down its barrel.

On a narrow ship such as the *Scorpion,* this presents problem four: room for the gun to recoil. The solution was to offset the cannon so they are not directly opposite each other.

Number five is heavier guns require a stronger ship's structure. Joshua Humphrey's diagonal riders and heavier/ stronger frame solves this problem and prevents hogging.

Problem six comes with the nature of the 18th Century manufacturing process for cast iron guns. Liquid iron is poured into a mold and allowed to cool. The bigger the mass, the longer the molten iron takes to cool. The larger the mass of metal, the greater the chance a large bubble forms in the gun which, under the stress of firing, may cause a cannon to fail catastrophically.

With all these known disadvantages, why the long 12-pounder? The answer: accuracy and "stopping power."

Prologue
Templeton's List

Northwest of Dorchester, SC, second week of April 1770

The distinctive crack of a bull whip greeted Miriam Bildesheim as she came around the smokehouse at the Garland plantation. A second crack followed by a guttural grunt made her sit up in the saddle and spur her Percheron to move faster. Chaya Delgado, the oldest of Miriam's seven daughters, set her Percheron to a canter next to her mother's. Behind the two women, Nero Haynes and Jonah Blanton, two former slaves who now managed farms owned by Miriam Bildesheim, urged their horses to follow.

This was supposed to be an informal visit before Miriam signed the papers to buy the plantation. She was there because the owner's widow, Martha Garland, had asked if she would buy the house and the land. Smallpox had killed Martha's husband, Charles Garland, as well as her oldest son and two daughters. Martha had moved her family to Charleston and turned day to day running of the plantation over to their foreman, Nate Willoughby, and his four assistants. But rice production had dropped, and after a poor harvest of indigo, Martha decided the time had come to sell the plantation that had been in the family since they arrived from Ireland in 1702.

Once past the oak trees that lined the access road, Miriam saw the plantation slaves gathered in a semi-circle 50 feet from a black man tied to a tree. Three armed white men stood watching the slaves while one she recognized as Willoughby was snapping a bull whip.

Miriam nudged her Percheron forward until the 2,200-pound horse was between Willoughby and the man tied to a tree. Willoughby flipped the handle of the whip and the tip cracked three feet from Miriam's leg as he snarled, "Get out of my way, old woman."

Even though she'd lived in South Carolina for 37 years, Miriam's English was heavily accented. Resting her hands on the pommel of her saddle of the Percheron that was 17 hands tall at the shoulder, she towered over Willoughby. She spoke in an even, but forceful tone. "You vill stop vipping zat man. Zat ist no way to treat a verker."

"He's not a worker, he's a slave and the property of the Garland plantation that I run. Therefore, I can do what I want."

Miriam glared at him, thinking that once she returned as the plantation's owner, he would be sent packing. *No man or woman or child should be considered or referred to as property.*

The foreman raised his whip again, then found himself staring down the barrel of a cocked .58 caliber pistol leveled at his chest. His arm froze. "You vill put zee vip down or I pull zee trigger."

The man lowered his hands to his sides but was still defiant. "I don't believe you will shoot me, old woman."

Miriam pointed the barrel to the side. "Drop zee vip and move avay!" Without taking her eyes off Willoughby, Miriam called out to the men and women gathered to watch punishment. "Cut zis man down, clean his back and take him to his hut."

"When you leave, old woman, I will whip him and everyone else who defies me!" Willoughby threatened.

"My name ist Miriam Bildesheim, and you vould do vell to remember me." Miriam kept the pistol pointed at Willoughby's chest. "I vill be back zoon. Venn I return, if any man or woman or child has been vipped, I vill vip you."

Willoughby laughed. "That, old woman, will never happen."

"Vee shall see."

Miriam nodded to Jonah Blanton and Nero Haynes. "Vee haf seen enough."

She gave one last look around before she tugged on the reins. The large horse obediently turned to head back down the road.

Three days later

Miriam and the others of the previous visit left Dorchester just after three in the morning, in order to arrive at the Garland plantation well before dawn. There was a quiet sense of purpose as they rode in silence.

No one was awake in the manor house as Miriam walked up the stairs. In one hand she held a pistol, and in the other she carried a bullwhip, which long ago she'd learned to use to herd cattle. A second cocked pistol was tucked in the belt around her waist. Jonah and Nero didn't have whips, but were armed with two pistols each.

The crack of the bull whip shattered the pre-dawn quiet in the room where Willoughby was fast asleep. Miriam prodded the still sleepy man with the handle as he stumbled from his bed. Miriam backed the cowering Willoughby against the wall, then Nero and Jonah pulled him into the hall while Miriam rousted the other three overseers out of their beds in the same manner.

Once Willoughby and his three assistants were gathered on the second-floor landing, Miriam again cracked the whip.

The tip snapped, ripping Willoughby's nightshirt and leaving a welt on his chest. The other three men jumped.

"You like zee taste off zee vip, no?"

Willoughby cowered, pressing his body into the wall. The whip snapped a second time, and again the night shirt was wrent.

Miriam pointed the handle of the bullwhip at Willoughby. "All of you vill pack your clothes. You are leaving zee Garland plantation zat I now own, und you vill never return. If I ever see you on von of my farms, you vill be shot."

Willoughby, the now former overseer, tried to keep his voice from cracking with fear. "What about our pay? Mrs. Garland owes me fifty pounds and each of my men forty!"

"Vat pay? Any man who vips another man bloody does not deserve to be paid."

There was nothing in any of the closing documents that required her to pay any of these men. If Martha Garland wanted to pay them from the proceeds of the sale, that was her business.

Miriam waited until Jonah and Nero escorted the four men to the manor house's wide porch. Each was carrying drawstring bags. She pointed with the whip to the access road. Willoughby started toward the barn.

Since she didn't respect Willoughby as either a man or a manager, she addressed him only by his last name, without either 'mister' or the German equivalent, 'herr'. "Villoughby, vhere are you going?"

"To get our horses."

Miriam walked to Willoughby and put the handle of the bullwhip under the man's chin and pushed up. Her ice blue eyes glared coldly into Willougby's and she could see fear alternate with defiance. "*Nein*. Zose horses belong to zis plantation, vich is now mine." Miriam pointed to the tree-lined access road. "Zee main road is zat vay. Valk! Und do not come back... Ever!"

By the time Willoughby and his three assistants started plodding down the access road, many of the slaves were standing outside of their huts, watching the scene unfold. Nero and Jonah went to all the huts and politely asked them to gather under the large stand of oak trees that were in the front of the plantation house where Miriam and her daughter waited.

Now that the sadistic overseer and his men were gone, and her dislike, even anger, at their behavior dissipated, Miriam Bildesheim stood with her hands clasped behind her, looking at the 47 black faces staring back. At 66, she was still over six feet tall, erect and accustomed to being very much in charge of what she referred to as the "*kollectiv.*"

Born in Konigsberg, Prussia, Miriam Bildesheim had arrived in Charleston in 1733 and with her husband Leo and two daughters – Devorah and Chaya. Leo was a well-known gunmaker who had provided weapons for the nobility.

Five more daughters—Yael, Adah, Eve, Leah and Rivkah —followed before Leo died of "the fever" in 1754. He had left Miriam with a very profitable gunsmithing business she knew little about other than the financials, and a deed to 500-acre farm north of Charleston. Miriam had to find a way to support herself and her seven daughters. She spoke with the four apprentices who worked for Leo. One wanted to own the business, so she worked out an agreement so that over five years he would own 49%. When she passed away, he could control another 31%, with the remaining 20% belonging to the *kollectiv*. The gun smithing business had grown and now employed two dozen men.

Having lived under Fredrick II of Prussia (Fredrick the Great) and George III, Miriam intensely disliked kings and royalty. She believed every man and woman deserved to find his or her own way in life. Kings, dukes and princes should not dictate what professions a man or woman could or could not practice, nor what property they could or could not own based on who their parents were or their religion. She and her husband had left Prussia because if the king woke up one morning and decided he didn't like a person or a group of people, they could be dispossessed of everything they owned.

Out of her beliefs came the concept Miriam called the *kollectiv:* an enterprise in which 80 percent of the profits were divided amongst the employees. Miriam's corporation was listed on the Royal Governor's tax and property rolls as Shayna Enterprises, Ltd. In Hebrew or Yiddish, *Shayna* translates as "beautiful."

She had started testing the idea in 1740 on her own farm. When Miriam dismounted from her horse at the Garland plantation, the Bildesheim *kollectiv* owned over 100,000 acres grouped in four small farming communities, an indigo processing factory, two inns, a dry goods store in Charleston, the original and very successful gun shop that manufactured well regarded rifled-muskets and pistols, and a gunpowder mill. Besides the crops grown to sell locally, the farms generated cash by producing indigo and rice for export. South Carolina rice was in high demand in Europe. Indigo plants were crushed and turned into a paste that was bought by dye makers in Europe who turned the paste into blue dye.

Even though farming was a labor-intensive business, slavery disgusted Miriam. The thought of claiming to own men and women and dictating every aspect of their lives was abhorrent to what she believed. But men and women like those in front of her had been sold to Europeans by their tribal leaders in Africa for gold and silver. These men and women or their parents had probably been brought to South Carolina against their will.

In many ways, Miriam saw herself as an escaped slave. Once the boat had moved away from the pier in Konigsberg, Leo and Miriam had felt and overwhelming sense of freedom they never wanted to give up.

Looking at the dark, upturned faces, Miriam could see uncertainty mixed with anxiety and fear. She sensed they were wondering, maybe even afraid that she would be worse than Willoughby and his assistants. Now her job was to placate their worries and begin to restore in them the sense of self-worth that the other members of her *kollectiv* enjoyed.

The irony of this Sunday moment was not lost on Miriam. Tomorrow evening, April 9th, there would be what she called "a gathering of zee tribe" at her house in Dorchester. Each of her daughters, husbands and grandchildren would come together for the first Seder of Passover. Everyone in her extended family were all descendants of the people Moses led out of Egypt and slavery under the Pharaohs.

Miriam cleared her throat. "Gut morning, I am Miriam Bildesheim und I haff not met many of you. Normally, I visit a plantation several times to meet all zee people before I buy. But zis time, zat vas not possible. Zee Garlands have sold zee plantation to me."

She touched the arms of the two men standing on either side of her. "Vit me are Jonah Blanton und Nero Haynes who manage two of my farms, and my daughter Chaya Delgado. Vee are zee new owners of zis farm und I vant to velcome you to zee Bildesheim *kollectiv* and Shayna Enterprises."

She bobbed her head for emphasis. "Zer are many zings you vill learn about my family und our business, but first I must tell you zat you are no longer slaves. No von owns you anymore. Zer vill be no overseers like Willoughby. Every person here ist now a free man, voman und child. Ven vee are finished here, I vill make a list vith all your names to be filed in zee royal governor's hall of records noting zat you are free men and women."

In front of her were stunned faces. One man who looked to be in his late 20s raised his hand. "Miss Bildesheim, does that mean we are free to leave and go where we choose?"

Miriam nodded. "*Ja*. I mean, yes. But please listen to vat Jonah and Nero haff to say. Zen you can decide whether you vill stay or leave."

She took a breath "Zo, each family who stays to work on zis farm gets a deed to vun acre of land on which we vant you to build a house. Zis land ist yours at no cost. I vill provide zee material zo you vill no longer live in a hut vit a dirt floor. Five days a week, a vagon will come in zee morning to take your children to a school, und in zee afternoon bring zem back. You vill still vork zee farm, und zee indigo vill be taken to our plant to be processed und zold. Zee rice vill be put in barrels und labeled vit zee name of zee farm. Eighty percent of vat zee rice is sold for vill be divided equally amongst zee families here, und eighty per cent of the profits from zee indigo vill be divided based on the number of acres farmed. Zee more acreage of zee farm, zee more money you make."

Miriam was sensitive that Chaya and she were pale faces. "Both Jonah and Nero each manage a farm and zey can explain how zis *kollectiv* verks. Vee vant you to stay, but if you decide to move, zen vee understand. But vonce you leave, you cannot come back, for zee land vill haf been divided up."

She turned to Jonah and nodded. His job, besides running the farm and taking care of the employees, would be finding someone here to eventually replace him as the manager, and identifying others who could help in other areas of the *kollectiv*. By turning to Jonah, Miriam was saying, "You've got the floor." As soon as he started talking, both Miriam and Chaya took several steps back to show they had confidence in what Jonah and Nero would say.

Nero spoke first, explaining the working hours, how they would get material to build houses and how the farming acres would be divided. He knew most of them could not read, but he showed them the papers that showed he was a free man. Answers to questions took almost an hour, then lunch was served and there was a chance to talk all together. In the end, none of the former slaves left.

Philadelphia, first week of October 1776

Gregory Struthers had been sailing on ships since he was 16. When the war broke out in 1775, he had just turned 21. He returned to New York as the first officer on the Merchant Ship *Ezra*. In port, he saw a flyer posted on small billboard near the pier, stating that the Continental Navy was looking for experienced seamen. A strong believer in the cause of freedom from England, the stocky, broad-shouldered Struthers offered his services. Commissioned as a lieutenant, Struthers was assigned to the frigate *Alfred*, where he became friends with then Midshipman Jaco Jacinto.

A large splinter ripped open Gregory's leg during the fight between *Alfred* and *H.M.S. Drake*. The wound became infected and, to save his life, the doctors amputated his leg. Struthers was lucky to survive the fever that followed the surgery. Jaco visited Greg in the hospital, and before he departed, he told his friend that if he ever needed a job, the Jacintos, who owned an import and export business in South Carolina, would hire him.

Still weak, Struthers took a small packet from New London to New York City, where his parents lived. The boat docked at a pier in the East River at the end of Murray Street wharf on June 3rd, 1776. A crew member was kind enough to carry his sea chest to the end of the pier, where Greg hired a wagon to take him to his parents' store on the corner of Avenue B and Houston Street. He was exhausted when he got into the seat next to the wagon's driver.

His parents, who hadn't seen him since he left to join the Continental Navy, were shocked by their son's gaunt appearance. They put him to work in the family store, where he sat at the counter and kept the sales ledger. In the evenings, he reconciled the books so that, on a daily basis, his parents knew how much money the store made. To regain his strength, every day he crutched to the tip of Manhattan and wistfully watched the ships coming and going, knowing that his seagoing days were over. Gradually, he became stronger.

Nearly everyone who lived on Manhattan heard the gunfire from Long Island on August 27th, 1776. Washington was soundly defeated, and the British Army occupied Greg's hometown.

Swinging along on his crutches, ignored by sailors, soldiers, and civilians, Greg alternated between the piers on the Hudson River and those on the East River. When he returned to the store, he updated his log with details of Royal Navy ships that arrived and those that left.

His parents and brothers hated the British but concealed their support of the rebel cause, because many of their customers were Loyalists. Some of their customers openly discussed their plans to seize property from those who rebelled. In September, a Loyalist offered to buy the Struthers' store. The amount was well above what the senior Struthers thought the business was worth. Rather than stay in New York, they also sold their house on 23rd Street to another Loyalist. Greg's parents and brothers bought four wagons to hold their belongings, and they headed up the Hudson River to Kingston, New York.

But Greg decided not to go north. Winter was coming, and living in the cold was not something he wanted to do. His parents gave him £100 and a horse, and he rode to Philadelphia, hoping Javier Jacinto was still a member of the Second Continental Congress.

When he knocked on the door at the address Jaco had given him, a stocky gentleman with swarthy features and gray streaks in his hair opened the door. He saw the missing leg and said, "You must be Greg Struthers. Please come in. My son has told me about you. I wondered if you'd ever come."

That night the two men talked for several hours, and the next day Greg Struthers accompanied Javier Jacinto to a session of the Second Continental Congress. Greg listened attentively to the debates and arguments.

Back at the house, Greg and Javier Jacinto warmed themselves by the fire and enjoyed a hearty meal; Javier had decided that this spare-framed young man had not been getting enough to eat. After supper, they retired to the library. Javier went over to a table that held gasses and bottles, and poured two glasses of port. Turning, he handed one to Greg and raised his own. "I have a proposal I think may interest you."

Greg took a sip of port and inclined his head. "Please go on."

"My brother and I, along with two others in Charleston, founded the Bank of South Carolina in 1774, which is chartered by the British Government and the Royal Governor of South Carolina. We need someone to run the bank and make it grow. I think you could do that. And, if we can agree to some goals, when the bank achieves them, we will give you ten percent of the bank's stock."

"Sir, I know nothing about running a bank."

"Neither did any of us when we were given the charter! But we knew the economics of shipping, importing and exporting goods, bills of exchange, letters of credit and farming. You know how to keep a set of books for a business, how to talk to customers, lead men, sail a ship, and negotiate with foreign businessmen. I think you can run a bank."

"May I ask why you created a bank?"

"Aye. We were tired of dealing with English banks and their usurious interest rates. Also, we wanted to buy land and ships, and we needed a bank willing to loan us money. We—the Bildesheims, Laredos and Jacintos—put up the capital. The Jacintos own fifty-one percent and the other families each hold twenty-four and a half."

Greg pondered. *This is a job I could physically do, and it's in Charleston, which Jaco told me is a friendlier town than New York or Philadelphia. And warmer.*

The elder Jacinto went on. "I must tell you that we, the owners of the bank, will not foreclose on any loans of anyone supporting the cause of independence. We simply find ways to restructure the loan. Once this war is over and we are free, we intend to use the bank to help our neighbors rebuild—and that includes Loyalists who swear allegiance to our country. If a Loyalist wants to leave, the bank will fund loans to those who buy their homes and businesses."

Greg leaned over and held out his hand. "I accept. When do I leave, and should we put our arrangement in writing?"

The older man shook the proffered hand. "Aye, I think that is a good idea. We can write out the terms and conditions right now. I shall have my secretary make copies in the morning and arrange your passage to Charleston. I will also write letters to my business partners and one to my lovely wife, Perla. Please honor us by staying at our house until she helps you find a place to live and introduces you to Charleston."

"Thank you, sir. That is most generous."

"Mr. Struthers, I must warn you about my wife and her friends. They will want to help you find a wife.

"That might prove difficult. I can be quite picky," Greg said, trying to sound light-hearted. In reality, he strongly doubted any woman would want to marry a cripple.

"Trust me, they are pickier than you—but not in the ways you might think. It matters less how a man looks than how he conducts himself."

Jaco, Greg reflected, had said much the same thing at the hospital. At the time, Greg had assumed his friend was just trying to cheer him up. Could he have been telling the truth?

On the way south on a packet named *Alacrity,* Greg spent the days on the schooner's deck, enjoying the warm end of summer. Already he was feeling better, even though all he had to his name were the clothes he wore and those in his saddlebags, the promised letters, and £88 and 6 shillings left from what he was given by his father.

When he'd knocked on the Jacinto door, he'd been an unemployed cripple. The moment he signed his contract, he'd become the new president of the Bank of South Carolina.

North Sydney, Nova Scotia, third week of February 1777

Inside the drafty barracks, the prisoners could hear the wind howling. No matter how much pitch and oakum caulk they crammed into the cracks between the planks of the walls and floor, wafts of frigid air flowed into the room. The barracks did have three stoves, one at each end and one in the middle. All were lit and the cast iron was radiating heat, but the pervasive cold seemed to devour it. Even if they could have opened the door, no one would have wanted to see the six inches of freshly fallen snow. Soon enough, they would have to trudge through it, barefoot, to the coal mine.

There were over 200 prisoners, and Eric Laredo was one of six officers present. He had been first lieutenant on the privateer *Duke,* sailing out of South Carolina. Born and raised in Charleston, he could not get used to the bone-chilling cold Nova Scotia. He had been a captive here for 12 months, and he was the ranking officer, now that Captain O'Rourke was dead. The incident that made Eric Laredo the senior officer happened four months ago.

Captain Edward O'Rourke had been commander of the privateer *Saoirse* out of Galway. He had been forced to surrender the private—named after the Gaelic word meaning *freedom*—to a Royal Navy brig and frigate that had boxed his ship in. Like many an Irishman, he hated the British, and he had staunchly refused to be pressed into service on either ship. So he had been set here, where prisoners of war mined coal for Britain.

O'Rourke had ordered the prisoners to stop working in the mine until they were given lumber to build frames to protect them from cave-ins. That had brought Major Timothy O'Dea, overseer of the mine, out from the nearby fort. O'Dea's temper was as fiery as his hair was red, and nearly all the prisoners feared him. But O'Rourke despised him; he regarded O'Dea as a traitor: an Irishman helping the bloody British.

Major Timothy O'Dea, Adjutant of the 2nd Battalion, Prince of Wales American Volunteers, ordered the prisoners to fall in to formation. Captain O'Rourke stood front and center wearing the crude woolen coat he'd fashioned, as had other prisoners, from a woolen blanket. The men stood shivering in the cold wind that originated from Hudson Bay and the Arctic. The six lieutenants made up a row behind him; the warrant officers were behind them, and the remaining prisoners formed 10 rows of 20 men.

Around the harbor, the trees were all bare. The leaves that had colored them in a riot of orange, red, yellow and green were all gone. Except for the evergreens, the branches of the deciduous trees were as barren as the rocky ground.

O'Dea rocked on his heels as O'Rourke explained that the prisoners would not work until the mines were made safe. Then O'Dea clasped his hands below his waist, pressing the thumbs together, and eyed his fellow Irishman. "So, *Captain* O'Rourke, are you telling me that your men will not follow my orders?"

O'Rouke's reply was civil, but emphatic. "Major, I am telling you that the mines are unsafe. If you want us to bloody well work in them, we need lumber and other materials to build frames to prevent cave-ins, so I don't lose any more of my men."

O'Dea sneered. "I don't give a damn whether you rebels live or die. You are here to work and to follow my orders."

"Then you don't give a damn if coal production drops."

The mine was expected to provide coal for the nearby town of Sydney, for other British settlements in Nova Scotia, and for Royal Navy ships stopping for provisions at the naval base in Halifax.

O'Dea's eyes darkened as his anger flared. He yanked his pistol out of his belt and held the barrel less than a foot from O'Rourke's head. The barrel quivered slightly as he pulled the hammer from half to full cock.

"O'Rourke," he whispered, "you and your rebels will do what I say, when I say it. Do you understand?"

The privateer glared back. "Sure and your mother must weep for the shame of you. Even a blind, shabbaroon traitor like you should know you can't mine coal with dead men!"

O'Dea's face convulsed in fury and his jaw worked. His anger got the best of him; he pulled the trigger. O'Rourke collapsed to the ground in a heap. Bits of blood and bone from the back of his head splattered onto Eric's face and stuck in the wood of his coat.

Not one prisoner moved as O'Dea looked around and began to reload his pistol. But the gunshot brought Major Johannes van Doorn, another Loyalist and commander of the Prince of Wales American Volunteers, running.

Van Doorn stopped short when he saw O'Rourke's bleeding body. He walked up to O'Dea and said, "Go back to the headquarters building and wait for me there."

O'Dea scowled and spun on his heel. Van Doorn studied the faces of the remaining officers. "What was this about?"

As senior remaining officer, Eric Laredo took a single step forward and came to attention. He described what had happened, repeating the officers' words verbatim.

Van Doorn said, "I see. And if I see to it the materials are provided, you will continue to work in the mine?"

"Aye, sir, with proper materials we can shore up the mine. But we'll also be needing warmer clothes, or we'll die of cold in winter."

O'Rourke's murder had been in October of 1776. Since then, the mines had been fortified and no more prisoners had died in partial cave-ins. However, none of the promised clothing had arrived. Their hands and feet and feet had itchy red patches and swollen joints make more painful by swelling and blisters. At night they huddled together around the stoves for warmth.

The door of the barracks flew open and a well-fed sergeant entered, wrapped in a warm woolen blanket over his red uniform. "All right, lads, up and out. You have work to do."

Snow blew into the barracks and what little heat was at that end went out the door. Eric walked forward, barefoot on the cold floor, willing himself not to shiver. "Sergeant Yale, would you go get Major van Doorn?"

"And why, pray tell, should I do that?"

"Because even sailors will freeze to death in the snow. If Major van Doorn wants coal, we need footwear and warmer clothing. And I am sure your storehouse has what we need." *After all, you confiscated it from us when we were brought here.*

An hour later, members of the Prince of Wales American Volunteers dropped several piles of boots, blankets and coats on the floor of the prisoner barracks.

Charleston, third week of November 1777

Rain poured down through much of the night as a line of thunderstorms drenched the town. Despite the breeze from the southwest, the humidity in the records room of the Royal Colony of South Carolina courthouse, at 84 Broad Street, was oppressive. Stocky, but not overweight, Bayard Templeton was sweating profusely. His muslin shirt was already soaked, even though he'd taken off his jacket and wig. His waistcoat, of fashionable raspberry with gold buttons, was also sweat-stained.

As a member of the bar, Templeton had access to the court records, from which he was compiling a list of properties owned by those he knew were actively supporting the rebellion. His document was now 12 pages long. He blotted dry the last of properties on this list and folded the pages in thirds. Back in his own office, he would spend the afternoon writing out three copies.

Already Templeton had written letters to Parliament, suggesting new laws that would grant the Royal Governor additional powers to go into effect once the rebellion was crushed. He planned to give one copy of the list to the new Royal Governor, then volunteer to assist in the prosecution of rebels for treason. If the new laws were passed, the governor could seize and auction rebels' property—which Bayard Templeton intended to acquire at bargain prices.

He extracted a pocket handkerchief and rubbed his sweating hands, then daubed his damp forehead. With a deep sigh of satisfaction, he contemplated the prospect of becoming the most substantial landowner in all of South Carolina. Humming, he stood and stretched his 5-foot, 6-inch frame. Templeton was average in height, but he wore shoes whose soles added two inches in height because he believed that being, or at least seeming to be, taller than his opponents was an advantage. His office chair, protected from view by a substantial oak desk, bore a thick cushion that elevated him over those who sat in the unpadded chairs at the front of his desk.

CHAPTER I
NEW COMMAND

Port Royal, first week of June 1778

Darren Smythe stood on the main deck of the 50-gun *H.M.S. Bristol,* eyeing his ship, *H.M.S. Puritan,* riding at anchor. The battered *Puritan* had dropped anchor in Port Royal a month before, carrying the survivors of the French frigate *Oiseau* captured in a bloody battle off Martinique. The fight had cost the Royal Navy frigate its captain, two lieutenants and 37 sailors.

Once the French sailors were offloaded, Smythe, as *Puritan's* first lieutenant, had supervised the repairs. As far as hulls and ropes and supplies went, the frigate was almost ready to go to sea. But before she could sail, the ship needed a captain and replacement crewmen.

Smythe guessed this summons to the flagship of the West Indies Station was to introduce him to his new captain. He'd been a lieutenant for almost two years, and *Puritan* was the second frigate he had sailed back to a friendly port. But as much as he would like a ship to command, Smythe was still very junior. Those lieutenants he knew who were given ships had held the rank for at least four years. Nevertheless, wartime sometimes made for accelerated promotions. Perhaps next year.... Smythe wondered how he would get along with the new captain, whoever he proved to be.

Looking out from under the awning that shaded most of *Bristol's* upper deck, Smythe studied *H.M.S. Liber*, a sloop of war anchored near *Puritan*. The name was a strange one. *Puritan's* surviving officers all hazarded guesses, but none of them knew the origin of the name. *Liber* had arrived four days ago; other than a boat going back and forth twice a day, the ship was just "there," so to speak.

Bristol, Puritan and *Liber* were the only Royal Navy ships in Port Royal's harbor. All the other ships assigned to the West Indies Station were off in the Caribbean hunting ships flying French, Spanish, Dutch, or rebel flags.

From across the bay in Kingston, smells of cooking with allspice, peppers and ginger wafted across the water. Darren had learned to like the spicy Jamaican food, especially a dish called *escabeche*. The technique of marinating a fillet of fish overnight in a spicy sauce had been brought to Jamaica in the 1500s by Spanish Jews.

A firm but friendly voice interrupted his study of the harbor. The speaker, another lieutenant, had been recently assigned to Rear Admiral Sir Peter Parker's staff. "Lieutenant Smythe, the admiral will see you now." Darren nodded and followed Lieutenant Horatio Nelson into Admiral Parker's cabin. Nelson, he'd found out during a previous visit when they'd had a few moments' private conversation together, was three years older than he. Nelson had arrived in December 1777, after commanding *Little Lucy,* a prize taken into the Royal Navy as a tender. At the time, Nelson had been the second lieutenant on *H.M.S. Lowestoffe*, a fifth-rate, 32-gun frigate.

Rear Admiral Parker came around from his desk. He wasn't wearing his uniform coat, and his shirt was opened down to his chest in recognition of the heat and humidity. "Lieutenant Smythe, thank you for coming." He turned to Lieutenant Nelson. "That will be all, Lieutenant." Translation —*"I want to have a private discussion with Lieutenant Smythe."* Nelson departed, gently closing the door to the admiral's cabin.

"Lieutenant, please take off your coat and make yourself comfortable in this damnable heat. Tea? Coffee? Or would you like something stronger?"

"Coffee would be wonderful, sir."

"Good." Parker pointed to a chair at the aft end of his cabin where the windows were removed to allow the gentle breeze to flow through the cabin. From where Smythe sat, *H.M.S. Liber* was in full view.

"I want to get right to the point as to why I asked you to come. Lieutenant, I have a dilemma to solve. Here in Port Royal, there are two ships without captains—*Puritan* and *Liber*. The sloop's captain became sick about two weeks out of Port Royal and died. Right after the ship arrived, *Liber's* first lieutenant slipped on a wet step and cracked his skull open in a nasty fall and may not be fit for duty for some time, if ever. Bad luck and all that."

Parker stirred his coffee with a silver spoon. Smythe dropped a spoonful of Jamaican sugar into his cup.

"*Liber* is a new build *Swan*-class sloop from the fertile mind of John Williams, the Surveyor of the Navy, finished last May. *Liber* had been designed for sixteen 6-pounders, but only has fourteen for reasons I don't have a ruddy clue. From what I can tell from reports from my surgeon and Nelson, the crew is a motley lot, mostly from the jails and dregs of the barracks ships at Portsmouth. I suspect that the ship may have some discipline problems. What I want you to do is go aboard, spend a few hours, and report back to tell me what you think of her. If you like what you see, *Liber* is yours—along with a promotion to Commander."

"Sir, may I bring an officer with me?"

"Of course."

"Sir, what reason shall I give to go aboard?"

"Do we need one?"

"I think so. I can't go on board saying, 'If I like you, I may be your commanding officer.' May I suggest that since *Liber* is a new ship, I am checking to make sure the hull is sound? From my experience with *Jodpur* at the yard in Halifax and the construction of *Puritan*, I believe I can carry the ruse off. And, when I report back to you, I will have a plan."

"I forgot about your yard experience. So then, will you take the command?"

"Not yet, sir. I would like to bring back recommendations on what, if anything, will be needed to make *Liber* the best performing sloop this side of the Atlantic."

"Well then, Lieutenant, I suggest you get on with it."

* * *

The boat being rowed from the pier out to *Liber* carried Smythe and *Puritan's* third lieutenant, Drew Rathburn. The two had known each other since they were cadets at the Royal Naval Academy. As they crossed the water, both lieutenants made a face at the foul smell, a mix of feces, urine, and filth. A stench of body odor became stronger as the boat neared the sloop. This was the same disgusting odor that had wafted over *Puritan* whenever the frigate was downwind of *Liber*. Once on board, the stench from rotted food, unwashed bodies, rats and human waste was almost overpowering. Both officers had to steel themselves not to recoil.

By design, neither Rathburn nor Smythe were wearing uniforms. They were simply Mr. Rathburn and Mr. Smythe from the Port Royal Dockyard, sent to have a look at *Liber* to determine if there were any defects that needed repairs while the sloop awaited its new captain.

Guided by the ship's carpenter Derwyn Evans, a burly Welshman from Cardiff, Smythe used a metal spike to poke the sloop's ribs, masts and planking. From his time on *Jodpur* and at the Hillhouse Yard, he knew how to spot rotted wood. Rathburn was conversing with the ship's warrant officers on the main deck.

Evans slapped the main mast with a meaty hand. "Sound and strong as she was when her roots were in the soil and her branches waved in the winds that blew ashore. She were born to be a ship's mast, this one." Then he led the way down to the bottom of the ship, where Darren intended to check the keel.

Bilges by their very nature were dark, dank and smelly, but *Liber's* were raunchier than any Smythe had known. The ship's stores were improperly lashed; beer and water casks were leaking; several containing dried peas, oats and flour were cracked. Rats had feasted on the unprotected food, leaving trails of droppings. The liquid in the bilges was a mix of stale beer, fouled water from the casks, urine and feces from rodents and possibly men, and the rain and seawater that drained down from the decks. The reek made Smythe's eyes water, but Evans seemed not to notice the putrid smell. Smythe was of two minds whether he was relieved or disappointed to find *Liber*'s ribs, decks and planking as sound as the masts.

The berthing deck was a jumble of sea chests, unstowed hammocks and general filth. The obnoxious smell told Smythe that the men were not using the ship's head. His suspicion was confirmed when he spotted piles of human waste on the deck between the ribs and next to a bulwark. Then he saw a sailor walk to a rib and relieve himself, unconcerned that the liquid spreading out on the deck was in their living space or that he was not following the Royal Navy's rules for sanitation—thereby violating the Articles of War.

He stopped in front of two seaman whittling on pieces of wood. From the shavings on the deck, one man had been using his knife for several hours. Both men looked up at the sight of the ship's carpenter and two strangers. "What are you making?" Smythe asked.

"Figurines. Heads of people. I sell 'em in port."

"May I see a finished one?"

"Certainly." The man stood and opened his sea chest, which doubled as his seat. The top was partitioned and padded with wool cushioning realistic figurines that, once painted, would command a fortune in a London shop.

"Does anyone on board build ship models?"

The man used his thumb to point to the man next to him. "Aye, he does. Made a right nice one of *Liber* on the way over."

Smythe looked at the second man. "May I see it?"

Without saying a word, the man opened his sea chest and held out a model of *Liber's* frame, partially planked, with decks and the lower sections of the masts.

"May I?"

Smythe examined the accurate model that was not quite to scale. "This is very good. Have you made models of other ships?"

"Aye, I have." The man peeled back several layers of clothing and revealed two other ship models. "That's my first ship, *H.M.S. Aldborough*. She was broken up in '72. This one is of *H.M.S. Liverpool*. The captain ran her aground in New York and our crew was distributed amongst many ships. I was the senior gun captain and was sent back to England. Here I am as *Liber's* gunner's mate."

"What's your name?"

"Jonathan Williams. I'm also gun captain for number 1 gun on the port side. My mate here is Gavin Dawson. He's captain for #3 cannon on the starboard side."

"So, when was the last time you fired your cannons?"

"On the way over here. We had gun drills, although when we'd fired ten balls from each cannon Captain said that was enough."

"Do the guns shoot true?"

"Aye, they do, out to about 200 yards. But them six-pounders ain't going to do much damage to a warship."

"Ever fire chain shot?"

"No, but the Frenchies fired a lot at us during the last war. Nasty stuff that rips up the rigging and sends chunks of iron all around."

Smythe's conversation with Dawson and Williams had drawn a small crowd, many of whom were eager to talk about the ship and their experiences. One sailor asked when *Liber* was going to get a new captain. Darren's truthful answer was, "I don't know."

Telling the men that the survey had to be finished, Evans pointed to the companionway to the main deck.

After taking a quick look at the forecastle, Smythe walked aft down the main deck to where Rathburn was talking with Bosun Innes Louttit by the mainmast.

Born and raised in Inverness, Scotland, Louttit had an accent as thick as an anchor hawser. Initially he was hard to understand, but Rathburn was quick to realize the bosun knew what he was about. *Liber's* sheets and braces were neatly tied, and ends were coiled and hung on spare belaying pins. The cannon and their carriages were spotless.

Smythe's last stop was the captain's cabin where he met with the remaining lieutenant and the two midshipmen. The cabin was dusty and needed cleaning. All three of *Liber's* remaining officers seemed nervous. The ship's Second Lieutenant, Virgil Soames, had a face that would have fit well on a woman. He also had long, delicate fingers.

Darren asked, "Did any of you or the late captain note any damage to the ship, or repairs that need to be made? I am to report my findings to the port master and Admiral Parker. They specifically want to know if the ship is seaworthy."

"On the way over, we had to replace a spar and some rigging. I believe Bosun Louttit covered that with Mr. Rathburn." Soames took the ship's log off the captain's small desk. He flipped a few pages, found the one noting the original damage and the another with the repair, then spun the book around so Darren could see.

The log included officers' and visitors' arrivals and departures. Darren noted that Lieutenant Horatio Nelson had been aboard for a few hours the day after *Liber* arrived.

I wonder why Nelson didn't take the command? Maybe Parker hadn't offered the ship to him. Or perhaps he objects to bad smells.

"Have you been on many ships, Lieutenant Soames?"

"This is my third. I spent three years as a midshipman on *H.M.S. Acquilon,* 28 guns, before I was transferred to the 50-gun fourth rater, *H.M.S. Romney*. I passed my lieutenant's board last fall on *Romney* and was assigned to *Liber,* which was under construction."

"The ship is as sound as a racehorse, but *Liber* is a bloody pigsty and a very unhealthy place to live. Do you not enforce the Royal Navy's rules?"

"I try, but the crew is a rough lot."

"Do you mean to say that the ship's crew does not obey a duly appointed lieutenant and temporary commanding officer?"

"Sir, I believe that they would, if I were officially in command."

"Well, then Mr. Soames, enlighten me, what are you?"

"In limbo, Mr. Smythe, in limbo."

I would have to agree with that assessment. However, Mr. Soames, you are an officer in the King's Navy and should have asserted yourself as the ship's commanding officer until such time as you were relieved. If you cannot get your men to obey your orders, what good are you? Looks like I'll have to instill some backbone in your spine! What am I missing? Was there a near mutiny?

Smythe looked at the midshipmen. He directed a question to the youngest, a lad with many pimples on his face. "How old are you?"

"Thirteen." Cyrus Tewksbury stood straighter. He was proud that he was a midshipman.

"Is this your first ship?"

"Aye, 'tis that. My uncle is captain of *H.M.S. Hero* and he arranged my appointment. This is my first ship, but I have been sailing around the River Mersey and the Irish Sea since I was a wee lad."

Smythe's eyes landed on the second and older midshipman. He was tall and lithe, and moved with quick, easy efficiency. "What's your name, lad, and what say you about *Liber's* readiness to go to sea?"

"Sir, I'm Chauncey Enfield. I think with a good cleaning and re-provisioning, we could be ready in a day or so."

"What sort of provisions does *Liber* need?"

"Food and beer mostly. We're down to less than a week of beer, and most of the food in the hold is spoilt. On the way over, we found every third cask of meat to be inedible. We stopped several times to fish and used the bad meat for bait. We caught enough to feed the ship. The hardtack in the casks are almost entirely devoured by weevils."

"You know a good bit about the supplies."

"I do math easily, so our late captain assigned me to be the purser.

"How old are you, and where did you get your commission?"

"Sixteen, sir. I graduated from the Royal Naval Academy a year ago and was assigned to *Liber*. This is my first ship."

Smythe and Rathburn asked a few more questions, then made their way back to the small boat.

Port Royal, three days later

At seven a.m. the flagship signaled *H.M.S. Liber:* "Send boat to quay immediately." No reason was given. The signal was part of Darren's plan to see if the sloop's crew had a watch that was paying attention.

Minutes after *Liber* acknowledged the signal, Rathburn and Smythe watched as six men climbed down and started rowing the cutter ashore. The individual in the stern wearing a blue coat was Midshipmen Tewksbury.

"Drew, are you ready for this?"

"Aye, I am. More importantly, are you, my good friend, ready?"

"I am, and I hope your confidence in me is not misplaced."

"Darren, you've already been a captain. For a change, you are going to command a ship with all its masts intact, one that is not in danger of sinking, and has the added bonus of not having to conduct funerals every day. 'Tis my honor to serve under you."

The cutter touched down at the base of the stone steps leading from the quay to a small platform. Tewksbury's eyes went wide with surprise when he saw Smythe's gold epaulet on his left shoulder, signifying that he was a commander. Worn, as Rathburn's was, on the right shoulder, the same epaulet identified the wearer as a lieutenant.

The 13-year-old midshipman gave his orders in a breaking voice someplace between that of a child and a man. "You two in the bow, give a hand there with Lieutenant Rathburn's sea chest and his belongings."

Rathburn's chest, two other boxes, a sword and a leather pouch that contained his correspondence and his journal, were carefully placed in the 20-foot boat, which then pushed off. His departure left Smythe alone on the quay with his baggage and thoughts.

All night long, Smythe had kept reminding himself that ever since he was a little boy, he'd dreamed of being the captain of a Royal Navy frigate. *Liber* wasn't a frigate but was one step closer to his dream. *If I do well with this sloop of war, one day I will command a frigate, maybe even a ship of the line.*

This was a bittersweet moment. Smythe was leaving *Puritan* and its crew. Master Bart Shilling and newly minted Lieutenant Alan Hearns had congratulated and encouraged him as they shook hands just before he left. What was most gratifying was that, given the opportunity, many of the crew would gladly serve under Darren again.

Puritan was now in the past. *Liber* was his future. Rear Admiral Sir Peter Parker had approved his plan to accomplish two tasks: clean *Liber* not only physically, but also the residue from the sloop's last captain; and get the sloop ready for sea. Only then, would Darren ask for his sailing orders.

Smythe allowed himself a glance at his left shoulder. The epaulet looked much better on that side. The uniform would look even be better if there were epaulets on both shoulders, signifying he was a captain.

He stood on the quay with his sea chest and a stack of three smaller wooden boxes. One contained a Dollond sextant, another protected a Dollond spy glass, and the third box had a brace of custom-made pistols from Samuel Galton. He also had two swords in scabbards, one given to him by his father. The other had belonged to Horrocks, the late captain of *H.M.S. Jodpur*.

John Dollond had been a London optometrist, the first man to make spyglasses, sextants and telescopes using achromatic doublet lenses which minimized distortion by bringing the wavelengths of red and blue light into the same plane. He did this by carefully grinding and mating a highly refractive, concave flint glass lens with an oval crown glass lens. The combination reduced distortion while at the same time letting in more light. Dolland's instruments were prized by sea captains, even though they were expensive. In 1772, after Dollond's patents had expired, the prices had dropped by as much as 50% for spy glasses and sextants with achromatic lenses.

The pistols had been an odd gift. A young American captain—Jaco Jacinto—had given them to Smythe, saying with a smile, "I hope you don't ever point them at me!"

Tewksbury's breaking voice interrupted Smythe's reminiscing. "Commander, are you ready?"

Darren waited until the cases were stowed on the bottom of the boat before he stepped in and sat on a thwart facing forward. Smiling, he said, "Good morning, Mr. Tewksbury."

As they crossed the water between, Darren looked at *Liber's* lines with a new perspective. The sloop was now entrusted to him. He would be responsible for how well the vessel and the crew performed. Do well, and he'd become a captain. Do poorly, and he would be a commander until he was killed, put on half pay, or cashiered out of the Navy.

At the base of the ladder on *Liber's* side, two of the oarsmen held the boat steady against the starboard side of the sloop. When he reached the hatch in the bulwark, Smythe paused until he heard Innes Louttit's booming voice, "His Majesty's Ship, *Liber*, ahhhhrrrriving."

Darren stood still while the ship's bosun played his pipe and rang *Liber's* bell three times. The crew, arranged in three groups, one aft by the mizzenmast, one forward by the bowsprit, and one on the port side, stood silently in ranks. The officers waited in a row on the quarterdeck.

Without saying a word, Darren strode purposely up the steps to the quarterdeck where he turned to face his crew. "I am Commander Darren Smythe, your new captain. Lieutenant Drew Rathburn is your new First Lieutenant. Mr. Soames is *Liber's* Second Lieutenant, and Midshipmen Tewksbury and Enfield are your other officers."

With that, he took off his coat and draped the garment, made from Georgia cotton, on the quarterdeck railing. He slipped off his shoes and slid them next to each other. With his hand, he waved the ship's crew toward the quarterdeck. Smiling, he said, "Everyone come aft and sit so I don't have to yell."

While the men moved aft, Darren considered what he planned to say. He'd spent most of the night scripting his speech, believing that first impressions in situations like this counted a lot.

Smythe brushed a lock of his unruly blond hair off to one side. He held onto the front of the railing as he spoke in as normal a tone as he could muster. "Three days ago, Mr. Rathburn and I toured *Liber*. I apologize if we came aboard under a false flag. We were sent by Rear Admiral Parker to determine what *Liber* required to be ready to go to sea. Before we can set sail as part of the Royal Navy's West Indies Squadron, we have work to do. First, we have to clean *Liber* from top to bottom. *Liber* is our home, but the best word to describe this ship is pigsty. We must clean every deck and the bilges. And from now on, we are going to follow the Royal Navy's policies on sanitation. Everyone—no exceptions—will use the heads in the bow of the ship. Once we have a clean ship, we are going to train. From what I understand, none of the guns have fired more than ten balls. We are going to practice gunnery so we can fire twice every four minutes. Once I can report to the admiral that *Liber* is ready, he has assured me that *Liber* will get a hunting license to take prizes where we can find them. If we are good at our job, there will be prize money for all."

Darren looked at the 120 faces looking back at him. "One last point. I can assure you that whatever happened before you joined *Liber* is of no consequence to me unless it affects your performance as a member of this crew. What *IS* important is what you do as a member of this crew under my command. You will find my officers open to suggestions. To succeed, we must all work together. However, do not take my openness as a sign of weakness. If needed and when appropriate, I will mete out sentences based on the Articles of War."

Darren could see that the men were listening attentively. "We start this morning. In less than an hour, lighters will show up and all the leaking casks and broken cases of food will be unloaded. We will then take on enough provisions for a week, including four sides of smoked beef"—faces perked up at this announcement—"before sailing to Lime Cay. There we will anchor and thoroughly clean this ship. Are there any questions? I apologize that I do not know your names, so please say your name before you ask your question."

Several men looked at each other before one raised his hand tentatively.

"Sir, I am Leading Topman Garrett Benson, sir. What ships have you served on?"

"Fair question, Benson. I served on *H.M.S. Deer*, 32-guns, as a midshipman, as a lieutenant on *Jodpur,* 32 guns, and on *H.M.S. Puritan*, 38-guns. After *Puritan's* captain was killed, I was acting captain. We captured the French frigate *Oiseau,* 36-guns, which unfortunately sank. We brought the Frenchies that survived back here to Port Royal."

Darren looked around. Another hand was in the air. "Sir, my name is Gavin Dawson. What about promotions? Some of us were promised advancement."

Darren turned to look at Soames, who nodded slightly, before answering. "I will read the captain's log and confer with Misters Soames, Tewksbury and Enfield. Those who have earned promotions will be given their due."

Another hand shot up. "What about some ruddy liberty? We've been on this ship for ten bloody weeks. Oh, sorry sir, my name is Ian Flagg and I'm a topman."

Darren heard muffled laughter. Liberty was rarely granted because Royal Navy captains were afraid of losing their crews to desertion. "Well, Flagg, that is also a fair question, but I don't think any of the dashers in Port Royal would be interested in this crew until every man jack of you cleaned up."

Laughter erupted at Darren's use of a slang word for whore. Not many officers were so plain-spoken. "Gentlemen, liberty is earned. Right now, we have a ship to clean and prizes to catch. Then, with a little prize money in your pockets, liberty for all of us will be much more enjoyable. Any other questions?"

No one else raised a hand. "Since our next steps are understood, dismissed."

A mile north of Lime Cay, Darren ordered the sails slackened. From the quarterdeck, he spotted the younger of his two midshipmen. "Mr. Tewksbury, take the cutter and find us a place to anchor on the west side of the island. We need thirty feet of water and room to swing."

The midshipman looked at Smythe quizzically, who answered the unasked question. "Take a quartermaster's mate with a line with a lead attached to take soundings. Bring them back on a slate so we can add the numbers to our chart. Meet us on the south side of the island."

Tewksbury nodded and started to issue commands to raise the topmost of the two boats off its cradle and swing it over the side.

A quartermaster's mate appeared with a wood-framed rectangle of dark gray slate and a white chunk of chalk in one hand, and a knotted ball of string with a lead weight at the end in the other. He stowed these in the boat and then, with the help of another sailor, stepped the mast and pulled the stays tight. On Tewksbury's command, the sailor raised the sail, letting Tewksbury pull in the boom as the boat fell away from *Liber's* hull.

Once the cutter cast off, Smythe sailed *Liber* down the east side of Lime Cay and around the southern side of the island. He ordered Louttit to slacken sail so the cutter could come alongside. Tewksbury tacked to bring the cutter within 10 feet of the side of *Liber's* quarterdeck.

Through cupped hands, the boy yelled, "Captain, there's a sandy bottom that shoals pretty quickly to a very nice beach. We can anchor safely 70 yards from shore where the water is six fathoms deep or more. On the west side, there's a reef about 300 yards away which gives *Liber* plenty of room to swing. Or, if you want, you can drop an anchor off the stern and keep 'er parallel to shore."

"Thank you, Mr. Tewksbury. Do you want to bring the ship in from the quarterdeck or lead in the cutter?"

"Sir, I'd like to come aboard and tell you when to drop the bow anchor."

"Then come along!"

Smythe stood on the forward starboard side of *Liber's* quarterdeck with his heart in his mouth as the sloop slowed to a crawl. He was trusting the judgement of a 13-year-old midshipman to select the spot to drop anchor. But then, his captains had entrusted him with even more dangerous tasks. *Were they ever as alarmed by me as I am now?*

Liber was barely making steerageway when Tewksbury yelled out, "Now, sir!"

Smythe didn't hesitate. "Let go the starboard anchor." A bosun mate yanked on the remaining lashing holding the anchor, and there was a loud splash. The four smoked beef carcasses hanging on the main sail spar barely moved. "Let go the port anchor." Another splash. "Slack all sails."

Smythe went forward and looked into the clear water. He could see both anchors on the bottom, their bills dug into the sand halfway up the flukes. Satisfied, Smythe turned to Bosun Louttit. "Furl the sails, but make sure we can easily loose them at a moment's notice."

"Aye, aye, sir."

"Mr. Soames, set the watch. Once we are squared away, feed the crew. Breakfast will be at sunrise, and then we will commence cleaning our ship."

Soames put the back of one hand to his forehead. "Aye, aye, sir."

Smythe studied what he could see of Lime Cay. The north end of the island was all beach. On the west side, about 150 feet away, sand was visible for about 20 feet before the trees began.

"Mr. Tewksbury, take four men ashore and explore the island. Look for some driftwood and a place to build a fire."

* * *

That evening, with *Liber* riding easily at anchor in the protected water between Lime Cay and Lime Cay shoal, Smythe invited his officers to join him for dinner in the captain's cabin. With Rathburn, Soames, Enfield, Tewksbury and Marine Lieutenant Peter de Courcy at the table, the space was full. The two midshipmen were sent to get their rations from the cook, along with two pitchers of beer.

When they returned and the food was dished out, Smythe spoke. "In the future, my preference is that those officers not on watch dine together, here in my cabin, for suppers and lunches. Objections?"

Soames looked at his new captain. "Sir, why? Our prior captain took his meals alone."

Smythe clasped his fingers and worked them. "We—all six of us, plus Quartermaster Evans and Bosun Loutitt—are responsible for the performance of this ship. We will have matters to resolve and plans to make. Meals are an excellent time to have those discussions. One of the more pressing items facing us is that about one quarter of the crew came from prisons. The rest came from barracks ships. Our job is to win them over so we can train them to meet and even exceed Royal Navy standards. This is critical, because in an action they must have confidence in us, as we must have confidence in them. So yes, Mr. Soames, I believe we should sup together. And when we are at sea, once a week I take supper in the messes and take questions from the crew. Does that answer your question, Mr. Soames?"

"Aye, sir, it does. Your answer is quite refreshing, I might add."

Darren started to say "Splendid" but didn't. There was nothing splendid yet about the state of *Liber* and her crew. But maybe, just maybe, he was beginning to win the crew over.

The next morning, with the entire crew on deck, Darren gave orders to bring up from the hold a dozen large, empty half-barrels taken aboard in Port Royal. Each mess took a turn pumping seawater into the barrels. Once they were filled with sea water, each eight-man mess was handed a bar of soap and ordered to wash their hammocks. Dirty water was dumped into a scupper and the barrels refilled with fresh seawater until the wash water ran clean. Wet hammocks were then hung on the rigging or draped over the bulwarks to dry. The officers, including Smythe and Rathburn, had a barrel of their own.

Smythe took the ugliest task with Midshipman Tewksbury: the hold, orlop decks and bilge. They directed the men to use soapy rope swabs to scrub down the inside of the hull. The dirty swaps were rinsed in small barrels of sea water. When the barrels were full of dirty water, they were carried to the main deck and dumped over the side. The process was repeated until the water was no longer dirty brown. Two four-man teams were assigned to pump the bilges.

While Darren was below, Drew Rathburn and Chauncey Enfield supervised the scrubbing down of the berthing deck. Soames and Stanhope had the main deck. By lunchtime, the ship was much cleaner and the pigsty odor, if not gone, was considerably lessened. The current in the channel carried the filthy water away from *Liber* and out into the Caribbean in a dark brown, oily looking smear that swirled in the current flowing between Lime Cay and the reef.

After the noon meal, the crew gathered on the now clean main deck. Smythe stood amongst them. "Now, gentlemen, we clean our clothes and ourselves. We will use the pumps to hose us down or, if you can swim, you can go over the side. Once you have washed with soap and are clean, put on your washed clothes and wash those that are dirty."

Again, Smythe led by example, stripping off the clothes he wore, washing them in a barrel with soap, laying them out to dry, then scrubbing himself with soap and rinsing off with sea water drawn up by the pump hose. The crew were quiet for his demonstration, but there were ribald comments, swearing, and laughter during the general cleaning that followed. About a dozen men went overboard to bathe, taking soap with them.

Once everyone was cleaned, Smythe again mustered the crew on the main deck. "Well done, men. Tonight we will feast on Jamaican smoked beef. With dinner, you will get an additional ration of rum. Enjoy and sleep well tonight, because tomorrow, we start training."

With the officers at the aft end of the ship and out of hearing, Ian Flagg tilted his back in made an exaggerated sniff. "Lads, perhaps our new captain thinks we're going to wash the bloody rebels to death! Now that we're bloody well clean, we can get dirty again."

CHAPTER 2
CHILD CAPTAIN WITH A TOY SHIP

Philadelphia, first week of July 1778

By March 10th, 1778, 10 of the 13 Colonies had ratified the Articles of Confederation that established the United States of America. New Jersey, Connecticut and Maryland were expected to ratify the document but had not yet done so. With the ratification, the Thirteen Colonies were now a country, but one at war struggling to free itself from British rule. Independence was still a dream, and victory over Britain was far from certain.

The mood in the Second Continental Congress was like a pendulum. One day, the delegates were happy and delighted with the progress of the war. The next, a rumor of another British success caused the mood to swing to doom and gloom.

To Jaco Jacinto, the Congressional mood swings were similar to the tides in the Delaware River. Incoming brought fresh water that slowly turned putrid. Then, as the tide receded, the water took the garbage down the Delaware

River and into the bay. And, once again, the air was fresh, at least for a few hours.

Even though Philadelphia's streets were laid out in a grid that made finding one's way around the city easy, he didn't care for the city that was the capital of the rebellion. He couldn't put his finger on a single reason, other than he often wondered whose side some of the delegates to the Second Continental Congress were on. In the end, Jaco decided that Congressional politics smelled like the Delaware River—putrid.

Scorpion, Jaco Jacinto's command, had moored at a pier in Philadelphia for re-provisioning. A debate within the Marine Committee over who should captain the ship and what tasks the frigate should be assigned kept *Scorpion* in Philadelphia.

One faction wanted to rotate captains to, as the chairman of the Marine Committee said, "give others a chance." His primary opponent in the matter kept saying, "Captain Jacinto has proven himself time and time again. Why change?"

And so the argument waged and *Scorpion* stayed moored to the pier, doing nothing while the summer season for hunting prizes that helped fund the war faded away.

Jaco chose to live on board the frigate rather than stay at his father's two-story house in Philadelphia, near the corner of Arch and Third Street. The senior Jacinto had bought the building as a place to live while he was a South Carolina delegate to the Second Continental Congress and a member of the Marine Committee.

One of the candidates that was put forward to relieve Jaco was Hoysted Hacker, formerly a merchant ship captain. As captain of the sloop *Providence,* he had demonstrated "indecision" in the course of battle. No one called him a coward, but officers who had served under him then flatly refused to do so again.

Scorpion's crew was owed prize money, and the men were demanding to be paid in gold or silver Dutch, English or Spanish coins, or in British pound notes. Jaco had firmly rejected a proposal by some in Congress who wanted to pay the crew in Continental dollars, which weren't worth the paper they were printed upon.

Jaco spent some days aboard *Scorpion*. On others, he met his father at Independence Hall to meet with delegates. Jaco was learning the Machiavellian world of national politics, where personal agendas sometimes became more important than sound decisions.

The bonding between father and son that had begun when Javier took his three sons—Isaac, Jaco and Saul—sailing on the Cooper River or hunting in the forests north of Charleston continued at a new level with his middle son.

Anyone looking at the three boys could tell they were brothers. They had similar facial features and stocky builds, and were about the same height. Of the three, Isaac had the lightest color skin and brown hair, and Jaco the darkest skin and jet black hair. Isaac, who was two years older than Jaco, had stayed in Charleston to help their uncle Gento run the family's business, South Carolina Import and Exports. Now 23, Isaac was the heir apparent to take it over when his father and Gento retired.

Their sister Shoshana was 18 months younger than Jaco, but she towered over the rest of the family. Shoshana had intense green eyes; a narrow, almost aristocratic face; and sandy brown hair that hung down to her waist, accentuating her height. By the time she had turned 16, Shoshana stood 6 feet tall in her bare feet. The family joke was that their mother must have slept with a Viking!

Jaco shared his father's passion for adventure. When he was 12, Jaco had asked permission to sail as a member of the crew to Europe on a ship carrying processed indigo and cotton. For the next three summers, Jaco had learned to navigate and sail a square-rigged ship. The vessels, owned by the Laredos, delivered and picked up cargos in London, Amsterdam, Brest, Lisbon and Cadiz.

Javier had insisted that Jaco keep a journal so he would have a record of his experiences and to note his emotions, the lessons he learned and the mistakes he made. At the end of each voyage, Javier would ask Jaco to describe what he had seen and the knowledge he had gained.

Jaco Jacinto had just turned 19. He had several options for continuing to fight the British, even if the Continental Navy was not going to retain him. One way was to return to Charleston, where consortiums that owned privateers would gladly give him a ship. Or he could join the Continental Army.

In a session on the topic of prize money, Jaco had reminded the delegates that Congress had the necessary gold and silver coins to pay his crew. *Scorpion* had brought back the equivalent of £15,000 in gold and silver Dutch guilders, along with £1,100,000 in British gold bars. The members of the crew wanted their payout before their enlistments expired on October 31st.

Using the table he'd submitted with his report, Jaco had explained the math that allocated each seaman £355, 5 shillings and 5 pence in prize money. Jaco reminded the delegates that the crew had voted to only take 10% of the value of the gold, instead of the 7/8s share they were entitled to divide. *Scorpion's* crew wanted the Congress to use the £990,000 to fund the war effort.

Since all of the delegates in the meeting were businessmen, the economics of the allocation were obvious.

Money Earned and Owed to the Crew of the Scorpion

Group	*Share*	*Madras & Cargo*	Madras' *Gold*	*Nevis & Cargo*	*Crew*	*Share*
Congress	1/8s & 90% of the gold	£1,875	£990,00 0	£2,375	N/A	£994,250
Ship's crew portion		£13,175	£110,00 0	£16,625		
Captain	1/8	£1,875	£13,750	£2,375	1	£18,063.66 *
Officers	1/8	£1,875	£13,750	£2,375	3	£ 6,063.66
Warrant Officers, QM, Bosun	1/8	£1,875	£13,750	£2,375	4	£4,563.66
Midshipmen & Mates	1/8	£1,875	£13,750	£2,375	12	£1,563.66
Seamen	3/8	£5,625	£46,875	£7,125	185	£355.55*
Totals		£15,000	£110,00 0		216	

The fractions of the pound amounted to the following: .66 equaled 12 shillings, 8 pence; .55 equaled 10 shillings, 6 pence.

The real roadblock to getting *Scorpion* back to sea was the Massachusetts delegation. They had, with the support of allies in Rhode Island and Connecticut and via parliamentary maneuvering, held up the decision on whether or not Jaco was to remain as *Scorpion's* captain until the issue of Edmund Radcliffe was resolved.

The young Bostonian had planned a mutiny to kill his captain and take over *Scorpion*. Based on the evidence, a three-man panel committee composed of lawyers from three different states had recommended that Radcliffe be tried for mutiny. The response from the Massachusetts delegation and its allies in Connecticut and Rhode Island had been to block payment of the prize money.

Jaco's had seethed with anger over the attempt to keep his crew from being paid the money they so richly deserved. More than ever, he regretted not trying and hanging Radcliffe when he'd had the power under the Articles of War to legally do so. He often wondered if that decision was going to haunt him later in life.

The compromise that emerged was that Radcliffe was released from the Continental Navy with prejudice, which meant that he could never hold a commission in the Continental Army or Navy or government office.

After lunch on the day after what Jaco dubbed "the Radcliffe Compromise" was approved, Joseph Hewes, the number two man on the Marine Committee, and Javier Jacinto walked to *Scorpion*. Seeing the two men approaching the gangway, Midshipman Earl Wilson, who had the deck watch, sent a sailor to the captain's cabin.

Jaco insisted that certain customs be followed, one of which was properly welcoming dignitaries. The bosun mate on watch blew his whistle before ringing the ship's bell three times. When the metallic tones from the brass bell died down, Wilson announced in a loud voice, "Congressmen, arriving!"

Again, protocol was followed. A Marine, resplendent in his dark green coat, led the two Congressmen to the door of the captain's cabin. A sharp knock resulted in a "Please come in." Had either man been over six feet tall, they would have had to duck under the beams that supported the quarterdeck to enter the small cabin.

Jaco shook hands with Hewes and gave his father a warm hug. "May I offer either of you some port, tea, or coffee?"

Joseph Hewes, as the senior of the two men on the Continental Congress's Marine Committee, spoke. "Whiskey, if you have some, would be appropriate."

Jaco reached into a rack and pulled down three glasses. "I'm sorry, I don't have any whiskey, but I do have some excellent Warre's port."

"I have good news," Hewes said, once they were settled into seats and savoring their drinks. "The Marine Committee has approved letting you stay on as *Scorpion's* captain. The official sailing orders will be delivered in a day or two, along with the crew's prize money—in English gold and silver coins, which you said would be acceptable to the crew."

Holding up his glass of port, Jaco tilted it in the direction of Hewes. "Sir, that is wonderful news. I was afraid that the Congress would insist on paying us in Continental dollars, which the crew views as worthless. Doing so would have caused the men to lose faith in Congress and make recruiting crews much harder."

Hewes nodded. "That was the very argument I raised."

"Repeatedly," murmured Javier into his glass. Jaco covered a grin with a sip of port. He had no doubt that some members had been willfully deaf to reason.

One problem solved, Jaco's mind shifted to the task at hand: getting *Scorpion* back in her element. "Sir, please thank the committee and the Congress for their confidence in me. Do you have any idea when you will want *Scorpion* to depart?"

"We expect by the end of the month. Can the ship be readied by then?"

"Once we receive the necessary provisions, we can be underway the following day."

"I expect that, with prize money still to be awarded, you will have little difficulty recalling most of the crew. Any misadventures?"

Jaco shook his head. "No, sir. If they had family here in Philadelphia, they mustered every evening. Most stayed on board *Scorpion* to maintain her. Occasionally, those who had some money went ashore to have a drink. They all know that if they wind up in jail for whatever reason, they forfeit their share of the prize money, which then gets distributed amongst the others."

"If I recall, your report has the muster sheet and the amounts to be paid, as well as the total."

"Yes, sir, that is correct. However, by his conduct, Mr. Radcliffe forfeited his share, and it has been re-allocated to the other lieutenants."

"Yes, that was included in the arrangement we made. It was a bit of a sticking point, what with his backers not wanting him to lose what they called 'his rightful share', but other members of the committee were less than pleased with Radcliffe's performance. May I ask how you plan to distribute and store the money?"

"Once the money is on board *Scorpion*, my officers and warrants will divide the money in front of the crew. Scorpion's carpenter made 216 canvass pouches and each is embroidered with a man's name. I have called muster the first Monday of each month to keep the crew informed of what progress was being made on their behalf regarding the award of prize money. They all have plans for the money. Some will buy land, others will pay off family debts, others will use the money to start a business."

Javier Jacinto nodded. "I cannot think of a better use for prize money."

Jaco had learned of the men's plans as he sat with them on the gun deck while they sewed the pouches and stitched names on each pouch.

"With all respect, these men have earned this prize money," Jaco said slowly. "They fought our enemies at sea, they quelled a mutiny. If it were not for their determination, I would not be here now, and the Continental Congress would be close to destitute. So if they take their prize money and depart, never to return, I will not fault a single one of them."

He took a deep breath and continued. "But I believe most of them *will* return. They did not go to sea as pirates, nor as privateers, seeking prizes. They came as men would sought something more precious than gold. That has not changed.

"And there is this." A quick grin flashed in the semi-darkness of the cabin. "There are three men ashore for every man on muster clamoring for a chance to crew *Scorpion*. She has a reputation, sir. It would not be difficult to replace able hands, or even officers."

"I think you underestimate *Scorpion*'s reputation, son," Javier rumbled. "I would estimate it as *five* men for every one. Even the warrant officers."

* * *

Jaco stayed on board *Scorpion* after his guests departed. He had an important task. His father had brought a letter from Reyna that needed answering. The schooner the Continental Congress commissioned to carry mail up and down the coast was leaving tomorrow morning for Hampton, Virginia, and then Charleston, and he wanted his letter in the mail pouch.

He placed her letter on the desk, then took out the six-inch long lock of Reyna's jet-black hair tied with a red ribbon that he kept in a folded piece of paper in his desk. Even after having the talisman for a year, he could still smell her scent. He read and re-read her letter, wanting to suck every thought and nuance off the paper.

My dearest Jaco,

Congratulations on the success of Scorpion! We—my family, your family, and our mutual friends—are very proud of you.

We have heard that the British have designs on Savannah because they reckon that if they can split Georgia, North and South Carolina from the northern states, they can defeat us. After we bloodied their nose when they attacked Charleston two years ago, they know taking our city will not be easy and will come with a large force.

I fear for my brother. Amos is still in the 2nd Carolina Infantry. They are part of the defense of our city, and you know better than I that musket and cannon balls do not care who they maim or kill.

Let me digress from the war and tell you of some exciting news. Dr. MacKenzie told me the other day that my apprenticeship is nearly over. Officially, I will be called a mid-wife, but for all practical purposes, I am a doctor.

We had an interesting visitor from Holland since my last letter. He showed us a set of surgical instruments that are far better than anything either Dr. MacKenzie or I had seen. They were made by a company called Smythe & Sons in Gosport, England. He had their catalogue, and before he left I ordered two complete sets, along with some of their medicines. Isaac was kind enough to allow me to use a draft from your parent's firm to pay for the instruments. When they arrive, I intend to give one set to Dr. MacKenzie as a thank you present.

Is this by any chance the family of that Royal Navy officer you captured and consider a friend, even though he is, at least until we win our independence, our enemy?

Also, the College of Charleston has loaned me a microscope and some other equipment which I have set up in the small shed behind our house. I now have a lab to conduct a little medical research.

Don't laugh, but one afternoon I was sewing up a wound and didn't have any clean water, but my patient had a bottle of rum. I washed the wound with the rum and then, after I stitched him up, used the rum to clean the skin. He said it stung worse than salt water, but smelled better than most wounds do. I sniffed, and he was correct. So as an experiment, each day, when I changed the bandage, I wiped down the sutures with rum, and there is no infection.

So, I went into my new little lab and looked at a drop of water from our well under the microscope. I could see all kinds of organisms. I dropped some rum onto the sample and most of them stopped moving. Therefore, I may be on to something but have to be careful about showing up with a bottle of rum to clean wounds. People might think I need the rum to fortify myself!

I miss you very much. Do you think <u>Scorpion</u> will be coming to Charleston soon?

All my love, and come home safe to me!

Reyna

Jaco smiled, then readied his writing materials. He made sure he had a clean blotter and plenty of ink. The quill scratched noisily on the paper as the words flowed from his heart.

My lovely and beautiful Reyna,

I fear you are right about the British changing their strategy. We have been winning our share of land battles in the northern states, and members of the Congress familiar with General Washington and the Army's strategy believe if we are not defeating, we are at least frustrating the British Army. They only control a small area around New York City and Rhode Island. General Sullivan has been ordered by General Washington to take back Rhode Island and that campaign is underway.

Congratulations on nearing the end of your apprenticeship with Dr. MacKenzie. I am sure you will be the best midwife in all of Charleston. When this war is over, my father and I will do whatever we can to help you attend medical school so you can officially be called Dr. Reyna Laredo Jacinto.

And yes, Smythe & Sons is Darren's family business. Even the surgeons on board our ships have heard of their fine surgical implements as among the very best available.

I too have news. The Marine Committee has voted to retain me as <u>Scorpion's</u> captain. Apparently, the decision was part of a compromise that let Edmund Radcliffe avoid a court-martial and probably the hangman's noose. My fear is that I have not seen the last of the disreputable

Mr. Radcliffe. I believe we are also going to receive our prize money in the next few days. My share is sizable and my father is going to issue a draft so the money can be deposited in our bank in Charleston. We should be able to afford a very nice parcel of land on which to raise our family. Unfortunately, once we all receive our money, Scorpion will go back to sea. I know not what our orders will be, but if my father has any say, we will be back in the hunting business. That is what Scorpion was designed and built for!

I will write as soon as I have more news. Continue the good work, Doctor Laredo—in my mind, one doesn't need a piece of paper to prove you are a doctor.

All my love, and I miss you smiling face.

Jaco

Philadelphia, second week of July 1778

Two days after Jaco posted the letter, a courier from the Continental Congress arrived saying that *Scorpion's* prize money would be delivered the next morning. Immediately, Jaco put in motion the plan he had worked out with the Marine Committee.

First step: everyone would be on board when the money was delivered. The fully provisioned ship would slip away from the pier and anchor in the Delaware River while the money was distributed.

"The counting", as it became known around *Scorpion,* took a little over four hours. With purses locked away in chests in the back of the magazine, *Scorpion* sailed down the

Delaware River, into Delaware Bay and then the Atlantic. With no Royal Navy ship in sight and *Scorpion* running due east with the steady wind coming over its stern, Jaco asked all the officers to join him in his cabin while he opened their sailing orders.

Jaco passed around glasses and put a bottle of port on the table. Jack Shelton, his first lieutenant, did the honors and filled each glass with two fingers of the burgundy liquid.

"Gentlemen, to our cause and to our success!"

Jaco picked up the folded document sealed with blue wax. "So, let us see what they really want *Scorpion* to do, and whether they differ from the discussions I had with Mr. Adams and Mr. Hewes." Jaco opened the letter and read it aloud. The penmanship was impeccable.

July 16th, 1778

Captain Jacinto,

You are to find the French fleet in our waters and offer your services as well as that of the Scorpion to the French Admiral, Charles d'Estaing. He is flying his flag on the 90-gun ship of the line Languedoc and is believed to be off Newport.

If d'Estaing refuses your offer of services, you are to find and seize British ships off the North American coast. Prizes shall be brought to either Boston, Philadelphia or Charleston for sale in Admiralty courts.

Plan your voyage so that you return to Kittery, Maine on or before October 31st, 1778 to have your ship refitted. During the re-fit, you are free to re-enlist those who wish to remain as a member of your crew or recruit men needed to man your ship. The Congress' intent is to send Scorpion south into the Caribbean in February 1779 with you as its captain if Scorpion is not being tasked by Admiral d'Estaing.

Good luck and Godspeed.
John Adams
Chairman, Marine Committee

Jack Shelton broke the silence. "That's a fine kettle of fish! Did Mr. Adams give you a letter of introduction, or a signal that we are to make once we find the Frenchies?"

Jaco shook his head. "My father said the French are supposed to be landing troops to help General Sullivan retake Newport, Rhode Island."

Hedley Garrison, who had begun his naval career as a midshipman and was now *Scorpion's* Second Lieutenant, rustled through the chart rack and found one showing the waters off Newport, Rhode Island, southern Cape Cod, and the islands of Nantucket, Martha's Vineyard and Block Island. Rolling out the chart, he spoke what was on his mind. "If the French are there, so will be the Royal Navy. How in God's name are we to determine whether or not a fleet is French or British? If we get close and they're British, we could be trapped and turned into splinters."

"Captain," Jack Shelton's tone was grave, "do we even know the French are actually there?"

Jaco took a deep breath. "Mr. Garrison is right. If the French are off Newport, we can assume the British are there too. Finding the ships is not the problem, finding the right ships is."

Empty glasses were put on the corners of the chart. "Let's start with an assumption that if the French Army is ashore, their ships are nearby."

Scorpion's captain drew a circle with his index finger east so' east of Nantucket Island. "Assuming the French fleet is in this area, we will have to either wait for favorable winds or tack back and forth to work our way to them. If the British admiral is smart, he has frigates stationed along a line from Long Island to Cape Cod to watch for the French fleet so he can bring them to battle."

Garrison handed over a pair of dividers, and Jaco adjusted them for distance using a line of longitude measured in degrees and minutes, then walked them along a possible course. "Gentlemen, let's go with the assumption that the British have got a line of frigates here or have the French boxed in. Let's plan our approach so that we pass through this line just east of Block Island at night so we arrive off Newport after first light. If we are lucky, we will be having croissants on the French flag ship for breakfast."

East of Block Island, third week of July 1778

With a steady wind out of the west nor' west, *Scorpion* tacked back and forth for a full day and night to reach the waters off the east side Block Island. The ship rode easily in the long swells, and as dawn broke, the ocean around *Scorpion* was empty. The lookouts hadn't spotted another ship since leaving Philadelphia.

On the quarterdeck, Jaco paced back and forth, trying to ease the tension in his back. Long Island and the Connecticut coast were on one side, and Cape Cod was to the north. The short distances limited his ability to use the *Scorpion's* speed to escape.

"Deck there! Four sails dead on the bow."

Jaco tried to look but was blocked by the rigging and the masts. "How far?"

"Ten miles at most."

"Mr. Shelton, send the men to quarters. No drums. Do not run out."

"Aye, Captain. Are you still planning to wear ship to the nor' nor' east?"

"Yes. In this haze, we'll be within two miles before they can recognize our flag."

Scorpion was loafing along under her mains and topsails. Jaco could see the swivel guns were all manned. The Marines in their green coats were lined up along the port and starboard bulwarks.

"Deck, two ships, frigates by their size, are bending on more sail and are headed our way."

The waiting was over. They were about learn if they were going to run or eat croissants. "Mr. Shelton, break out our flags and prepare to wear ship to east nor' east."

Soon he heard the flap of the Continental flag overhead. Jaco studied the strange ships bearing down on them. One was clearly a frigate with its guns run out. The other was a much larger two-decker that had not yet run out.

He studied the rigging though the Dollond spyglass, searching for a flag. Slowly the two-decker began to turn. He could see seamen on the decks hauling on the braces to turn its yards around. It was the French tricolor; they had found the French fleet.

Through a speaking trumpet, Jaco asked to be led to the flagship and was instructed to follow the frigate *Engageante* toward the forest of sails.

As they cruised in parallel 200 hundred yards apart under slackened sails, *Scorpion* was dwarfed by the three-decker *Languedoc*. The lower deck gunports were closed, but the black snouts of its 24-pounders on the upper gun deck were run out. A single broadside could turn *Scorpion* into matchsticks.

Deciding that he and Garrison should go unarmed to D'Estaing's flagship, Jaco left his sword in the cabin. The cutter, with one of *Scorpion's* quartermaster's mates at the helm and a sailor in the bow, swiftly covered the distance between the two ships.

A hatch in the lower gun deck opened and the two men climbed up to where Jaco and Hedley could enter the 1,750-ton ship-of-the-line. A French officer introduced himself as *Capitaine du Frigate* Jules Devereaux, and welcomed Jaco and Hedley to *Languedoc*. Devereaux was so thin he looked emaciated, and Jaco wondered if the French fleet was on short rations.

The admiral's cabin was sumptuously furnished and huge, spanning the beam of the ship for about 50 feet. Against one wall there was a buffet of smoked meats and cheeses, and the cabin was filled with a rich aroma of freshly baked breads.

Vice Admiral d'Escadre Jean Batiste Charles Henri Hector d'Estaing was standing in the center of the cabin, smiling. He was about Jaco's height and weight, wearing a silver-gray wig. Jaco thought that D'Estaing had so much gold trim and so many medals on his uniform that if the French admiral jumped in the sea, they would take him to the bottom like a stone.

The French admiral took Jaco's proffered hand in both of his and said in French, "Welcome to my flagship, Captain Jacinto. Please, let us have something to eat, and then you can explain why you are here."

Unlike the wooden plates used on the *Scorpion*, a servant handed Jaco one made of fine china. A servant expertly plated the food Jaco selected. He was offered a choice of coffee or tea, and another servant held out a chair, indicating where hie should sit at the large table. The officers exchanged pleasantries, and the admiral enquired, "*Capitaine* Jacinto, where did you learn to speak French?"

"I visited France when I was learning my family's trade, and then several times during our war."

"And you, Lieutenant Garrison?"

"My mother is from Montreal, and we speak both French and English at home."

"Ah! So tell me, *Capitaine* Jacinto, about your ship. Have you ever taken on an English frigate in battle?"

Jaco gave a précis of how *Scorpion* had sunk one 28-gun frigate in battle and put three others out of action. He did not mention his frigate's hull was made from alternating layers of oak, pine and oak that caused Royal Navy 12-pound balls to bounce off, or that *Scorpion* could easily sail at a steady 10 to 12 knots or that his long 12-pounders outranged and were more accurate than those used by the Royal Navy.

D'Estaing leaned back in his chair, listening politely but with an air of superiority. "Pray tell, what do you think your little ship can do for my squadron?"

"I was sent to offer my ship and my services to you. *Scorpion* is faster than anything the Royal Navy has near her size. We know these waters and we can scout for you."

"*Capitaine,* how old are you?"

"Nineteen."

D'Estaing was silent for a moment, then said, "You do realize that the French Navy has been sailing around North America for the past century. We have been battling the Royal Navy for much longer. We know them. My king sent my fleet here to help you defeat the British. Your Congress asked for my country's help. So, again, why you are here?"

"Sir, we know our—"

D'Estaing cut him off. "France has the best maps in the world. The British keep trying to copy our *Dépôt des Cartes et Plans de la Marine* charts. My orders come from the Marquis d' Lafayette and your General Washington." D'Estaing smeared soft cheese onto a piece of bread. "Before you say anything about tactics, might I remind you that the French Navy has tried many different ways to defeat the

Royal Navy and have an idea of what works and what doesn't. I hardly think that, after a few battles, the Continental Navy can add anything to this knowledge."

Jaco leaned forward. "Sir, I realize *Scorpion* is just one frigate, but there are things my crew knows about our coast and our weather that you, with all your experience, may not."

As soon as the words came out of Jacinto's mouth, d'Estaing's body language changed. He was not used to being contradicted, particularly by an officer still be wet behind the ears. His tone turned sarcastic. "I am surprised that your navy sent a boy to offer his assistance to me. So.... I suggest you take your little toy boat and go play. My squadron is strong enough to deal with the Royal Navy. We have defeated them in the past and we will do so again. Good day, *Capitaine* Jacinto."

* * *

Scorpion must have sensed that the French admiral did not think much of the ship or its captain. As soon as Jaco ordered the top gallants, top and main sails set, the frigate moved away like a racehorse allowed to run free instead of being confined to a track. Neither he nor the ship could get away from the French fleet fast enough.

As *Scorpion* moved east into the Atlantic, Jaco felt free to hunt. He was not going to be shackled to the demands of a French admiral who clearly didn't think much of *Scorpion* or of him.

Charleston, fourth week of July 1778

Of the things Miriam Bildesheim disliked in her life, riding sidesaddle was near the top on the list. Her disdain for fashion that rendered one helpless was topped only her scorn for lazy people who did not want to better themselves and expected others to serve them.

At 74, Miriam still had the agility to place her left foot into the stirrup and swing her right leg over the back of the saddle. When one of her daughters told her that for a brief second her unmentionables showed, the septuagenarian simply said, "No vun vill zee anything zat zey haff not seen before."

Miriam was fluent in Polish, Lithuanian, and Russian in addition to her native German. For reasons she never understood, speaking the King's English was still a struggle.

The house Leo and Miriam had built in Charleston as a home for seven daughters had been expanded and converted into the Charleston Inn, with 11 rooms. It was run by their daughter Rivkah and her husband, Levi Navarro.

Yael and her husband Jorge Delgado ran the Dockside Inn, built on land at the tip of the peninsula where the Cooper and Ashley Rivers join. The Dockside had 22 rooms, a tavern, a hall for special events, and a restaurant.

Miriam was six feet tall, and slender as a stick. She still stood erect without any stoop to her back, but her formerly chestnut-brown hair had turned a mix of gray and white. Some days she braided it; on others, like today, she let her hair hang loosely as she rode her Percheron, named Frederick after the Prussian King. The name was not intended as a compliment to the ruler of Prussia. Miriam's Percheron cantered down the road from what she liked to call "the family farm" in Dorchester to Charleston. In some places, the road was bordered by oak trees with trunks three feet in diameter and tall pine trees that stayed green all winter. Their shade made the ride pleasant. In other sections, where there were no trees to block the sun's rays, the marsh grass was chest high even though the soil had begun to dry out in the summer heat.

Once a week, Miriam made the journey to see her children and grandchildren, and to go over the books of the businesses in the provincial capital.

With the rebellion now in its third year, Miriam's recommendation to the members of the *kollectiv* had been to grow more food. Now eighty percent of what was planted were rice, beans, corn, and other crops, and only 20% was cotton or indigo. As she had explained, "If zee price for a bale of cotton or a pound of indigo dropped, vee could go hungry. If we grow food, vee vill always haf enough to eat. Und customers always vant to buy food."

Miriam rode ahead of two men who, while not officially bodyguards, were nonetheless there to protect her. In South Carolina society, women did not travel unescorted. Both men, former slaves, were now foremen in the indigo processing plant.

The ride back Charleston gave her time to think. The war was coming to South Carolina, and it would no longer be what the English called "a family affair" between Englishmen. Now that the French and the Spanish had declared war on England, the rebellion, which she fully supported, was about to become what she feared: an uglier and even more brutal war.

The additional animosity had already begun. The South Carolina legislature was about to pass laws that would disenfranchise Loyalists, which she thought was wrong. Better to try to win them over. With no Royal Governor to protect the Loyalists, Miriam was afraid that the fighting, pitting friends against friends and family members against family members, would become more bitter and divisive.

The clop of her horse's hooves on the stones at the back of the gunsmith shop brought a smiling Ezekiel Raskins out of the shed where he was forging gun barrels. A neat row of new barrels lay on rack, ready for boring. The gun shop was building muskets for South Carolina units in the Continental Army as fast as they could be produced. Raskins had fashioned dies and molds to make parts that minimized the amount of hand fitting needed to assemble a new musket similar to what the British Army used, and for the long barreled, rifled versions preferred by South Carolina soldiers. These rifled muskets, improved versions of the German jaeger rifles, were time consuming and costly to make. Their advantage was that an average marksman could easily hit a man at 200 yards and a skilled shooter could drop an enemy soldier at 400.

"Ezekiel, vee must talk."

"Aye, I know. You want to move the shop north, someplace between Dorchester and Columbia."

"Ja, dat ist correct. Und zoon."

"I have a plan, but I need wagons. I propose that I, along with four of our workers, move to the new building. That leaves Josiah, my main assistant, and two others here in Charleston. They can take care of customers here and fix anything we have made, but new guns will be made in the new location. The workers will be moving with their families. I will come back to Charleston if needed. And if Charleston falls, then I will stay at the new place."

They agreed to present his plan to the employees. As an incentive, Miriam offered the workers who would relocate an acre of land and money to build a house.

"How many vagons vill you need?"

"With six we can move the shop supplies in two trips. Then the workers can use the wagons to move their families. Have you found a place?"

"Ja. I bought zee blacksmith's business zat I told you about. It ist on a small river zo you vill have plenty of vater. Venn do you vant zee vagons?"

"Next Monday."

"Gut. Vee make zee food delivery to Fort Moultrie on Monday. Venn zay are empty, zee vagons vill come here."

Satisfied with their plan to move the gun shop her husband had started, Miriam remounted her horse. Her next stop was dinner with her daughter Adah and her granddaughter Reyna.

Chapter 3
UNPLEASANT CONVERSATIONS

West of Tortuga, fourth week of July 1778

Liber sailed through the Windward Passage to the water between the Turks & Caicos Islands and north of Hispaniola. This area was where Rear Admiral Sir Peter Parker wanted Smythe to hunt for prizes. The Commander of the West Indies Station suspected Smythe would find rebel, Spanish and French privateers wanting to prey on British merchant ships carrying raw sugar, rum and spices from British held islands of Barbados, St. Kitts, Nevis and Grenada north to New York, Halifax and England.

Early in the revolution, Britain, France, the Netherlands, Spain, the Continental Congress and some of the Thirteen Colonies had issued letters of marque to consortiums that owned armed vessels. Letters of marque were, according to the First Sea Lord, legalized piracy. Some menbers of Parliament wanted to hang foreign privateers as pirates, but the First Sea Lord cautioned against doing so because Parliament had also issued letters of marque.

One wag in the Continental Congress had said privateering was war for fun and profit. And indeed, rebel privateers were having an effect on British merchant shipping. On the Lloyds Insurance Exchange, cargo insurance rates were up by half, and merchants were adding surcharges to the insurance premiums to goods bought on letters of credit to cover potential losses.

His Majesty's ships couldn't be everywhere at once. Merchant ship captains and the owners of their cargo had two choices: either wait for a Royal Navy convoy to cross the Atlantic, or sail across the Atlantic alone, hoping that the "little ship, big ocean" theory of privateer avoidance worked.

The Royal Navy's experience battling privateers during the Seven Years War was that privateers followed one of two models: sally forth from their base and bring their prizes home for sale, or hunt in waters near where cargos were loaded and bring captured ships to a friendly or neutral port to sell. Both strategies worked.

Rear Admiral Parker had used a chart to show Smythe where rebel and French privateers had been based in the Caribbean during the Seven Years War. Smythe's orders directed him to put as many privateers as he could out of business, and to capture Spanish, French or rebel cargo ships.

Smythe was studying a bay on the tree-lined north shore of Tortuga, an island on the north side of Hispaniola. The afternoon sun was at his back, and he was debating whether to sail *Liber* east through the *Canal de lat Tortue* (Tortuga Channel) that separated Tortuga from Hispaniola or go around the north side of the island when he an outcry from near the mainmast.

"What the hell arrrrrr ya dooooing, lad?" Louttit's Scottish accent and loud voice could be heard by everyone on the quarterdeck. Smythe walked to the front railing to see what had generated his bosun's bellow.

A seaman whose name he didn't know, but soon would, replied, "Taking a piss. What does it bloody well look like?"

"Yerrrr suppoooosed ta use the heads in the fooorwarrrd paarrrrt of the ship, not a ruddy gun carriage!"

"I'll piss where I damn well please."

"No ya won't, Flagg. I'm bringing you up on charges. This is the second time in two days I caught you pissing on a gun carriage. Now you'rrrre going to clean them both up."

Virgil Soames showed up out of nowhere. "Bosun, what's going on here?"

"I caught Flagg pissing on the number 4 porrrt gun carriage for the second time in two days. He's like a bloody dog marrrrking his turf. I warned him yesterday that the captain would take a dim view of not using the heads. I also found a pile of shite back by the porrrrt number five gun. Not sure who crapped, so I had some of the lads clean it up this morning."

Soames was skinny as a nail and about half as wide as the seaman he addressed. "Flagg, did you relieve yourself on the gun mount?"

"Aye, that I did."

The Second Lieutenant stood with his hands clasped behind his back and rocked on the balls of his feet. "Captain Smythe has a standing order for everyone to use the heads. You are aware of his and the Royal Navy's policy, are you not?"

"Aye, that I am, but a man should be able to piss, and shit, where he pleases."

The men who crew number 4 gun on the port side may disagree with that assumption. "You are about to face charges for disobeying a direct order. Do you understand, Flagg?"

Flagg's eyes became bright with defiance. "No man should be punished for following nature."

"Dogs follow nature. Men can exercise restraint." Soames turned to the Scotsman. "Bosun, clasp Flagg in irons and put him in the hold. The captain will decide his punishment."

Satisfied that he didn't have to intervene, Smythe walked to where the quartermaster was standing at the wheel and looked at the binnacle while he pondered. *Flagg is clearly testing me. I wonder if he was acting on behalf of others? I can hold a trial in my cabin with just Louttit, Rathburn, Soames and Flagg present, along with an armed Marine for security. Or I can try Flagg in front of the entire crew. If I don't keep control of the trial, it might turn into a circus that leads to ridicule of me and my authority. Sailors who have witnessed court martials before will spot any missteps. If I am too lenient, I could lose the respect of men just as easily as if I am too harsh. Either way, I can't let the infraction stand. If I do,* Liber *would be on its way to becoming a pigsty again!*

"A penny for your thoughts, Commander." The soft voice was Drew Rathburn's.

Smythe turned so he was facing his First Lieutenant. "Join me in my cabin. Find Soames, Bosun Louttit and Quartermaster Stanhope and bring them along. Young Tewksbury can fill in for you for a bit."

With the men gathered in his cabin, Smythe got right to the matter. "Gentlemen, I'd like to take your counsel on whether I should hold Flagg's trial in my cabin or on the main deck in front of the assembled crew."

Bosun Louttit was the first to speak. "You have no choice but to hold the trial on the main deck, captain. From the moment you took command, you said you wanted a clean ship. He's testing you to see if you are all bark and no bite."

Stanhope, who had started out as a powder monkey and was now a quartermaster, nodded vigorously. In the former captain's log, Smythe had found a note recommending that Stanhope be promoted to ship's master. "Captain, I agree. Some of the men think you are young and inexperienced and want to see what they can get away with. Once you show you have steel in your backbone, this kind of nonsense will stop."

Smythe looked at Louttit and then at Stanhope. "Do you think there are more who want to test me?"

Louttit was quick to answer. "Aye, there be. But if you send a message that you are fair and not to be trifled with, the men will respect you and this will end here."

"Bosun, what if the others in his mess discussed this and Flagg said he would be the one to put me to the test. Is that possible?"

"Sir, it is not only possible, but likely. Men like Flagg don't do something like this unless he and his messmates have discussed it."

"Do you know Flagg's messmates?"

The bosun answered with a definite nod of the head. "Aye, I do."

"Good. Bring them here right now. I want to get to the bottom of this before I stand in front of the crew."

The seven other seamen who ate with Flagg were ushered into the now crowded cabin. Each sailor stood trying to look anywhere but at their captain.

Smythe moved so he was standing in front of the center man. "All of you, look at me. I want to know if you encouraged Flagg to crap and piss on our ship." He had first intended to say *my,* but the word *our* came out.

One of the men answered immediately, "Sir, I didn't think he would actually do it, what with the ship being so clean and all. Our former captain didn't care where we went."

"What's your name?"

"Garth Vanders, sir. I'm a top-man, and I man one of the forward swivel guns."

"Vanders and the rest of you. *I* care because a clean ship is a healthy ship. Your former captain might have gotten sick from the filth. His log says on the voyage to Port Royal that sometimes as much as a third of the crew was sick at a time. That's what you get if you live in a pigsty."

Vanders looked at his captain. He was clearly worried. "Is Flagg going to be tried?"

"Yes, he is. Article 11 of the Articles of War gives me broad powers on what punishment I order. What I am trying to decide right now is what do I do with the seven of you. Do you know of any others who thought this was a good idea?"

Vanders and the others shook their heads. "No, sir."

"Bosun, take their names. I will enter them into my log in my entry about Seaman Flagg's trial."

Vanders swallowed. He asked, "Sir, are you going to have Flagg flogged?"

"If he is found guilty of disobeying a direct order, I will punish Flagg based on what is allowed under Article 11 of the Articles of War."

"Sir, please don't have him flogged. Not for pissing on a gun mount and taking a shit on the deck."

"It's not that simple, Vanders. He disobeyed a direct order. Repeatedly. His actions jeopardized the health of everyone aboard ship. Dismissed."

The seven men filed out of his cabin. Once the door closed, Drew Rathburn, who had been standing in the corner watching, spoke up. "That could be a storm in a teacup. Sir, are you worried about those men talking with the other sailors?"

"No. Right now they are talking amongst themselves, feeling guilty and trying to assign blame for Flagg's behavior. But soon the story will be all over the ship. Then we can have a trial and I can play God, or maybe King Solomon. Flagg is going to be charged under Article 11 and the article states the captain can order any punishment, including death. Assuming he is guilty, what punishment do I give, Lieutenant?"

"What does your instinct tell you?" Rathburn returned.

"Three or four lashes is not enough. Five, plus a cleaning detail, should send a message. Six seems too much. This is a small ship and crew, and we need every man jack. My fear is that others will test me."

"That they may. And if they do, we will deal with the situation. This punishment should be enough to be a deterrent."

"Drew, pass the word we are going to hold Flagg's trial on the main deck just before supper tonight. Louttit, stay a bit. I want to ask you a question."

Liber was running with the wind under just her mainsails when the crew mustered on the main deck aft of the mainmast. This let Smythe hold his trial at the front of the quarterdeck so every member of the crew could see and hear what transpired. His position also let him look over his crew and sent the message that he was "over" every one of them.

"Bring the prisoner forth," Smythe commanded. The drummer started a staccato beat as Flagg, with iron bands connected by chains around his ankles and wrists, climbed awkwardly up the companionway to the main deck. He was flanked by two marines.

Smythe felt sick at having to order a sailor to be flogged for something as stupid as fouling the gun deck. But this was a matter of discipline as well as crew health, and an example had to be made.

"Seaman Ian Flagg, you are charged with disobeying a direct order from the captain of His Majesty's Ship *Liber*. This is a crime under Article 11 of the Articles of War as amended by Parliament in 1757. The order was that every man aboard this ship follow the Royal Navy's sanitary policies, which require you to urinate and defecate using the heads at the bow of the ship. You were caught relieving yourself on one of the King's cannons and admitted to doing so several times before, as well as defecating on the deck just forward of the number four port gun mount. What say you?"

Flagg was defensive, if not sullen, when he spoke. "A man should be able to piss and shit where he wants." There were a few snickers from the crew. Darren had instructed De Courcy, Stanhope, Louttit and Evans not to react unless the crew got unruly. They were, however, to remember names.

"Not on a King's ship. Your actions make His Majesty's Ship *Liber* an unhealthy place to live and work. That is probably the reason why so many of your fellow sailors fell ill during the voyage from Portsmouth to Port Royal."

Smythe looked at the crew to see if his words caused a reaction. So far, the men were stone-faced. He suspected that many had thought their captain would overlook Flagg's indiscretion. "Flagg, do you admit to the crimes as charged, or do I need to call witnesses?"

"I did take more than one piss and crap."

"Do you understand that you are admitting your guilt in this crime?"

"Aye. But it felt good." More snickers from the crew. "Are you going to flog me, Captain?"

"No, Flagg, I am not, and neither is Bosun Louttit. Your messmates are. I find you guilty of violating Article 11 of the Articles of War. Your punishment is five lashes administered by your messmates. You will choose the five, and each man will apply one lash. If they do not do it properly, the man's stroke will not count. In addition, you and your messmates will clean up any human waste found on this ship for the next two months. And the eight of you will scrub the ship's heads every day. Bosun, bring Flagg's messmates aft. Lieutenant De Courcy, prepare the prisoner for punishment."

Smythe could see the sailors looking at each other. Those who had thought that Flagg would get away with this had horrified looks on their faces. Others who thought he was getting his just deserts for his prior infractions were smiling. One man took a step forward. "Beggin' the captain's pardon, but sir, what if we all promise to use the heads? Would you stay Flagg's punishment?"

"A promise of future behavior does not undo past actions. Every man on this ship must obey the Royal Navy's regulations. This is a matter of obedience as well as cleanliness." When Darren finished speaking, he wondered if his words were too harsh.

Flagg was being lashed to the bulwark between two racks of belaying pins on the starboard side. His wrists were tied to the ratlines and his legs spread and tied to nearby racks. Louttit made sure that the lashings were tight. Once Flagg was secure, a bucket of seawater was placed next to his right foot.

Almost reverently, Louttit took the cat-o-nine-tails out of its red cloth bag. The woven rope handle branched into nine thin lines of rope, two feet long with knots every six inches.

He handed the cat to Vanders and showed him how to swing the cat so the tips cracked in the air. After several clumsy attempts, Vanders said he was ready. Smythe stood at the front railing of the quarterdeck. "All stand to witness punishment. Bosun, you count the strokes only if they are properly administered."

Louttit held a tightly folded cloth in front of Flagg, who opened his mouth. The bosun pulled the cloth tight before tying the ends at the back of his head.

"Commence punishment."

Vanders glanced at Louttit, who nodded. "Make it good, lad, or you'll keep going until you lash Flagg right!"

The smack of rope against flesh was the loudest sound on *Liber*. Darren could see the welts raised by the rope ends.

Flagg grunted when the second lash slapped his back, raising another set of red lines. Each of the five messmates did their duty, and Smythe could see the pain on their faces. He was sure that administering the punishment to their friend, whom they had encouraged to disobey an order, was almost as hard on their minds as the lashes were on Flagg's body.

After the fifth lash, Flagg's back was a mix of red welts and broken skin. Louttit splashed the seawater onto Flagg's back and then gently wiped it down with a clean rag.

"Take Flagg to the surgeon mate's cockpit," Smythe commanded, "and see he returns to duty as soon as possible."

Charleston, first week of August 1778

From his office in a building overlooking the waterfront, Bayard Templeton looked down at ships tied to piers or anchored in the Cooper River. A gentle breeze carried the smells of the marshy land and slow-moving water on the other side of the Cooper River, along with the yells of men loading cargo. The clopping of horses' hooves on the cobblestones pulling a wagon down a pier had interrupted his thoughts. Templeton's heart was not in the work for the moment, and the noise from the harbor had provided a welcome distraction.

August in Charleston was known as "the sickly season" because this was the time of year when "the fever" struck men and women and children without warning. This mysterious disease was one of Charleston's dark secrets, and the reason why many of the wealthier families moved out of town in August and September.

Templeton rested his hands on the windowsill to watch the goings on below his third-floor window. The sight of *Ranger*, a Continental Navy frigate once commanded by John Paul Jones, riding at anchor with her flag streaming in the light breeze made Templeton mad.

The rebellion, Templeton thought, was an affront to every man who'd served in the King's army during the Seven Years War, called the French and Indian War in North America. When the Royal Governor had called for men to form provincial units, not enough South Carolinians had volunteered, so Templeton had joined the North Carolina Provincial Regiment.

The unit had been attached to Braddock's army, ordered to take Fort Duquesne. The French and Indian forces had intercepted Braddock's men near the Monongahela River well short of their target. As the British Army units were pushed back, Lieutenant Colonel George Washington had taken command of the Virginia and North Carolina troops and formed a rear guard that held firm. The colonists were comfortable fighting from behind trees and taking aimed shots at their enemy. Their stand had covered Braddock's British Army units' retreat.

A lieutenant, Templeton had distinguished himself in the battle and subsequently joined the Royal American Regiment, hoping to earn a commission in the British Army. But when the Treaty of Paris was signed in 1763, Templeton was told his service was no longer needed despite his desire to serve his king in the British Army.

Restless, Templeton had traveled to England to study law in 1764, and his service record helped him gain entry to Gray's Inn, one of the four Inns of Court that prepared men for the practice of law. He had returned to his native South Carolina in 1769 and hung out his shingle.

It had been tough in the beginning, but Templeton had managed to make ends meet helping his father, a builder, negotiate contracts. This led to work filing deeds and other documents with the Provincial government. In court, Templeton came face-to-face with the other four English-trained lawyers in Charleston. The most successful was Edgar Barrows, who had been practicing law since 1753.

Templeton's own practice had tapered off since the war began. He was an outspoken Loyalist, and in Charleston, most people wanted independence from Britain.

What puzzled Templeton was that King George III had not named a new Royal Governor for South Carolina. William Campbell, the last governor, had fled after Britain's first attempt to capture Charleston in 1776. Without a royally appointed governor, Templeton's plans to confiscate the properties of rebels had stalled. He would, however, be ready to strike the moment Britain's victory was achieved.

Looking out the window, Templeton decided to do his part to bring the rebellion to a swift and ignominious end. He would close his practice and travel to New York to offer his services to the British Army, which was forming more regiments of Loyalists. The sooner the King's authority was reestablished, the better.

North of the Bahamas, second week of August 1778

Jaco stared out his cabin windows into the inky blackness of the Atlantic Ocean night. With a full moon and a cloudless sky, one could read a chart on the quarterdeck, and tonight was one of those nights.

He had just completed his entries into his journal and the captain's log. Two sharp knocks on his cabin door he answered with a "Come in," and Jaco turned his chair around to face the visitor.

Jack Shelton entered. "Jaco, the first watch just took over. Sails are set, God willing, for a nice night of sailing. We are not, as per your instructions, showing a lantern."

"Jack, sit for a minute and have a drink." Jaco reached over to the bulkhead and slid a glass from the rack across the table to his first lieutenant. Then he held up two bottles, one of port and the other of madeira.

"Like you, I enjoy a taste of port at the end of the day."

Jaco filled his guest's glass and topped his off. "Jack, do you ever wonder if this war is worth the cost?"

"That's like Moses wondering if he should lead his people out of Egypt. Where did that come from? I never took you for a doubter."

"I'm not. But think for a minute. Three years ago, Massachusetts militiamen pulled the triggers on their muskets, and suddenly we're at war with the country many would say is the richest and most powerful in the world. We had no army or navy, only a few poorly equipped and under-trained militia units. The Royal Navy had 350 rated ships and we had none. Both the Royal Navy and the British Army are much bigger, better trained and better equipped than anything we could dream of forming. And yet, here we are three years later. The British hold New York and Newport. That's all. How much longer they will keep Newport is anyone's guess. Their attempt to cut New England off died when Burgoyne surrendered. Now the French are in the war on our side. After meeting D'Estaing, I think the French are more interested in avenging their losses from the Seven Years War than helping us. To them, we are a side show in the battle to regain some of their colonies. Frankly, I don't trust the French. So where does that leave our rebellion?"

Shelton smiled. He'd spent two years at Yale College taking philosophy and divinity courses before he joined the Continental Navy. "Still at war. At the moment the war is a stalemate. Like a scale of justice. Washington can't defeat the British Army and the British Army can't defeat Washington. We, and I include privateers in the *we*, can't defeat the Royal Navy, but we certainly can make things miserable for them."

"Exactly. And that, my friend is what keeps me going. I like to think *Scorpion,* by whatever we can do, will add enough weight on our side to end the stalemate in our favor."

"Jaco, I'll drink to that. Every ship we sink or capture adds weight to that scale in our favor."

Chapter 4
Fortune Sometimes Smiles on the Innocent

North of the Mona Passage, second week of August 1778

Because of ship's small size, only 96 feet long, *Liber* only had two full length decks. The main deck was where the sixteen 6-pounders were mounted. The captain's cabin, at the extreme aft end of the main deck, and the officer's compartments forward of the captain's cabin, were on the main deck and under the quarterdeck.

The next deck down was the berthing deck, where the crew of 125 men lived and ate. Below the berthing deck, there was a partial orlop deck that extended from the bow to the forward mast. In the stern, another partial deck extended from the stern to the mizzen mast. The magazine was just forward of the main mast. In the hold, one was standing on the bottom of the ship.

During the day, sea chests were stacked and lashed along the bulwarks, and stowed hammocks hung from black-painted iron rings screwed into the oak crossbeams. At night, the berthing deck looked like a sausage factory, tightly packed with hammocks containing sleeping sailors.

Bosun Loutitt's job was to keep the men busy during the day when his captain wasn't conducting drills. The ship's rigging and sails always needed maintenance, and Captain Smythe's orders were to wash the main deck daily and swab the berthing deck once a week. Quartermaster Stanhope taught a daily class for the midshipmen and the men who aspired to become quartermasters on ship handling and navigation.

Then there was "keeping the peace" for which the bosun, the quartermaster, and newly promoted Gunner's Mate Gavin Dawson, were responsible. The berthing deck was a cramped, volatile place; scuffles were common, and their job was to make sure these didn't explode into brawls.

Loutitt had most of the crew on deck re-tarring sections of ratlines. Satisfied the work was progressing well, the bosun went down to the berthing deck to look for shirkers.

As he descended the aft companionway, he heard voices rising in pitch and volume. By the foremast, there was a cluster of six men, their voices raised in anger. Loutitt paused and listened. He recognized one as Vanders.

"Herring, you ruddy arse, what are you sayin'? This captain is one of the fairest I've been around. He's no lobcock!" Three of the other men nodded at the gun captain's words. They agreed; their captain was not a limp-dick.

Owen Herring, who often needed "encouragement" to do any assignment, replied sullenly, "I think he's wet behind the ears. He'll run home to momma at the first sign of trouble, dragging us behind him like he was sick of the idles."

Vanders shoved Herring in the direction of the forward companionway. "No one wants to hear your whining. Flagg got what he deserved, and if you continue to wag your tongue

I will turn you in. Now get your shag-bag arse up on deck and get to work with the others."

Loutitt watched the group break up and retreated up the aft companionway.

Smythe was studying an Admiralty chart depicting the north coast of Haiti and western Cuba. He was debating whether to stay near the old pirate base on the island of Tortuga northwest of Hispaniola or to search near Santo Domingo on the southeast side of the island. Parker's Flag Lieutenant Horatio Nelson had heard rumors that several privateers took refuge there. A knock on the door stopped him. It was the gunner's mate, Gavin Dawson. "Beggin' the captain's pardon, sir, but Mr. Soames would like you to come on deck, sir. Right now."

On the quarterdeck, Soames handed Smythe a spy glass, saying, "Take a look three points off our port bow."

In the distance, Smythe could see two sets of sails, but they were close together. If the ships were moving, they were doing so slowly.

"Do we know if they are French or British?"

"Not yet, sir. Tewksbury is up with the lookouts."

"Let's go find out. Mr. Soames, break out the top gallants, royals, the flying jib and fore staysail. Mr. Stanhope, wear ship port to a new course of nor' east."

Men scampered up the three sets of ratlines, worked their way out along the spars. On Bosun Louttit's command, all three royals dropped in unison. The flying jib was hauled up and sheeted home, and *Liber* pitched down slightly from the added push. The sloop had been cruising at what Smythe called a "stately" speed of six knots under mains and topsails. In the light but steady breeze, he figured the extra sails were worth three knots.

"Permission to come onto the quarterdeck."

Smythe recognized the squeaky voice of Tewksbury, who was standing by the quarterdeck's port companionway. "Granted."

"Sir, one is a two-masted brig. The other is full rigged, a very large merchantman. The brig looks to be French; I saw the Tricolor."

"How far away?"

"Four miles away at most, sir."

"Ask the other officers, Bosun Louttit, and Quartermaster Stanhope to join me on the quarterdeck."

Tewksbury nodded and ran off.

Waiting for his officers to assemble, Smythe felt totally alone. As a lieutenant, Captains Horrocks, Tillerson and Davidson had let him make suggestions and carry them out. As captain of *Liber,* he was the one accepting suggestions. Responsibility for success or failure now rested on his shoulders, not on his lieutenants'.

When all seven were convened, Smythe had Tewksbury pass along what the lookout had seen before the lad returned to his post, then addressed his officers. "Let us proceed under the assumption that we have a French privateer armed with 9-pounders, and a British merchant ship just taken as a prize. We will beat to quarters straightaway, but don't load or run out until I give the order. Let's see what the Frenchman decides to do and then we will finalize our plans. However, we want to avoid trading broadsides or a boarding action."

"Captain," Tewksbury called down, "both ships look to have taken in their sails. The Frenchman is moving away from the merchantman which is now flying a French flag. We're about two miles."

We have the wind at our back, so neither ship can turn toward Liber. *Are they going to split and run, or are they going to try to box* Liber *in and take us as a second prize?*

Darren went below to get his Dollond spyglass, sword, and pistols. Two bells rang, alerting the crew that they were an hour into the forenoon watch. *I wonder if I am going to live to hear them later in the day?*

Back on the quarterdeck, Smythe saw that the brig had tacked to the nor' west. The other ship was falling off to run with the wind. Through his spyglass, he counted six guns sticking out the brig's port side. He watched the French ship's sailors trimming sails; this long after a tack was sloppy. *Or he's short-handed.*

He could feel the eyes of his men on him. This was his first action as their captain. "Mr. Stanhope, hold your course."

Smythe buckled his sword belt on and checked the flash pans to make sure the pistols were loaded before he stuffed them into his belt. Now, even though he was wearing only a shirt and breeches, he felt properly dressed for the coming action. As he walked aft, he could feel a tightening in his gut.

"Gentleman, we're going to wait until the French ship passes us and then tack to port, as close to the wind as we can get. What I envision is a set of circles. *Liber* has a clean bottom and a well-trained crew who can shoot and handle sails at the same time. Lieutenant De Courcy, keep your men on the deck to help handle lines. Mr. Soames, load chain shot and aim, as we practiced, at the base of the ratlines. I am going to avoid exchanging broadsides because he has 9-pounders to our sixes. Understood?"

Soames nodded, then Tewksbury asked, "What about the other ship?"

"We take the brig first, then we run down the merchantman. What says our lookout?"

"Deck, I can see gun smoke coming from the merchantman."

Darren and the other officers studied the fleeing merchantman through spyglasses, but even Smythe through his Dollond couldn't tell what was happening. He shifted his glass to the French ship, wondering, *How many of your crew did you put on the prize?*

"Deck, the brig is tacking to the so' west."

The French ship was now heading toward *Liber* to angle across *Liber's* bow.

"Gentlemen let us go to work. Mr. Stanhope, standby to wear to starboard. Course due east. Bosun Louttit, get the braces and sheet loose."

Loutitt had already positioned himself by the main mast. "Aye, sir. We're ready."

"Mr. Stanhope, wear ship to starboard."

"Aye, sir, new course due east."

With the change course, *Liber* pitched down slightly at the bow. If his sloop and the French brig maintained their respective courses, they'll pass more than three-quarters of a mile apart, beyond extreme range for a 9-pounder and well out of range of a six.

I expect you think that I want to get alongside and trade broadsides. Sorry, I am about to take a page out of my friend Jaco's book instead.

"Mr. Stanhope, hold your course until we're just inside a mile. Then we are going to wear to port to a course of due north."

"Aye, Captain."

Smythe cupped his hands to his mouth, "Bosun, we're going to wear ship to port again shortly, on my command."

Louttit waved an acknowledgement from his position, midships next to a rack of belaying pins at the base of the mainmast.

Darren looked through his glass at the French ship's captain. He could see the crew moving around the deck, getting ready to hand the braces for the yards and the sheets for all the sails. *I need to circle to get behind. This is harder to execute than describe. My hat's off to you, Jaco, for having the balls to use these tactics. If I get this wrong, my ship will be in splinters. What are you thinking, Frenchman?*

The bow of the French brig began to move to starboard as the ship began to turn toward *Liber*. Darren forced himself to wait until the ships passed, going in different directions. Turn too early and the brig could slow down and rake *Liber* from the bow. Turn too late, and *Liber* would lose ground. The French brig began to tack to starboard, through the wind.

"Mr. Stanhope and Mr. Louttit. Wear ship to port now! Smartly. Keep the ship turning until I tell you to stop. We're going to dance in a circle until we get in position to rake this French brig."

Like a well-trained horse, *Liber* came around. "Mr. Stanhope, I am going to cheat a bit to the west, so steer nor' nor' west."

The braces creaked around in unison. Louttit kept them stacked and the sloop lost little speed. To Darren's eye, he had gained a bit of advantage once the sails were trimmed. Instead of being on opposite sides, *Liber's* bow was now on the Frenchman's rear quarter. *Splendid!*

Stanhope saw the advantage. "Well done, sir. One more turn and we'll be able to shoot up the stern!"

"That's the plan, Mr. Stanhope, that's the plan!"

The captain of the French brig had probably also worked out the geometry. Darren suspected the French ship would again turn to starboard and invite a broadside-to-broadside exchange. That move, however, would expose him to the risk of *Liber* not taking the bait and crossing his stern.

"Deck, brig is tacking to starboard."

Louttit was up near the bow, talking to a swivel gun crew. Darren cupped his hands around his mouth. "Stand by to wear ship to starboard!"

He got a wave in return and Stanhope asked, "Captain, what is the new course?"

"I'm thinking so' by west and let's see what that gives us."

Darren turned away to wipe the sweat off his brow, the result of a combination of heat, tension and concentration. One mistake and the Frenchman could take his ship. Or he could die. He was more afraid of the former than the latter.

"Deck, the brig is having problems with its jibs. They're both fouled."

Darren looked at the sails first with his naked eye and then through the spyglass. Both jibs were wrapped around a stay, and even a good crew would take minutes to get them free. Better to let them fall to the deck and then untangle as you raise them. The French brig's trouble meant the ship couldn't sail as close to the wind as before. Instead of heading in a northerly direction, the brig fell off, headed so' so' west. *Now is the time to pounce.*

"Mr. Stanhope, change course to so' so' west. Bosun Louttit, Mr. Soames, make sure the guns are loaded, run out, and the matches are lit. We're about to test the skills of our gunners."

There were rumbles from the gun deck as the guns were run out. Soon afterwards, the bosun's voice could be heard. "Ready to fire on your command."

The French crew's struggles with the ship's jib and fore staysail almost put the brig in irons as Stanhope aimed *Liber's* bow at an imaginary spot in the ocean where the sloop would pass about 50 yards from the French brig's stern. Smith could read the gold letters, which spelled out *Éternité. What an interesting name!*

"Mr. Soames, you may fire when you bear!"

Darren looked up at the mainmast. "Lookout, can you still see the merchantman?"

"Aye, sir. She's about five miles away under full sail."

The bang of the number one 6-pounder on the port side caused Darren to wince in surprise, and he turned his attention back to the French brig. As the other cannon fired in succession, he saw stays and braces fly apart as the chain linked between two small iron balls ripped through the hemp ropes. A section of the quarterdeck railing disappeared in a shower of splinters. Glass and wood flew as ball and chain shattered windows in the captain's cabin as a fourth shot hit home.

Liber was 100 yards past *Éternité's* stern when Darren ordered the sloop to come about to the starboard. The French crew had finished untangling the two jibs and men were sheeting them home when there was a loud crack. The upper two sections of the brig's mizzenmast came tumbling down.

Darren went to the front railing of the quarterdeck and yelled down to his port gun crews, who almost finished reloading. "Splendid, lads, just splendid!"

He turned to his grinning quartermaster. "Mr. Stanhope, change of plans. Continue on this course. We'll come back to *Éternité* later. They are not going anywhere."

Cupping his hands, Darren yelled to the lookouts, "Where away is the merchantman?"

"Three points astern to starboard. Still about five miles."

"Mr. Stanhope, come port to east nor' east. Mr. Louttit, we're going to come to port, so you'll have to trim the sails."

Thoughts raced through Darren's mind as he revised his plan. "Mr. Rathburn, get a boarding party ready. Mr. Soames, you lead the boarding party and when we take the ship back, you will have a chance to be a captain. Then, we'll go back and capture *Éternité*."

By the time the sun had set, the British merchant ship *Shropshire* was back in its crew's hands. *Éternité* had surrendered, and Darren put a small prize crew on board, with the privateer crew confined in the hold. With only one mast, the former French privateer was the slowest ship in the convoy.

North of the Bahamas, third week of August 1778

Scorpion's bell rang two times, which was the signal that the watch team was into the second hour of the first dog watch. The sound was also the signal for the crew to assemble on the main deck, for what Jaco referred to as a "captains call". This was a nothing-off-limits question and answer period; any crew member could ask anything without fear of retribution.

The night before, after Abner Jeffords had finished his turn on watch, he'd gone over to the Starboard Perfecto Corner. "Beggin' the cap'n's pardon, may I have a word?"

"Certainly, Mr. Jeffords, what's on your mind?"

"Sir, the last cap'n's call was three months ago. You used to have one on the first Sunday of every month. Bosun Preston and I think you ought to have one."

"Are then any problems on the berthing deck?"

"None I know of, sir. And the fact you eat in a different mess every week is a good thing, but I think the crew likes to hear the cap'n's plans from, well, the cap'n. This way, no rumors start because everyone heard the same words."

Jaco had nodded in agreement. "Aye, you're right, Mr. Jeffords. Schedule the call for tomorrow evening during the first dog watch. I will do a better job of keeping to the monthly schedule. Thank you for reminding me."

Once the men were gathered around the mainmast, Jaco climbed onto a large box that someone had thoughtfully placed on the grating between the main and foremasts so everyone in the crew could see him. The sun was well down in the west and the temperature was pleasant.

"Crew of *Scorpion,* on our first cruise, I held one of these sessions every month. This time we haven't been as regular. But from now on, we will hold this important meeting on the first Sunday of every month. The format is simple. I give you an update on what my plans are for *Scorpion* based on our sailing orders, which are to find and capture English ships off the Bahamas, Turks and Caicos, and the Windward and Leeward Islands. Where we take the prize depends on where we capture the ship. Sometime in September, we will start working our way north so that we dock in Kittery by the end of October or early November. So, lads, any questions?"

A sailor sitting against the bulwark raised his hand. "Aye, I have one. Does the captain think we will win this war?"

"Yes. But not tomorrow." Jaco waited until the laughter died down. "Seriously, winning our independence may take a few more years before the English come to their senses."

Another sailor raised his hands. “Sir, now that we are down where it warm, can we hang our hammocks on the gun deck and open the hatches?”

Jaco glanced at his Bosun, whose nod was imperceptible unless one was looking for it, then replied, “Aye, we can do that. I’ll have Mr. Gaskins and Mr. Preston make sure we have enough rings. If we don’t have enough, we can take some from the berthing deck and put them back when we return north. Understand that if we have to tack or wear ship, you will hear your shipmates tramping around the main deck.”

The last question was one about promotions. Jaco’s answer was that they would schedule the exams next week, assuming they were not in action, and a note would be made in the log so that those who passed would receive the additional pay beginning this month.

Port Royal, third week of August 1778

Liber was the last of the three ships to anchor. The first was the merchant ship *Shropshire*, carrying barrels of refined sugar and rum. It, like many of its sister ships, had originally been built for the British East India Company in a shipyard in Massachusetts, then sold to the current owners, who plied *Shropshire* between the island of Dominica and Bristol in England.

The next ship to anchor was *Éternité*. Without enough spare masts on board to make repairs, *Liber’s* carpenter Derwyn Evans had lashed two spars together to extend what was left of the mizzenmast.

Within minutes of *Liber’s* anchor splashing into the water, the ‘Captain repair on board immediately’ signal was hoisted on *H.M.S. Bristol’s* rigging. Smythe gathered his officers at the aft end of the quarterdeck. “Mr. de Courcy, you have the responsibility of turning our prisoners from *Éternité* over to the prison, where they can cool their heels until they are shipped to a French base."

The Marine Lieutenant nodded, and Smythe issued his next instruction. "Mr. Tewksbury, please make a boat ready to take me across, and then go to *Shropshire* and tell Mr. Soames that, once everyone is off *Éternité,* he is to go ashore and find the Admiralty Court in Kingston and ask them to survey our prizes to value them for auction. Can you remember all that?"

"Aye, sir." The 13-year-old recited his instructions flawlessly.

"Mr. Enfield, please liberate all the wine from *Éternité* and bring the bottles and barrels along with any cheese and salamis to *Liber* before you update our provisions list, then go to the victualing office and get us some new supplies." The young midshipman bobbed his head appreciatively. "Aye, aye, sir. I will take care of getting our bar restocked. And while I am ashore, I will see if I can find more of that smoked Jamaican beef."

"Excellent." Turning to his First Lieutenant, Smythe continued. "Mr. Rathburn, you have command of *Liber* while I pay my respects to the admiral." Grinning, he added, "I shall endeavor to do my best to survive the encounter."

The boat ride from *Liber* to *Bristol* on the calm water of Port Royal's harbor gave him time to compose his thoughts. As the quartermaster's mate sailed the boat, Darren enjoyed in the pleasant aromas of meats being smoked wafting across the bay from Kingston.

This was the first time he had to report on his actions as a ship's appointed captain. On prior occasions, he had been required to appear before boards of inquiry to describe the death of a captain or explain severe damage to—or the loss of of—a ship. Now as then, his responsibility was to tell the truth.

A grinning Horatio Nelson waited until the tones from the bosun's whistle had died down. "Well done, Smythe, well done. The admiral is looking forward to hearing the details of your exploits."

"Thank you, Mr. Nelson. I am glad to see you are well and enjoying your time on Admiral Parker's staff. And, yes, we did have some good fortune. But tell me, shouldn't *Liber* have been yours?"

"If the truth be told, I did want the sloop, but Parker preferred me to stay on his staff. Cleaning the ship was a wizard idea. Not only did you get rid of the filth, you symbolically cleaned the ship of old habits and the memory of dead officers."

Darren mumbled another thank-you as the ebullient Nelson led the way to the admiral's cabin. Rear Admiral Sir Peter Parker was smiling as he walked toward Darren with his hand outstretched. "Commander. I see you retook one of our own and captured one of theirs."

"Aye, sir, that sums up the action nicely."

The admiral's post-captain and chief of staff offered their congratulations as well.

"Please, sit and tell us the details. My cook will be bringing some sweet rolls and tea."

Darren put his official report, his journal, and *Liber's* log on the polished table, along with a diagram of the skirmish with *Éternité*. When Rear Admiral Parker finished asking questions, he announced that Smythe would resume his sailing orders after the sloop replenished its provisions. Once that pronouncement was made, Parker looked at the other three men. "Gentlemen, if you'll excuse us, I have a personal matter to discuss with Commander Smythe."

The admiral waited until the others left his cabin before going to his desk and bringing four documents to the table. His demeanor softened, as a father talking to a son. "Please, relax. I need to share some things of a private nature about Captain Horrocks. We served together when we were lieutenants. I remember when he was given a sixth rater, and then a fifth. He captured half a dozen prizes that I know of from letters he sent me, as well as from reports to the Admiralty. He was a very good friend."

Smythe sat with his hands in his lap. This unexpected turn of the conversation evoked his own memories of Captain Horrocks and a lump formed in his throat.

"The day after you left, Smythe, this letter from one of England's oldest and most respected law firms—Scoons—arrived. They sent the letter to the Admiralty, who forwarded it on to me with a cover note. Apparently, Captain Horrocks thought enough of you to make you the beneficiary of his estate. The unopened letter is from the law firm; I suggest you read the document straight away and respond as best you can. I'll ensure your response will be on the next packet to England." Parker slid both the opened letter from Scoons and the sealed one across the table.

"Thank you, sir."

"That is not all. Apparently, you have friends in high places."

Smythe blurted out, "I do, sir?"

"Yes, the Duke of Somerset was selected for promotion to Rear Admiral. He thinks highly of you and wrote, asking how you were doing. Now that you have returned—and successfully—I have some good news to pass on to him. So, as with my young flag lieutenant, Mr. Nelson, the Royal Navy has plans for you. I suspect if your next hunting trip yields results, you will be given a fifth or sixth rater to play around with. If you keep your wits about you, one day you may be sitting in the captain's cabin of a first rater, or better yet, flying your own flag."

"Sir, I don't know what to say, other than I will do my best not to disappoint."

Parker stood up and extended his hand. "The sturdiest ship of the line is no more than a floating hulk if she is not crewed and commanded by men of capability and good spirit. You seemed to have grasped that."

* * *

Smythe waited until after supper and when he alone in his cabin to read the unopened letter from Henry York, a solicitor from Scoons and Partners. Daylight was fading fast when Darren broke open the letter. The wax seal fell onto the table. York, Darren noticed, had excellent penmanship.

Dear Lieutenant Smythe,

My name is Henry York and I am a partner at Scoons and Partners, which is one of England's oldest, and I dare say, one of the most respected law firms. While we have some clients who are members of the court, most are businessmen or successful Royal Navy and British Army officers.

The purpose of this letter is to inform you that the late Captain Horrocks, RN, was my client and I am the solicitor assigned to settle his estate. In his last will and testament, he designated you, Lieutenant Darren Smythe, RN, as his beneficiary for all his property and assets. The will was duly filed with the Probate

Registry in the City of Portsmouth by Scoons and Partners and a copy retained by this firm. Upon notification of Captain Horrocks passing, we contacted the Admiralty for help in locating you.

The following is a list of Captain Horrocks' assets:

1. 3.9% interest bearing account with the Bank of England in the amount, as of May 2nd, 1778, of £12,178, 11 shillings and three pence;

2. House on the coast in Langton Herring located at 1 Coast Guard Road. The house comes with 50 acres of land, and is appraised at £2,123 not including the furnishings.

3. A separate interest-bearing account at Barings Bank which, as of the date of this letter, has £1,934 from farm income. Barings is a well known merchant bank. The farm generates approximately £173 per year in profit.

Langton Herring is a small town on the coast about four miles west of Weymouth. The land and property are being managed by Ned Jernigan, who lives on land sold to him by Captain Horrocks.

Our fee to probate the will was £25 plus court fees of £25, which we deducted from your bank account. Your inheritance tax of 25% (5 shillings per pound) must be paid before you are allowed to take possession of the assets. To pay the tax from your funds, Scoons needs authorization in writing by you to proceed.

We also need your instructions as to what you want us to do with the house, furnishings and your funds. Until we have this discussion, the money will remain in the interest-bearing Bank of England and Barings Bank accounts in Captain Horrocks' name. When the inheritance tax is paid, they accounts will be transferred to your name.

Upon your return to England, please contact our office so we can provide an update and copies of all the documents.

Henry York
Partner
Scoons and Partners

Smythe read the letter and sat back in his chair speechless and in shock. Assuming this was not a cruel joke, he was rich! As rich as his parents, maybe more so. As he sipped a glass of a French burgundy taken from *Éternité*, he remembered Horrocks' death on the quarterdeck of *Sorcerer*. He wondered at what point Horrocks had revised his will, and if he had felt any bitterness as he lay dying that he'd had so little occasion to enjoy his wealth. The thought that the money might be cursed ran through his mind.

He had two letters to write. One to Henry York, which would be simple. He would tell him to proceed with the probate of the will, pay the inheritance taxes, and hold onto the house and land. He added four questions. Would York:

1. Send him details, including drawings, of the house and the land?
2. Describe the arrangement withNed Jernigan?

3. Act as his agent to deposit future prize money checks?

4. Continue to manage his legal affairs until he returned to England?

The letter to his parents was much more difficult to write. Just before he'd left for Bristol to supervise the construction of *Puritan,* he had signed an agreement with his parents that upon his father's death, his two brothers would each receive 35 percent of the stock in the company. His sister would receive 20 percent, leaving 10 percent to him. If Darren ever decided to enter the family business, he would be a minority partner. Assuming what was in York's letter was true, any thought of joining Smythe & Sons was now moot.

So, what do I write? He brushed a lock of his wavy blond hair back so it wouldn't block his view. After deciding not to say anything about the inheritance until he returned to England and met with York, Smythe dipped the quill pen in the ink well. He wrote of his promotion to commander, his captaincy of the sloop-of-war *Liber,* and the taking of *Éternité.*

* * *

Two days after *Liber* anchored, the surveyor valued *Éternité* at £4,000, providing its mast was replaced at a shipyard. Built in 1777 as a privateer, *Éternité* was in excellent condition and the surveyor believed the repaired brig would bring top dollar.

Soames brought back news that Lloyds of London was paying a £3,000 bounty on ships it insured that were re-captured from a foreign navy or a privateer. With that information, Smythe compiled a table for *Liber's* log and his personal journal.

Group	Allocated Share %	No. of Participants	Shropshire Return Fee	Eternite	Total Pool	Individual Share
Admiral	12.50%	1	$ 375.00	$ 500.00	$ 875.00	$ 875.00
Ship's captain	25.00%	1	$ 750.00	$ 1,000.00	$ 1,750.00	$ 1,750.00
Lieutenants, Surgeon, Royal Marine captain, Master	12.50%	3	$ 375.00	$ 500.00	$ 875.00	$ 291.67
Warrant officers - Carpenter, RM officers, Quatermaster, Bo'sun	12.50%	4	$ 375.00	$ 500.00	$ 875.00	$ 218.75
Midshipman, mates, RM sergeants	12.50%	6	$ 375.00	$ 500.00	$ 875.00	$ 145.83
remainder of the crew	25.00%	113	$ 750.00	$ 1,000.00	$ 1,750.00	$ 15.49
		100.00%	$ 3,000.00	$ 4,000.00	$4,000.00	$7,000.00

Darren composed the report that he would take to the flagship, so the amounts would be entered into the admiralty's records. Studying the numbers, he was struck by the inequality they represented. Rear Admiral Sir Peter Parker earned £875 for issuing sailing orders. As captain, he received a quarter, while the crew who shared the same risks as he did split 25% amongst them. Splinters and musket balls strike at random and do not know who their victims are.

I believe Horrocks' bequeathment is changing my perspective. The amount of prize money I will receive no longer seems immense. It covers just two-thirds of the inheritance taxes I must pay to keep the fortune left to me.

CHAPTER 5
RETURN TO CANADA

East of Halifax, Nova Scotia, fourth week of August 1778

In the Western Atlantic, August meant good sailing weather. After not finding any potential prizes in the waters around the Bahamas and the Turks and Caicos, Jaco sailed *Scorpion* north. The frigate cruised off the east coast of North America to east of Halifax with the steady wind coming over the port side. At an easy nine knots and occasionally pushed by the Gulf Stream's two knots, the 1,500 nautical mile trip took just seven days.

Jaco's strategy was based on his knowledge of merchants' desire to get their goods in Europe as quickly as possible. In the early fall, cargo ship captains headed toward Europe could take advantage of the steady winds out of west to shorten the transit time. Furthermore, the waters off Nova Scotia were right near Kittery, whereas venturing into the Caribbean meant he would have to set aside at least two weeks to get back to Kittery. With the crew's October 31st end of enlistment looming, *Scorpion* only had six to seven weeks left in its hunting season and Jaco wanted to make the most of the time left.

During the transit north, he promoted two sailors to quartermaster mates, three to bosun mates and two more to gunner's mates. The men who passed their tests made their marks or signed their names in the ship's log.

Three times, lookouts had spotted sails on the horizon. Each time, however, the merchant ships had been escorted by at least two Royal Navy frigates, so *Scorpion* sped away. Jaco could sense the crew's frustration mounting, as was his.

A sharp knock on his cabin door caused Jaco stop writing in his journal. "Come in."

One of the junior bosun's mates stuck his head in the door. "Captain, sir. Mr. Patterson would like you to come to the quarterdeck. The lookouts have spotted two ships, dead on the bow."

Jaco picked up his Dollond spyglass, a gift from the Marine Committee, and followed the seaman to the quarterdeck. "Well, Mr. Patterson," he called out, "what have we?"

"Sir, Landry spotted a British merchantman and frigate."

"What do you propose?"

"We wear ship to course of nor' nor' east and see what they are about?"

"Take us there."

The third lieutenant turned to the main deck. "Mr. Preston, alert the watch. We are about to wear to starboard. Mr. Jeffords, new course will be nor' nor' east."

Patterson waited until the sailors were in position and ready to handle the braces that controlled the angle of the spars relative to the centerline of the ship and the sheets to the sails. He yelled out through cupped hands, "Stand-by to wear ship!"

"Wear ship to starboard, Mr. Jeffords."

"Aye, Mr. Patterson."

"Helm a-lee, Mr. Jeffords."

As soon as the bow started to move, Preston ordered the sheets released on the two jibs, and had them re-sheeted to maximize the push *Scorpion* would receive now that the frigate was on its new course. At the same time, the yards were pulled around in unison by the braces so that the wind, which was coming over the port side, was now pushing the ship from the port quarter.

Now Jaco could see the tops of the unknown ships' taut sails. He couldn't estimate their speed but was confident that *Scorpion* would run them down.

Long, four-foot swells sent spray onto the main deck each time *Scorpion's* bow plunged through the water. Some droplets landed on Jaco's face, and he enjoyed the taste of the cold, salty water. The creaking of her yards and masts showed no signs of stress.

Each time the watch turned over, Jaco had the oncoming watch team record the frigate's speed. *Scorpion* was loafing along at nine knots. When they had closed the distance somewhat, Jaco cupped his hands as he yelled toward the mastheads. "Lookout, can you tell me the size of the frigate? The ships were still hull down to those on either the main or quarterdeck.

There was a slight delay. "She has twelve ports, sir."

Twenty-four guns. Probably a sixth rater with 9-, maybe 12-pounders. "Mr. Patterson, send for all the officers."

"Deck, the frigate is headed our way. The merchantman has not changed course."

The British frigate captain has something to protect. So we need to take the ship and find out what is so precious.

"Mr. Shelton, clear for action and let's show them who we are. With the order to show their colors given, Jaco turned to his officers. "Here's what I want to do." He quickly explained how he saw the action unfolding. When he finished, he asked if anyone had any suggestions.

Hedley Garrison always looked at events differently. "Captain, what about the possibility that merchant ship is the frigate's prize?"

Smiling, Jaco looked at his second lieutenant. "Indeed, that would explain the British captain's strategy, but doesn't change how we fight the frigate. Mr. Patterson, I have the deck, everyone to their stations."

Jaco studied the on-rushing Royal Navy frigate. Its cannon were already run out and protruded from both sides. *Damn*, he thought, *the frigate is angling towards us.*

"Mr. Jeffords, fall off to starboard half a point, if you will."

Jaco estimated they would pass at about 400 yards, and ordered everyone off the quarterdeck except himself and the two quartermasters. Garrison was told to load ball, and Jaco could hear the rumbling of the wooden wheels of the cannon trucks on the gun deck.

What Jaco had not seen was the British captain had his port bow chaser trained as far to port as possible. Suddenly, smoke obscured the Royal Navy frigate's port side, and just as everyone heard the boom which followed, there was the thump of a cannon ball striking the hull, and then a loud banging sound, as if *Scorpion's* hull were an immense drum and something was striking it. Bosun Preston ran forward, peered over the port side and untied an axe lashed to the bulkhead, stored there in case the crew had to cut an anchor cable, sheet, shroud or brace in a hurry. The bosun swung the axe three times, and the banging stopped.

Before Jaco could ask what happened, *Scorpion's* port side long cannons bellowed a reply. Even though he should have been anticipating the blasts, Jaco was startled.

Wood flew from the British ship's bulwarks as, one after another, the 12-pound balls struck home. On *Scorpion,* the British cannon balls made dull thumps on the hull or high-pitched screeches as they passed over head. Two popped through the mainmast's mainsail.

The bow of the Royal Navy frigate began to turn towards *Scorpion* to run with the wind. Jaco ordered Jeffords to fall off to starboard to open the distance yet stay roughly parallel to the enemy frigate's anticipated course.

Again, the British ship got off the first shots of what promised to be a slugging match. Each time one of *Scorpion's* cannon answered, a wave of concussion passed over the quarterdeck.

An English ball ripped out a section of the railing on both sides of *Scorpion's* quarterdeck. Luckily no one was hurt by the flying shards of wood. Another turned one of the boats into splinters. Two men on the main deck, hiding below the bulwarks and waiting to handle sails, were injured and taken below.

Jaco kept his attention focused on the British frigate. He watched the beak disappear into a cloud of splinters and the bowsprit sag, held in place by the stays, as 10 of the 11 balls fired by *Scorpion* hit home.

British 9-pound balls continued to thump against the "sandwich" of *Scorpion's* oak-pine-oak hull. As each impact pushed on the outer layer of oak, the pine layer compressed, dissipating the ball's energy. The strength of the inside layer of oak prevented penetration, and cannonballs dropped harmlessly into the sea.

On the Royal Navy ship, there were now gaps in the bulwarks and smoke rising from the forward part of the ship. Without the push from its jib and fore staysails, the British frigate slowed.

The firing continued until *Scorpion* pulled ahead. Jaco gave the order to wear the ship to starboard to cross the bow of the British frigate. He needed to keep *Scorpion* far enough from the Royal Navy frigate to take advantage of the longer range of his cannon. Jaco studied the British ship through his spyglass. There were holes in the bulwarks for all three decks. He could see British seamen pulling the wounded away, and even the sea chests on the berthing deck. He wondered how many guns on the Royal Navy ship's port side were still functional.

Scorpion turned like an obedient racehorse, and the first two guns on the starboard side bellowed. The first ball slammed into the frigate's bow, just under the port bow chaser, disabling it. The second took out the top of the bulwark on the forecastle before expending itself on the structure that supported the quarterdeck. As the smoke dissipated, Jaco saw the Union Jack fluttering down. Dark grey smoke was rising from the British ship's forecastle.

"Cease fire, cease fire!"

Jaco yelled to Bosun Preston to slack all sails, then told Jeffords to wear the ship to port and adjust the course so that *Scorpion* was within 100 yards of the frigate. Hedley Garrison on the gun deck was ordered to keep the guns manned and loaded. If the British opened fire, he was to hammer the Royal Navy ship until directed to stop.

Jaco's next order was to First Lieutenant Jack Shelton, to get the three intact boats in the water and cross to the British ship to see what assistance was needed. The first boat back brought a wounded midshipman who was all of 14, along with eight wounded crewmen. The midshipman said that the fire on *H.M.S. Inquest* was already out of control.

By now, flames were visible forward of fore mast. English seamen who could swim were jumping into the cold North Atlantic. Gunners tossed ropes out of the gunports so uninjured sailors could clamber from the boats onto *Scorpion.*

Jaco saw Midshipman Wilson descending after a man in a blue coat into the last boat, which quickly pulled away from the burning *Inques*t. When the boat drew close to *Scorpion,* Jaco leaned over the railing and called out, “Wilson, how many more left on board?”

Wilson shook his head vigorously and yelled, “None we can help!” He pointed to the man in the blue coat sitting in front of him. “Their captain ordered me to leave the dead. He figures the fire will reach the magazine within 20 minutes.”

Jack Shelton climbed to the quarterdeck. “What do you want me to do with the prisoners?” he asked.

“Detail the Marines to hold them forward on the main deck until you and I have a word with their captain. Once Wilson and the boat are back on board, we’ll set sail. I want to catch the merchant ship as soon as we can.”

The table in *Scorpion’s* cabin had been taken apart and put in a rack along the port wall; the chairs were stacked and lashed to fittings on the forward bulkhead. What was left was an open area the width of the frigate and about 20 feet fore and aft.

The Royal Navy captain entered, carrying his hat and sword. “Welcome to *Scorpion,* I am Captain Jaco Jacinto, and this my First Lieutenant, Jack Shelton.”

The Royal Navy captain bowed his head and held out his sword horizontally. "I am Captain Oliver Glanville, captain of His Majesty's Ship *Inquest*, 24 guns."

Jaco took the sword gently. "Captain Glanville, I shall return this to you when you leave my ship. But I have some questions that need immediate answers."

Glanville inclined his head, watching the faces of his captors.

"Do you know how many of your men we saved?"

The British captain shook his head. "My third lieutenant should be taking muster. I estimate about 125."

"That is going to make spaces on *Scorpion* crowded for a few days. What is the name of the other ship and where were you going? I ask because, while you are not obliged to reveal information, your answer may affect the outcome. Do I fire into the hull if the commanding officer refuses to surrender, or attempt a boarding action?"

Glanville looked stoical. "I do not think your countrymen will thank you if you fire into the hull. *H.M.S. Bear* is carrying prisoners, about 200 of your sailors are being transported to a prison camp at North Sydney, Nova Scotia. *Inquest* was her escort."

Jaco forced himself not to react. His best friend, Eric Laredo, had been taken prisoner. He wondered if he had been sent to Glace Bay or North Sydney or someplace else; he did not know if Eric was alive or dead. "Captain, that solves a lot of problems for me. Assuming we take *H.M.S. Bear*, my plan is to swap your prisoners for ours. I expect they will be delighted to sail your ship and augment *Scorpion's* crew. And I promise that, as long as they cause no problems, we will treat your men well. To begin, we'll help your surgeon any way we can."

On Jaco's order, Jack turned Glanville over to the two Marines at the door. As soon as Glanville was out of earshot, Jaco said, "Bring all our officers to my cabin immediately. Tell Jeffords to keep us on course toward *H.M.S. Bear*."

Shelton grinned. "Are you thinking what I think you are thinking?"

"And that is?"

"Raiding the prison at North Sydney?"

Jaco grinned back. "Am I that predictable? A raid maybe, prisoner swap more likely. But before I tell our officers the good news, I want to find out what that first cannon ball did to our port side."

Jaco found Bosun Preston in the shade under the quarterdeck. "Bosun, talk to me!"

"Aye, sir. Well, we no longer have a port anchor. That first ball hit right on the head of the port anchor and sliced some of the lashings, which allowed anchor's iron flukes to bang on the hull. I cut the lashings and the anchor dropped into the sea. Mr. Gaskins says he has a spare set of flukes in the hold, along with enough wood to make another."

"Well then, I suggest you tell him to get cracking on making a new port anchor. We'll need it in about two days."

* * *

Scorpion easily overtook the much slower *H.M.S. Bear*. Besides rescuing their countrymen, Jaco was anxious to put distance between *Scorpion* and the burning frigate as swiftly as possible. *H.M.S. Inquest* exploded in a series of bright red flashes. Each explosion was felt on *Scorpion* a mile away. As the smoke cleared, all that could be seen by the lookouts was flotsam on the water.

When the frigate's bow pulled even with the quarterdeck of *Bear*, Jaco raised the speaking trumpet to his mouth.

"*H.M.S. Bear*, lower your flag so no one is hurt. We know what you are carrying, and we will take your ship by force, if need be. I have given all my best riflemen instructions to aim at your officers."

Bear's flag came fluttering down and the sheets were let go, letting their sails luff. Now Jaco had to find out what they had just captured, and whether any of the captives were fit for duty. With 125 prisoners already on his hands and more to follow, he felt distinctly short-handed.

Jack Shelton was the first man from *Scorpion* aboard the prison ship, followed by two armed sailors. The captain of *Bear* was a portly, bacon-faced man in his 40s. When Shelton climbed up onto the main deck, he was standing in front of the prize crew in the bow.

Shelton recoiled from the smell—a mix of feces, urine, body odor, and rotting garbage—rising from the hatch in the center of the ship. The putrid stench made him suddenly angry. He was in no mood for polite introductions. "How do I get those men out of the lower decks?" he demanded.

Bear's captain responded pleasantly, as if nothing was wrong. "Knock the pegs out of the hatches and lower the ladders down into the hold."

"Where are the hammers?"

"Lashed to the bulwark amidships."

Shelton was doing his best to control his anger as he answered. "You get the hammers and knock all the pegs out immediately. Then you go down into the holds and explain to my countrymen that they are being freed. Once my countrymen are on deck, you and your crew will go into the hold."

"But I am the captain of a king's ship! I am entitled to separate quarters and parole!"

Shelton, a preacher's son, had been taught never to use blasphemy. This time, his anger got the better of him. Like most of the crew, he had heard of the horrible conditions on the British prison ships in New York harbor, and what he saw on *Bear* was, in his eyes, an abomination. "Damn your eyes! You are now a prisoner of war, and I am going to treat you as you treat my countrymen."

The captain and one of Bear's officers did as they were told. Slowly, the Americans filed up the ladders and stepped into the fading sunlight. Additional sailors who came over from *Scorpion* guided the Americans into a group. They were filthy. Their clothes were in tatters, and many of them were emaciated, or looked as though they had been beaten.

Shelton's jaw worked as he looked them over. He strode over to the side and called out to *Scorpion's* men who were lowering a cutter. "Bring soap back, along with Mr. Patterson."

After inspecting the prison ship, Shelton ordered the British seamen to empty their sea chests until he had enough clothes for the Americans he'd just freed. In the captain's cabin, he found a chart that showed the ship's route from New York with its load of prisoners from the Continental Navy frigate *Raleigh*.

When Lieutenant Patterson climbed over the side. Shelton explained the situation. "They'll need to wash, using soap and sea water. Have the British seamen from *Bear* man the pumps. I know the water is cold, but we have no better choice. Toss all the dirty clothes over the side. The British sailors are donating their clothes for our men. Once they're clean and dressed, we'll divide them up. I'll be back with the *Inquest's* captain to start the prisoner transfer. Glanville needs to see how our men were treated by the Royal Navy."

"The captain doesn't like us hanging about."

"Can't be helped."

Back on board *Scorpion*, a still furious Jack Shelton told Jaco of the on conditions on the prison ship. "There is some good news. Many of the men on *Bear* were taken from our frigate *Raleigh*. We should be able to put them to work once they clean up and get a proper meal or two."

Jaco sent for Captain Glanville, and when the Royal Navy captain knocked on the door to Jaco's cabin, the two Americans were waiting. The Royal Navy officer was a head taller than Jaco, and had to stoop slightly to keep his head from banging into the overhead beams.

"Captain Glanville, I apologize in advance, for I understand the conditions where our prisoners were kept on board *Bear* are disgusting. Unfortunately, I have no other place to keep your men. This much I can promise. While we sail to where I hope to be able to release you, your men and those of *Bear* will be properly fed. You can, if you so choose, clean the hold where you will be kept. There are two decks and plenty of space for the 175 of you to hang your hammocks, so you will not be crowded. Any resistance, of course, will be dealt with harshly."

Glanville sighed. "I understand. You are doing what you have to do. But what about my wounded?"

"They will be kept on board *Scorpion* with your surgeon until they are well enough to be moved. I will treat them as if they are my own sailors."

"Thank you." Glanville held out his hand. "Perhaps we shall meet again under more pleasant circumstances."

Jaco took the offered hand. "We should be allies, not enemies. I wish you good luck."

* * *

Hedley Garrison and a half dozen sailors from *Scorpion,* plus most of the American prisoners, were more than enough to sail *Bear*. The former captain and first lieutenant of *Bear* were ferried to *Scorpion* along with *Bear's* log, which indicated the prison ship had made many trips to North Sydney. Jaco hoped *Bear's* captain might tell them where the prisoners were kept.

Graham Picard was sweating profusely when he was ushered into Jaco's cabin. His clothes were dirty from cleaning the hold, but nowhere near as bad as what the American prisoners had been wearing when they were freed. Jaco did not invite him to sit down but saw to it that a cup of hot tea was offered. The portly officer guzzled it down. Then Jaco got right to the point. "Captain Picard, what can you tell us about Glace Bay?"

Picard glared at the young captain. "I don't see how it's my business to tell you anything! You're a bloody rebel and look like a damned Spanish pirate. That makes you the ruddy enemy twice over."

This was going to be a very different exchange than the one with Captain Glanville, Jaco reflected. But he had prepared for this.

"Mr. Picard, I shall be blunt with you. Whether you tell us or not makes no difference in my plans, but it might make a difference in whether or not you are exchanged for an American officer or drown in *Bear's* hold. Your former ship is now our prize and, if I have no reason to revise my tactics, will fly a Continental Navy flag as we approach. So, unless I know how to plot a safe passage to our destination, your ship with you locked in the hold will take the heaviest fire, and the most casualties. While I would prefer a civilized exchange of prisoners, to everyone's benefit and satisfaction, I am both willing and able to do what is necessary to free our prisoners at Glace Bay. And after seeing how our men were treated as *your* prisoners, I hardly feel the need for patience or for*bear*ance."

Off to one side, Jack winced.

Graham Picard's jowls moved and he pursed his lips while he deliberated. Then he spoke abruptly. "The prisoners are not at Glace Bay. They're outside a settlement called North Sydney."

The chart from *Bear* was already rolled out on the table. Jaco pointed to the northern shore of Cape Breton Island. "Show me."

With a thick forefinger that had dirt under the nail, Picard indicated where *Bear* anchored to unload, and where the fort was located.

"What kind of cannon does the fort have, and how many men are there?"

"There's a small, undersized regiment under the command of Major Timothy Van Doorn. He's a Loyalist from New York. From what I understand, he's a very capable soldier who doesn't like you rebels."

Jaco ignored the jab. "Cannon?"

"Four, all four-pounder field guns."

"The fort, what are the walls made from?"

"Logs. It's more a stockade to provide shelter from the winter than a proper fort."

"Where are the prisoners kept?"

Picard looked directly at Jaco. "In a building by the mine."

"How many prisoners?"

"Maybe two hundred. Doorn told me that every few months a Royal Navy ship needing sailors comes in and offers the prisoners a choice: work the mine as a prisoner or join the Royal Navy. There's always some as see the good sense in rejoining the flock, as it were. We anchor *Bear* in Lloyd Cove and row the men ashore. Van Doorn's soldiers take the men from there to the prisoner barracks."

"What other ships are usually there?"

Picard looked like he'd rather spit than speak, but a hard stare from Shelton settled him.

"Every week, a coal ship anchors in Lloyd Cove. Lighters moored in the cove ferry coal out to the collier. The prisoners help load the bags onto the lighters."

"What about Royal Navy frigates?"

"Rarely do they stop in Sydney. They prefer Halifax, where they can get supplies and sometimes enjoy a bit of shore leave."

"And defenses?"

"For a coal mine that far north?" Picard scoffed, but Jaco noticed that his eyes turned shifty and he shuffled his feet.

"Very well. That's enough, and perhaps it is enough to prevent unnecessary loss of life," Jaco said, and signaled the guards to return Picard to the prisoners' deck.

In a separate interview with *Bear's* first lieutenant, Jaco's suspicions were confirmed. Picard had not been entirely truthful. The first lieutenant, who had a markedly different view of matters, was more forthcoming. Van Doorn, he said, was building small stone forts with cannon overlooking the bay. The first one was being constructed at Chapel Point and by now was probably completed.

The lieutenant seemed genuinely appalled by how the American prisoners had been treated. Jaco sensed that the captain and first lieutenant of *Bear* had not gotten along especially well.

North Sydney, fourth week of August 1778

Just after dawn, *H.M.S. Bear* glided into Lloyd Cove and dropped anchor where she normally did. A heavily laden collier named *Yarmouth* rode at anchor with its sails furled.

Scorpion dropped one anchor from the bow and then the new one made by Gaskins off the stern to keep its port side guns pointed at the fort. Jaco assessed the Chapel Point battery through his spyglass. To his intense relief, it did not look finished. *Scorpion* was not showing a flag, nor were its guns run out, but they were loaded and ready.

A red-coated officer ordered a boat readied and headed to *Scorpion*. Lieutenant Cornelius Giffords, Royal Nova Scotia Volunteers, greeted Captain Glanville, who gestured to Jaco and said, "I think you need to speak to this chap."

"Lieutenant, I am Jaco Jacinto, Captain of the Continental Navy frigate *Scorpion*. On board *Bear*, we have 196 Royal Navy sailors. I propose that we exchange them for all, and I do mean *all* of my fellow countrymen held here. This way no one gets hurt and we'll be gone once they are on board."

At first Giffords' face was shocked, then he regained his composure. "I cannot make such an arrangement."

"Then take me to the man who can."

"He.... He... is not in Nova Scotia."

Jaco's coal-black eyes bored into Giffords'. "Don't lie to me, Lieutenant. We can make this exchange peacefully. Or I will take our men back by force—and take our Royal Navy prisoners with us. Based on what I know about how you treat prisoners of war, I may decide to kill every British soldier I find, and then burn Sydney to the ground. Now, again, who can agree to the exchange?"

Giffords swallowed, visibly. "Major Van Doorn."

"Good. Take me to him. Where is he?"

"In the stockade."

Jaco drew a pistol and put the end of the barrel under Giffords' chin. A little upwards pressure pushed the cold steel into the soft place under the lieutenant's jaw. "Excellent. Now, once we are on shore, we will go under a flag of truce. And bear in mind, Lieutenant, if there is any trickery, you will be the first man I kill."

The stockade was up a slope, 100 yards from the rocky shore and only 400 yards from *Scorpion's* long 12-pounders. On each of the corners facing the cove, a tower made from logs rose about 10 feet above the stockade wall that was about 15 feet tall. Giffords carried an oar to which a white piece of cloth was tied. The gate opened and Giffords, Jacinto and Garrison entered.

They followed Giffords to a small building on the far side, which was the only structure made of stone. All around them Jaco could see soldiers eying the two men in dark blue frock coats.

Major Johannes van Doorn stood on the porch, awaiting the small procession. He was wearing a sword and had a pistol stuck in his belt. A second officer came out of the building and stood next to Van Doorn, scowling at the two Continental Navy officers.

Van Doorn rested his hands on his hips, close to both his weapons. "Who the bloody hell are you?"

"Captain Jaco Jacinto of the Continental Navy Frigate *Scorpion*. This is my second lieutenant, Hedley Garrison. Major van Doorn, we are here to discuss an exchange of prisoners."

"Seems to me I could throw you in with the other rebels we have as prisoners. Or I could kill you."

O'Dea came down the steps and walked to the side of the two Americans. He acted as if he was inspecting them for a future purchase.

Jaco ignored this until O'Dea started to walk behind him, then he whirled and faced O'Dea. "Honorable men don't walk behind those with whom they are negotiating in good faith under a flag of truce."

Van Doorn waved to O'Dea, who retreated to the porch a step behind his commander.

"Major, if I do not return to my ship within the hour, my first lieutenant has orders to open fire. I think being on the receiving end of my ship's 12-pound cannon balls would be unpleasant for you and your men. I do not think your fort would be able to withstand a barrage of 12-pound balls fired from long guns. Then my crew, whether I am alive or not, will land and kill every man Jack of you before they take back our men you are holding as prisoners. Now, Major, you can avoid all this unnecessary bloodshed by giving me all your prisoners. In exchange, I will turn over the one hundred and ninety-six Royal Navy sailors presently in the hold of *H.M.S. Bear*."

"Gadzooks, you're a ruddy arrogant sort, aren't you?"

Jaco said nothing and glared at Van Doorn, waiting for an answer.

"If I agree, then what do you do?"

"*Scorpion, Bear* and the coal ship, which I will take as a prize, will depart without firing a shot. How many men do you have as prisoners?"

Van Doorn looked at Giffords, who answered. "One hundred and ninety-six."

"Don't fence with me, Major. I want all the American prisoners. I shan't be leaving any behind, so tell me the real number."

"Two hundred and twenty-one as of last night's count."

"Thank you. This brings me to my last point. You will allow the prisoners to bathe with soap and fresh water and provide them with clean clothes."

"Captain, you are making ridiculous demands to which I may not agree. We can fight an interesting battle over a few prisoners of war. The skirmish wouldn't make the history books and, in the end, I think you will lose."

Jaco refused to take the bait. "Major, time is being wasted."

"I need time to consider your proposal."

"Major, you have just a few minutes before the first 12-pound ball rips through this fort."

"Young man, I think you're bluffing. Even if your popguns can reach this far, the ball they fire may kill you just as easily as me."

"Aye, that is a possibility. Please understand, Major, I don't play games with my crew's lives. If there is a risk to take, it is mine to accept."

"I don't think your cannon balls will damage my fort, so I suggest that you go back to your ship under that flag of truce and see if you can take your prisoners by force."

"Major van Doorn, you are making a mistake. Many men, but mostly yours, will die unnecessarily."

"Yes, but you won't get your prisoners. So, to use your own words, that is my risk to accept. Several privateers and Continental Navy ships have tried to claim them. ALL, repeat, ***ALL*** have failed. I will gladly add your ship's name to the list. We may or may not succeed in taking your frigate as a prize, but we can sink it."

Jaco turned to Hedley. "Lieutenant, we have nothing left to discuss."

His statement was punctuated by the sound a cannon firing, followed by the cracking noise of wood splintering. Jagged shards, some of them as long as a spear, hissed overhead. Van Doorn jerked around and saw a large hole just beneath the forward wall of the guard tower. A second cannon boomed and a section of the wall next to the open gate disintegrated into a mass of splinters. The third ball punched a hole in the stockade and hammered into the stone wall of the building where Van Doorn had his office. When the dust cleared, there was a hole a man could crawl through.

O'Dea put a hand on one of the posts that held up the roof over the porch. He looked at Jaco, then down at his ample stomach, where a large splinter had run him through. O'Dea's eyes glazed over and he fell face forward.

By the time a fourth ball screamed a few feet over Jaco's head and slammed into the stone building's roof, both he and Hedley were running for the open gate. A few musket balls sang over their heads and others kicked up the dirt.

Ball five hit the guard tower on the left front corner of the fort. Jaco and Hedley were less than 20 yards from the front gate of the fort when they heard Giffords yelling. Jaco turned and saw Giffords running towards them and waving. "Signal them to stop! Major Van Doorn has changed his mind."

Hedley waved the oar just as a ball left the number 7 starboard gun. The fighting position on the right front corner of the fort disintegrated.

Jaco spoke calmly. "Lieutenant, have Major Van Doorn tell me that to my face, so we can work out the details of the prisoner trade. I'll wait by the boat we used to come ashore."

Walking towards their boat, Hedley looked at his captain. "Damn that was close."

"Shelton was confident that our guns would make mincemeat of the stockade. Unless I signaled, he was to begin firing ten minutes after we entered the fort."

"Why didn't you tell me?"

"Because I didn't want to scare you!"

Van Doorn was covered with dust and dirt and brushing his sleeve off as he approached the two Americans. "Captain, meet me with a detail of your men at that red building over yonder. You bring a boatload of Royal Navy sailors ashore and you can return with a load of your men."

"First, I want to tell my countrymen what is happening. And you have the bathing and clothes to attend to. Then the exchange can begin."

"Very well. Agreed."

Jacinto insisted the prisoners be led out into the sunlight where he could address them all. As they gathered, he looked for a tall, blond man about his age. Not seeing anyone who looked familiar, he began to speak.

"Gentlemen, I am Captain Jaco Jacinto of the Continental Navy and commander of the frigate *Scorpion*. After you bathe and are given clean clothes, you will board the ships out in harbor and we will take you to Boston. The war is not over so we will do our best to avoid the Royal Navy."

Van Doorn's men already had buckets and bars of soap standing by. Cold well water was being pumped out of the well and the men were washing the coal dust and dirt from their bodies.

"Jaco, is that really you?"

The soft, South Carolina accent was very familiar. He turned to see a man who looked aged. "Eric?"

"Aye, 'Tis I. And you, my friend, are a sight for sore eyes."

* * *

The northeast tip of Cape Breton Island was well astern of *Scorpion* when Eric Laredo knocked on the captain's cabin door. Jaco had asked him to come aft for a drink once the ship's sails were set for the night. Between the rescue and this moment, Eric had kept his distance to let Jaco 'the captain' run his ship. Now Jaco wanted a chance to talk privately with the man who had been, and he hoped still was, his best friend.

Jaco put down the quill pen he was using to write in *Scorpion's* official log. "Come in."

When Eric entered, he walked over to his friend and gave him a manly hug.

"Good God, Eric, I was so happy to see you! I was afraid you were sent to one of those horrible prison ships in New York. How'd you wind up in North Sydney?" Jaco poured two glasses of madeira and handed one to Eric.

"It was a nightmare, Jaco. *Duke* was carrying two tons of gunpowder we'd picked up in Spain when we lost a mast in a storm. The next day, *H.M.S. Jodpur* spotted us. We couldn't run, and one of the balls from *Jodpur* must have hit a barrel stave, for a spark set off the powder. One minute I was standing on the quarterdeck and the next I was swimming." His face worked. "Only six of us survived."

"How were you treated?"

"On *Jodpur*, I dined with the officers. The captain, a chap by the name of Horrocks, was very civil, very professional. All the officers were."

"And so you met Darren Smythe."

Eric's expression became one of astonishment. "Do you know him?"

"I do. At one point I captured Mr. Smythe and we took him to Brest. We had many interesting discussions, and after we win our independence, I'd like to get to know him better. In an action against three Royal Navy frigates where we managed to escape, I'm pretty sure I saw him on one."

"According to Hedley Garrison, that day you gave the Royal Navy a lesson in gunnery, tactics and seamanship."

"We had a good day."

Eric smiled. Both Garrison and Patterson had already told him about the raids at Aberdeen and Stornaway, and the taking of *H.M.S Coburg*.

"Smythe seems to be a decent sort. I think if circumstances were different, we'd be good friends. He is not like some of the Loyalists back in Charleston."

"Perhaps. Jaco, I have to ask. I saw van Doorn but not that sadistic gundiguts O'Dea. What happened to him?"

"O'Dea is dead. A splinter ran him through."

Eric absorbed this. "Good. He was an ill-tempered man who liked to hurt people." Eric described O'Dea shooting Commander O'Rourke, then he became pensive. "I was determined to survive. Not just to return home, but to spite Van Doorn and O'Dea.

Eric took a long swallow from his glass of madeira. "This is good. Where did it come from?"

"The incredibly well stocked captain's pantry of the armed merchant ship *H.M.S. Madras*."

"So, Jaco, congratulations on being a captain of a frigate."

"Thank you." Jaco hesitated, then decided now was the time. "There is... something I need to tell you."

Eric looked apprehensive. "And that is?"

"Reyna and I are engaged."

Eric laughed so hard he almost fell off his chair. "Congratulations! I haven't seen her in two years; she must be all grown up."

"She is. I don't think you would recognize her."

"Well, the two of you are perfect for each other. Although it was not so long ago that I thought she would kill you after you rubbed mud in her hair. Does Reyna still want to be a doctor?"

"Oh, yes. She's apprenticed to Dr. MacKenzie and is already better than most doctors you and I know."

Jaco took a sip of wine and continued. "I saw your parents in February and they are well. They know you were captured but nothing more. Amos is an officer in the 2nd Carolina Infantry."

Eric ran his finger around the glass until it hummed. "What do you know about the war?"

"Well, the French and Spanish have declared war on the British. With them on our side, I hope the English will get tired of fighting. But who knows? They're a stubborn lot."

Eric thought for a few seconds. "When are you and Reyna getting married?"

"When the war is over."

Eric grunted softly. "That may not be for several years."

Jaco nodded. "Aye." After a few seconds, he asked, "Eric, when we get to Boston, what do you intend to do?"

"Go back to Charleston as soon as I can. Then I want to figure out how I can help beat the British. I am not sure how, but I don't want to fight from the deck of a ship anymore."

Jaco held up his glass as an acknowledgement and savored the moment; his best friend was alive and well. And he understood why Eric didn't want fight at sea. The quarterdeck was a dangerous place in a battle.

Chapter 6
Return of the Duchess

South of the Turks & Caicos, first week of September 1778

Coming out of the Windward Passage between Cuba and Hispaniola, Smythe set *Liber's* course to transit the Florida Strait. At the northern end of the Bahamas, he planned to turn east for 100 miles before sailing south toward the Turks & Caicos Islands. The route would let *Liber* search for privateers hiding in the sparsely populated islands, which were transit lanes for ships.

Dawn broke on the sixth day out of Port Royal just like the prior five—bright blue sky and an aquamarine sea—with one big difference. Sunrise revealed a large Spanish merchant ship under full sail five miles in front of *Liber*. Although armed with six 9-pounders on each side, *Cadiz* surrendered without a fight. Nassau was only 100 miles away, and at the stately speed of six knots they reached the Bahamas' capital in 16 hours.

The sloop stayed in Nassau for three days, long enough to replace the provisions they'd consumed and to turn *Cadiz* over to the Admiralty Court to sell the ship and the 100 tons of refined Cuban sugar in its hold. Soames was smiling when he came back on board. Based on the clerk's advice, Darren valued *Cadiz'* cargo at £20,000 and the ship at £4,000 in the table in his log and journal.

His quill pen scratched noisily as he made the calculations and wrote the list of estimated prize money. Smythe thought that even the pen didn't believe the amounts.

Admiral Parker—£3,000

Captain—£6,000

Each lieutenant—£1,000

Quartermaster, carpenter, bosun—£750

Each mate and midshipman—£500

Each seaman—£53 1S

The seaman's share was more than four times the £12 the Royal Navy paid them each year. So far under his captaincy, the men of *Liber* were doing quite well.

Once the formalities of handing over *Cadiz* were completed, *Liber* left Nassau and sailed east. Three days out of Nassau, they were passing Providenciales Island, the northernmost of the Turks and Caicos. Smythe was quieter than usual, remembering his first cruise as a midshipman on *H.M.S. Deer*. In these waters, he had seen his first action against a privateer named *Duchess,* which had fired a devastating broadside, crippling *Deer* and killing its captain, master, and first lieutenant.

So far, the only ships they'd seen were in a British convoy of four merchant ships escorted by two frigates. He let one frigate sail close enough so their captains could see the recognition signals and *Liber's* flag.

Each day, *Liber's* lookouts squinted in the bright sun as they checked coves and harbors that had been pirate havens

50 years ago. From the deck, Smythe wasn't looking for ships, he was scrutinizing the horizon for signs of an onrushing hurricane. If one appeared, the direction his ship sailed was critical. Guess right and *Liber* would spend a night in rough seas pelted by rain. Guess wrong and *Liber* could lose a mast or capsize and sink.

With daytime temperature in the 90s, within two hours of hosing the main deck with sea water the wood was uncomfortably hot. The black-painted cannons were so hot that by late afternoon tendrils of steam curled up when water was splashed on them. Yet, despite the heat, everyone on board agreed that the weather in this part of the world was better than cold northern seas.

Occasional afternoon squalls provided relief from the heat. Rainwater was captured in half barrels so the crew could enjoy a drink of the sweet tasting fresh water. Once the shower passed, tendrils of moisture rose from the hot deck.

The westerly wind let Smythe keep *Liber* a mile off the coast of Mayaguana Island, the southernmost cay in the Bahamas. The sloop's lookouts could see across the flat island with its scrub pines and palm trees and spot any ships transiting to the nor' west.

Suddenly, "Deck there, two sails going nor' west, two points aft the starboard beam." Both ships were fully rigged, running with their royals sheeted home, cruising as fast as they could sail.

If Liber is to have a chance at catching them, I have to either reverse course or come around the south side of the island. In any case, I need more sail. "Mr. Louttit, let's get our royals and top gallants out smartly. If nothing else, we'll dry them out. Then fly the fore staysail and both jibs."

The bosun waved, issued a stream of commands, and men started climbing the rigging. *Liber's* spars for its royals were relatively short and needed only two men on each side to free the gaskets.

Darren issued his next command. “Bosun, let the royals loose, get them sheeted home. We’ll be on this tack until we clear the reef.”

The flying jib and the fore staysail came next, and *Liber* surged ahead, pushed by wind against five more sails.

Darren turned to his midshipman on the watch. “Mr. Tewksbury, tell me, which is the fastest way to catch those two ships? Reverse course and go around the north side, or go around the south side of the island?”

The 13-year-old glanced at the sails of the unknown ships. “Sir, if we reverse course and they’re watching us, they will know we’re interested. I’d go around the south and then see if we can catch them. The sun will be gone in three hours, so if they’re hanging a lantern on their stern like they’re supposed to do, they should be easy to follow.”

“I like your thinking. Now figure out when to tack.”

The sun was a nearing the horizon when *Liber* came around the reef at the southern tip of Mayaguana Island and turned north. The two mystery ships were close to the visual horizon, about 10 miles ahead.

“Mr. Tewksbury, pass on to your relief that we will continue flying the royals and top gallants and flying jib for two hours after sunset, then we’ll reef them for the night. Make sure the lookouts know to keep track of the lanterns, if they hang them.”

* * *

However, neither of the unknown ships hung a lantern. They were in an area where four nations—Spain, France,

England and the rebels—were at war, and a lantern can be seen for miles on a clear night.

As dawn lightened the sky from black to grey, a steady but not heavy rain started. Smythe kept *Liber* on the east side of Andros Island so the westerly wind wouldn't push the sloop towards the island.

During the afternoon watch under Lieutenant Soames, *Liber* emerged from the clouds and rain, and the lookout called down that the two unknown ships were less than three miles ahead under shortened sail. Like *Liber*, now that they were clear of the rain and gusty winds, they were hanging more canvas.

Smythe studied the two ships. One ship was clearly a merchantman, and the other looked vaguely familiar. He couldn't read the names on the back yet, nor tell what flag either ship was flying.

Liber surged ahead, gaining ground because the slower merchant ship was setting the pace. Inside two miles, Smythe rested his elbow on the forward railing to steady his Dollond spyglass. He still could not discern the name of the merchantman, but the frigate was starting to tack and he had a clear view of the ship's name. His heart sank and fear knotted his gut. It was the *Duchess*.

Suddenly, Smythe was in a hurry. "Are you ready, bosun?"

The Scotsman waved.

"Stand by to wear ship to starboard. Mr. Stanhope, new course will be so' east."

A high voice piped up behind Smythe, "Sir, why are we running?"

"I'll explain in a minute. Mr. Tewksbury, gather all the officers at the aft end of the quarterdeck. Bosun. When our course is set and the sails are sheeted home, come join us."

When they were assembled on the quarterdeck, Smythe pointed to *Duchess*, now three miles behind them. "That, gentlemen, is the *Privateer Duchess,* armed with at least sixteen 9-pounders. *Duchess'* captain a very capable seaman who makes subtle moves that you don't notice until too late." As Darren told the story of how the privateer had crippled *H.M.S. Deer*, the memories scared him.

"Gentlemen, we will not take on *Duchess* at this time, not with a sloop, not when we are heavily outgunned by a ship that can match our speed. Maybe later, with a bigger ship. Carry on."

Boston, second week of September 1778

Scorpion led *H.M.S. Bear* and *H.M.S. Yarmouth* into Boston's harbor to an anchorage between Spectacle and Castle Island. While waiting for the ships to drop anchors and furl sails, Jaco had time to watch a cutter sailing out from Charlestown where the Port Captain had his offices. Ebenezer Brinley was about to pay them a visit. Jack Shelton called out, "Mr. Preston, rig a bosun's chair to hoist Captain Brinley aboard."

Brinley declined the offer of a ride up the side of the frigate. It may have been a matter of pride to show that he was still fit and spry enough to make the climb up the ladder on *Scorpion's* side, but he was huffing noticeably when he reached the deck. When Brinley saw a row of six sailors standing at attention on either side of the hatch, he smiled.

Bosun Preston blew General Call on his brass bosun's pipe and one of his mates rang *Scorpion's* bell three times. Then Preston bellowed, "Boston Navy Yard, arriving."

The 60-year-old Ebenezer Brinley was still grinning at the ceremony and warmly greeted Jaco. "I see *Scorpion* has brought us prizes to sell.

"Aye, sir. Please join me in my cabin, for we have much to discuss."

Jaco had set out three glasses—one for his guest, one for Jack Shelton and one for himself—and a bottle of madeira wine taken from *H.M.S. Inquest,* whose bell now hung next to those of *H.M.S. Coburg* and *H.M.S. Cutlass*. After a toast to their cause, Brinley settled in the chair at the forward end of the table.

Jaco began describing the sinking of *H.M.S. Inquest* and ended with the prisoner exchange. "Some of the men are now on *Scorpion's* muster. The rest are from Massachusetts, Rhode Island and New Hampshire. I hope you can find a way to get these men paid and on their way home."

Brinley nodded vigorously. "Consider the matter done. As for *Bear,* the collier *Yarmouth* and its load of coal, my brother Absalom runs the Admiralty Court here in Boston, and there are many ship owners who will be interested in these ships."

"Thank you. I am sure he will get a fair price."

"You know, Captain Jacinto, you are making a lot of men rich."

"We will be richer when we are free of British rule, not by seizing prizes but by cultivating our land and businesses. And, yes, I am aware that many of my men are going to be very well off."

"What's next on your list?"

"One of the men who was retaken at Sydney is Eric Laredo. We grew up together in Charleston, and I'd like Eric booked on the packet that runs up and down the coast."

"Done."

Perfecto! "Thank you."

"Do you have a list of provisions that you need?"

"Mr. Patterson, my third lieutenant, will give you our list."

"And how long do you plan to stay in Boston?"

"Not long. The sooner *Scorpion* can be re-provisioned, the sooner we can resume our assignment. By now, the Loyalists in Boston know we are here and have probably sent riders to their British friends in New York."

"Yes, I rather think the seizing or sinking of Scorpion has become a priority for the British, so we shall expedite your departure."

The day turned foggy and rainy. In the cutter taking them ashore, Jack Shelton and Jaco Jacinto huddled in their greatcoats as waves of the gray-blue water slapped against the sides of the boat.

A stale smell of fish rose about them, getting stronger as they neared the pier. The source, they soon saw, were rows of gutted and butterflied cod hung from ropes to dry.

Jaco guessed that weather would delay the drying process, before the fish could be packed into barrels between layers of salt and shipped to Europe. Before the war, dried fish was a principal export of the northern Colonies to England, France, Portugal and Spain.

Ashore, the rain and drizzle made everything wet, particularly the slick cobblestones, and the footing was treacherous on the narrow streets. Unlike Charleston or Philadelphia, whose streets were laid out on a grid, Boston's streets followed no pattern at all. Learning the city's layout was difficult, unless one had a map. This morning their destination was the Green Dragon, a coffee shop on Union Street.

The two Continental Navy officers were walking on North Street when Jaco was shoved in the back and sent sprawling.

Jaco turned and sat up, his hands bleeding and dirty, his clothes very muddy about the knees. Seeing who had shoved him, he remembered that it wasn't only loyalists who held a grudge against Scorpion's captain.

Edmund Radcliffe stood there, waving a silver-topped cane and glowering at him. "That's where you belong, Jacinto, in the gutter."

Shelton was wide-eyed and frozen with alarm, his eyes darting from one man to the other.

Slowly, Jaco stood up, not taking his eyes off Radcliffe. His first impulse was to pummel his former second lieutenant senseless. Another part of him said, *Walk away*. For a moment, Jaco considered challenging Radcliffe to a duel. Instead, he wiped the mud and filth off his coat.

Radcliffe now had an evil, malevolent grin on his face. Jaco forced himself to speak civilly. "Instead of attacking me, you should be thanking me for not hanging you when I had the chance." Jaco turned to Jack Shelton, who had his hand on his sword. "Let's go."

Radcliffe put his hand on Jaco's shoulder and started to pull him around, but Jaco, who was shorter but more sturdily built, used his thumb and forefinger to remove the offending hand. As he did, Jaco whispered, "Radcliffe, don't ever touch me again. The next time you do, you will not like what happens. Do I make myself clear?"

"And I," snarled Radcliffe, "will see to it that any prizes you bring to Boston rot unsold -- or sell for pennies on the pound."

"You would sabotage the means of financing independence out of a spiteful grudge? I'll be sure to mention that to the Marine Committee. I'm sure John Adams will be delighted that you undermine his authority. Go off and play with the squires of Alsatia with whom you are friends. Spending any time with you is a monumental waste. Good day."

Jaco stepped away, refusing to turn his back on what seemed to him a rabid jackal in human form. Radcliffe screamed, "You bloody bastard!" and drew the blade from his cane.

Radcliffe's first lunge went wide, giving Jaco time to draw his own sword. His first parry knocked Radcliffe's blade to the side. Jaco suspected Radcliffe's anger was getting in the way of his sword fighting skills. Out of the corner of his eye, Jaco could see a crowd gathering. Sword fights on the street were not common, particularly with one contestant wearing the uniform of a Continental Navy officer.

Seeing the cold face of Jaco Jacinto, the warrior, Shelton was afraid that if his captain ran Radcliffe through, he would be jailed. "Jaco, don't kill him!"

Another lunge by Radcliffe, easily parried by Jaco, who used the slide of the blade to slap his attacker's forearm hard enough to cause his opponent to lose his grip. The sword clattered to the cobblestones.

Jaco put the tip of his sword under Radcliffe's chin and pushed him three steps back, while Jack Shelton picked up Radcliffe's weapon. "Edmund, don't come near me again. The next time, I won't be nearly this restrained." Jaco extended his left hand, into which Jack Shelton put the handle of Radcliffe's weapon.

Jaco stepped back, sheathed his sword, then bent the blade over his knee until the metal snapped. Jaco held out the two pieces. "Now, Radcliffe, be a good rat and go back to whatever hole you came from. And stay the hell out of my way."

Chapter 7
Scorpion on the Loose

Philadelphia, third week of September 1778

Eric Laredo noticed that every port had a unique smell. On the way up Delaware Bay, the fresh sea air of the Atlantic changed to the musty smells of brackish water. Near Philadelphia, the odors changed again, smelling of a garbage filled, dirty river.

This was much less pleasant than how he remembered Charleston harbor, but typical of ports that were well inland. Even in South Carolina, when the wind was blowing from the nor' west, the smell of rotting vegetation from the wetlands north of Charleston filled the sky. To most Charlestonians, the smell was welcome because the odor meant that the rice paddies would be full.

When Eric Laredo stepped off the schooner *Alacrity,* shortly after nine in the morning, he was planning to spend only the day in Philadelphia. The packet's captain had said the schooner was leaving just after dark, and if Eric intended to continue his voyage to Charleston, he'd best be back on board.

He had to ask directions, but eventually he found the house of the father of his best friend. He knocked, then waited on the steps until the door was opened by a man with greying hair.

Javier Jacinto's jaw dropped. "My god, man, come in. Eric! I'm sorry, but you...."

"I know, I look different. I just spent two years in hell."

"Let's go to the kitchen where I can fix you something to eat and we can talk."

"Thank you, something to eat that wasn't stored in a barrel would be most appreciated!"

Javier laughed and led the way. He sliced two apples and put a loaf of crusty, dark bread on the table, along with a jar of honey. Then he brought to the table a board with a knife and a wax-coated wheel of hard, white cheese. "Tea, coffee?"

"Either."

While they ate, Eric recounted his story, from the time *Duke* blew up until he knocked on the door. He ended by saying, "I don't know who I hate more, the British or their Loyalist friends. The British are waging war on us. Loyalists treat us like rabid dogs, or worse, rats. I swear to God, if I ever meet Johannes van Doorn again, I will kill him. And, after the war is won, I will have a hard time trusting anyone who was a Loyalist."

Javier didn't respond to Eric's raw emotion. He could only imagine the horror that Eric had endured in Nova Scotia, but he understood his anger toward Loyalists. He also knew the anger was mutual. Loyalists regarded the war as unnecessary and wrong. Some argued that rebellion broke the commandment to honor one's father and mother.

Eric changed the subject, "How is my father's business? Jaco said the British have taken many of his ships."

Jacinto sighed. "In his last letter, he said he had lost eight of his sixteen ships. And he is not alone. The British have captured many of our merchant ships."

"I do not want to stay in the Navy. I do not wish to sail the seas anymore. So what then can I do to help our cause?"

Javier glanced at the shelf clock. The hands on the David Rittenhouse timepiece indicated it was just past 11 in the morning. "Come with me to a meeting with Count Klaus Olafsson. He is a member of the court of the Swedish King Gustav III. His monarch is interested in our rebellion and wants to help. Perhaps we can find work for you."

Off Cape Hatteras, NC, third week of September 1778

Scorpion was headed due south. Jaco was scanning the horizon in front of his ship, just after forenoon watch began. The swells seemed larger than usual; the frigate loped along, rising up and then plunging down, sending spray aft and wetting the main deck.

"Mr. Shelton, what do you make of the weather to our south?"

"Captain, in the New Testament, the Book of Mark, Chapter 4 Verse 39, it is written: "*And he, being God, awoke and he rebuked the wind and said to the sea, 'Peace, be still.' And the wind ceased and there was a great calm.*" Jack paused. "Sir, I don't think that will happen. We're in hurricane season and I'd say we're looking at the northern edge of one."

"Exactly what I am thinking. If this storm parallels the coast, we should be safer if we head east. We are not anchoring in Chesapeake Bay where *Scorpion* could be blown onto a sand bar. Call the watch, let out royals and fore staysails until dark. We have about twelve more hours of daylight, and at 10 knots we should be one hundred and twenty miles from here."

"Aye, Captain."

For the next few hours, the wind picked up. Heavy rain soaked the ship as the frigate plunged through eight-foot swells, and Jaco came close to regretting his decision. But then, just before dark, the wind slackened, the rain ended, and the seas became calmer. He had the royals reefed but kept the top gallants sheeted home, wanting to sail as far away from the storm as possible.

All night long, Jaco visited the deck at close intervals to monitor the wind and direction of the waves. Just before dawn, the men on deck could see stars, and Jaco ordered another sighting. *Scorpion* was 110 miles nor' nor' east of Bermuda. After breakfast, he ordered the ship to change course to so 'west. Off in the distance to the nor' west they could see the back end of a hurricane darkening the skies and water. Months later, when he returned home, he learned this very hurricane had prevented a battle between the Royal and French Navies off the North Carolina coast.

The sun was well up when the lookout called, "Deck, two sets of masts, two points off the larboard bow."

Jaco, who was napping in his cabin, didn't hear the call. A hard knock on his cabin door woke him. He swung his legs out of his bunk and stood up, calling out, "Come in."

A young Marine entered. At 6' 4" Private Elias Marchais was the tallest man on the ship. He had to stoop to avoid the overhead beams. "Captain, two ships about five miles away. The watch asks if you want to change course to investigate."

"Aye, of course we should take a look. Tell the watch I'll be on the quarterdeck shortly."

Even with the steady breeze and the movement of the ship through the air, the bright fall sun warmed the deck. The liquid in the thermometer was at the 85-degree mark and everyone on deck was dressed in shirts and breeches. The wood on the main deck was hot underfoot, and Jaco ordered the main and quarterdecks to be hosed down to cool them.

As the seamen worked the pumps, they sang a shanty known as “Drunken Sailor”. Rhode Islander and Leading Seaman Colin Landry led the chant while the eight men pushed the bar up and down to suck sea water through a canvas pipe.

All the men sang—

> Way, hey, up she rises,
> Way, hey, up she rises,
> Way, hey, up she rises
> Early in the morning!

Then the seven sang—

> What shall we do with the drunken sailor?
> What shall we do with the drunken sailor?
> What shall we do with the drunken sailor?
> Early in the morning?

Landry supplied the replies, each line repeated three times by the seven men for a verse:

> Put him in the scuppers with the hose pipe on him...
> Hoist him aboard with a running bowline...
> Put him in the long boat 'til he's sober...
> Pull out the bung and wet him all over...

Heave him in the scuppers with the deck pump on him...
Tie him to the taffrail when she's yardarm under...

After he finished "Drunken Sailor," he switched to "Blow the Man Down."

Jaco admired two things about Landry. One was his voice, which was a resonant baritone. The other was the number of sea shanties he knew. At night, when he wasn't on watch, Jaco often asked him to serenade the crew accompanied by two seamen who'd brought fiddles. The singing stopped abruptly when a call came from Newton Lofton who, along with Landry, was one of *Scorpion's* best lookouts. Jaco was sure if there was a bird riding a wave at 10 miles, either man could see the creature.

All the officers gathered on the quarterdeck had a good view of the ships, less than three miles away. One, a large merchant ship, had lost a mast; the other was a 36-gun frigate flying a Royal Navy ensign. But why were it sails furled?

"Mr. Shelton, show our colors and clear for action. No need for drums. Do not load or run out. If these ships are disabled and are in need of help, we are obligated to provide it, war be dammed."

As *Scorpion* approached neither ship made any attempt to maneuver. The merchant ship's name was *Chennai,* which suggested British East India Company ownership. *Chennai's* bowsprit was only a few feet above the water, and sailors were transferring barrels to the frigate *Aries.*

Scorpion glided to a noisy, slack-sail flapping stop less 75 feet astern and perpendicular to the two ships. As Jaco picked up the speaking trumpet, Jeffords warned him, "Cap'n, we're not going to be able to hold this position long.

We'll have to fall off, then sail down wind and come back around.

Jaco nodded and headed to the forward port corner of the quarterdeck. The seamen referred to both forward corners of the quarterdeck as Perfecto Corner, because when their captain was on the quarterdeck, he would stand at the upwind one. The name came from Jaco's frequent use of the Spanish work *perfecto*.

Four men in royal blue coats stood at the aft railings of the frigate's quarterdecks. "*Aries*," Jaco called over to them, "how may the Continental Navy frigate *Scorpion* provide assistance?"

"Are you going to try to take us? We won't surrender without a fight," one of the men called back.

"If I had intended to take you right away, I would have opened fire. What is wrong with your ships?"

"In the storm, *Aries* lost her rudder and several planks in *Chennai's* forward hold gave way. We are trying to build a new rudder and transfer *Chennai's* cargo."

Jaco pondered. Aries *is helpless without a rudder, and if they can't hang a new one, the frigate will have to be towed or sunk. Can we keep* Chennai *from sinking? At three knots, we're eight to 10 days from Charleston. If I take both ships, then their problems become mine and* Scorpion *is saddled with several hundred prisoners and two crippled ships. Are these two prizes worth the risk?*

"You are about one hundred miles directly south of Bermuda. We'll leave you alone. Good luck." Jaco turned to Bosun Preston and Quartermaster Jeffords.

"Mr. Jeffords, let's fall off so we are sailing downwind. Mr. Preston, haul in our sails. We'll tack back toward the west after we are out of sight of these ships."

North of Havana, fourth week of September 1778

Rather than heading east up through the Windward Passage, Darren took *Liber* west, past the Cayman Islands and up through the narrow Yucatan Channel. Cuba was just over the visual horizon to the south. He was hoping to catch a Spanish ship headed back to Spain. Rear Admiral Parker had said that Spanish cargo ships often carried a mix of gold and silver; cacao, which was becoming popular in England; the anil plant which produced indigo blue dyes; and barrels of dead insects from cactus plants used to make red and orange dyes.

Months in the Caribbean had tanned Darren's face and arms and bleached his blond hair almost white. The more he sailed in the Caribbean, the more he liked this part of the world. The winters were warm and pleasant, and if the summers were hot and humid, he preferred the discomfort of extreme heat to the achingly cold, gray, damp winters that lasted from November to April in England.

Smythe still didn't know what the house in Langton Herring actually looked like, nor did he know if or when he would live there. The money from Horrocks' estate was more than enough to live well for the rest of his life anywhere he could imagine, and still leave much to his heirs—if he ever had any.

"Sail ho, one point astern on the starboard quarter. We can see 'er royals, so the distance is about eight miles."

"Captain, aye." Even though his rank was commander, he was still "captain" of His Majesty's Ship *Liber*.

Having the mystery ship astern and upwind presented an interesting problem. To investigate, *Liber* would have to either luff and wait or work to windward.

Young Tewksbury, who had just celebrated his 14th birthday, had the watch and was standing next to the quartermaster. Darren studied the young man. *When I was his age, I was in my second year at the Royal Naval Academy. Tewksbury's a good one. If he wasn't so young he could stand for Lieutenant.*

"Mr. Tewksbury, what do you recommend?"

"Sir, I'd come about to nor' west by nor, which should be as close to the wind as we can sail *Liber*. Then, if you want, we can fly our staysails. We'll need them when we turn so' west to intercept. When our bow is even with theirs, we tack to so' west by south and hold that course until we are behind her, then come back east to run her down."

Smythe nodded. "I agree, Mr. Tewksbury; execute."

From Captains Tillerson and Horrocks, Smythe had learned that letting one's junior officers make and carry out recommendations is excellent training that builds their confidence so that if they ever were in command, they would know what to do. Presently, when they had draw closer, he asked the midshipman, "What if the unknown ship changes course?"

Tewksbury took a look through his spyglass and confidently answered, "Sir, I don't think this one will. The ship is riding very low in the water, which tells me she's heavy and slow to turn. Probably a merchantman."

"Here, Captain, take a closer look." Drew Rathburn held out the Dollond spyglass.

The high quarterdeck and forecastle were characteristic of Spanish shipyard construction. The ship continued sailing to the east. In Darren's mind, if he were the captain of the Spanish ship, *Liber's* actions should set off alarm bells, yet from what he could see the merchant ship was sailing serenely along. Darren wondered if maybe he was missing something and should be alarmed. This was his first encounter with a Spanish merchant or warship, and he didn't know what type of armament a Spanish merchant ship might have.

"Sir, permission to come about to port? I plan to position on the starboard side of her wake," Tewksbury said.

"Granted."

Stanhope, *Liber's* quartermaster, joined them on the quarterdeck, on the assumption that the sloop was going to clear for action and his station was at the wheel. Darren turned to him and asked, "Every fought a Spaniard before?"

"No, sir, but I have heard that they will fight to the death. And they are not known for treating their prisoners well."

"That's a cheery thought, Mr. Stanhope. Perhaps one of the reasons they fight so hard is they assume everyone else treats prisoners inhumanely. Perhaps we shall have occasion to prove to these Spaniards, at least, that such an assumption is unwarranted."

As *Liber* passed the Spanish ship at a distance of 500 yards, Darren counted six gunports along the port side. "Mr. Louttit, show them our colors."

Above his head, the cloth of a 4' x 6' Royal Navy ensign snapped before streaming in the wind. Almost at the same time, the unknown ship unfurled a large white flag that had a crest in the middle and several wavy lines, which Darren recognized as the Spanish ensign.

"Mr. Louttit, please beat to quarters. Mr. Tewksbury, you've got us this far, now what do you recommend?"

Cyrus Tewksbury nodded vigorously. "We load ball and run out as we come up on her starboard stern quarter. When we get close enough, you can hail her from the beak and ask the ship to strike and heave too. If not, we tack back and forth along her stern and hammer away with our popguns—sorry sir, our 6-pounders, using a mix of chain shot and ball until she strikes."

Darren looked around at his officers, all of whom had gathered on the quarterdeck. From the deck below, the staccato beat of a snare drum sounded that the crew was clearing for action. “Anyone speak Spanish?”

Lieutenant De Courcy raised his hand, “Aye, I speak some, seeing as my best friend’s parents were from Spain. My problem is understanding when they speak fast, as Spaniards tend to do.”

“Good. You get to hail the captain.”

“Deck! The Spaniard has run out!”

Tewksbury, Rathburn and Smythe focused their spyglasses on the side of the ship. “Looks like nine-pounders, sir,” Rathburn said, “and any captain who commands nine-pounders should be reluctant to surrender.”

“Even so, I would like to avoid bloodshed if we can, so we will ask the question. If he says no, then we persuade the captain of the error of his ways. Mr. De Courcy, make sure your Marines on the swivel guns on the masthead focus on the quarterdeck first, and then on the gun crews.”

“Aye, Captain, that we will.”

Darren could now read the name on the stern. They were about to take on the *Alhambra,* headed due east.

“Mr. Tewksbury, I now have the watch. Mr. Stanhope, fall off a bit to starboard so that, when we tack to port, we can maximize the time we have to fire into his stern.”

After hearing his order acknowledged, Darren focused his spyglass on the men he could see on the quarterdeck of *Alhambra.* One man was issuing orders. He was broad shouldered, and when he finished speaking, he strode to the side of his ship and stood with his hands gripping the railings, staring at *Liber*.

When *Liber* was about 50 yards off *Alhambra’s* port quarter, Darren handed the speaking trumpet to De Courcy.

The position put the sloop in the Spaniard's "blind" spot where neither a stern chaser nor the main battery could hit *Liber*. De Courcy called over, speaking Spanish slowly and carefully. "*Alhambra,* this is His Majesty's Sloop of War *Liber*. Please heave to so we can take your ship as a prize. We do not want any bloodshed."

The man on deck shook his head and responded in English. "If you want my ship, you will have to take it by force." Then he grabbed a musket that had been hidden by the railing and fired at *Liber's* captain. The ball flew past his right shoulder.

Under his breath, Darren muttered, "Cock and pie," then spoke aloud. "He wants a fight, so we give him one."

Numbers ran through his head. *Nine-pounders, effective range, at best 500 yards. Alhambra is making about six knots. With the sails Liber is carrying, we can easily make nine or 10.* His sloop's six pounders wouldn't do much to the structure of the merchant ship. *We need to rip up the rigging or send balls through the captain's cabin to kill or maim the men manning the cannon on the main deck.* But something was bothering the back of his mind. *What am I missing?*

"Mr. Stanhope, Mr. Louttit, stand by to come about to port. New course will be so' so' east. I want to stay within 100 yards of *Alhambra* when we cross her stern."

Hearing acknowledgement, Darren walked to the forward edge of the quarterdeck railing, "Mr. Soames, you may fire as you bear into the captain's cabin." Looking up at the rigging, "Mr. Tewksbury, you know what your job is." Getting a wave in response, Darren looked around the quarterdeck, feeling very uneasy.

"Ready about, Mr. Louttit, We do this smartly so we don't lose too much speed or distance. Mr. Stanhope, helm a lee."

Liber's yards creaked and groaned as the ship started to come around. The ship heeled noticeably to starboard and Darren was suddenly afraid they wouldn't be able to elevate the guns. "Mr. Louttit, ease off the sheets and trim so we are level."

The Spanish ship's quarterdeck was 20 feet higher than *Liber's,* which meant the Spanish officers were closer to the swivel guns on each of *Liber's* mastheads; but the Spanish gunners could shoot down at *Liber*.

Darren figured his number one port gunner was within seconds of firing when Midshipman Enfield yelled, "*Alhambra* has a stern chaser!"

The opening gunport revealed the largest gun Darren had ever seen, and it was pointed directly at him. The gun had to be a 24-pounder or bigger. He shouted, "Aim for the gunport!" just as *Liber*'s first six-pounder fired. In the huge gunport, he could see the crew pulling the enormous cannon into position.

Liber's second 6-pounder barked, and the ball shattered glass in the captain's cabin. But Darren's gaze was riveted by the sight of flame coming out of the bore of the cannon. An instant later, *Liber* shuddered from the impact of the heavy ball. He looked down at the gun deck and saw the gun crews carrying on as if nothing happened.

"I'm going to see the damage." Midshipman Enfield jumped to the main deck and disappeared down the aft companion way.

Gun number seven fired, and there was cheering on the gun deck. Overhead the swivel guns barked. Darren was counting the seconds before he could order the ship to tack either to port or starboard to get away from the big cannon's field of fire. *Alhambra* was beginning to slowly and ponderously turn to starboard to trade broadsides.

"Mr. Stanhope, Mr. Louttit, come about to starboard and pull in the sails! We need all the speed we can get!"

The sloop responded, and *Liber* sailed away from *Alhambra*. At most, Darren hoped, the Spaniard was going to get off four shots with their nine-pounders.

Enfield appeared, breathless, at his side. "Sir, the ball destroyed a rib just forward of the mainmast. The splinters shredded many of the hammocks. A few sea chests were blown apart before the ball broke into pieces."

"How far above the waterline is the hole?"

"About five feet, sir."

"Get Mr. Evans to give you an estimate of how long he will need to fix the hole."

"Aye, sir." The midshipman walked quickly below.

The boom of the first of *Alhambra's* 9-pounders brought him back to the tactical situation. The first ball made a row of waterspouts, the last of which geysered 50 yards behind *Liber*. The mainsail on the foremast popped, punctured by the second ball. *Alhambra's* third ball slammed into *Liber's* hull, causing the sloop to quiver. The last one hissed behind the stern and splashed into the water harmlessly, 200 feet from where Darren stood.

"Mr. Louttit, Mr. Rathburn and Mr. Stanhope—"

"Captain!" called out Lieutenant Soames. "Sir! Gunner Dawson is pretty sure his ball hit the carriage of the Spaniard's 24-pounder! He saw the gun fall on its side."

"Was that what the cheering was about?"

"Aye, sir."

That changed everything. The tactical course of action was no longer to run, but to engage.

Each time *Liber* maneuvered to get astern of *Alhambra*, the Spanish captain countered with a turn in an attempt to get into position to fire his main battery. Darren used the sloop's better handling to stay out of the Spanish merchant ship's field of fire. The deadly dance continued along a base course of due east, bringing the two ships ever closer to the Spanish base in Havana.

Darren had a choice. He could continue the dance, occasionally get a broadside into *Alhambra's* bow or stern in the hopes of disabling the Spanish merchantman. Or he come alongside *Alhambra* and fight a traditional battle against a ship with bigger guns. In that fight, *Liber* could be crippled, taken, or even sunk. Or he could sail away and save his crew to fight another day, recognizing that *Liber* didn't have the firepower to overpower *Alhambra*. Before the gunport to the 24-pounder was closed, Darren and several others confirmed through spyglasses that the gun was pointed at an odd angle. *Alhambra's* stern was defenseless. He had just decided to continue the dance, focusing all his available guns at the wide stern, when the lookout called down, "Sail ho! Looks like a frigate two points off the port bow at about five miles."

Darren turned to his first lieutenant. "Mr. Rathburn, the frigate is likely Spanish as well. I think discretion is the better part of valor. Today the Spaniard got the better of us only because *Liber* doesn't have the weight of broadside to defeat *Alhambra*. Let's fall off to port and give this oncoming frigate a wide berth."

For a second, he was tempted to fire a broadside at the Spanish galleon in frustration, but at this range it was a futile gesture. And, with an unknown frigate close by, he didn't want to alert its captain that a potential prize—*Liber*—was nearby. "Once we get clear, we'll fire the guns to empty them and secure from quarters. We need to go back to Port Royal to get the damage repaired."

90 miles east of Charleston, fourth week of September 1778

Leaving the two disabled Royal Navy ships to fend for themselves, Jaco adjusted *Scorpion's* course and speed so the ship would arrive at the harbor mouth an hour before sunset the next afternoon. This would give *Scorpion* time to work up the river and anchor or tie up to a pier by dark. Jaco was excited by the prospect of spending a few days with Reyna. The crew were excited because they would get a few days of liberty ashore.

Just after dawn, Jaco heard the call, "Sail ho. Two ships, two miles on the 'larboard bow. Both English." He pushed aside his bowl of oatmeal mixed with honey and dried apples. So much for breakfast. Jaco made his way to the quarterdeck. "What do you see?" he asked his first lieutenant.

"One frigate, one cargo ship, if direction, size and speed tell true." Through his Dolland, Jaco saw that the frigate had already started toward *Scorpion*. "Mr. Shelton, what do you make of her?"

"I think this Royal Navy captain wants a fight. Either he is shielding a merchant ship or sees a small frigate and thinks, 'Ha! an easy prize.'"

"I agree. Beat to quarters and show them our colors. Load ball and run out. Hmm, looks like she has guns on the main deck as well. Let's keep our distance. Mr. Preston, get the top gallants loosed and sheeted home smartly."

Tuning to the man at the wheel, Jaco issued his next command. "Mr. Jeffords, he has the wind gauge so we will hold our course and make him come to us. We're not going to show him *Scorpion's* speed or our ability to maneuver just yet. I want to stay at least 500 yards off until we know what kind of guns those are on the upper deck. Most likely, he will try to get close and pound us into submission, but we don't have to accept his invitation. Every man jack on this ship wants to go home and enjoy their new wealth, so we will only engage if we have the advantage and can quickly disable this frigate. If the other ship is another frigate, we may need to show our heels. If, on the other hand, this one is an escort for a cargo ship, we can decide whether or not to go after the merchantman once we are clear."

The Royal Navy ship continued to close the gap. *Scorpion* fell off two points to starboard to open the range, heading directly into the long Atlantic swells. The up and down movement would make long range gunnery harder, but at least the ship was not pitching and rolling.

Jaco studied the Royal Navy ship's armament. On the gun deck, he counted 13 cannon that looked like 12-pounders. The main deck had three guns that he thought might be 9-pounders, but the big hole at the end of the short barrels suggested they were a new type of cannon he'd heard about, called a carronade. The short barrel of the carronade made them lighter than a traditional naval gun of comparable bore. The heavier ball that came out of the barrel was slower and far less accurate but devastating at close range. *So we'll just have to stay out of range*—their *range*. The British captain might be counting on the surprise of superior firepower. *It's our superior range against your superior weight, and our weight is still impressive.*

"Mr. Shelton, pass the word to Mr. Garrison that he may open fire as soon as his guns bear. Do remind him that at this range and with the ship's movement, timing and aiming the shot is more important than rate of fire."

Jaco stared the Royal Navy frigate, running through the options his enemy could choose. With *Scorpion* outgunned almost two to one, tactics were crucial. The cargo ship, now well north of them, was the real prize, but first he had to disable, not necessarily take, the English frigate.

The four watchwords of effective naval officers that John Paul Jones had drummed into his head ran through his mind like a checklist.

Leadership—my crew are trained, experienced and ready to fight like devils.

Seamanship—we can maneuver and shoot accurately at the same time.

Strategy and tactics—I have a plan to turn this fight into a turning melee that will give Scorpion the advantage.

Courage—I hope I have the nerve. If my plan doesn't work and I survive, I will have my crew's blood on my hands.

The British frigate fired first. Smoke billowed from the side of the Royal Navy ship as its cannons fired one right after another.

One 12-pound ball hit the water 100 feet from *Scorpion*, skipped three times and sank to the bottom. The second landed short, skipped and thumped into the hull.

Scorpion's gunners returned fire, and the first ball slammed into the Royal Navy frigate just aft of its foremost cannon on the main deck. Ball two also struck the side, and Jaco saw splinters fly. Then three balls from the Royal Navy ship hammered into *Scorpion*. Two hit the bulwark just below the main deck. The third carried away a chunk in the bulwark and chewed up the grating that let light onto the gun deck before expending itself in a rack of belaying pins. Splinters flew everywhere, but none of the Marines or sailors who'd flung themselves face down on the main deck were seriously hurt.

The two ships were now almost side by side at 500 yards. Jaco yelled at Jeffords to fall off two more points to open the distance back to 600 yards. Both ships' crews were firing at will. Thumps from the British balls could be felt on *Scorpion's* hull, but so far, none of them had penetrated the three layers of planking. *Scorpion's* gun crews kept up their rate of fire of one aimed ball every two minutes.

Jaco could see two gaps in the British frigate's bulwarks and large holes in its side. Not all of its port side 13 guns were firing, but those that were kept hitting *Scorpion*. None of the three guns on the main deck had spoken.

Jaco crossed over to the U-shaped enclosure set up around the quartermaster's station to protect the helmsman from splinters and musket balls. "Mr. Preston and Mr. Jeffords, we need put an end to this foolishness. Are you ready?"

Jeffords replied, "Aye, Cap'n, ready when you are."

Preston, the ship's stocky, well-muscled bosun, didn't duck as an English cannon ball whistled through the ship's rigging 20 feet behind him. "Aye, sir." He faced forward and bellowed, "All right, lads, on your feet. Let's show the bloody Royal Navy how we Continentals handle a ship."

Jaco heard the splintering of wood and turned, expecting to see someone on the quarterdeck torn apart or seriously wounded. What he saw was a gap in the railing and Jack Shelton pulling small splinters from his arms and thighs.

"Mr. Preston, slack all sails. Mr. Jeffords, fall off to port."

"Aye, Cap'n, turning to port now."

On the main deck, the sheets to the three sails—main, top, and top gallant—on the masts, as well as the forestaysail and jib, were released. Preston's men and Patrick Miller's Marines held onto the lines. *Scorpion* slowed noticeably and the masts groaned loudly in protest as the ship turned in a tight radius. "Mr. Jeffords, new course west by north."

Jaco walked to the port side and studied the British ship, now almost a half a length behind *Scorpion*. He could see several blue-coated men on the quarterdeck looking at his ship and wondered if they knew what was coming. "Mr. Preston, get those sails sheeted home, *now!*

Hedley Garrison came out of the aft companion way. "Captain, we'll have the cannon loaded with ball and chain shot when we cross her stern. We've got casualties from splinters off the edges of our gunports, but all the cannon are fully manned."

A man on the Royal Navy frigate's quarterdeck was shouting orders and gesticulating. Sailors released the sheets to the main and mizzen staysails so they could tack the ship to port. *Scorpion* now had the wind gauge and was maneuvering for a straight stern shot, or worse, from a rear quarter. Either way, the tables were turned on the Royal Navy frigate, whose name Jaco could now read. *Scorpion* was fighting *H.M.S. Pondicherry. What kind of name is that?*

Jaco looked for Lieutenant Garrison, but he was back down on the gun deck. He did see Third Lieutenant Philip Patterson standing just aft the bowsprit. Jaco cupped his hands to focus his voice over the noise of battle. "You may fire as you bear. Make them all count."

Patterson waved and stayed in his position. Jaco guessed he wanted a better view of the target to estimate the range.

Now *Scorpion's* starboard side guns could go to work. Each cannon was double shotted with ball and chain shot. The first ball and chain smashed through the windows of the captain's cabin, destroying the frames as they headed down the deck. Gun two fired and the ball splintered the starboard railing of *Pondicherry's* quarterdeck before destroying two racks of belaying pins where the starboard sheets for the sails on the mizzenmast were tied. Immediately, the main and top sails on *Pondicherry's* mizzenmast, partially freed, began flapping.

The chain shot from cannon three amputated the legs of the helmsman before carrying away the ship's wheel and binnacle. The body parts ended their flight in coils of rope for the braces of *Pondicherry's* mainmast. The 12-pound ball blew out a chunk half the diameter of the mizzenmast.

Balls four and five along with their chain shot went down *Pondicherry's* gun deck. One hit the number three gun on the Royal Navy frigate's starboard side and disintegrated against the breech of the cannon. Shrapnel shredded four men and knocked the cannon off the carriage. The fifth ball embedded itself in the mizzenmast and blew enough wood out of the far side that, for all practical purposes, the weight of the mast was sitting on the cannon ball.

By the time ball six entered *Pondicherry's* gun deck, a fifth of the men manning the ship's cannon were either dead, dying, or wounded. After ball five hit the mizzenmast, the frigate's pitching motion broke the remaining wood above the main deck and the mizzenmast came down, landing with a loud thump before toppling to the port side, pulled over by the port stays. Balls and chain shot from *Scorpion's* starboard cannons six through 10 continued the carnage. Most of the rigging holding what was left of *Pondicherry's* mainmast in position was shot away. Two of cannons on the port side of the main deck and one on the starboard side were lying at odd angles. One was split open by a *Scorpion* cannon ball; the other two sat on what remained of their carriages.

Scorpion emerged from the gray-white smoke of its cannon fire. Jaco could now see the damage its guns had caused. *Pondicherry,* he deemed, was so badly damaged that *Scorpion* was now free to go after the cargo ship. Fighting on for the sake of taking the frigate as a prize was problematic. *Pondicherry* still had formidable guns and a larger crew. If the captain was stubborn enough, *Scorpion* might have to inflict so much damage that the larger ship would be all but worthless, and at a terrible cost of life. If his purpose was to take prizes to fund the war effort, the merchantman was clearly the better choice. Staring at the Royal Navy frigate, he wondered what the butcher's bill already was *on Pondicherry*. Putting the visions of the human carnage out of his mind, Jaco cupped his hands and yelled toward the maintop.

"Lookouts, can you still see the other ship?"

"Aye, Captain, two points on the port side astern. She's got all her sails out. Best guess is we're about four miles apart."

"Mr. Jeffords, Mr. Preston, get ready to fall off to nor' by east. Have the lads set the royals." Jaco waved to his First Lieutenant. "Mr. Shelton, have the gun crews come up on deck so they can see the results of their training. Then go find the cooks. We have about an hour, so have them pass out a ration of beer and some biscuits soaked in rum. I'll bet they're a bit thirsty. Tell the lads 'Well done.'"

Scorpion needed almost 90 minutes to run down His Majesty's Merchant Ship *Cochin*. Jaco positioned his ship so *Scorpion*'s bow was just off the starboard rear quarter. Jack Shelton balanced himself on the bulwark and the bowsprit before speaking through a speaking trumpet. "*Cochin,* please heave to so we can take you as a prize. If not, we will take you by force."

A tall man in blue coat stood by the railing and frantically waved both hands. "For God's sake, don't fire on us or you'll bloody well blow us both to kingdom come!"

Cochin's flag came down, and Philip Patterson took 12 men over to board the English ship. There he learned *Cochin* was carrying 10 tons of coarse grain gunpowder for cannon and five tons of fine grain powder for muskets and pistols, along with 10,000 musket balls, 1,000 muskets and 100 pistols.

The East India merchantman's crew was brought over to the *Scorpion* and Philip Patterson had his first command. His mission—wait while *Scorpion* finished taking *Pondicherry,* then follow the Continental Navy frigate to Charleston. Jaco thought that *Pondicherry's* captain would most likely surrender, once he saw that continued resistance would only cause the death of his men without securing the escape of *Cochin.*

Westchester County, NY, first week of October 1778

The trees on the rolling hills around him had just started to turn orange and red. Mixed with those which were still green, it provided a beautiful vista to Bayard Templeton. This was his first time he'd seen the color change that several natives had told him formed a riot of color in late October.

As a newly appointed captain, Templeton rode next to the commander of 2nd Troop of A Squadron of the Green Dragoons, Captain Lionel Scarsdale. The British Army had welcomed his service because he'd fought in the French and Indian War. He felt good to be in uniform again, and he could now do his part in putting down the rebellion. And after this war was won, he'd execute the second part of his plan—acquiring rebel property at bargain prices. He'd already made it known to several British officers that he could arrange for them to buy very desirable properties.

Behind the two officers, 50 men, resplendent in dark green coats with pewter buttons and white breeches, rode their war horses. Each man had a carbine length musket and two loaded pistols, along with his cavalry saber. 'Two Troop,' as Bayard Templeton referred to the group of men, was assigned to search Storm's Bridge, a town west of White Plains, reported to be hiding a large store of muskets, balls, and gunpowder for local militia units. The town was near the site of the Battle for White Plains where, almost two years ago in October 1776, the outnumbered Continental Army had held off a superior British force under General Howe. It was past time to balance the score.

A half mile from the town, Captain Scarsdale halted the column and studied what he could see of Storm's Bridge through his spyglass. Collapsing the brass tube with a smack, Scarsdale turned to Templeton. "What do you think?"

"Sir, if you cannot see anyone, there is probably an ambush. I suggest we divide the troop into two columns and come in from different directions on foot. If we have a fight, we'll be better prepared."

Scarsdale leaned on the pommel of his saddle. His parents were wealthy merchants in New York and avid supporters of the king—and so was he. "Dragoons don't fight on foot."

Bayard Templeton bit back a retort. He'd learned the hard way during the Seven Years War, known as the French and Indian War in the thirteen colonies, how effective an ambush could be. He didn't want to argue with his superior officer who had been conducting searches such as this one for two years. Yet something in his stomach said danger lurked in the town.

Here he was outranked, and he had to remember that. No matter how ridiculous or foolish an order was, it was to be obeyed. Still.... "Then, sir, I strongly recommend we start searching houses on at one end of the town to flush the rebels out. I saw enough ambushes fighting the French and their Indian allies to recognize one when I see one."

Scarsdale was adamant. "Nonsense, Templeton. The rebels won't challenge the Green Dragoons if they know what is good for them. And if they do resist, we'll teach them a lesson they won't forget."

Scarsdale edged his horse forward. The horsemen cantered into the town in two columns and, on the captain's orders, in the center of the town, formed a square with the men facing outward. Scarsdale eased his horse out so he could clearly be seen and bellowed, "Residents of Storm's Bridge! Please come out of your homes and muster in front of my men. Do it now!"

No one came out. The hairs on Templeton's neck stood up. All around him he could see open windows. Those on the second floors would let any decent marksmen easily pick off the Dragoons. Scarsdale repeated his demand. A voice came out from one of the houses with a distinctly Scottish accent. "Goooo back to yer camp, lads. Yer not wanted around heeerrrr!"

Scarsdale stood up in his stirrups and looked around. He had been one of the first to offer his services to General Sir Henry Clinton, the British Commander in Chief for North America, and he took his duty to king and country very seriously. "We're here to search your houses for weapons. Come out so we can do this peacefully."

The same voice responded, "Goooo home, lads. That is the smaaaarrrt thing to do. Or this could end baaadly for the British Army and the Green Dragoooons."

"Damn your impertinence! Come out now, or we will burn you out."

"I dooon't think so, laddie. Yer flogging a cat's tail. Go home. This is the laaaast time I'll warn ye!"

The informality of address infuriated Scarsdale. He drew his sword and pointed to a three-story building, the largest in Storm's Bridge. "Sergeant! Take four men and search that building. Bring out whoever is in there and then burn it."

Before the men could swing their legs over their saddles, the first volley of musket fire erupted from the south side of the square. Then the west side was enveloped in gunsmoke, followed by the north side, and lastly the east side of the square. Smoke obscured the buildings as the second volley followed right after the first, telling Templeton that each marksman had two or three loaded muskets, probably with a helper to load. The Dragoons were out in the open, well within range. If they didn't get out of the square quickly, they would be massacred.

As lead balls sang all around, Templeton bent low over on his horse. He saw Scarsdale lying on the ground, bleeding from three balls in his chest. A dozen other dragoons had fallen from their horses. Others were clutching wounds while trying to stay on their saddles as terrified horses backed or reared. Templeton screamed and pointed to the road closest to where the troop was gathered. "Take the east road, men!" He grabbed one of his pistols and fired at a window, then did the same with his second. The third volley started just as what was left of the troop galloped away.

Once outside the village, Templeton gathered the 20 remaining men of Two Troop. Of those, five had to be helped down from their horses because they could ride no further. Templeton looked back at the village square, where green-coated men were lying on the ground. Already the villagers were gathering their horses and weapons. With an awful certainty, he realized the ambushers had aimed high to avoid hurting the horses.

Port Royal, first week of October 1778

The hole in *Liber's* side made by the 24-pound ball from *Alhambra* required a rib and a deck buttress to be splinted with thick planks on both sides. The work took two weeks before *Liber* was ready for sea. When the repairs were completed and *Liber* was taking on fresh provisions, Rear Admiral Parker summoned Darren to *H.M.S. Bristol*. The admiral's flag secretary, Horatio Nelson, was in the cabin and came forward to welcome him. "Commander Smythe, I have been following your exploits on *H.M.S. Liber*. I must say, I am impressed. To take a ship that is smaller or bearing fewer guns is the goal of some commanders, but there is more honor and glory in taking on superior adversaries—and defeating them!"

"Thank you, sir. We've been lucky."

"Bloody hell, man, there is not that much luck to be had, save it be augmented by skillfulness. I hope someday we can sail together as captains in the same squadron. Wouldn't that be a nightmare for the rebels! Or better yet, for the French and the Spanish."

Nelson was about the same age as Smythe. For an admiral to select such a junior officer as his flag lieutenant meant that either he had connections, ability, or both. Nelson, Darren suspected, was out to make a name for himself, just like he was.

"Commander Smythe..." Rear Admiral Parker's voice brought him back to the proceedings, "I have your orders. The Admiralty wants *Liber* back in Portsmouth to add two more six-pounders. You are to leave immediately, sail north and find Admiral Graves' fleet off New York. There you are to collect whatever dispatches and mail he has, and then sail for Portsmouth as fast as *Liber* can go. I also have a package of letters and reports *Liber* can carry back to England."

"Yes, sir. We can be underway in less than an hour after your dispatches are delivered to *Liber*." Darren almost said *my ship;* but, in reality, the sloop was owned by King George III.

"I will have the pouch delivered." Parker turned around and picked a letter off his desk. "Meanwhile, there is this. Fortunately for you, this letter came in on the packet which arrived yesterday. Had it arrived after you departed, months or even a year may have passed before it caught up with you."

Darren took the proffered piece of paper and began reading.

Commander Smythe,

It is my pleasure to inform you that you have been selected to command a new, sixth rate frigate, H.M.S. Gladius, 28 guns. The ship is being built in Portsmouth at the Royal Navy Dockyard and should be ready for sea by early February 1779.

When you arrive in Portsmouth, you are to report to the Admiral commanding the naval base. At such time, you will be promoted to captain. Up to 30 days leave is granted as long as your time away does not delay Gladius going to sea.

Congratulations.

Hugh Montagu

First Sea Lord

Fourth Earl of Sandwich

Darren read the letter a second time and felt his eyes brimming. Ever since he was 10 years old, he'd wanted to be the captain of a Royal Navy frigate. Now his dream was coming true. All he had to do was get back to England.

"Commander, soon to be *Captain* Smythe, I think a toast is in order. Lieutenant..." Nelson brought over a bottle of madeira and handed each man a glass that he filled with the burgundy liquid. "To Captain Smythe: your success. May you bring fame, fortune and victories to our country."

Darren allowed the two officers to toast him, then raised his own glass and said, "Success and victories for England."

He was already wealthy. Fame may or may not come, but already he was developing a solid reputation as a captain. Darren emptied the glass and hoped his hands didn't shake.

"Before you go, these two letters also came yesterday. One is from your solicitor and the other is from Admiral Davidson. I hope they, too, contain good news."

The heft of the package from Henry York suggested the drawings he'd requested of house in Langton Herring were inside. They could be studied later, and in about a month, he could visit the property in person. Any correspondence from Rear Admiral Davidson was very important and should be read and answered immediately. Smythe suspected that Davidson had been behind his promotion and new command.

Chapter 8
Homeward Bound

Charleston, first week of October 1778

Before the war had started, South Carolina's busiest port had ships at the piers and anchored in both the Cooper and Ashley Rivers. Some would be waiting to come dockside to unload, others used lighters to carry cargo both ways. Those ships who were at a pier were always under pressure to unload, reload and put back to sea to make room for other ships waiting in the roadstead.

When *Scorpion* arrived just before dark, trailed by *Pondicherry* and *Cochin,* Jaco counted 10 empty piers. He had never seen so few ships in Charleston. *Scorpion* then *Pondicherry* docked on opposite sides of an empty pier, ending a frustrating nine-day voyage of tacking back and forth as they worked their way toward the port. *Cochin,* because of its cargo, was anchored out in the Cooper River.

Scorpion was moving just fast enough so Jeffords still had rudder control when the lines were tossed to the dock hands. The frigate bumped the pier gently and stopped, and lines looped around the pier's bollards secured the Continental Navy to the pier. *Pondicherry* did the same five minutes after.

The time needed for the ships to sail up the Cooper River and dock had been enough for word to fly around Charleston that *Scorpion* was bringing two prizes. As Jaco waited for his crew to lash the gangway in place, he spotted Reyna, her mother Adah, his mother Perla, and his younger brother Saul standing in a small group off to one side away from the crowd, waiting to escort him home.

Jaco recognized two of the three men approaching the gangway—General Moultrie and Benjamin Wood, Charleston's port captain—but not the third waiting impatiently to board *Scorpion*. Moultrie was the first to be "bonged" aboard. He started speaking as Jaco and he shook hands. "Welcome back to Charleston, Captain Jacinto. I see you tweaked the British Lion's nose again." The general gestured and said, "Please allow me to introduce Colonel Rufus Blackthorne, my commissary officer. He is the man to take care of *Scorpion's* needs."

Jaco looked at the rail-thin man with a hawkish face and immediately thought that Blackthorne would buy and sell own his wife and children without thinking twice. "We will need provisions and ammunition as soon as possible." He waved in the general direction of *Cochin*. "What is on board that ship is very important. You will also need to figure out what to do with the *Pondicherry's* and *Cochin's* crews. There's almost as many wounded as there are healthy seamen."

They were standing a few steps beyond where the braces for the mainmast were tied to the belaying pins and the extra ropes were neatly coiled. Moultrie again spoke, willing to be the straight man. "And Captain Jacinto, what is on board *Cochin* that is so special?"

"Ten tons of course grain gunpowder for cannon, five tons of fine grain powder for muskets and pistols along with 10,000 musket balls, 1,000 muskets and 100 pistols.

"Oh my, that's cause for jollification!!!" Moultrie rubbed his hands and actually grinned. "That is a very nice haul. And is the ship is intact?"

"Yes, and I think Laredo Shipping would be happy to buy *Cochin* straightaway to replace some of the ships the English have taken."

"Aye, they and a few other ship owners. How badly damaged is the Royal Navy frigate?

"The hull is intact, but my 12-pounders tore up the bulwarks. I don't know if *Pondicherry* is worth repairing and sailing as part of the Continental or the South Carolina Navy."

South Carolina had formed its own sea-going navy, and its legislature had offered Jaco a commission as a captain of one of its frigates any time he wanted to accept one. Their most recent offer had been to send him to the Netherlands with a crew to man a ship being built in Amsterdam. The 40-gun frigate, named *South Carolina,* had the scantlings of a 74-gun third rate ship of the line and was armed with twenty-eight 36-pounders and twelve, 12 pounders. But, the British Government, recognizing the potential of the ship, had engaged in diplomatic maneuverings that kept it in the Dutch port.

"Our surveyors can make that determination. Blackthorne here will take your victualing order and have the supplies delivered. When do you intend to put to sea?"

"In two days, maybe three, to give my crew some time in town without giving the British Navy time to box us in. I don't want to have to fight my way out of Charleston."

Jaco wasn't worried that men would desert because in *Scorpion's* magazine were the chests with the purses of prize money. Money from *Pondicherry* and *Cochin* would add to their individual shares that were to be paid out at the end of their enlistment. If a sailor deserted or were in jail, he would forfeit his share. And there were only a few weeks left.

* * *

Dinner with his family and Reyna was a festive affair. Even though they had heard the story from Eric, they insisted that he describe from his perspective the raid that had freed Reyna's brother.

As one of their servants were clearing the table, Perla Jacinto put her hand on Jaco's arm. "Go spend time with Reyna. And if Miriam is here in town, take the time to see her. She is determined to make sure our rebellion succeeds."

Jaco found Miriam Bildesheim in the back office of the well-stocked Bildesheim's General Store, the place everyone referred to as "The Store." Besides being the largest in Charleston, "The Store" had the best selection and prices. Miriam's face lit with a big smile when her Reyna and Jaco walked in.

"Jaco! and *mein engel* Reyna! I am zo glad to zee you. Come, come, Jaco, tell me about zee prizes zat you just captured."

Miriam posed probing, exacting questions about the ships, their crews and cargoes, and listened intently to his replies. Then she took Jaco by the hand and sat him in a chair in the middle of the store. She announced to all the men and women present, "Come, ask your questions of our own Jaco Jacinto, captain of zee frigate *Scorpion,* zee best ship in zee Continental Navy."

Embarrassed, he did as requested while Miriam went out into the street and invited in passersby to come meet one of the Continental Navy's best captains, Charleston's own Captain Jacinto. While he greeted people, Reyna and her grandmother stood in the back, beaming.

Tarrytown, NY, second week of October 1778

The unseasonably warm weather, called by some "Indian summer", had Bayard Templeton sweating in his forest green wool tunic. Looking through his spyglass, he surveyed the small town in the valley below, calculating how his men should approach the cluster of farmhouses built around a church. The village looked peaceful, but appearances could be deceptive. The debacle at Storm's Bridge was fresh in his mind

Snorts from several horses vocalized the restlessness of the 50 men of Two Troop, B Squadron, Green Dragoons, who constituted what was now Templeton's command. The men lost in prior skirmishes had been replaced by Loyalists from New York, New Jersey and Connecticut eager to serve their king. Two Troop's mission was to seize any weapons they found and arrest those who had them. Supposedly, this cluster of farms were the homes of men in the Continental Army. Templeton's orders, from General Sir William Howe, were to send a strong message to the rebels: Stay home. Look after your families, and if required, quarter the king's soldiers. How he delivered that message had been left to Templeton to determine.

Templeton studied the village and the people, women and children for the most part, who were at work in the fields and outside the barns. It was time, he decided, to move. He directed one of his lieutenants to take six pairs of men and approach the village from the east. His other lieutenant was to bring another six pairs by way of the west. "I'll enter from the center with the rest. Approach at a walk. Remember, these people are our neighbors. Do not draw your weapons unless we meet resistance. If we do, only kill those who resist."

Almost as soon as Two Troop came out of the stand of woods, men, women and children started running for their wood and stone homes. Templeton wondered if they were going to fight or if they would submit to having their homes and barns searched.

When Templeton arrived in the center of the village, there was not a human in sight and it was eerily silent. He dismounted, then banged on the door of the first house with the hilt of his sword. "Open up and be searched. We are looking for weapons, nothing else."

The door creaked narrowly open, revealing a pregnant woman, a young boy, and two smaller children. "There's nothing in this house that the British Army wants or needs," the woman said quietly.

Templeton slowly but firmly pushed the door open. "That, ma'am, is for me to decide, not you."

He paced around the three-room dwelling, poking and prodding with his sword. Finding no firearms, he walked out and commanded, "Search all the houses according to our plan."

At each house, a four-man team went inside while four others dismounted and stood guard, ready to react to any resistance. Templeton waited in the town square. None of Two Troop's men found anything of note, nor any men of military age to impress. The few muskets were old hunting pieces, not military grade firearms. Templeton walked over to an older man who stood outside his house while it was being searched. Templeton guessed the man was in his 50s.

"Where are the husbands and brothers of the women?" he demanded.

"Gone."

"Where have they gone?"

"Some joined the army." He did not specify which army. "Others are away hunting. Once harvest is in, they hunt for furs and meat."

"Who tends the farms?"

"The rest of us."

Templeton didn't believe him. He walked over to a large barn, carefully avoiding droppings from horses and cows. Inside, he found six horses in stables and piles of hay. He poked at these with his sword, but nothing squirmed or clanked. Shafts of light filtered through cracks in the walls making his search easier and casting shadows on the dirt floor. *Thank God I'm not a farmer*, he thought. *What a wretched existence. Barnyards, animals, shit everywhere. No refinement*. He returned to the village square, remounted his horse and surveyed the town.

Women and children were looking at him. Their glares and surly expressions made Templeton uncomfortable. He put his right hand on the brim of his dragoon hat. "Good day, ladies. We may be back. And if we return, pray that we don't find arms and ammunition."

150 miles east of New York, third week of October 1778

When *Liber* left Port Royal, Smythe had a half a dozen small barrels purchased from the market, containing cinnamon, ginger, turmeric, peppercorns, cloves, and thyme, lashed to the bulkhead in his cabin. They would be worth a fortune in London—if they ever reached England's capital—but they were destined for his mother's kitchen to be used in dishes she prepared for his father. The aromas filled his cabin and wafted down the passageway. The ship's cook also had a supply and knew how to use spices to improve the taste of the rations.

Admiral Parker had admitted he didn't know where Graves or the British fleet were, but he'd recommended three possible areas—near Halifax, off New York, or off the Carolinas. Logic said start with the southernmost location before heading to the next one north. Darren's greatest concern was food. *Liber* only had space for six weeks of rations, seven if he had the cooks stretch what they ate.

Finding no sign of the fleet off the Carolinas, *Liber* sailed north on a zig-zag course that took the sloop about 150 miles off Cape Hatteras, then back to a point about 30 miles from the shore. The only ships the lookouts saw was a convoy of four merchant ships being escorted by two Royal Navy frigates.

Near the end of the second week of searching, the lookout called, "Deck, ho! There's a whole bloody forest of sails three points off the port bow." As *Liber* closed on the fleet, Darren signaled that his ship was carrying dispatches for the admiral. *Liber,* dwarfed to insignificance, slowly picked its way through the formation to come alongside Admiral Richard Howe's flagship, *H.M.S. Eagle,* 64 guns. Nervously, the officers on the *Liber's* quarterdeck joked that a single fouled line or unhandy tack and their Royal Navy careers were over. Darren went to his cabin to put on one of the uniforms that Davidson had had specially made for his officers when he had been captain of *H.M.S. Puritan*. In the waters of the Caribbean, the only time Darren wore the coat was when he visited a flagship. The rest of the time, he wore a shirt and breeches and went barefoot, virtually undistinguishable from his crew. Not only was such clothing more comfortable, it was practical for the times he climbed the lines to get the feel and scent of the prevailing winds.

Sometimes he wished he could simply pretend to be a midshipman and go skylarking.

Eagle, a 1,400-ton, third rate ship-of-the-line, towered over *Liber*. The two-decker's upper gun deck was 15 feet above the quarterdeck of Darren's sloop. Darren stepped from the cutter onto the ladder without getting either the dispatch pouch or himself wet, then climbed up the ladder to the hatch on the lower gun deck. A bosun piped him aboard and Commander MacLeish from Howe's staff led him to the admiral's cabin.

Sunlight drenched the spacious, well-appointed cabin. The windows were all open, letting in a fresh breeze. The admiral was standing at the aft end near the windows. Smythe approached, packet in hand. "Admiral Howe, sir, I bear dispatches from Admiral Parker. And he has instructed me to carry any dispatches you have to Portsmouth. *Liber* is to proceed at best speed to England."

"Very well, I shall have some for you presently. After you leave, keep your ship alongside until I send them over. But first take some refreshment." Howe waved at the table, where cookies and sweet rolls waited on a platter.

"Aye, sir." Darren approached the table and selected a roll redolent with cardamon. He wondered if the Admiral had an oven and a personal cook. That was what Davidson had wanted on *Puritan*, but there simply hadn't been room.

"Smythe, have you heard about *Pondicherry*?"

"No, sir."

"*Pondicherry* was captured along with *Cochin*, a ship full of gunpowder and arms, by the rebel frigate *Scorpion*. Both are now in the hands of the rebels in Charleston, and we are hard pressed to supply all of our ships. Admiral Davidson says you are the Royal Navy's expert on *Scorpion* and its captain. What can you tell me?"

Damn. "Sir, the captain of the ship is Jaco Jacinto, from Charleston, South Carolina. He is a competent seaman and tactician, and he knows the waters of the Atlantic better than many a British captain. It is my understanding he served on merchant ships for several years before joining the Continental Navy. That would be enough to make him formidable, but there is more. The frigate *Scorpion* is several knots faster than our frigates, and armed with very powerful, very accurate 12-pounders that outrange our cannon of similar size. One on one, he can best any captain of a fifth- or sixth-rate frigate in the Royal Navy. I doubt, however, that Captain Jacinto would engage a fourth rater; his ship carries only 20 cannons."

Admiral Howe stood still, listening intently. He had good reason to be attentive; *Scorpion* was operating in the waters he was supposed to control.

"Sir, I realize this sounds hard to believe, but *Scorpion*'s construction seems to make the ship's hull all but impervious to our nine- and twelve-pound balls. Unless a ship has very heavy guns at short range, a captain will waste his fire trying to punch through that hull; it is as if the hull were made with iron plates. Even so, Captain Jacinto prefers to outsail his opponent so he can rake a ship from the bow or stern and take apart the rigging."

Howe huffed and clasped his hands behind his back. "You make this Jacinto chap out to be some sort of naval genius."

"No, sir, he is not. But he knows what he is about and has a very capable ship manned by a well-trained crew. That, sir, makes him a formidable adversary."

"How would you take him down?"

"Sir, I'd concentrate fire on *Scorpion*'s rigging. But you'd need at least three fifth-rate frigates with captains working together to box *Scorpion* in so Jacinto has no choice but to stand and fight. Then our captains might have a chance."

"I don't have three frigates I can spare. I have one new ship—*H.M.S. Dilettante* —that the Admiralty decided to experiment with by putting forty-eight of those new 18- and 24-pound carronades on her gun decks. Carronades, I am told, are smaller and lighter and need smaller gun crews, which is another reason why they are attractive to the lords in the Admiralty. *Dilettante* has a clean bottom and I intend to pair the two-decker with a brig and a sloop. That should do the trick. Thank you, Commander. I will send my pouch over to *Liber* before sunset."

CHAPTER 9
BIG GUNS AND A CLUMSY SAILER

East of Cape Cod, third week of October 1778

Scorpion's course was a direct line from a point 50 miles east of Charleston to a point 120 miles east of Cape Cod. The route kept the frigate far from where the Royal Navy's North American Squadron was supposed to be sailing, and away from the British frigates watching Hampton, VA, Delaware Bay, and the entrance to Long Island Sound.

Jaco had assured the crew that with good weather and fair winds they would be back in Kittery before their enlistment was up on October 31st. They had stayed in Charleston two extra days, and now the payment in British pounds for *Cochin* was locked in the chests with the rest of their prize money, to be distributed when they landed at Kittery.

At this time of year, hurricanes and squall lines with violent thunderstorms and strong, variable winds were as much a threat to *Scorpion* as the Royal Navy. *Scorpion* was sailing under its main sails with the jib parallel to a squall line that was moving nor' west to so' east, almost perpendicular to their course The rain reduced visibility to at most three miles. Given their current course, Jaco estimated the squall line would overtake *Scorpion* in a few hours and force him to change course.

Once the ship felt the gusty winds that precede squall lines, he ordered the watch to furl sails, leaving only the mainsails on each mast and the jib. Experience suggested the frigate would be pelted by rain for about three or four hours before the squall blew past. For all Jaco knew, the Royal Navy could be waiting on the other side of the squall line. He hoped that when *Scorpion* emerged, the sea would be empty.

He'd guessed wrong. The heavy rain lasted about five hours, leaving being low clouds and mist that reduced visibility to less than a mile. As the wind slackened and the base of the clouds lifted, Jaco found himself staring at a Royal Navy two-decker and two smaller ships, a sloop and a brig, less than a mile away, 2 points off his port bow.

Jaco yelled out, "Bosun! Get all hands-on deck to make sail. Mr. Miller, beat to quarters."

Jack Shelton came up on deck, glanced at the Royal Navy fourth rater, then shook his head. "Well, Captain, to quote the Book of Joshua, Chapter 10 verse Nine, in the New Testament, which I am sure you have never read, 'Joshua came upon them by marching all night from Gilgal.' That Royal Navy two decker is a very ugly surprise."

Jaco made a wry face at his first lieutenant's attempt at biblical humor. "Aye, Mr. Shelton, we need to keep our wits about us and not act as if we were the cat's Uncle Gringog. Get the topsails, the top-gallants and the royals out smartly, along with the fore staysail, or we will soon become guests of the Royal Navy."

Scorpion's captain watched sails dropping from the two-decker's yardarms to the beat of drums. Closer by, the rattle and staccato beat of *Scorpion's* drummer sang out, drowning out any sounds from the Royal Navy ships.

Jaco studied the two-decker, and then eyed his sails. "Mr. Jeffords, wear a little more easterly to get the wind over our port quarter. Steer east so' east."

"Aye, Cap'n. east so' east it is."

With *Scorpion's* sails sheeted home and the sails trimmed for maximum speed, Jaco now had time to consider the Royal Navy brig and sloop-of-war. Their 6- and 9-pounders were sticking out both sides, and both were unfurling their royals. Signal flags went up and down the halyards of all three Royal Navy ships. *We have about seven hours of daylight left. I need a plan in a hurry.*

On board H.M.S. Dilettante

Captain Brendon Byrne had not expected to see a ship of any kind, much less his quarry, less than a mile away as *Dilettante* emerged from the squall line. But when the unknown frigate turned east, he read the name through his spyglass. By luck and the grace of God, he'd found *Scorpion.*

He was about to test the mettle of the two lieutenants who commanded the smaller ships. Byrne liked Alan Hearns, the young lieutenant who'd just been given command of the 12-gun sloop *H.M.S. Kittywake.* Hearns had come highly recommended, and already *Kittywake,* the fastest of his three ships, was a mile off *Scorpion*'s left rear quarter. The 14-gun brig, *H.M.S. Derry,* was under full sail and gaining on *Dilettante,* after losing ground during a tack while its crew unsnarled its forestay sail and jib.

The c*hase is on. Captain Jacinto, make your move.*

On board Scorpion

Scorpion was heeled slightly to starboard as the ship rode the long swells. Based on their last sighting, the frigate was on the western edge of what Benjamin Franklin had charted and named the Gulph Stream. According to Franklin, the wind and currents would generally carry his ship to the nor' east—away from where Jaco wanted to go.

From the quarterdeck, Jaco could see all three Royal Navy ships, which had bent on as much sail as they dared. The sloop's captain had even hung out his studding sails to get more speed and close the gap. The two-decker was losing ground to the much faster *Scorpion,* but the brig, with all the canvas it could fly, had passed the two-decker.

Jaco faced his officers, "Turn around and take a good look, gentlemen. I'm open to suggestions on what to do before dark."

Hedley Garrison sized up the situation. "Sir, we may be dragging some weed, and while we may be fast, I don't think we can run away. So how and when do we pick a fight?"

Scorpion's captain turned to his first lieutenant. "Jack?"

"Sir, I would run for as long as possible to separate the two smaller ships from the two-decker. Then I'd force a fight with them one at a time. If we can cripple them, they can't rake us if we have to fight the two-decker. I haven't worked out how to do this without keeping the two-decker from closing on us."

Jaco nodded grimly. "That, gentlemen, is the crux of the matter. Let's keep running and maybe we can find a golden bridge and get away without a fight."

On board H.M.S. Kittywake

Lieutenant Alan Hearns studied *Scorpion* through his spyglass. The last time he'd seen the rebel frigate had been in

January, when he'd been on *Puritan*. *Scorpion* had shot *H.M.S. Griffin* to pieces, damaged *Puritan* from long range, then pummeled *H.M.S. Hussar*. Now, with a fragile sloop and its puny 6-pounders, he was supposed to herd *Scorpion* toward *Dilettante*—without being sunk in the process. He felt like a terrier sent to rout a lion.

On board Scorpion

Jack Shelton and Jaco estimated that the sloop on *Scorpion's* starboard quarter was within 1,000 yards, while the two-decker was at least three miles behind. Hedley Garrison was standing on the starboard bulwark on the main deck just forward of the quarterdeck. Jaco joined him. "Mr. Garrison, if we tacked now, the sloop would be about five to six hundred yards away. Can your men hit a ship that size bow on?"

"Aye, Captain, the lads hit those sloops off Scotland, and they were smaller and the seas rougher. We should get four, maybe five hits at this range, possibly more."

Jaco nodded. "Let's hope that will be enough." He turned to his bosun. "Are we ready?"

"Aye, Captain. We are awaiting your command."

Jaco walked back to the ship's wheel. "Mr. Jeffords, stand by to come about to starboard, new course south."

Jeffords acknowledged. Jaco took another look at the onrushing sloop, sails taut and straining against their sheets. He didn't think the sloop could fly any more canvas.

"Helm a-lee."

The bow started to come around, and on the main deck the fore staysail and the jib slipped through the forward stays. The two sails were sheeted home as the sailors from the port gun battery and the Marines hauled on the braces. The yards came around, first the foremast, then the main and finally the mizzen. The sails stayed perfectly aligned and *Scorpion* began to regain the speed lost in the turn.

When Jaco saw their ship was nearly at right angles to the sloop, he leaned over the quarterdeck's forward railing. "Mr. Garrison, you may fire when you have a target."

Garrison went down the aft companionway and strode to where the mainmast rose from its step on the ship's keel through the gun deck. "Lads, let's not shoot as if we were drunken emperors. Take your time and aim. Range will be five to six hundred yards. Fire as you bear."

On board H.M.S. Kittywake

Lieutenant Hearns didn't need a spyglass to see what was happening. He had assumed that *Kittywake* was gaining on the rebel frigate because it was faster. The idea that *Scorpion* would deliberately slow to draw his sloop into a trap had never entered his mind. Until now. "You bloody sly bastard!!!" he whispered. *Kittywake* was now in mortal danger.

He had two choices: turn port and head north to escape *Scorpion*, or turn to starboard and angle away from the rebel frigate. If he went north the gap between the ships would widen, and when night fell he'd lose sight of *Scorpion* in the darkness. Duty dictated his course. Hearns cupped his hands and yelled, "Stand-by to come about to starboard, new course so' west by so'. Helm a-lee. Gentlemen, let's be quick about this."

On board H.M.S. Dilettante

Byrne was hoping he could steer his ship on a course toward where he thought *Scorpion* was headed and gain ground. As he gave commands, the way the two-decker handled was another reminder that she was a "clumsy sailer." *Dilettante* was designed for one purpose only: sail in the battle line in order to get within 200 yards of a French Navy third or fourth rater so its crew can shatter the enemy ship's bulwarks with 18- and 24-pound cannon balls from its carronades. *Dilettante* was not designed to chase a nimble, well-captained frigate.

Byrne watched *Kittywake* turn to starboard, thinking, *Brave lad, this way you stay within sight of* Scorpion. The safe thing would have been to head north. He waved for his senior midshipman. "Signal *Derry* to follow and stay in position."

On board H.M.S. Kittywake

Hearns saw a puff of smoke, then a ball announced itself with the scream of wood being torn apart. *Kittywake's* bowsprit was at an odd angle, and the martingale and jib boom guys flapped in the wind.

Hearn's evaluation of the damage was interrupted by the double boom of two more cannons fired one right after another. The port bulwark abeam the foremast erupted in a shower of splinters. One 6-pounder barrel spun like a pinwheel before crashing to the deck. Another collapsed on its destroyed carriage. Men wounded by shrapnel from the shattered cannon ball and jagged splinters screamed in pain.

Balls four and five screamed overhead, punching a hole in sails on each mast. Ball six blew a hole in the berthing deck, a foot over the waterline before taking a large chunk out of the mainmast.

Balls seven ended its career in the water, but ball eight slammed through the bulwark and shattered on the barrel of a six pounder. Shards of cast iron flew around, cutting sheets and braces as well as ripping more men apart.

A part of Hearn's mind kept counting the number of cannon balls. Number nine whistled through the rigging and didn't hit anything. Ball ten hit right below him and he could feel the quarterdeck quiver as the 12-pound iron ball went through the bulwark and blew a hole in the aft bulwark of his cabin before dropping in the water.

Kittywake was slowly turning and he wondered how much longer Scorpion's 12-pounders could target his ship. What alarmed Hearns was that just after gun 10 fired, *Scorpion's* forward most gun fired again. *Damn, the rebel gunners are good! Kittywake* shuddered as a ball slammed through the bulwark, blew through the foremast, hit the number one gun on the starboard side and broke apart. A chuck of cast iron thudded into the deck just in front of Hearns.

The foremast hung in space for a second before toppling to port. Popped stays hissed overhead as they whipped through the air.

Men ran toward the sheets and stays that were still attached to the mainmast and began to hack at them, hoping to save the other two masts. The canvas from the mainmast's sails that fell into the water slowed *Kittywake*. The quartermaster tried in vain to keep the sloop from slewing to port but the pull from the sails in the water overpowered the sloop's rudder

The inadvertent turn presented *Kittywake's* side to *Scorpion,* but the rebel frigate was now sailing to the south. His ship, albeit crippled, was safe. He had survived.

On board Scorpion

From the aft end of the quarterdeck, Jaco studied the enemy brig and then the two-decker. Jaco had never been in a night action and didn't want his first to be against a two-decker. His best option was to keep running.

"Mr. Shelton, bring us around to port to a course of dead north. Let us see if the two-decker follows us."

On board H.M.S. Dilettante

Byrne snapped his spyglass shut, having just seen *Scorpion* reverse course after savaging *Kittywake.* He worked out the geometry of the four ships and said aloud to no one in particular, "Damnation." Upon spotting his senior midshipman he said in a louder voice, "Signal *Derry* to close on *Dilettante.*" Then,"Quartermaster, stand by to come about to port, new course nor' by nor' east."

While his ship was turning, Byrne signaled *Kittywake* to ask if the sloop needed assistance. Hearns hoisted flags, replying that they were not in danger of sinking and would head for New York. Byrne, who had served as midshipman and captain on sloops of that size, tried to estimate how many dead and wounded were on board, and gave up. Visualizing the carnage was unpleasant.

He again aimed his spyglass at *Scorpion* as his mind worked out a strategy to win. Unfortunately, the reports were proved true—the rebel frigate's cannons were capable of hitting ships at 600 yards. He had thought that hardly credible, but there was no arguing with the evidence of his own eyes. This presented a problem; the only way *Dilettante* could win this fight would be to get close enough so its carronades could be effective.

On board H.M.S. Derry

So far, Commander Simon Varney had been a spectator of the action. He had not been present when Commander Smythe had given his report, but what he had been told had more than worried him; it had made him very afraid. Now he was terrified.

When he'd taken command of the 14-gun brig 10 months ago, Simon had just turned 24. Patrolling off the coast of France in May, *Derry* had captured a rebel merchant ship loaded with £10,000 pounds worth of tobacco and cotton. At auction, the ship had brought another £2,000. His share had been a tidy £1,800, which he'd deposited in his new account at the Bank of England. But this action was against a warship and the outcome looked to be very different.

The rebel captain's strategy was obvious—take out the smaller, faster ships so he could run away from *Dilettante*. *Derry* had to delay *Scorpion* long enough for *Dilettante* to get within range and bring its carronades to bear.

His own 9-pounders might do some damage, but he decided his best option was to ram *Scorpion,* knowing in the ensuing boarding action his small 100-man crew might be overwhelmed. But if he could sacrifice his ship by grappling, *Scorpion* could not get away from *Dilettante*.

Simon looked at the upturned faces of the gun crews on the main deck. They had seen *Kittywake* hammered by *Scorpion's* mystery 12-pounders. He knew his crew was wondering the same thing he was. Would they survive?

Commander Varney turned to his senior midshipman, who was all of 16. "Signal *Dilettante*, am going to attempt to grapple."

The dark-haired boy looked at his captain with wide open eyes.

Varney tried to conceal his irritation at the delay. "Do it now. Let me know *Dilettante's* response." He looked down at his hands. His fingers were white from tightly gripping the railing. Simon let go and flexed his fingers, then watched *Scorpion* while he waited for an answer from Captain Byrne.

"Sir, *Dilettante* approves and wishes us good luck."

Of course he does. I am making his job easier by sacrificing my crew and my ship. "Thank you." Varney turned to the man at the wheel. "Quartermaster, on my command, come port to a heading of nor' nor' east. We shall attempt to ram *Scorpion.* That will slow that bloody frigate down so that *Dilettante* can do its job."

Derry's captain leaned over the railing and yelled at his bosun. "Once we finish our tack to the nor' nor' east, get everyone below and behind the stove. Make a wall of hammocks to absorb the splinters. I want only myself, the quartermaster and the first lieutenant on deck."

The bosun, who'd been in the Royal Navy far longer than Varney, put the back of his hand to his forehead with genuine respect.

Varney was counting down the seconds as he waited for the right moment. "Quartermaster, ready about. Helm a-lee. New course, nor' nor' east."

May God help us all!

On board Scorpion

The turn by the Royal Navy brig caught everyone on the quarterdeck by surprise. Once the brig was steady up on its new course, the relative bearing between the two ships didn't change, which meant only one thing: the brig was on a collision course with *Scorpion.*

Jaco didn't have time to ask his officers for their ideas. The Royal Navy squadron commander's strategy was clear. One option was to alter course so that the brig had to chase *Scorpion* from behind; but if the brig had bow chasers they could shoot up Scorpion's stern. Option two was to fall off to the west, cross the bow of the brig at close range, and then turn back to the north. This option would bring *Scorpion* within a mile of the slower two-decker. Option three was to reverse course, pass close to the two-decker and head south. Jaco quickly rejected options one and three.

His first lieutenant had been reasoning along the same lines. "Captain, let's cross the bow of the brig and let our cannons do their work. Even if we don't cripple the brig, we'll at least put the fear of God into its captain."

Jaco quickly answered. "I agree. Unless we lose a mast, we should be able to run and hide from the two-decker. And the Royal Navy trains gunners to aim for the hull."

Hedley Garrison's head bobbed up and down. "Sir, if you get my gunners within 200 yards, we'll double-shot the cannon. They already have balls in them so we can easily add chain shot. Trust me, when my men get done, that brig won't have all its masts standing."

Jaco hesitated before replying. The risk of losing one of their own masts was the problem. Lose a mast and they'd be captured. Jaco looked at his officers. "Jack?"

"I say we cripple the brig and then run."

"Mr. Patterson?"

"Anytime we can give the Royal Navy a bloody nose, I say we do it."

"Mr. Miller?"

"I am only sorry that my Marines won't have a part. I say teach the British another lesson."

"Mr. Wilson, what do you have to add?"

"I don't like running. Once we cripple the brig, I'm for having a go at the two-decker. We can out sail the damned ship and let Mr. Garrison pound away from a distance."

"I like your pluck, Mr. Wilson, but a two-decker is more than *Scorpion* is designed to battle. Those higher guns might surprise us in a most unpleasant way. I prefer that *we* keep the advantage of range, and we shall use our speed to do so.

So, we will fire as we cross the bow of the brig, at a distance that favors our long twelves and keeps us out of range of any bow chasers, then sail away into the night."

On board H.M.S. Derry

The brig was inside 600 yards and Varney was growing uneasy. If Jacinto turned *Scorpion* to cross his bow, he could pound the hell out of *Derry*. But that was a risk he had to take.

He ordered his quartermaster to aim *Derry* to hit *Scorpion* between the bow and the foremast, which allowed some room for error. The two ships, Varney estimated, were now less than 400 yards apart.

Suddenly, the relative angle between the two ships began to change. Varney glanced at his ship's wake—straight as an arrow, therefore *Scorpion* had to be turning through the wind. Varney's heart sank. *Derry* was about to be battered and his crew's courage would be wasted.

Smoke billowed out of *Scorpion's* number one and two gunports at the same time, and Varney felt a ball hammer into *Derry's* hull. At the same time, he heard the whistle of chain shot ripping up his ship's rigging.

The first two 9-pounders on *Derry*'s starboard side disappeared in a dark haze of splinters. Both barrels lay on the deck 10 feet from their shattered carriages. With the halyard severed, the jib fluttered to the deck. The port ratlines for the foremast along with several stays were flaying in the wind. But *Derry* hadn't slowed. Momentum and the wind in the remaining sails carried the ship forward.

Varney gripped the forward railing on the quarterdeck. His heart was pounding with both fear and excitement. *We still have a chance.*

Derry's hull shuddered again. The sound of splintering of timbers in the hull was muted by the main deck, and Varney's attention was distracted by a loud crack as the mainsail yardarm on the foremast split.

Varney felt the wind but didn't hear the ball that ripped the wheel out of his quartermaster's hands, filling his hands with small splinters. He ordered him to go below and tell the bosun to rig the alternative steering. *We can't change course now, even if I wanted to!* Then he looked for his first lieutenant.

The man's upper torso was on left side of the quarterdeck and his hips and lower legs were lying in bloody heap kept onboard by the railing.

The brig was now was falling off to starboard and downwind, away from *Scorpion* as ball after ball struck the hull and chain shot tore at the remainder of the rigging. Varney was alone on the quarterdeck, watching the ships head in opposite directions.

On board H.M.S. Dilettante

Byrne leaned over the main deck bulwark, 20 feet above *Derry's*. He'd slackened sail so he would have time to talk with Commander Varney. "Do you need assistance?"

"No, sir. We have two holes in the bow and are plugging them. Our foremast won't last the night, so we are putting a splint around the damage before we head for New York. I'm sorry, sir; we failed."

"You nearly succeeded, and you slowed him. The frigate is probably headed to Boston. We'll try to intercept him."

Dilettante would patrol a line east of Boston along 71° 30' W longitude and hope *Scorpion* showed up.

On board Scorpion

Jaco took *Scorpion* 50 miles to the east before he resumed his base course to the point north of the tip of Cape Cod. They spent the night tacking back and forth as they worked their way into the wind from the nor' west. Around midnight, he agreed with Jack Shelton and let *Scorpion* sail nor' by east until dawn. The plan was to then head west by so' to get to the mouth of the Piscataqua River.

Unfortunately, the winds didn't cooperate and forced *Scorpion* far south of where Jaco wanted the ship to be. Scattered rain squalls again obscured visibility, and when the frigate broke into the clear, less than half a mile away was a large, familiar looking two-decker. This time, the Royal Navy ship was to windward and the lookout must have spotted Scorpion's sails through the rain, for the drums on the two-decker were already beating.

"Mr. Shelton, beat to quarters and gather the officers."

As the two-decker's gunports opened, Jaco studied the barrels. He recognized the 9-pounders on the upper gun deck, and he was expecting 18- or 24-pounders to stick way out of the side. Instead, the cannon on the lower gun deck didn't poke out as far. A look through his Dollond spyglass showed the gun shape he'd seen on *Pondicherry*.

In Charleston, the British captain had said the Royal Navy was beginning to equip its ships with carronades, named after the Carron Company in Scotland. They fired a heavy, slow-moving ball that was ideal for smashing ship bulwarks. Apparently, this two-decker was armed with them.

On board H.M.S. Dilettante

When the lookout yelled that *Scorpion* was half a mile away, Captain Byrne's first thought was, *Bloody hell, I guessed right*. Jacinto was running for Boston, and *Dilettante* had the frigate pinned against the north coast of

Cape Cod. *Now all I have to do is bring you to battle to teach you a ruddy lesson. By taking* Scorpion, *we'll put an end to this rebel captain's career and end this scourge that has been embarrassing the Royal Navy.*

On board Scorpion

Jaco ordered the fore staysail, jib, mains, top and top gallants sheeted home. He hoped the added sails would increase *Scorpion's* advantage in speed.

With the officers gathered at the aft end of the quarterdeck, Jaco followed his custom of making sure they all knew what he had in mind. This way, even if he were killed, the other officers knew the plan and the tactics he intended to employ. "Gentlemen, my plan is to get past this two-decker by forcing her to maneuver. We will use our speed and agility to stay at least 500 yards away to keep well clear of those big carronades, unless we can get a clear stern or bow shot. Our goal is to get back into the Atlantic by sailing nor' east, then try to reach Kittery before the end of the month."

The two-decker's bow was making white water. Jaco saw a gap between its masts, which showed that the larger ship was wearing to starboard to cross *Scorpion's* bow.

Jaco waited until the two-decker was committed to its turn. "Mr. Preston, stand by to fall off the wind to port and run west."

After seeing a waved acknowledgement, Jaco turned to his quartermaster. "Mr. Jeffords, fall off now. New course is due west."

"Aye, Cap'n. New course due west."

The Royal Navy ship's port side bow chaser boomed, and the ball raised a waterspout 100 yards from *Scorpion's* starboard side. Jaco figured they were in the two-decker's blind spot—too far forward for the main armament along the sides, and too far aft for the bow chasers to fire at his ship.

On board H.M.S. Dilettante

Captain Byrne gave the order to fire the bow chaser more out of frustration than anything else. From the quarterdeck, he could tell the ball would miss, but at least *Dilettante* was in gun range.

The game of cat and mouse had begun. Byrne wanted *Scorpion* headed west so the land would keep the smaller frigate contained. He did not want Scorpion to escape into the Atlantic.

Byrne kept *Dilettante* on the north side of *Scorpion's* wake.

On board Scorpion

Jaco watched the two-decker slowly falling behind. If *Scorpion* was making eight knots, the two-decker was making six at most. The two-decker's main deck was at least 15 feet higher than *Scorpion's,* which to Jaco's way of thinking just made the ship a bigger, easier target. He wondered if his long 12-pounders could, at 600 yards, punch through the thicker bulwarks. He also wondered if *Scorpion's* layered hull would stand up to carronades. He'd rather not pay the price to definitively find out.

The cannon on the two-decker's main deck worried Jaco more than the mysterious carronades. He knew the reach on those guns, and the damage they could inflict.

"Captain? What are your plans?"

Jaco turned around to his officers. This was their first engagement with a two-decker, and the concern showed on their faces.

"We need room to maneuver so we can get away without leading them to Kittery. The north shore of Cape Cod and the coast around Boston to the west will force us to turn. The captain of the two-decker is no fool. He's using the land as a wall to box us in. We are going to tack to nor' nor' east, and I assume the two-decker will try to cut us off."

Shelton spoke up. "You're assuming that the Royal Navy captain wants to get broadside to broadside."

"Yes. I am gambling that is the Royal Navy captain's plan, because if we are broadside to broadside inside three hundred yards, I fear what will happen to *Scorpion*."

"So you aim to force him to play our game."

"Aye, Jack, I do."

Hedley Garrison was already in the fight. "Where do you want us to aim?"

"The upper gun deck. If we miss high, we rip up the bulwarks on the main deck, tear up some of its rigging and maybe and kill some of the two-decker's officers. We'll have a better view from the quarterdeck, so Mr. Shelton and I be there and advise accordingly. If we do not order you to adjust your aim, keep firing accurately as fast as your crews can. The gun crews have shown they can fire two accurate balls every four minutes. Now is the time to show the Royal Navy how good our gun crews are. Just make sure the hammocks are in the nettings along the bulwarks of our gun deck. We've never been hit by balls as big as that two-decker is going to throw at us. Carry on, gentlemen."

Jack Shelton remained behind. He spoke softly, as a friend. "Jaco, I've seen you take on risks before, but a two-decker is a big mouthful. This is like Jonah wanting to swallow the whale."

"No, my friend, I don't want to eat the two-decker, just give it a bloody nose so we can escape. I know it looks bad. I just don't think we can get away except by going north. I am counting on the Royal Navy captain thinking the same way. He wants to close on us, so we are going to let him—but not in the way he wants."

He turned away from his first lieutenant, determined to again show His Majesty's Navy that Continental Navy captains and their ships were a small but formidable enemy. *And our mettle in a fight is not to be underestimated.*

On board H.M.S. Dilettante

Tension and fear tightened the muscles in Captain Byrne's back and gnawed at his gut. He was determined not to show fear as he walked along the starboard side. On his route to the beak of the ship, he stopped to encourage his main deck gun crews. He'd just returned to the quarterdeck from his walk down the port side when his first lieutenant yelled out. "Captain! *Scorpion* is tacking to starboard."

Byrne watched as the rebel frigate appeared to steady up on a nor' east course. At six knots, his ship was covering roughly 167 yards every minute. *Scorpion* seemed to be running two knots faster, so the rebel frigate would travel 100 yards more every minute, or 267 yards per minute. He rounded the number up to 300 to be on the safe side.

If he wanted to turn inside and angle toward the rebel frigate, he had to turn *Dilettante* now to allow for his ship's slow response. Byrne turned to his bosun and helmsman, who were standing near each other on the quarterdeck. "Stand by-to come about to port. Aim to a point about a half mile in front of that frigate. We'll give him a taste of British iron and see how he likes being on the receiving end, the rebel bugger!"

On board Scorpion

Jaco walked to the enclosure that housed the helmsman, where Jeffords was taking his turn at the wheel, and asked Preston to join him. "Call all hands. We're going to fall off the so 'east and run with the wind to force the two-decker to tack again. With luck, we should pass in opposite directions with the range opening."

"We're going to take a broadside from the Britisher, aren't we?"

"Aye, Mr. Preston, we may. But I think we will be at the extreme range of his guns. If our layered bulkheads are true, we should survive. Now, Mr. Jeffords, fall off to starboard. Make your new course so' east. Mr. Preston, get those sails trimmed and then get everyone onto the gun deck. I want only Mr. Shelton, Mr. Jeffords, Mr. Preston and myself on the deck for this. Those not manning guns firing on the enemy need to be ready to come on deck to handle the sails."

The range between the two-decker and *Scorpion* was about 500 yards as the Royal Navy captain adjusted his ship's course. The two-decker was now on a converging course with the Continental Navy frigate.

Almost immediately, gun flashes lit up the side of the two-decker, first from the lower deck, then the upper. Smoke filled the air as *Scorpion's* long 12-pounders fired in reply.

Jaco had never seen a two-decker fire a broadside. Waterspouts, too many to count, erupted well short of *Scorpion*. The two-decker was obscured by gray-white smoke billowing to midway up the main sails. Only the aft third of the two-decker's quarterdeck and the bowsprit were visible.

Jaco was just about convinced that his ship was out of range of the carronades when the bulwark aft of the beak caved in, sending chunks of wood flying through the air. Another heavy ball carried away the steps leading from the main deck to the quarterdeck. The next 24-pound ball dropped through the grating that let light into the center of the ship and expended itself on the berthing deck.

Hits by the heavy balls from the carronades sounded different from 9- and 12-pound balls. They made a duller, deeper thunk as they struck the port side of *Scorpion's* hull. Jaco couldn't tell how much damage they were causing.

Wind and each ship's movement let them sail momentarily out from the pillowy clouds of smoke. The two-decker's guns were firing as fast as they could be reloaded, not broadsides. With much less smoke, Jaco could see that his ship wasn't the only one taking hits. Wood flew each time a 12-pound ball from *Scorpion's* gun struck the bigger ship. *Hard to miss anything that size.*

"Mr. Jeffords, Mr. Preston, fall off two more points to starboard. Once we pass this big bastard, tack to port and get behind him!"

Mr. Garrison came up on deck to say something, but Jacinto yelled before his subordinate could speak. "When we start tacking to get behind, I want your gunners to fire ball to tear up the two-decker's gun-decks."

"Aye, Captain. So far, we don't have any major casualties."

"Good, get back to your guns. If I can manage to get us behind the two-decker, aim for her stern-chasers. This fight is far from over."

Now that *Scorpion* was ahead of the two-decker and neither ship's guns could fire at each other, Jaco call out. "Mr. Preston, Mr. Jeffords, get the starboard gun crews up on main deck, we're going to come about to port and cross the two-decker's bow. New course, Mr. Jeffords, is nor' nor' east. We'll adjust once we turn."

Mr. Garrison hastened to the main deck, and Jaco yelled out, "Ready about, now!"

"Aye, Cap'n, helm a-lee."

"Mr. Wilson, take enough Marines aloft on each mast to get the swivel guns manned and loaded. They should be close enough to fire at least once. Make their main and quarterdeck an unpleasant place to be."

"Aye, aye, sir."

On board H.M.S. Dilettante

Byrne didn't know who to damn more, the designers of his adversary's ship, its captain, or those who designed and built his ship, which handled like an unruly bull calf. He knew what was coming as soon as he saw *Scorpion* turn to port. Swiftly, he ordered the crews of the two 9-pounder bow chasers to shove a bag of grape shot down each barrel. "Both crews, fire at the quarterdeck as you bear, nothing else." Byrne fervently wished that a sufficient number of the one-inch diameter balls might find Captain Jacinto.

As the two ships fought their way through the waves, the seaman in Byrne assessed the work of the rebel sailors. He found himself nodding as he watched them skillfully tack *Scorpion. An Englishman doesn't cease to be a good sailor when he turns traitor, that's the hell of it.* The yards on each mast moved together and the sails were quickly trimmed. Ropes were swiftly coiled and hung on belaying pins. Then the men went below, leaving only four on the quarterdeck.

Now he had to accept the drubbing *Dilettante* was about to get. Unless he could make one more move.

"Bosun, prepare to tack to starboard. Quartermaster, new heading south." *If I am lucky, and if Dilettante responds, we'll have suckered Scorpion into an exchange of broadsides at less than 300 yards.*

"Ready, about to port. Let's get this ship turned."

On board Scorpion

Both Jaco and Jack Shelton saw the two-decker's crew release the jib and fore staysail. *Damn. The Royal Navy captain is playing his cards well.*

Shelton ran forward and jumped down to the main deck, shouting for Preston to get the port gun crews ready. Garrison came up and, seeing him, Jaco yelled, "We're going to turn back toward the west and cross this two-decker's bow. Mr. Jeffords, Mr. Preston, tack the ship to port, helm a-lee now! We need *Scorpion* to turn on a farthing!"

Dilettante was about halfway through its turn to the south as the handier Continental Navy frigate finished its turn. Now, with the wind over its port side, the ship was heading east as it crossed the two-decker's bow.

Smoke billowed out from the two-decker's bow chasers, 300 yards to the north of *Scorpion*. Most of the lead balls turned the water between the two-decker and *Scorpion* to a froth. A few smacked into the ship's hull just before the number one gun on *Scorpion's* port side fired.

Hedley Garrison's gunners were spot on in their aim. The gallery that housed the two-decker's bow chasers was a splintered mess of wood and body parts by the time the number four gun on the port side fired. Of the 11 balls fired, not one missed, but the two-decker sailed on, bruised but clearly not battered.

The sails were pulled in as tight as possible to get the most push from the wind. *Scorpion* leapt ahead as if the ship knew that every knot it made through the water carried them farther from the heavy carronades. Scorpion's captain already had his next move planned. As soon as his ship was beyond 600 yards, Jaco tacked Scorpion to sail due north.

On board H.M.S. Dilettante

Byrne didn't like the way the fight was going. He wanted to get into a slugging match in which the weight of his broadsides would carry the day. He now found himself in a maneuvering fight with a ship that was faster and handier. *Dilettante* was now on the defensive and he didn't like it.

In a moment of weakness, Byrne admitted to himself that this rebel ship and its captain was indeed the formidable adversary described by Royal Navy captains who survived their encounters with *Scorpion.* Now he now understood why the captains who faced this rebel captain and his ship spoke of the pair with respect, bordering on awe.

Still, Byrne was not going to give in. His ship was bigger and designed to take punishment from 24-pounders. All he needed was one broadside inside 200 yards and he was sure the fight would be over—with *Dilettante* the winner.

He impatiently watched as his two-decker slowly turned with the wind to a heading of nor' east. The fight had shifted into a turning melee. *Scorpion* could stay out of range, accelerate ahead and again cross his bow, or slow down and cross his stern. All Byrne could do was order his helmsman to keep the ponderous two-decker turning. Hopefully, he would have enough momentum to finish the turn to the west, catch some wind and regain some speed.

Dilettante, however, wasn't responding to the helm well. As the ship lost speed, the fourth rater also lost rudder effectiveness. Byrne could sense his ship was in for another pounding. He cringed when the saw the jet of flame spit out of the forward most starboard 12-pounder. Byrne forced himself not to close his eyes or imagine what was about to happen to his ship.

The second of *Scorpion*'s 12-pound balls slammed into the rudder post and severed the rope connection to the tiller bar, which split into two pieces. One fell into the water, the other into the hold. *Dilettante* no longer could be steered and began to weathervane. Yardarms that were being pulled around to catch the wind on a new course now flapped in the wind as the rudderless two-decker slowed to a stop, dead in the water.

More cannon balls from *Scorpion* flew down the upper and lower gun decks, shattering as they smashed into gun carriage, beams, ribs and carronades. Wood splinters and iron shards filled the air, stabbing into the bulwarks, shredding and impaling men. The upper gun deck, hit by three cannon balls, was slippery with blood, severed limbs and human tissue.

Byrne wondered why his ship was luffing, until he saw the wheel under his quartermaster's hands spinning without any resistance. Then the swivel gun on *Scorpion's* foremast barked. All but one of the aft 18-pounder carronade's gun crew on the starboard side fell, bleeding from musket balls. Next the swivel gun on *Scorpion's* mainmast spoke, and the crew on the port 18-pounder carronade lay sprawling, bleeding, some dead, the rest wounded. The balls that missed tattooed the quarterdeck, sending small splinters through the air as they embedded themselves in the wood.

Byrne had started toward his main deck when he heard another swivel gun fire. The helm erupted in splinters and his quartermaster crumpled to the deck, bleeding from two musket balls, one in his chest and one in his stomach. When Byrne looked around, he was the only one left standing on the quarterdeck. His first lieutenant lay motionless on the starboard side, bleeding from a hole where his nose used to be.

During a lull in the shooting, the ship's bosun's head appeared by the companionway, like a turtle's coming out of its shell. "Captain, the tiller is shot through. The carpenter says we need hours to find out what we need to fix and make repairs."

Byrne felt and heard an explosion beneath his feet that he thought was one of *Dilettante*'s stern chasers firing. Smoke billowed up from the stern gunport, but he paid no attention, assuming the gun crews were doing their job. He was more focused on getting his ship, only 20 miles from the north shore of Cape Cod, under control. If *Dilettante* drifted downwind for more than a few hours they might run aground.

Suddenly the cannon fire stopped, leaving only the cries of the wounded, the creaking of the yards and clacking of loose pulleys to fill the air. Byrne yelled at his bosun, "Get all the sails furled until we get the rudder fixed."

A glance at his adversary told Byrne *Scorpion* was headed west under full sail. The rebel frigate was no longer his worry; saving *Dilettante* from running aground and being captured was.

His second lieutenant came on the quarterdeck, his right sleeve bloodied from where a fragment of chain had gouged out the muscle in his forearm. "Where are the other officers?" Byrne demanded.

"The first and third lieutenants are dead and the fourth lieutenant is wounded. Our midshipmen are helping sort out the gun decks, sir."

Byrne closed his eyes for a second. "Find a quartermaster and toss a lead out; see how deep the water is out here. We'll take soundings every twenty minutes until we are in less than one hundred feet of water. Then, if we don't have a rudder, we drop both anchors."

His lieutenant hurried off, leaving Byrne to start an inspection of his ship. His first stop was the upper gun deck where, except for the cannons on their sides, there was little visible damage, until one looked at the ribs and bulwarks. Jagged chunks of metal and splinters were imbedded everywhere. With all the wounded carried below, the bosun's mates had the surviving gun crews sloshing down the decks with sea water to wash off the blood.

His next stop was the officer's wardroom, where the carnage made him turn away. Instead of men, there were body parts. He could see where the breech of the port stern chaser had blown apart. The explosion had killed all 22 men, but the blast had been contained within his cabin, or what was left of it.

His last stop was the orlop deck and the surgeon's cockpit. Amputated limbs were in buckets to be carried to a gunport on the lower deck and dumped over the side. The surgeon had no idea what the butcher's bill will be, but for Byrne, whatever the cost, it was way too much, and it was his fault.

Kittery, Maine, fourth week of October 1778

The process of removing *Scorpion's* cannon and all the remaining stores on board so the ship could be inspected took three days. James Hackett, *Scorpion's* designer and builder, sent a list to Congress of what needed to be repaired and replaced, along with a cost estimate. *Scorpion* would also be hauled out of the water, its bottom cleaned and, where needed, the copper plating replaced.

Jaco gathered the crew around him on the empty gun deck, lined with their sea chests they were using for chairs. Off to one side were two tables, behind which were the chests from the hold that contained the purses of prize money. In the battle with *Dilettante,* four members of the crew had been killed outright or died of their wounds. All were from Boston. Their purses would be removed from the chest. Before he headed south, Jaco planned to find their families and deliver the purses.

Jaco walked back and forth in front of the men. "Gentlemen, your enlistments are up tomorrow, the last day of October 1778, and as such you have no obligation to return. Your contributions have made the Continental Navy better and brought us closer to the day when we are no longer ruled by King George. We have taken prizes, damaged, sunk or captured Royal Navy frigates, many larger and more heavily armed than *Scorpion.* You, gentlemen, have done your duty well."

He took a few steps and resumed speaking in measured tones. "When you leave this ship, you will all have a purse of gold and silver guilders and English pounds. You are richer not because of the money but because of what you accomplished as part of *Scorpion's* crew."

Jaco paused, wishing to be honest. "I understand if some of you believe you have done enough. But until we are free from the British, *Scorpion's* job, our job, is not done. The frigate will sail again under my command next February when the refit is completed. In January, we will start signing on the crew, and I hope many of you return. I would be honored to have every one of you back aboard to write another chapter in our ship's history. In the meantime, I wish you and your family's success and good health. May God keep you and watch over you."

Jaco unlocked the chests. Hedley Garrison reached in and called out the first name. At the table, the man was shown the page in the muster when the money was originally divided and what his share was. The stitching was cut and the purse dumped on the table and counted. Satisfied, the man either signed or made his mark in the column next to his name on the ship's muster. The coins were returned to the purse and pocketed by the sailor. Before each man left the ship, Jaco shook each his hand and said, "Thank you for sailing on *Scorpion.*" With each man, he exchanged a few words wishing the man well. Jaco was gratified by the number who said they would be back. Yet, while he believed their commitment was genuine, he suspected that many would have a change of heart and not return.

After the sailors and mates had left the ship, Jaco asked his officers to join him in his cabin for one last drink together.

Garrison held up his glass. "To Captain Perfecto, may he lead many more ships to victory." Jaco smiled at the nickname.

Once they took a drink, Garrison spoke again. "Captain, I think I speak for all the officers as well as Bosun Preston and Quartermaster Jeffords when I say that, barring something unforeseen, like being given our own ships, we will all be here in December."

CHAPTER 10
WEALTH ISN'T EVERYTHING

Gosport, England, first week of November 1778

Three weeks and three days after leaving the North Atlantic Squadron, *Liber* anchored at the Royal Navy's main base in Portsmouth, England. The oh-so-familiar smell of the mudflats outside the port, coupled with smell of kelp and the sulphureous odor of the dying seaweed known as gutweed chorophyta or sea lettuce, was a potent reminder that he was home.

With the pouches of dispatches delivered, Darren went to the shipyard and saw that the keel for *H.M.S. Gladius* had been laid. The yard manager informed him that the tentative launch date was February 19th, 1779.

H.M.S. Gladius was an *Enterprise*-class frigate, another of prolific ship designer John Williams' designs. When finished, the full-rigged ship would be 120.5 feet long, have a beam of 35.5 feet and displace 593 tons. Planned armament was a main battery of twenty-four 9-pounders on the gun deck and four 6-pounders on the quarterdeck. Under full sail and with a clean copper bottom, *Gladius* could make 10 knots and needed a crew of 200 men.

Back at the Port Admiral's office, Smythe asked the captain in charge of personnel assignments how many officers and sailors he could take from *Liber* to his new command. Smythe was curtly told to wait until he was officially promoted and *Gladius* actually needed a crew. When he reminded the captain that *Liber* was going into the yard and he had a letter saying he was to be promoted when he arrived in Portsmouth, the captain gave him an icy stare as if to say, *Don't push. Wait and you'll get what I assign.*

All of which left the question of when to visit the property in Langton Herring. As soon as he'd landed in Portsmouth, he'd posted a letter to York asking to meet and schedule a visit. In the meanwhile, he would see his family.

On his way to his parents' house, Darren stopped at the rock where, as a little boy, he had watched ships coming in and out of Portsmouth, dreaming that one day he would be the captain of one. Today, as he sat on the rock, the view and the intoxicating smell of the sea was the same. The 10-year-old boy's dream had come true. He was a commander in the Royal Navy and the captain of a sloop of war. The next time he put to sea, he would be Captain Darren Smythe, commanding officer of *H.M.S. Gladius*, 28 guns.

Commander Darren Smythe stood at the door to his parent's house, debating whether he should knock or just go right in. The house was no longer where he lived. Even though his mother had said there would always be a room for him, in Darren's mind his home was a captain's cabin, or possibly the estate in Langton Herring. Here he was a guest.

Darren rapped twice, loud enough for his mother to hear, assuming she was home. If Olivia Smythe was following what he remembered as the family routine, she would be in the kitchen preparing dinner.

A woman wearing a kerchief to hold back her graying hair opened the door and studied his tanned face for what felt like an eternity. She spoke one word, softly. "Darren?"

"Aye, mother, 'tis I."

Olivia Smythe took both his hands in hers and stepped back, gently pulling him into the house. "Let these old eyes look at you. I was wondering if we would ever see you again."

"Mother, I was home less than a year ago."

"Yes, but to an old woman, that is forever." Olivia looked at Darren as if she was inspecting him. "You look good in that uniform, I must say. So, now you are a commander?"

"Yes, and I am being promoted to captain. I will be given command of a new frigate, *H.M.S. Gladius.*"

"Congratulations! You have done well in the Navy. I always knew you would. Can you stay for dinner and the night?"

"Aye. A boat is picking me up at seven-thirty tomorrow morning."

"Your father will be delighted to see you. Can you come for Sunday dinner at Emily's? We have started to rotate. One week at Bradley's, next week at Gerard's to save wear and tear on an old lady."

"You look like a plump currant!"

Olivia smiled at the analogy that meant she looked healthy. Darren followed his mother on the familiar route from the front of the house to where the kitchen was located in the back. The floors, originally built in 1640 and then added on several times, still creaked. The oak table was still in front of the great hearth and stove where his mother baked breads and pies. There were no servants to ease her workload.

His mother sat him at the table and prepared a plate of bread, smoked meat, and stilton cheese. "This will take the edge off your hunger until supper. Eat, and tell me about your adventures. It will be a change from what I hear every night at the dinner table," she said with a smile.

At supper that night, for the first time in his life Darren was alone with his mother and father and could share his world without competing for attention. Conversation was about Darren and his life, not about the family business.

Later, Darren and his parents were sitting in the drawing room, where the heat from the fire had taken the chill out of the evening air. Each had a glass of Spanish sherry. Lester Smythe held out his glass, not to offer a toast, but to make a point. "Darren, all of us in the Smythe family are very proud of you. From that moment on the rock when you asked me to help you become a midshipman, I knew that one day, if you were not killed or crippled, you would have your own ship."

"Thank you, father."

Darren thought he could see, by the flickering light, a wry smile. "And I think that had I not gotten you an appointment at the Royal Naval Academy, one of two bad things would have happened. Either you'd have joined Smythe & Sons and we'd have had a very unhappy employee, or you'd have run away and joined as a seaman. And either way you'd been very angry at your mother and father."

Lester Smythe rarely revealed his inner thoughts, and Darren thought his statement was a revelation. *He was right. I would have been very unhappy and the unhappiness would have transitioned to anger every time I saw a ship. I would have left to join.*

"Well, Father, let us drink to something that never happened!"

Charleston, second week of November 1778

The offices of the Bank of South Carolina were in an imposing two-story red brick building at the corner of Church and Broad Street. The bank's headquarters was intended to give viewers an impression of strength and stability. Inside, the reception area was tastefully paneled and modestly furnished. On the first floor were three offices and a conference room off to the side for private conversations. The second floor consisted of eight offices, one of which could be used for large meetings.

Five 3-foot wide, 4-foot tall windows let customers see into Greg Struthers' office. He felt seeing his presence gave them confidence to do business with the bank.

Money, loans, and collateral documents were stored in a walk-in vault in the back of the bank, constructed from sheets of iron joined by hot rivets hammered into place. Three hard to pick warded locks, for which there were only three sets of keys, added to the security. One set was kept in a small safe at the Jacinto home. Another was kept by Struthers in his office at the bank, and the third kept locked away at Miriam Bildesheim's house north of the city.

Gregory Struthers was studying a loan document for Calvin McManus to make sure the words reflected what the two men had agreed to earlier in the week. Calvin was the head of a family that owned a cotton plantation north of Charleston and was coming in to sign the documents this afternoon. The loan was being offered because the two ships carrying the cotton to mills in the Netherlands had been seized by the Royal Navy. Without the loan the McManuses would go bankrupt.

He glanced up as an exceptionally tall woman walked into the lobby he recognized as Shoshana Jacinto. Besides being spectacularly beautiful, Jaco's sister had piercing, intense green eyes. She was also one of the smartest human beings he'd ever met.

Shoshana had been apprenticing at the law firm of Burrows & Soriano since she was 15 because none of the law schools at the Inns of Court in London would accept female students. Recently, Raphael Soriano and her father had prevailed upon the judges who examined prospective members of the South Carolina bar to let her sit for an examination. Law school attendance was not a requirement to be a member of the bar, knowledge of the law was. If Shoshana passed, she would be admitted as the first female member. The exam was scheduled for February 1779.

After apologizing for the interruption, Shoshana said, "Mr. Struthers, these documents just came in on the packet. The Laredo ships can now fly the Swedish flag and therefore, unless they are carrying munitions, are exempt from being seized by the Royal Navy. This will lower their insurance rates and make loans to the Laredos less risky."

Shoshana laid out documents registering several Laredo ships as being owned by a Swedish firm, Laredo Shipping AB, based in Stockholm. AB, she explained, stood for *Atkiebolag*, the Swedish equivalent of incorporated. Next, she placed the notice to Lloyd's Register and Lloyd's of London of the new ownership on the desk. "We have a set of documents for the Laredos here in Charleston at our offices, as well as documents showing the Swedish company's ownership. One copy goes on each ship."

"How did you carry this off?"

"To be honest, the idea came from a discussion Eric Laredo had with a Swedish count. The project took over a year, mostly to send documents back and forth. So this makes me a bit of an expert in Admiralty Law. Sweden was the neutral nation we needed; France, Spain, the Dutch, seven German states and Britain are all at war. Oddly enough, they all use Lloyds to insure their ships despite trying to take them from each other." Her green eyes twinkled.

There was a knock at the door, and one of the bank's five employees, a mature woman in her forties, entered. "Mr. Struthers, there's a Curtis Armstrong from the Royal Governor's office who says he must see you."

Greg saw a look of displeasure cross Miss Jacinto's face and said, "Give us a few minutes and then send him in." Then he asked Shoshana, "What do you know of him?"

"Before William Campbell, our last Royal Governor, fled and later died, Armstrong was an officious clerk on his staff who issued business licenses and collected taxes. We don't have a royal governor, but businesses in Charleston, including the bank, still pay taxes as assessed before the war. He's a dedicated Loyalist and my father refers to him as 'that addlepated idiot Armstrong'."

"Do you have any idea what he wants?"

She sighed. "I can guess. The charter for the Bank of South Carolina was issued by the Bank of England and signed by King George in 1774. Since the rebellion started, Armstrong had tried at least once a year to shut the bank down on the grounds that if we do not recognize King George, the charter is no longer valid."

"Would you mind staying?"

"No, 'twill be my pleasure."

The door opened and in strode Curtis Armstrong. He was short, on the plump side of stocky, and sweating heavily in the humid, 80-degree heat. The word golumpus came to mind when Greg first saw Armstrong. The clerk shot a hostile look at Shoshana, who was casually leaning against a bookcase full of books that the bank owners bought to help the owners of a bookstore stay in business.

Rather than rise and offer his hand, Greg clasped his hands in front of him and stayed seated at his desk. "I apologize that I do not stand; I am missing one of my legs." Greg almost said, "thanks to a Royal Navy cannon ball," but didn't. He simply let the words hang in the air and let Armstrong use his imagination to determine how he lost a leg. "What can the Bank of South Carolina do for you, Mr. Armstrong? Does the office of the Royal Governor need a loan?" Shoshana turned away to conceal her smile.

"I am here to officially notify you that the office of the Royal Governor has discovered that the Bank of South Carolina has been issuing loans to rebel businesses so they do not go bankrupt. Since these rebels are traitors in the eyes of King George the Third, the Royal Governor intends to revoke the Bank's charter." Armstrong placed on Greg's desk a sheet of paper on which the red wax seal of the Royal Governor was clearly visible.

Greg kept his hands clasped in front of him, leaving the note untouched. "Pray tell, Mr. Armstrong, would you please provide an example?"

Curtis Armstrong sniffed derisively. "You have loaned money to plantations whose owners have joined the Continental Army. Those farmers sell their produce to the Continental Army's commissary-general."

"The last time I checked, the bank, according to its royal charter issued and signed by none other than King George the Third and the former Royal Governor, is free to loan money to *any* individual or business deemed, after investigation, creditworthy. One's political views are not relevant when we consider a loan application. What is important to the bank is the borrower's ability to repay the loan. So, we've committed no crime, unless King George the Third through Parliament has passed a law requiring us to take into consideration one's loyalty to the crown as part of our process."

"The men who signed the loan documents are rebels! That means they are traitors and, as such, guilty of treason."

Greg held up a hand. "Mr. Armstrong, I am a bit baffled. So far, I have not seen any news about trials in which some of my fellow South Carolinians have been charged with treason. Have you, Miss Jacinto?"

The tall woman was smiling broadly as she shook her head.

"Mr. Armstrong, as I am sure you know, Mr. Campbell, our last Royal Governor, left this colony on September 15th, 1775. And I have heard that he recently passed away—in England. So I am also puzzled as to how he could have signed such a document or applied a seal. Would you enlighten me?"

Before Armstrong could respond, Greg continued. "And I believe our current governor, Mr. Henry Laurens, is now a guest of King George the Third at the Tower of London. Therefore, I doubt he signed your document either."

Armstrong tapped his right forefinger on the sealed and unopened letter. "You have been officially notified that the Crown is revoking the Bank of South Carolina's charter. As of this moment, you are no longer a chartered bank."

"Really, Mr. Armstrong." Greg turned to Shoshana. "Ms. Jacinto, I understand you clerk for one of Charleston's oldest law firms. Please correct me if I am wrong, but to do something this drastic, doesn't even King George have to have evidence which his barristers must present in a court? Then and only then, a judge or jury rules on the validity of the charges and decides whether or not to convict. Or did I miss something?"

Shoshana responded coolly. "No, Mr. Struthers, you didn't. No one in the history of the Royal Province of South Carolina has ever been charged with treason. Nor has anyone ever presented any evidence that would support revoking the charter of the Bank of South Carolina. If they did, my law firm, which represents the bank, would have been notified."

Greg nodded his head several times. He looked at Curtis Armstrong, who mopped his damp brow with a handkerchief. "Mr. Armstrong, I dare say there are some folks in Charleston who would consider those loyal to the king as traitors. That is a matter for the court to decide, not a banker. Forgery is also a matter for the court to rule upon. By the way, who *did* sign your notice?"

"I did, on behalf of the Royal Governor. Signing is well within my power as the Royal Governor's new first secretary," Curtis snapped.

Shoshana smiled as she spoke. "Mr. Armstrong, you may think issuing this notice is within your power, but we can have a very interesting discussion in front of a judge to determine what legal orders you can and cannot issue as a clerk. I for one, would like to see the document from King George, or from Parliament, or the Royal Governor that gives you such power."

Curtis's eyes narrowed to slits, and he tapped the document again. "My office will find enough evidence to support charges of treason and gain a conviction. Your assets will be forfeited and you, sir, along with the other owners of the bank, will hang."

Struthers was not cowed by Armstrong's threat. "Sir, those are strong words. But any legal action you initiate will take time. Perhaps I should inform you that I have reviewed every performing and non-performing loan in our portfolio. The loans that give me pause are held by Loyalists, many of whom have left Charleston, most likely not to return. Their departures leave the bank with non-performing loans because these individuals have not met the terms and conditions under which they were loaned money. However, because the Bank of South Carolina is a nice neighbor, we have *not* yet foreclosed on their property put up as collateral, but we have the notices ready. If we are provoked, we *will* foreclose and legally take the property to sell to recover what funds we can. The rest, alas, we will have to write off."

Greg glanced at Armstrong's document. "I suspect that many of these Loyalists who owe the bank large sums of money want to close us down so they don't have to repay their loans. Several of these individuals have come into my office and threatened to use their influence with your office to shut the Bank of Carolina down. If you are interested, I can share my log of those who have made those threats, the time and dates they made these threats, and the amount they owe the bank. We are a profitable, well-funded bank with access to capital both here in South Carolina and abroad. This makes us able to defend ourselves in court if need be."

Curtis Armstrong flushed and used the handkerchief in his pocket to again wipe the sweat off his forehead and cheeks.

Greg smiled and continued. "If we went to court, Mr. Armstrong, you would be asked to recount any conversations you may have had with those individuals—under oath. Just so we are clear, Mr. Armstrong, if you continue to pursue this path, it increases the risk that the bank will not be repaid. Therefore, we will have no choice but to *immediately* foreclose on those who are past due and seize their property. The only legal way to prevent this would be for these Loyalist debtors, who are past due, to pay the bank what it is owed plus the penalties outlined in their loan agreements." Greg's tone was soft, but Shoshana could sense the steel behind the words.

"Mr. Armstrong, please take your notice and leave. You are wasting my time. I will forget this conversation took place—unless the Royal Governor's office continues on this course. Miss Jacinto is my witness to your threats. It may interest you to know that Miss Jacinto is an intern at Burrows & Soriano and may soon be a member of the South Carolina bar."

Mr. Armstrong's pudgy face flushed bright red. He looked at Shoshana, clearly surprised by the revelation. "I didn't know you were planning to sit for the bar exam. I did not know the association would allow a woman to become a member of the bar."

She gave Armstrong her best debutante smile. "If given a fair hearing, I am confident I will pass and become the first woman member of the bar."

Shoshana watched the bureaucrat leave the bank. "I'll add a record of this meeting to the file in my office. If Mr. Armstrong does attempt anything more than bluster, let my firm know. Now, on to the second and more important reason I came here."

"And that is?"

"Do you remember Phoebe McManus, Mr. Shelton?"

"I do. She is Calvin McManus's daughter."

"Yes. She would like to meet you socially."

"I beg your pardon?"

"Miss McManus, who is twenty-two and someone I have known and admired since I was a little girl, thinks you are handsome, and a gentleman with excellent prospects. And you come highly recommended—by my mother and Adah Laredo."

"She does know I am missing a leg."

"Aye, she does, and says that what is in a man's heart and head is what matters. So here is how we in Charleston, proceed in such matters, assuming you are interested. Before you leave for the day, you will receive a formal invitation to dinner on Saturday night at our house, to which you should respond formally. Only her parents, my parents, my younger brother Saul, you, Phoebe, and myself will be at the table. After dinner, Phoebe and you will be left alone in the parlor or outside in the garden to talk. If there is interest on both sides, then she will allow you to call on her."

"I see. Your mother is playing matchmaker."

"Aye, that she is. The Spanish word is *casamentera* and the Hebrew word is *shidduch*. Jaco and my father told us to find you a good woman, and we enlisted Adah Laredo in the hunt. Phoebe qualifies in many ways. She is educated, smart, beautiful, comes from good family, and is very eligible."

Greg felt as if the ground were slipping away from under his feet but managed to answer. "I will be there."

Shoshana was grinning as she picked up her briefcase and stopped in the doorway. "Good. Just make sure you send a formal response to my house. And remember, Mr. Shelton," she intoned, "we southern women of all religions are raised by our mothers to be ladies in the parlor, chefs in the kitchen, and... harlots in the bedroom. See you Saturday." The last words were spoken in a cheerful lilt.

Portsmouth Royal Navy Base,
third week of November 1778

Darren waited for the bureaucratic wheels in the Admiralty to turn. *Gladius* was framed but still a long way from being launched, and he was still *Liber's* captain until officially relieved. Therefore, he allowed one third of *Liber's* crew to go ashore each day. Before they were rowed to the personnel landing, he admonished the sailors that if any of them caused a disturbance, liberty for all the crew would end. He didn't want to risk his captaincy on the stupidity of a drunken sailor.

With nothing else to do, Darren studied the plans of the manor house, sent to him by Henry York. He was trying to visualize the inside of one of the rooms when there was a knock on his cabin door. Quickly, Darren folded the sheets and put them in his desk. He had told no one, not even Drew Rathburn, about his sudden wealth. "Come in."

Midshipman Tewksbury entered. "Sir, a boat has arrived from base headquarters saying you have a meeting with the Port Admiral. There is a messenger waiting to meet you as well."

"Thank you. I'll be along directly."

Messenger? For me? Strange. Maybe he is from Scoons.

The rain had slowed to a light drizzle. Before he entered base headquarters, Darren shook off his cape and hat under the portico. The two Royal Marines guarding the door brought their muskets to the vertical, present arms position when they saw his single gold epaulet. Inside, a clerk offered to hang his cape on a rack near the door.

The lieutenant on duty came to attention in front of Darren. "Commander Smythe, the gentleman at the table is here for you. Once you finish your business, I am to take you to the Port Admiral's office."

Darren thanked him, then approached the table. The stranger stood and said, "Commander Smythe?"

Darren replied a hesitant, "Yes, I am Commander Smythe."

The man offered him a pouch full of papers.

"I am Phineas Harrods, one of Mr. York's law clerks. Mr. York sent me with the papers you requested and asks when you would be free to accompany him to Langton Herring. He understands you will be in Portsmouth until your new ship is completed." Harrods then bowed slightly and handed Darren a card. "This is the address of our office in Portsmouth. We have couriers who go back and forth to our main office every day, and Mr. York can be reached there. Have a good day, sir."

Mr. Harrods departed, and Darren turned to follow the waiting lieutenant. He was led to a corner office with large windows on both sides through which one could see ships in the graving docks, and ships being built, and ships further out in the harbor. Rear of the Blue Admiral Davidson was in the room, as well as Rear Admiral of the Red Arthur.

At the Royal Naval Academy, there was a course on the Royal Navy's organization and rank structure. There were three levels of rear, vice and full admirals—blue, white and red. Blue was the most junior and red the most senior at each level. As Darren shook Davidson's hand, the admiral put his hand on his shoulder. "Commander Smythe, I am glad to see you again. I hear you have done well with *Liber*."

"Thank you, sir. We had some success."

"Well, Admiral Arthur has a draft for substantial amount of prize money, which is much more than some success!"

"Splendid! And thank you, sir. May I ask, when is the crew to get their share?"

Davidson smiled. "Tomorrow. We asked you here to officially promote you, and to discuss what we should do about your friend Jacinto. Have you heard the latest, Smythe?"

"No, sir."

"*Scorpion* bashed about three of His Majesty's ships: *Dilettante,* a fifty-gun fourth rater, the sloop *Kittlywake* and the brig *Derry*. Captain Byrne was quite candid in saying that Jacinto schooled them."

Sorry as Smythe was for the captains and commanders of the three ships, he couldn't help thinking, *I tried to warn Admiral Howe*. And part of his mind rejoiced that Jaco Jacinto was alive and well. If only they could be allies instead of enemies! "Sir, I recommended to Admiral Howe that he send at least three fifth-raters with 12 pounders to hunt *Scorpion*. That would be essential to match the range of his guns, and only numbers can offset his ship's speed."

"Brilliant, Smythe. That's the second reason you are here. Now, winter is almost upon us; *Scorpion* will probably be laid up somewhere for re-fitting and repairs, and so we suspect the rebel frigate won't be out until the spring. You sir, when you leave here, will have a set of orders directing Admiral Gambier commanding the North American Station to provide you with two more fifth-raters whose sole purpose is to sink or capture *Scorpion*."

"Sir, that's splendid, but *Gladius* is only approved for 9-pounders. To take on *Scorpion*, I recommend we adjust the number of cannons to twenty 12-pounders." Against *Scorpion*, 9-pounders would be all but useless.

"That's a wizard idea. I will see if it can be done." Davidson stepped back with a satisfied nod.

Admiral Arthur took a box from his desk. "In the name of King George the Third, I have the honor and pleasure to present this second epaulet to you, Captain Smythe."

"Thank you, sir."

Davidson pinned the second epaulet on his right shoulder. "Now, Captain, would you join us for a spot of lunch?"

"I would be honored, Admiral."

Rear Admiral Arthur turned to pick up a letter from his cluttered desk. "First, we have two other matters to discuss. As of tomorrow, you are no longer captain of *Liber*. Rathburn is going to take over *Liber,* and Soames will become his first lieutenant, so you must move ashore."

Darren was very pleased for his friend. "If you will allow me, Admiral, I will personally deliver Rathburn's orders. He deserves a command."

"That will be fine. Next, there is the matter of who you may take with you to *Gladius*. You can have both midshipmen and either Louttit or Stanhope, but not both."

"What about some of the crew?"

"How many?"

"A dozen."

"Give me their names."

Darren rattled off 12 names, starting with Jonathan Williams and Gavin Dawson, then said, "Sir, Midshipman Enfield is ready for the lieutenant's exam and so is Tewksbury, but Tewksbury won't turn 15 until next February."

"No matter. If he passes, he passes. We are starting a one-week preparatory class next week followed by the exam. Make sure both men are there. My flag lieutenant will deliver the formal orders tomorrow. If they pass, you have your lieutenants; at worst, you'll have two midshipmen and I'll have to find you a lieutenant or two."

"Thank you, sir. And if I may, I would like to officially request some leave."

"How about 30 days, starting the 26th? Not much will happen with *Gladius* while we wait for shipments of wood. All the construction is held up because ships couldn't get through the Skagerrak due to bad weather."

"Splendid, sir."

After lunch, Smythe held back and asked Rear Admiral Davidson for a few minutes to discuss a private matter.

"Sir, this is a bit awkward, but are you familiar with the Scoons law firm?"

"I am. Why? Are you in some sort of trouble, Captain Smythe?"

"Oh no, sir. Captain Horrocks left me his estate. Henry York at Scoons is the executor. I just want to be assured that they are not a bunch of scoundrels."

Davidson laughed. "No, Captain Smythe, they are not. There are many peers, including myself, who use them. Henry York is one of the partners."

"Thank you, Admiral Davidson. That is good to know. Do you know Mr. York?"

"I've met York at least twice, I think. If you are working with a partner, the Horrocks estate must be large. Scoons is very good. They have me invested in two breweries in Germany, a glass maker in Holland, and two wineries in France. The profits go into a bank in the source country—Rothschilds in France and Germany, ABN AMRO in Holland. Scoons' attorneys are reputable and top-notch; I suggest you heed their advice."

"Thank you, sir."

"Have you met York yet?"

"No, sir. We are going out to the manor house Horrocks left me."

"A manor house! Where?"

"In Langton Herring, along with 30 acres."

Davidson put both hands on Darren's shoulders. "Young man, of all the people I know, you best deserve this good fortune. If I may make a recommendation, consider it seriously. Enjoy your wealth, but don't waste it."

"Aye, sir. I have my work cut out for me. This is something they don't teach at the Royal Naval Academy."

Davidson laughed. "There is much about life they don't teach young officers. Now as it happens, I'm beached here in Portsmouth until my new three-decker is fitted out. We're heading to the West Indies to see what mischief I can create in December. Let's sup one day later this week and talk of this. Managing wealth and making money grow is not easy."

"Thank you, sir. I would appreciate the advice."

"Do your parents know?"

"No, sir. Not yet. I intend to tell them at Sunday dinner. Right now, I have more questions than answers."

The walk back to the pier and the wait for the boat back to *Liber* gave Darren time to contemplate what life as a wealthy man could mean. His parents' were considered well-to-do, but not wealthy, a distinction Darren didn't understand. Where was the line?

* * *

Lieutenant Soames was the officer on watch when Darren climbed up the side of *Liber* and onto the deck. Virgil Soames' eyes got as big as saucers when he noticed the second epaulet on Darren's shoulder.

"Mr. Soames, please gather the warrants and all the officers in my cabin immediately."

"Aye, aye, Captain."

Smythe proceeded to his cabin. He put the ship's log on the table, then beside it Rathburn's orders, and the sheet transferring the two midshipman, Bosun Louttit and twelve sailors to the new frigate *H.M.S. Gladius*. He was setting out glasses when there was a knock on the door. "Come in."

One by one, the officers filed in, each one looking alert and curious. None of them looked astonished, so Smythe deduced that Soames had already told them their sloop's captain had been promoted.

This was a bittersweet moment, but Darren was determined to be cheerful. "As you can see, gentlemen, I have some news."

He waited to the chuckles died down. "The most obvious one is that I have been promoted. Tomorrow I will leave *Liber* to take command of *H.M.S. Gladius,* which is a phantom ship because it has not yet been built. Lieutenant Rathburn will take over as captain of *Liber;* the official turnover ceremony will take place tomorrow morning. Mr. Rathburn is on the new Commander list."

There was a round of handshakes and congratulations. When these died down, Darren continued. "Mr. Soames, you will be Rathburn's first lieutenant. Midshipmen Enfield and Tewksbury, both of you have been invited to attend a lieutenant's exam preparatory class beginning next Monday. Should you pass, you will be assigned as the second and third lieutenants on *H.M.S. Gladius*. Should you either of you fail, which I do *not* anticipate, you will be midshipmen on *H.M.S. Gladius*." Darren looked around and tried to keep his voice matter of fact. "Are you with me?"

There were nods and several ayes. "Splendid! Next, we have a crew to divide. Much as I would like to take every man with me, that would hardly be fair to Commander Rathburn or to *Liber*. Mr. Louttit, it would be my pleasure to have you as *Gladius'* bosun."

"I would be delighted, sir."

"Splendid! I have a list of twelve men from *Liber's* crew who will transfer to *Gladius*. All those who are leaving *Liber* will have to move to a barracks ship tomorrow. I will accompany them to make sure the barracks ship's log and muster reflects their assignment to *Gladius*."

He handed Drew Rathburn two envelopes. One held his assignment as a captain of *Liber*, and the other his orders to supervise a refit and be prepared to leave once it was completed. "Mr. Rathburn, you earned this command. Good luck and Godspeed." Darren next told the midshipmen that their orders to the preparatory class billeted them in a brick building on the base. Then he held up a glass. "Gentlemen, to your success."

That night, after dinner, Darren asked his mother and father to join him in the study. In the background, the crackling fire offset the damp cold from the outside. Darren told them about his inheritance and his plans to visit the house in Langton Herring. Olivia gasped audibly but didn't say a word. Lester asked, "What do you propose to do with the house and the money, son?"

Darren took a deep breath. "Invest the money wisely. The house, I am not sure. Right now, the land makes a profit. I have no expenses other than the fee I pay for a manager, for there is no staff. This is why I want to spend a few days in Langdon Herring."

Lester Smythe rubbed his chin. Fourteen thousand pounds was a large fortune, and he was not sure his son realized how big. "Darren, you could leave the Navy and live well on the money. Your wealth makes you an excellent prospect as a husband. You would find yourself invited to the best gatherings and introduced too many fine young women. You'd have the privilege of choosing one to be your wife."

Olivia understood the value of money; for decades she'd been the company bookkeeper. But her son's new wealth was not the uppermost concern in her mind. "If you left the navy and lived in Langton Herring, we would get to see you more often," she said quietly.

"Mother, I am a naval officer. I just made captain and, unfortunately, we are at war. My duty is to stay in the Navy." He wanted to add that he didn't want to choose a wife as one would a horse. He wanted to love her.

Olivia felt her fear for her son's life and well-being rise to the surface. "Duty be dammed! You've done your duty and more. Duty will get you killed in this stupid war. We should give the rebels their liberty and be done with it!"

"Aye, Mother, I agree, but whether or not the war continues is out of my hands. Only the King and his friend Lord North have the power to end this war, and Lord North thinks we shall win. Talk to your member of Parliament, because until Lord North's government falls with a vote of no confidence, the war will continue, whether father, you or I like it or not."

Neither his mother or father responded. To change to what he thought was a more important subject, Darren showed the drawings of Langdon Herring to his parents, then asked the question that had been vexing him all evening. "What do I tell Bradley, Gerald and Emily?"

"The truth. You have been bequeathed an estate and some money. The amount is none of their business."

"Should I ask Emily's husband Francis if he knows Henry York?"

"That is up to you," his father answered. "Francis is from Bournemouth, which is not far from Langton Herring. He may know the house."

Chapter II
Frustrating Liberty

Charleston, late November 1778

The mail packet schooner's route started in Boston and made stops in Philadelphia, Hampton, Charleston and Savannah. The two-masted ship *Alacrity* carried mail, cargo, and up to a dozen passengers up and down the cost on a "regular" schedule. The captain timed his arrivals in port for early morning and departures after dark to minimize the risk of encounters with prowling Royal Navy frigates.

Alert for possible fares, wagon and buggy drivers waited at the end of the pier where *Alacrity* docked in Charleston. Jaco flagged a wagon driver who was delighted to be paid with a silver English shilling coin rather than a paper Continental dollar. The driver eagerly helped Jaco load the heavy box that contained the ships' bells from *Coburg, Sorcerer, Inquest and Pondicherry*. They would hang next to *Sorcerer's* in the sitting room of his parents' house until he had a home and a study of his own. His sea chest was the next to be loaded, then the boxes with his sextant, spy glass, and his brace of pistols.

On the ride, Jaco was not in the mood to talk. Thankfully, the man didn't ask any questions other than where were they going. When they arrived, the wagon driver helped Jaco stack the boxes on the front port, and Jaco handed him a second silver shilling.

Jaco looked at the stack of boxes, reflecting that when he'd left to go to Philadelphia as a prospective midshipman, he'd brought only a half empty sea chest. Now the chest was full of uniforms, and made much heavier by £5,400 in prize money.

The sweet smell of cornbread and eggs cooking drew him up the steps. He knocked, and a moment later a tall young woman opened the door.

"Welcome home, Captain Jacinto." Shoshana smiled at the look of astonishment on his face.

The last two times Jaco had visited Charleston, Shoshana had been at Yael Bildesheim Delgado's farm north of town, where the Jacintos kept a dozen horses. The last time he had seen his sister, she had been gangly. Now she had grown not only grown taller, she had filled out.

Shoshana laughed as she looked down at her older brother. Emphasizing her height was a way of getting back at him for all the teasing she'd endured when they were younger. "Hi, Shorty, why don't you come in?"

Once inside, they hugged tightly. "*Mamá* is in the kitchen making breakfast. Go surprise her. I'll bring in your belongings."

Perla Jacinto was a petite woman whose jet-black hair was streaked with gray. Jaco snuck up behind and tapped her on the shoulder. She jumped in surprise and almost lost her grip on a cast iron skillet that held several eggs.

She hugged her second oldest son fiercely, then held him out to arms' length so she could look at him. "I should have known that was you! *Papá* wrote, saying you might arrive in December."

"I am glad to be home. I planned to spend only a week in Philadelphia with *Papá* but had to stay two weeks because *Alacrity* was booked full."

"How long can you stay in Charleston?"

"I have to be back in Maine by the first of the year, so I booked a passage on the packet Monday, December 28th."

With his older brother Isaac married and living in a house down the street, the only others living at home were Shoshana and the youngest Jacinto. "Where is Saul?"

Saul was five years younger than Jaco. At age eight, Saul had come down with a disease that left his left arm useless and weakened his left side. "Upstairs, probably sleeping. He was up late reading last night."

His mother turned her attention to the cast iron skillet and the stove, which was also made of cast iron. "Sit, sit. You can have these eggs, along with the cornbread in the oven. Shoshana, you may have the next plate." She cracked two fresh eggs into the pan.

While Jaco ate, his mother asked questions about *Scorpion* and his life at sea. Then she asked, "Does Reyna know you are here?"

"I sent her a letter as soon as we docked in Kittery."

"Good."

Jaco looked at his sister and then his mother. "So, what is the latest gossip?"

Shoshana giggled. "We introduced your friend Greg Struthers to Phoebe McManus, and sparks flew. Every day since, she has been bringing him lunch at the bank."

"Good for Greg! I mean, both of them. She is *perfecto* for him."

Perla's face turned grim. "Bayard Templeton went to New York and joined Tarleton's Green Dragoons."

"The lawyer Bayard Templeton?"

Shoshana nodded. "The one and the same. He left for New York, then he turned up and started making inquiries among the Loyalists in town as to how big a regiment they thought they could raise in South Carolina."

"Does Father know?"

Perla wiped the iron skillet with a cloth. "He does. So does General Moultrie. Both men expect the British may be able to find two or three hundred Loyalists to join them. I fear the war is coming to Charleston."

Shoshana finished her wedge of cornbread, slathered with butter that was partially melted into the crumb. "This morning, Reyna and Dr. MacKenzie are going to the hospital being built at Fort Sullivan. Eric is at his father's shipyard, supervising the building of a ship named *Stockholm*."

"Why that name? All their ships have been named after women."

Shoshana explained the Laredo's Swedish subsidiary that effectively made their ships "neutral" and therefore not subject to seizure by the Royal Navy. "They bought a cargo ship that the owners couldn't afford to complete, and Eric hopes to sail to Europe in March. They already have a full load of cotton waiting in our warehouse."

"So Eric will still sail, but as a merchant, not a naval officer. And Shoshana, what about you? Any prospects?"

His sister shook her head solemnly. "I am not interested in anything other than work and studying law until I pass the bar exam."

Gosport, first week of December 1778

The iron rims of the large wheels of a carriage rattled noisily on the cobblestones outside, alerting Darren that York had arrived for their drive to the property. Despite the pre-dawn darkness and the falling rain, the solicitor greeted Darren warmly.

York was in his forties, a bit paunchy, and of middling height. He had a round face and his graying hair was tied loosely in a ponytail that ended just below his neck.

Cold rain splattered on Darren's dark blue cloak as he handed his saddle bags to the coachman. Unlike the quarterdeck of a ship, the carriage would keep the two passengers dry for the 80-mile trip to Langton Herring. Darren then watched the coachman hitch one of the horses owned by his family to the back of the carriage. The saddle and tack gear went into the covered boot.

Once they were underway, York showed him a fully equipped writing desk that could be assembled in place. Darren thought writing legibly would be very difficult as the carriage bucked and bounced on the uneven road; at the same time, he was impressed by the lawyer's determination to put travel time to good use. The other item in the cabin was a picnic basket stocked with smoked meats, cheeses, bread, and several bottles of good wine. *At least we won't starve!*

At first, their conversation was stilted and awkward. York inquired about Darren's experiences and Darren, who'd never retained a lawyer before, asked how York supported his clients. The more Darren heard, the more comfortable he became. After a natural pause in the conversation, Darren asked the question that had haunted him ever since he'd received York's first letter. "How long were you Horrocks' solicitor, Mr. York?"

York looked at the young naval officer. "Are you asking me how long Captain Horrocks had been my client before he was killed? Or how did he become my client?"

"Both."

"Well then, the tale goes back many years, to the last war. As a new lieutenant, Horrocks was not much older than you when he received his first large draft of prize money, almost a thousand pounds. He went home to see his family after two years at sea, intending to share his new wealth with his parents. But when he got to Brighton, he found that his parents had died, and his sister had sold the house and the store and moved away. Horrocks spent the rest of his leave locating her. She not only refused to make him welcome, she refused to give him a farthing from the sale of their parents' estate. So there he was: homeless and disowned."

York looked at Smythe. "Horrocks returned to his ship and talked to one of his fellow lieutenants, a chap you know now as Rear Admiral Sir Peter Parker. Parker sent him to Scoons. Horrocks wanted a share of what he regarded as his rightful inheritance. I made a deal with Horrocks. Scoons would take on the case on the condition that he became a client and allowed the law firm to invest his prize money conservatively on his behalf. This was in 1758, when the law firm was still owned by the Hooper family, who founded it in 1659. The current owner, Charles Scoons, acquired the law firm in 1759. Over the years, Captain Horrocks earned about seven thousand five hundred pounds in prize money, which we increased in value to fourteen thousand, so you can see we managed his money well. The receipts for the deposits are in my files in Tunbridge Wells."

"What happened with the lawsuit?"

"His sister had sold nearly everything of value, both monetary and sentimental. She had kept a painting of their parents and one of her and Horrocks as young children. The rest was gone—sold for whatever she could get. Lieutenant Horrocks settled for £100 and the fees for one of Scoons' barristers. And after that, he never wanted to see or speak to his sister again."

Darren recollected that Captain Horrocks had been reticent on the subject of family; he hoped his own family never became so divided over inheritances. He let the implications of what York said run through his mind before he spoke. "I would like to invest some of the money, but not take much risk. Can you make some suggestions?"

"I can. Scoons has a staff who evaluate potential investments we recommend to our clients. I come to Portsmouth once a month for several days. On my next trip, we can meet and discuss my firm's recommendations."

"Thank you." Darren looked out the window. The rain had stopped. With luck, he would see the house before nightfall, but the December days were short.

Sunset was still an hour away when Darren asked the coachman to stop in the village of Langton Herring, less than a mile from his property. He jumped out and saddled the horse. When York asked what he was doing, Darren responded, "I will see more from the back of a horse, and it will convey a better message to whomever we meet."

Darren looked around. They had stopped beside the village blacksmith's work yard. Across the street lived a cooper, as Darren could tell by the parts of barrels stacked neatly. The largest building was a stone church that looked to have been built several hundred years ago. He counted 11 one-story houses, all made of stone with a mix of thatch and wood shingle roofing. The lone two-story building bore a painted sign, faded by the weather, depicting a green and spreading tree. York said this was the Oak Tree Inn.

The wind shifted slightly, replacing the smell of the English Channel with the odor of cow manure being spread in the nearby fields. Several villagers came to their doorways or paused in their work to see who had arrived.

At the entrance to the road of the estate, Darren pulled his horse to a stop. The largest house he'd ever seen stood on slight rise and faced the English Channel. It seemed to fairly glow in the fading light of the westering sun. He nudged the horse forward to stay ahead of the carriage and rode towards the entrance.

A man came out of the building and walked towards them, tipping his hat as he came up to Darren. "You must be young Captain Smythe, then. I be Ned Jernigan, the man who farms your land and caretaker of the house."

Darren bent over and clasped Jernigan's offered hand. "I am happy to meet you." The skin on Jernigan's hand was rough like the bark of a tree and his grip was strong. Darren felt as if his hand disappeared in Jernigan's.

Jernigan nodded to the solicitor, who had disembarked from the carriage. "Mr. York, good to see you again. I have the books ready for you to inspect. We had a good summer and fall."

Darren wanted to learn more. "Mr. Jernigan, what did you grow?"

"Wheat, barley, oats and peas this year. We rotate what we grow on each field among our four crops so the land has a chance to recover. If you wish, tomorrow I will show you."

In Gosport's lending library, Darren had read a treatise on how a four-crop rotation helped improve the yields. He was pleasantly surprised that Jernigan practiced the technique.

"I'll give you a tour of the house. There is not much inside; Captain Horrocks never finished buying the furniture he wanted. Many of the rooms are just four stone walls."

Self-consciously, Darren pushed back the lock of his hair that always seemed to fall down to his eyebrows. "As long as there are beds for York, his driver and me, we'll be fine."

"Aye, there are. My wife and I will bring supper tonight and breakfast in the morning."

"Thank you."

In the foyer, York remarked, "The marble flooring is from Italy. The building was constructed from stones brought down from Scotland. The walnut paneling in the rooms that are finished comes from our colonies in North America, and the light birch is from Russia."

Jernigan was right, there wasn't much furniture in the house. A 12-foot-long table with eight chairs looked lost in the dining room. The parlor had a single large couch and two wooden chairs. The room York said was the library had two large brown leather chairs and a small table in front of the fireplace. Against one wall, a painting in need a frame sat on the floor.

Darren studied the painting of a naval battle between Royal Navy and French ships. York walked up beside Darren. "That's Richard Paton's painting of the Battle of Quiberon Bay. Horrocks was there, you know. When he heard about the painting, he authorized me to buy it."

Horrocks had mentioned being fourth lieutenant on *H.M.S. Resolution*, a 74-gun third rate ship of the line that captured *Formidable* early in the battle. When Darren was at the Royal Naval Academy, the course on the service's history had covered Admirals Hawke's and Duckworth's decisions and tactics in detail. The painting brought back memories of Horrocks and his calming presence on the quarterdeck. Smythe tried to emulate the man, often imagining what Horrocks might do in any difficult situation. Darren said, "That should be properly framed and hung in a place of honor in this house."

The tour continued as Darren followed York up the broad stairway that turned 90 degrees on the second floor and another 90 before it ended on the third floor. A wide, varnished banister on the inside of the curve was a convenient place to rest one's hand going up or down. On the upper two floors, the layout consisted of three bedrooms, each with a large sitting room and a smaller room for clothes. The sitting rooms all faced the English Channel. *What I am going to do with six bedrooms, each of them ten times the size of my captain's cabin on* Liber? *It would cost a bloody fortune to finish and fully furnish this house, to say nothing of paying the servants to staff it.*

Langton Herring felt cold and impersonal, and Darren wondered, as he trailed York and Jernigan, if that impression would change over time.

Discussion over supper with the Jernigans focused on what the land grew, how Jernigan sold the crops, and what taxes he paid on the sales. Then the Jernigans retired for the night, and Darren held up a half-finished bottle of madeira and suggested to Henry York that they have a nightcap in the parlor.

Once they were settled, he asked, "Do you know why Captain Horrocks bought this place?" Darren couldn't imagine why such a solitary figure would choose such a huge estate. On the other hand, the view of the channel was splendid.

"He said he wanted someplace peaceful, where he could sit and watch the channel yet be far from the Royal Navy."

"But why this house?"

"The owner was in desperate financial straits and needed cash right away. Captain Horrocks offered a thousand pounds. When he took possession, the owners had sold much of the furniture to pay their debts. The farm was a mess; for two years the prior owner hadn't had the money for seed or to pay someone to farm it. Jernigan, who was living in Bournemouth at the time, approached Captain Horrocks with a proposal. He would farm the land and give Captain Horrocks 20% of the profits, less the cost of seed. However, as an incentive to relocate, he also wanted to purchase ten of the fifty acres on which to build a house and farm of his own."

"Where's his land?"

"The strip along the northern boundary. Horrocks negotiated a ten year note with Jernigan for £75 per year. If Jernigan fails to make his payment, Horrocks had, and now you have, the option of taking the land back."

Darren's brow furrowed. "Hold on, sir. You just told me that Horrocks had paid £1,000 for the house and land and will collect £750 from Jernigan for his ten acres. So, in the end, the house cost Captain Horrocks £250, and he's been earning money from the farm every year."

"Yes. Your math is correct. Captain Horrocks was a shrewd businessman."

"How much does my forty acres produce?"

"A good income. Last year, your twenty percent was £174. The amount has increased every year under Mr. Jernigan."

"Where's does the money go?"

"You have £1,900 in a separate account at Lloyd's Bank where Jernigan's payment for the mortgage and crop sales are deposited. When Captain Horrocks was alive, he allowed Jernigan to use the funds as collateral for seed loans, if they were needed. My firm's fee is £50 pounds per year for managing the accounting and a quarterly visit. That fee comes out of this account, which Horrocks set aside to see if the farm could be a successful venture and turn a profit."

"And if I sold the house and the land, I could take every shilling."

"Aye, you could."

"I see."

As long as there was no cost for a household staff, Horrocks' estate made money without Darren having to attend to it. But he struggled with the idea of living in such a cold house, and the prospect of the cost to furnish it and pay for servants to maintain it make him shudder. Yet, Horrocks had seen potential in Langton Herring. Given time, would he as well?

* * *

The next day, Smythe listened as York went over the books with Ned Jernigan. Satisfied, York said that he would leave for Tunbridge Wells after lunch and stay at an inn along the way.

York's departure gave Smythe time to tour the farm with Jernigan and take his own measure of the man. At the edge of a field of barley, Smythe asked, "Ned, what do you need to increase the yield of the farm?"

The answer came without hesitation. "Buy more land. If you bought another fifty acres, I could hire a family or two to work the land and pay them a living wage."

"Do you know of any land nearby that may be for sale?"

"Aye, I do. There's land on both sides of Horrocks' House that the owners want to sell because they are losing money.

What the bastard fools—sorry, sir—what the landowners don't understand is that as long as a tenant farmer has enough to feed his family and pay his share of the taxes, he doesn't care about yields or profits. The landowners need to provide some incentive for the farmer to increase the farm's yield, something to offset the extra work the farmer will have to put into the land. That, sir, is the genius behind my arrangement with Captain Horrocks and now you. The more the farm produces, the more we both make."

Darren took a deep breath. *Jernigan's hostility to the landed gentry who live off the backs of their tenant farmers just surfaced.*

"Do you know how many acres are available?"

"If you want the land and houses, over one hundred and ten acres are available."

"Do you know what they want for the land, not the houses?"

"They may not sell the land without the houses, sir."

"I think if we took most of the land off their hands and left them with a summer cottage, so to speak, they might accept an offer."

Ned Jernigan squeezed his jaw with his beefy right hand. "Methinks they'll ask twenty pounds per acre, but if you ask them what their yield per acre is by crop, you'll find the amount is about half ours. So I would offer them ten per and settle for any number under fifteen."

"If you had the land, do you think you could bring the production up to what you are producing?"

"Aye, I could, but it will need a year, maybe two. And, to work the land, I would need one or two more families. The land is the same. If they own ten acres and a house and we share eighty percent of the profits of what we farm, they'll work their arses off, just like I do, and be better for their effort."

It is much the same way on a frigate, Darren reflected. *The prospect of prize money does more to motivate men than the threat of punishments, appeals to honor, or talk of glory.* "Do the landowners live on the farms?"

"No, one lives in Portsmouth and the other in London. The people from London come down in the summer and the one from Portsmouth comes about once a month, stays for a few days and then goes back."

"Can you get me their names and addresses? I can have Mr. York contact them."

"Aye, I can." Ned chewed his lip. "Sir, one more thing."

Darren cocked his head and waited.

"Sir, my son Bartholomew wants to become an officer in the Royal Navy. Captain Horrocks said he could procure him an appointment as a midshipman when he turned thirteen. He is now almost fourteen. I have a letter from Captain Horrocks making that commitment."

"Where is your son now? I would like to speak with him. And may I read the letter?"

"Let us go back to the house. He was repairing a plow earlier this morning."

Charleston, second week of December 1778

Learning that Jaco was in Charleston, General Moultrie invited him to visit the forts that guarded the entrance to Charleston's harbor and offer suggestions. After taking a tour, Jaco made two recommendations. The first was to build an oven for every two guns to heat cannon balls to create "hot shot." The fort only had one oven, and Jaco was concerned that the balls would cool before they were fired. The second, mount the cannon on platforms that could swivel. This way they could track a ship over a longer distance and fire more times.

Events such as the trip to Fort Sullivan kept Jaco busy while Reyna worked at what she called her "medical doctor apprenticeship." Every evening around five, he met Reyna and either escorted her to his house or stayed with the Laredos for dinner. Around ten in the evening, they would part company.

Some afternoons, weather permitting, Jaco took Saul out sailing after he returned from school. The 16-foot sailboat had been in the family since Jaco was four, and he knew every inch from bow to stern. Sailing gave the brothers time to talk as they enjoyed being on the water. Saul's questions about how Jaco captained *Scorpion* and battles he fought came one right after another.

In the privacy of the boat, Saul asked for advice as to what career he should pursue. Jaco knew his younger brother spent his spare time devouring the writings of Daniel Dafoe, Jonathan Swift, Shakespeare, Chaucer, and Miquel Cervantes in Spanish. He also knew Saul felt awkward, having only one functioning arm and a pronounced limp. He suggested that Saul would make an excellent professor of literature, so he could share his love of books.

One afternoon while they were sitting shoulder to shoulder on a long tack down the Cooper River, Saul placed his paralyzed hand in his lap. "Jaco, do you think a school like Kings College in New York or Yale or the College of New Jersey would accept me after the war?"

"Why wouldn't they?"

"Because...." He looked down at his limp hand.

"Look, you're very smart, you're well read and well-qualified. Your physical limitations shouldn't have anything to do with your ability to learn."

"But they may require I come for an interview."

Jaco swallowed hard. "Saul, if you go for an interview, you will impress them. If they do not accept you, not having you as a student is their loss. Listen, my First Lieutenant Jack Shelton was attending Yale when the war broke out. I can ask if he will help you."

Saul spoke in a low voice. "I don't want to be accepted out of pity or nepotism. I would always wonder if I were there on my merits or another man's word."

Jaco put his arm around his younger brother's shoulder and pulled him close. "Saul, everyone needs help in some way. Father helped me get a commission when he deemed I was ready, and then it was up to me to demonstrate I was worthy. Shoshana is studying law because Raphael Soriano opened his door to her. Reyna is studying medicine because Dr. MacKenzie believes she will someday be Dr. Reyna Laredo."

Tears flowed down Saul's cheeks. "I just don't want them to help because they feel sorry for me."

"Little brother, we are not feeling sorry for you. We are proud of you because of what you do well and what you wish to do with your knowledge."

After dinner that evening, Reyna led Jaco by the hand out to the swing in the back yard of the Laredo house, the place where he had proposed marriage. The air was cool, and Reyna took both of his hands in hers.

"Jaco, my love, I am sorry I have not been able to spend more time with you. I wish to, but there are many sick people in Charleston. And mother, as you know, is very strict. She won't allow us to be together unless properly chaperoned."

Jaco nodded. *I didn't realize my moping around waiting for you was that obvious.* "I know the rules. Oh, Reyna, I feel badly, leaving you for months at a time."

"Jaco, we both see the signs. War will come to Charleston and we must both do our part. There will be wounded to help and fighting to be done. We both understand this, my love. We must survive so we can enjoy our life together."

Portsmouth, third week of December 1778

The clippety-clop of horses' hooves on cobblestones came to an abrupt end when Darren reigned in his horse and dismounted. Next to him, on a second horse, Bartholomew Jernigan hesitated, prompting Darren to say, "We're leaving the horses here. My parents own the stable. Get down so we can take the saddles off, then we'll walk to their house."

Darren had hoped to secure young Bart Jernigan an appointment as a midshipman on *Liber,* for with Tewksbury and Enfield gone, Rathburn needed two midshipmen. The sloop, however, had already sailed for North America, so he'd asked that Jernigan be assigned to *Gladius.* He was confident that Bosun Louttit would be an excellent but demanding instructor.

Darren's mother gave Bart Jernigan the once over before showing him to one of the empty bedrooms where he would stay until Darren found acceptable quarters for the young man. Darren could tell Bart had passed muster with his mother because the young lad was invited into the kitchen for something to eat and drink. As she prepared a plate of bread and cheese she said, "Darren, there are several letters for you on the table in the parlor."

"Splendid!" He sensed his responsibility for Bart had been transferred to his mother and he had been dismissed, so to speak.

Darren spotted the letters, neatly stepped on the varnished oak table that had been in the family's possession since the early 1700s. One was from Henry York, one had the Admiralty crest, and the third bore the Royal Navy emblem. He broke the wax seal off the Royal Navy note, opened it, and read.

Captain Smythe,

This letter is to inform you that both Midshipman Enfield and Midshipman Tewksbury passed their lieutenant's exam. They will be receiving their formal orders to H.M.S. Gladius in due course. Of the 27 lieutenants who participated in the preparatory course, 20 took the lieutenant's exam and 14 passed. Mr. Tewksbury, despite his young age, had the highest score. Mr. Enfield finished fifth.

Respectfully,
Thaddeus Fullerton
Captain
Royal Navy

Darren grinned. *Splendid! Now I can turn young Jernigan over to my two new lieutenants.*

The letter from the admiralty was next.

Captain Smythe,

This letter is to inform you that the armament of three Enterprise-class frigates, H.M.S. Gladius, H.M.S. Pilum and H.M.S. Hasta is being changed from twenty-six 9-pounders to twenty 12-pounders. Furthermore, an additional layer of oak is being added to the bulwarks on the gun decks.

The drawings and funding have been approved. The launch date of H.M.S. Gladius is still scheduled for February 9th, 1779. We expect that by the time Gladius is fitted out and finishes a week of sea trials, the modifications to both Pilum and Hasta should be completed. All three ships should be ready for sea by February 26th, 1779.

Edward Hunt
Surveyor of the Navy

So Davidson had got his way. Darren wondered if he would be given command of the three ships, or if they would assign a senior captain to act as commodore.

He poured a glass of madeira from the decanter before he sat down to peruse York's letter.

Captain Smythe,

I have contacted both families about the adjoining property and both have agreed to a price of £12 4s per acre. Moreover, the Templars have an additional adjoining 50 acres they are willing to sell at the same price per acre. This would bring the total to £1,860 even for the 150 acres.

If you agree, I will prepare and file the necessary documents and advise Mr. Jernigan who will, as you have instructed, manage the combined properties. For his efforts, he receives 5% of the profits from the new 150 acres. The current tenant farmers of the new acreage will be given the same offer as Mr. Jernigan and their mortgages will enable them to keep their land if you sell the property as long as they make the annual payment and pay off their mortgage.

Scoons' fee to prepare and file the documents and complete the transaction £21 8s. Funds for the land purchase will be taken from the farmer's account at Lloyds Bank.

Please notify me of your approval to proceed. I will be in our office in Landsea Tuesday through Thursday of the third week of every month until the first of the year. The office is a short walk from the naval base. There is a law clerk in the office full time and a courier going back and forth to our offices every day. Once the documents, assuming you agree to the transaction, are completed, I will send them to our Portsmouth for you to sign. If I am not there, one of the clerks can assist you..

I am waiting on several proposals for investments on the continent. Are you interested in investing in the same companies as Rear Admiral Davidson?

Henry York
Partner
Scoons and Partners

Darren opened the writing desk in the parlor and took out a quill, ink and paper. He scratched out a quick letter, authorizing York to buy all the land, requesting to be notified when the purchases has been closed, and stating that *Gladius'* departure date was currently set for the end of February 1779. He would sign whatever documents were needed as soon as they were ready. And yes, he would consider being involved in the same companies as Admiral Davidson.

As he sealed and addressed the letter to York, Darren wondered if he should resign from the Royal Navy and enjoy life as a wealthy, eligible young man. He had a place to live, income from the farms and plenty of money. Then he rejected the idea. Living on an estate would be tedious compared to being captain of a frigate. *I am not ready to be beached. Perhaps someday I'll tire of the life as a naval officer, but not anytime soon.*

Charleston, fourth week of December 1778

Jaco's next to last day in Charleston was ideal for a sail on the 16-foot sloop, and this time he'd invited Reyna. It was the only way Reyna and he could truly be alone. But first there had been the uncomfortable and all but one-sided conversation with Reyna's parents and elder brother. Adah Laredo had explained the terms while Reyna's father and brother had loomed silently until Jaco convincingly said, "Yes, ma'am." He'd had to promise that they would sail, anchor for a picnic lunch, and then return to Charleston. Nothing else. If Reyna became pregnant before they were married, there would be hell to pay.

Thankfully, the weather cooperated; it was a lovely day for a sail. When they pulled away from the dock, Reyna was wearing a light grey busk and a pair of sandals. Her jet-black hair billowed in the breeze, forcing her to frequently brush wayward strands off her face. The most important thing for Jaco was she was relaxed and smiling. And so was he!!!

Reyna helped with the sheets as they sailed down the Cooper River to the inlet where ships enter the harbor. Jaco tacked to keep the boat parallel to the shore of Sullivan Island, letting them sit shoulder to shoulder to help counter the boat's heel. In a little cove on the southern end of Capers Island, Jaco tossed the anchor over the side.

He held Reyna and she rested her head on his shoulder. "This is peaceful. I am glad we could do this."

Jaco rested his forehead on hers. "I look forward to being married, when we won't have to ask for permission to be together!"

"Our time will come..." Reyna let the words tail off and fell silent before she asked, "Do you really think the war will come to Charleston?"

"I do. My father said the consensus in Congress is that the British have given up trying to split the Northern colonies away. They are now going to try to break the country in two by taking Georgia and the Carolinas. That makes Savannah and our Charleston targets."

"Do you have any sense of when?"

"My father thinks this spring. The British generals in New York will use the Royal Navy to bring troops south. We don't have the ships to stop them, so I suspect that *Scorpion* will be assigned to harass the British."

Reyna looked into Jaco's eyes, as if she was searching for an answer. "I fear for my brothers, and for you. I do not want the war to take them from me. The war is making all of you old men before your time. I cannot explain how much Amos has changed, and as for Eric... well, perhaps you know even more about that than I."

Jaco pulled Reyna close. "I do know. But I also know that Amos, Eric, and myself, and many others, believe that independence is worth the price we pay. You know as well as I do that our ancestors were not allowed to own land in England or Spain. If Britain continues to treat the colonies as resources to be plundered, we will continue to lose the rights we have so far enjoyed. So if we are injured, or killed while defending our liberties, we accept our fate."

"Eric's experience in the prison camp changed him. He often withdraws into himself. And you, my love, are no longer the carefree one who was always pulling pranks and who loved to sail as a merchant captain apprentice. Both of you have become very, very serious. Promise me that after the war is over, you will not be so dour."

"This war has changed us all in ways I don't think we will ever fully understand. I cannot promise I will be as carefree as I was, but I think I can promise that, when I am spending more time on boats with you—" he dared to press his lips to the top of her head; that wasn't the sort of kiss that had been forbidden—"instead of on ships of war, I will be less serious than I am now."

Reyna kissed her forefinger and touched Jaco's lips. "I believe that too. And I wish to see you happy again. I want to have your babies and grow old with you."

Amelia Island, Florida, fourth week in December 1778

Bayard Templeton, newly promoted to major, was glad to set foot on dry land. He hated ships. Standing on the light brown sand as the first British Army officer ashore meant the sea journey was over. Now he was back in the warm south, out of the penetrating, damp cold of New York.

He was met and greeted by Colonel Martin Walsh. The Irish-born Walsh commanded both the garrison at Fort Clinch on the northern end of Amelia Island in Georgia, and the one at Fort Prince William on Columbia Island in the British Territory of Florida. Walsh gave directions on where he wanted the Green Dragoons bivouacked and then strode off, leaving Templeton on the beach to oversee the lighters as they ferried Two Troop, their horses, 200 infantrymen and their *materiel* ashore. Templeton was watching the choreographed ship to shore movements when Cornelius Vickers, a man he had not seen in two years, walked over and called out, "Templeton! It is good to see you. Merry Christmas!"

Vickers was a wealthy rice broker from Charleston and one of Templeton's former clients. Most of the rice he bought and sold went to Spain and Portugal where it was in high demand, but also England, France and the Netherlands.

"Aye, it is good to be back. Merry Christmas and Happy New Year to you. As you see, our campaign to run the rebels out of Savannah and Charleston is about to begin, which will make 1779 a much better year. With luck and hard campaigning, we will put a swift end to this ridiculous rebellion. My job," he puffed his chest out a bit more, "is to conduct a reconnaissance of the rebel defenses of Savannah and Charleston."

Vickers watched as men in green coats led horses out of the lighters. "I have some welcome news. We have over three hundred men who have volunteered. Some of them," he hesitated, then continued, "are former slaves, who have been offered their freedom in return for their service. And more are joining every day. Lord Dunmore's Proclamation of 1775 encouraged slaves in Virginia to leave their rebel owners. However, many of our friends who are loyal to the king are losing their slaves as well."

"Three hundred!!! That's a very good start to raising a regiment."

"Why don't you join us for dinner this evening? Agnes will be delighted to see you."

Templeton bowed his head slightly, as if he was talking to one of his "betters." Vickers was one of the pillars of Charleston society. "Thank you, you are most kind. I must see to my men first. Say about seven?"

"That will do very well." Vickers strode off, and Major Templeton smiled. The evening ahead promised to be pleasant. Vickers was famous for his well-stocked liquor cabinet.

He should be able to begin his sortie into Georgia in two days. Savannah was 125 miles to the north, three or four days by horseback. His Dragoons would travel light with only their arms and food for eight days. After those supplies were consumed, he had English pound notes and gold coins to buy food from local farms. His written orders from Lord Cornwallis authorized him to confiscate livestock and whatever else they could find to feed themselves and their horses from rebel farmers who refused to sell food and fodder to his dragoons.

Gosport, fourth week of December 1778

A cold rain pelted the canvas top of the carriage. Darren felt as though he were sitting inside a drum as he and his parents rode around the harbor from Gosport to Portsmouth. The reason for the hour-long journey was the annual day-after-Christmas reception by the Fitzmaurice family. Invitations were both coveted and very limited.

Darren had reluctantly bowed to his mother's insistence that he attend and wear his uniform. Many senior Royal Navy officers would be there and making a favorable impression, Olivia Smythe opined, would be good for his career. There would also, she pointed out, be eligible ladies in attendance. Darren reminded his mother that how his ship performed in battle was the best way to impress an admiral. Nonetheless, he had agreed to come along. If nothing else, it was a break for the routine and a chance to see what "society" was all about.

While he was not opposed to meeting a member of the opposite sex, he wasn't sure he would know what to say after the initial hello. He knew none of the niceties of idle conversation, of fashion or the gossip of Portsmouth and London society, or the goings on in the King's court. His life revolved around leading men and all the tasks required of a captain commanding a warship.

Fitzmaurice and Sons, Ltd., his father reminded him, was one of the largest construction firms south of London. The family's first major contract had come with a King's commission in the 1620s to rebuild the fortifications guarding Portsmouth Harbor. The firm had also built the graving docks in the port, as well as ones in Bristol and Liverpool. And, Lester Smythe stressed, hobnobbing with the wealthiest families in southern England and being seeing by them in a favorable light would serve Darren well once he retired from the Royal Navy.

The carriage stopped under a large portico and a footman opened the door. Darren was first out, then his father, who gallantly held out his hand to help his wife step down. Well into her fifties, Olivia was a handsome woman who still moved easily. They were Darren thought, a fine couple whom age had treated kindly.

Darren waited until his parents were announced by the Fitzmaurice's majordomo, then he heard, "Captain Darren Smythe, Royal Navy," pronounced in a deep, carrying voice. Darren strode into the room. Already his parents had disappeared into the crowd. He stood for a moment, trying not to panic and not sure what to do.

"Ah, Captain Smythe, you look well in your uniform."

Darren knew the voice instantly, glad there was someone he really knew at the reception. Smiling, he turned to see Rear Admiral of the Blue Stacey Davidson, Duke of Somerset, standing next to a strikingly beautiful woman who was almost as tall as the admiral. She too had blonde hair, blue eyes, almost as if she came out of the same mold as the duke. "Good evening, Admiral, I am delighted to see you...."

Davidson smiled and finished the unsaid sentence. "So you could have someone to talk to you."

"Aye, sir. I don't have much in the way of formal graces."

The rear admiral waved his hand. "Fear not, neither do most of those here. They just pretend they know. My suggestion, Captain Smythe, is to charge ahead under a full head of sail, and if you offend anyone, apologize and carry on. Now before I earn the ill will of the woman at my side, may I introduce my wife Belinda, Duchess of Somerset."

Darren bowed and took the offered hand to acknowledge royalty. "It is an honor."

The duchess smiled and said, "My husband has spoken well of you. He said that your habit of dressing like any sailor on deck would probably keep you alive long enough to earn the rank you deserve."

To his horror, Darren felt his face blushing. The admiral covered his confusion by saying, "Captain, you are one of the few to whom I would turn over my quarterdeck with the assurance they would do a better job than I in any situation. So, come, let us have a drink and celebrate your new command. And I want to hear your latest thoughts about Captain Jacinto. The mere mention of his name is enough to cause faint-heartedness in battle-hardened captains and apoplexy in the halls of the Admiralty."

But the Davidsons were soon whisked away by Malcom Fitzmaurice, leaving Darren standing in the middle of the floor with a glass in his hand and feeling out of sorts. His mother walked over, accompanied by a woman her own age and an attractive young woman with brown eyes and chestnut brown hair.

"Son, I see you are alone for the moment, so I thought I would introduce our hostess, Mrs. Virginia Fitzmaurice, and her daughter, Miss Clementine Fitzmaurice."

A servant materialized at their side bearing a tray with glasses of madeira and port. Darren waited until the women selected glasses before putting his empty one on the tray and taking a full one, thinking, *I am going to need fortification.*

Clementine Fitzmaurice looked as nonplussed as Darren felt at being thrust upon a stranger. He took her proffered hand and bowed slightly. "It is my pleasure to meet you, Miss Clementine."

A swirl of persons descended up Mrs. Fitzmaurice and bore her away along with Darren's mother, leaving Darren standing awkwardly with the lovely Miss Fitzmaurice.

"Please, call me Clemmie. I hate my first name."

Darren smiled, thinking, *She's a bit rebellious, like me.*

"Aye, so Clemmie it is."

"Your mother has told us about you. I'd like to hear of your adventures first-hand if I may. But only if it won't bore you to tell me."

Darren said that he had recently turned over command of *Liber* and was waiting for *Gladius* to be built. He didn't want to go into the details of what it was like to be a scared midshipman on a shot-up frigate, finding one's captain dead and the surviving senior officer not willing to take command. Or a lieutenant on the deck of a frigate with chain shot and 12-pound cannon balls whistling around. Or the sickening, sucking hydraulic sound of a man hit by a musket ball.

Another servant came by with crackers and bits of cheese and smoked meat. He waited until the young woman sampled two before he took one. Clemmie's eyes sparkled. "Captain, please, don't be so hesitant. There's enough food here to feed an army."

Darren took one more and the servant stepped away. Clemmie's expression became serious. "How well do you know the Duke of Somerset?"

Not *Rear Admiral Davidson*, but *the Duke of Somerset*. Clearly, for the Fitzmaurices it was the man's social standing that mattered, not his accomplishments; whereas, on board *Puritan* the duke had let it be known that he preferred to be addressed by his rank, not his title. He'd only resorted to his title during official visits, or on rare occasions when he was annoyed or irritated by someone he viewed as incompetent who had behaved stupidly. Clemmie's use of his title sent off alarm bells in Darren's head.

"I was his first lieutenant for almost a year."

"So you know the Duke well?"

Darren said, "I do," then fell awkwardly silent. *I am not going to tell her that he may be one of my mentors and benefactors. If I tell her that I address him as Rear Admiral Davidson, not the Duke of Somerset, will she think I am more familiar with the man than I am, or the reverse, that I hardly know him at all?*

"Would you make an introduction?"

Is she social climbing? What am I supposed to do? "I believe your father knows Rear Admiral of the Blue Davidson and his wife Belinda well enough. They would be in a better position to make introductions, than I." Feeling slightly panicked, Darren changed the subject. "Are you involved in your father's business?"

Clemmie's eyes sparkled with mirth. "If you asked my father, he would say all I do is spend his money. If you asked my mother, she would say I work hard at running off suitors who want to marry me for my inheritance. What say you, Captain?"

"Well, I'm not one of your suitors, nor am I interested in your family's money."

"That's so dashing and gallant, to say nothing of being quite different, Captain Smythe." Clemmie put a hand on Darren's sleeve. "Do you have a woman in every port?"

Darren laughed. "No, not a one. Normally, I don't stay long enough to be involved in social activities. In some of the places my ships have been, we have stayed only long enough to take on provisions. And I'm not sure there are many families who would like their daughters marrying Royal Navy captains, given that we have a high mortality rate."

"Why is that?"

"England always seems to be at war, and the Royal Navy is, in many ways, the world's constable. On the quarterdeck, we are quite visible to our enemies' marksmen."

"Ohhhh, that is very morbid, Captain Smythe. Now it is my understanding that many Royal Navy captains became very wealthy through prize money. What say you?"

"That, Clemmie, is a true statement. I know of several captains who have made tidy fortunes." He deliberately didn't say, *including myself.*

The two spoke for a few minutes until Virginia Fitzmaurice returned and put a hand on her daughter's arm. "Pardon me, Captain, but I need to introduce my daughter to someone. If you will excuse us."

Again, Darren was left standing in the middle of the room alone. A servant held out a tray as if to say, "You could use another glass of wine."

Darren took the wine, sipped it, wondering if he had just sailed through a thunderstorm. He wasn't sure if all his masts were still intact.

Chapter 12
Stabbing at the Rebel Underbelly

Boston, first week of January 1779

On the journey north, the lateen rigged mail packet schooner *Alacrity* twice had to race away from Royal Navy frigates. The first time occurred coming out of Chesapeake Bay. The second time, *Alacrity* had just exited Delaware Bay when dawn revealed a Royal Navy frigate scarcely 500 yards away with 9-pounders run out.

Awakened by the sound of gunfire, Jaco ran out of his cabin, pulling on a heavy coat. Only *Alacrity's* speed and ability to sail closer to the wind allowed the schooner to escape—with two new holes in her main sail.

Standing on deck watching the Royal Navy frigate attempt to catch *Alacrity*, Jaco worried and fretted. If the British captured *Alacrity* they would confiscate the British pounds meant to pay for *Scorpion*'s repairs, recruiting sign-on bonuses, and supplies of foreign currency, while his uniforms and sailing orders would mark him as a rebel officer. In the tense moments before *Alacrity* was out of range, he wondered how Major van Doorn would treat him if he wound up in the coal mines in North Sydney, Nova Scotia. And, who, if anyone, would come to rescue him?

Alacrity arrived in Boston on Wednesday, January 7th, 1779. A smiling Jack Shelton was waiting on the pier wrapped in a cloak, seemingly impervious to the biting wind that chilled Jaco to the bone. After hugging his friend and First Lieutenant, Jaco said, "Happy New Year, Jack. But what are you doing here? I thought you were going to get your own command."

"I was supposed to take command of the 28-gun *Trumbull,* but the captain ran the frigate aground in Long Island Sound. The ship is still there, kept afloat by empty barrels. Lord only knows when they will get the frigate freed or how long the repairs will take. Then I was offered the *Andrea Doria*—just before the crew burned the ship off Red Bank, New Jersey to keep her from being captured. We seem to be losing ships as fast as they are built. I turned down *Cutlass* because that would mean carrying dispatches back and forth to France. I've done that, and it is tedious, unless one is forced to fight a Royal Navy sloop-of-war. And while there are many merchant captains who know how to sail fast, not so many know how to command a ship of war, or serve on one. So here I am!"

"Well, Jack, fate seems to be taking a hand. In any case, I am glad to have you back."

"Thank you. But I'm not the only one. We have 146 of *Scorpion's* crew that were paid off. Jeffords and Preston said we'll have about 160 men back by the end of the month, which means we'll only have to recruit 50 or so to sail with a full crew. They recommend recruiting in Boston if Congress will pay their expenses."

Jaco put the box with his sextant into the bed of the wagon. "If Congress won't, I will."

"I thought you would, and told them so."

"Are the officers are back as well?"

"Everyone except Wilson. He passed his lieutenant's exam and is on *Deane,* a French built 24-gun frigate. She's leaving in a few days."

Jaco grinned. "*Perfecto!* Shall we get the rest of my boxes on the wagon and get going?"

"Did you bring the bells back?"

"No. I didn't. We're going to collect a new set."

"Just as well. Your cabin was getting crowded."

Gosport, first week of January 1779

This week, the Sunday dinner was held at Darren's older sister's house. Over plates of roast chicken stuffed with onions, plums, and the last of the Spanish almonds, his sister Emily chided him about his reluctance to be introduced to eligible women. His firm "Not now" and a vigorous shake of his head put an end to that topic of discussion.

On the way home in the carriage, however, his mother hoisted that sail. "Tell, my Darren, what happened between Miss Fitzmaurice and you? Her mother and I think you would make a fine couple."

"Nothing happened, Mother."

"What do you mean by nothing."

"Just that, nothing. She and I are from different worlds."

His mother looked baffled. "You are from very similar backgrounds," she said.

"Mother, I think Cle—errrr, Miss Fitzmaurice is more interested in my relationship with Rear Admiral Davidson than anything else about me. By her own admission she does nothing but spend her father's money." He didn't want to say, *What kind of life is that? Why would I marry a woman who might spend me into destitution?*

"The duke is very well-connected and in good favor with the king. Knowing him could prove useful to you some day in the future."

Darren took a good breath and measured his words carefully, not because he was angry, but because he wanted to be precise. "Mother, my relationship with Rear Admiral Davidson is not a piece of material that can be used for barter. He respects me for my ability as a naval officer and has, I suspect, used his influence to help my career. My intent is to keep giving him reasons to help me advance. I see the Rear Admiral Davidson as a mentor and would never, except in dire circumstances, ask for a personal favor."

Olivia Smythe leaned across the coach and gently put her hand on her son's knee. "Darren, you are so naïve. Relationships such as the one you have with the Duke of Somerset are extremely valuable. He knows, and you should know, that someday you will need a favor from him that will benefit you. When the time comes, do not be hesitant; just pick your time wisely."

Darren wanted to end the conversation. He'd already asked for a favor by asking Davidson's advice about Scoons and investments. "Aye, mother, I will keep that in mind."

Northwest of Charleston, second week of January 1779

After several days of easy riding, the 92 riders of A and B Squadrons, Two Troop of the Green Dragoons, were 30 miles northwest of Charleston. According to Templeton's map, Two Troop was paralleling a road that connected Charleston and Savannah. The dense woods forced the men to ride single file. At a clearing large enough for the entire command to gather, Templeton passed the word that they were going to take a break. He now had to decide how much closer to Charleston his unit should push before returning to Amelia Island. Templeton was sure the rebels would not leave Savannah and Charleston undefended. He had expected to run across patrols before getting this far, but they had met nothing in the way of resistance. So where were the rebels?

The voice of one of his sergeants interrupted his musing. "Sir, the scouts spotted a group of farmhouses a half a mile ahead." Implied in the sergeant's statement was a suggestion that it was time purchase food. While they still had rations, fresh fare would make a welcome change.

"Any sign of the rebels?"

"No, sir, but the scouts stayed on the edge of the fields."

"Sergeant, let's go take a look." Templeton folded his map carefully before sliding it into the map case tied to his saddle. He put a foot into the stirrup. "Pass the word that we are to act as gentlemen."

The sergeant nodded and Templeton heard the words being murmured down the line before he mounted his own horse. Entering the cleared field, skirmishers fanned out 50 yards on either side of the column.

Ahead, Templeton saw three small homes and two large barns. In one pen between the barns were goats, nibbling at anything in reach. In a larger pen, pigs snorted in alarm at the approach of strangers. Templeton stopped in front of the home in the center, and his men formed an arc behind him. So far, no one had drawn a weapon.

Two women along with several young children emerged from the barns and the homes. A young boy was holding a rope tied to a cow who followed meekly behind. Tendrils of smoke rose from a small building off to the side and the scent of meat being smoked filled the air.

Templeton addressed the woman at the fore. "Good afternoon, I am Major Bayard Templeton of His Majesty's Green Dragoons. Who might you be?"

"Leah Bildesheim Fonseca. And I know who you are, Mr. Templeton. You are a lawyer from Charleston showing his true colors." Her tone was not threatening, nor was her statement an insult. She was merely stating facts.

I've stumbled on one of the outlying farms of the Bildesheim holdings. I represented the Royal Governor when they acquired this land. Both women standing in front of him were tall, wafer slim, and had a proud, erect bearing. They bore a resemblance to Miriam Bildesheim; he concluded they were two of her daughters.

"Where are your menfolk?" he said peremptorily.

"Out plowing our fields to get ready for spring planting. They will be back before dark."

"We'd like to purchase food—hams or bacon if you have some, and any fresh or dried vegetables."

"Nothing here is for sale. We barely have enough for our own needs."

"I'll pay you in English pounds."

"You heard my wife. Nothing on this farm is for sale."

Templeton turned around at the sound of the male voice to see a burly looking man approaching. He was leading a plow horse, and was followed by a boy leading another horse. "And who might you two be?" Templeton demanded.

"Emory Fonseca. My son, Michael."

Templeton gestured at the men behind him. "I can seize your land in the name of the king if you refuse to support his army."

"You can threaten to do that, but to be legal, you need an order signed by King George the Third or the Royal

Governor, neither of which I think you have. As a lawyer, Mr. Templeton, you should know that."

"I can take you prisoners for supporting the rebel traitors."

"Again, you can do that, but since you have no evidence, the charges won't stand up in court. So, I suggest, Major Templeton, you move on. We have nothing here to sell."

"My men need provisions. I can either pay for what we require or take the food by force."

"Suit yourself, Captain, but if you take what you want by force, our neighbors will hear of it, and the next time you come you will do so at your peril."

"Are you threatening me, Mr. Fonseca?"

"No, Captain, just telling you what will happen."

Templeton drew one of his pistols and turned to his sergeant. "Search the barn and the house for food we can use. And take their horses and this cow."

Michael held fast to the rope and yelled, "No!

A Green Dragoon dismounted and tried to take the rope, but the 10-year-old boy, tall and strong for his age and determined, pushed the Dragoon away. The cavalry man looked to his commander for orders. Templeton fired his pistol. The ball stove in the boy's chest. Michael gasped and fell, bleeding and very dead.

Leah Fonseca rushed to her son's side, dropped to her knees and cradled his head. Then she looked up, rage in her eyes. "You just killed my ten-year-old boy, Templeton. I swear you will not live out this war."

"You Fonsecas are full of predictions." He addressed his sergeant. "Burn their house. Take the cow and any food in the smoke house and that you can find elsewhere." Turning back to face Leah and Emory Fonseca, he added, "Kill anyone who resists."

Portsmouth, second week of February 1779

The copper sheathing, which had been slow to arrive, was now in place on *Gladius'* bottom, gleaming in the winter sun. As Darren climbed the scaffolding around the ship in dry dock, he could see *H.M.S. Plum* and *H.M.S. Hasta* at the fitting out piers where they were being modified to replace their twenty-six 9-pounders with twenty 12-pounders. The work to strengthen their bulwarks and deck was almost complete.

Both their captains, *Pilum's* Dyer Taylor and *Hasta's* Hamilton Meegan, had gone home on leave. Their crews were on barracks ships in Portsmouth until the ships were ready, to keep them from disappearing into the countryside. Both captains were due back next week, and then Darren would begin discussions on how they could capture or sink *Scorpion*.

Smythe walked aft on *Gladius'* main deck. He saw the door to his cabin was open. Entering his cabin, he found a man standing there with his palms on the table, looking at the ship's plans. He was a tall, gangly stranger wearing a blue coat, his long, jet-black hair neatly braided.

"Good afternoon, sir. May I help you?" Darren said.

The stranger turned around and took in the sight of Darren and his epaulets. "Sir, I am Nathaniel Watson, your new First Lieutenant. I'm sorry I was not here sooner, but both my parents fell ill and passed away. I had to take care of their affairs."

Darren wondered if the man's parents had died while he was at sea, or if he had been with then during their last days. He hoped the latter. "Mr. Watson, I am sorry to hear about your parents. Will you need to be going home again before we sail?"

"No, sir. They were farmers and my brother is taking over the farm."

Darren held out his hand. "Then welcome to *H.M.S. Gladius*. What ship were you on before?"

"My last ship was *H.M.S. Juno*, 32 guns. We scuttled and burned her in Narragansett Bay to keep her from being captured by the rebels."

"Well, we're going right back to America to put a rebel frigate called *Scorpion* out of business."

"Yes, sir. I've heard of *Scorpion*. I came back aboard *H.M.S. Dilettante,* which is now being refitted in Bristol. They're taking the carronades off the lower gun deck and replacing them with 24-pounders."

"Then you know we have a formidable task. *Gladius*' other officers are joining me for dinner at my parents' home in Gosport tonight. Would you care to join us?"

Watson clearly regarded the invitation as one he shouldn't turn down. "I would be honored to attend, sir."

"Mr. Watson, you should know that *Gladius* is going to be the flagship of a squadron of three frigates.

"Who is going to be the commodore?"

"I am."

Darren noted the look of surprise on Watson face, then went on to the next item on his mind. "Do you know any young men wanting to become officers?"

"No, sir. Why?"

"We need a midshipman. I plan to raid the Royal Naval Academy tomorrow, even though the class doesn't graduate until June. Please come along so you can help make the selection."

"Aye, that I will."

"Is this your first new construction?"

"Aye, 'tis."

"Then let's take a tour before the ship gets all cluttered up with casks of food and beer, hammocks, barrels of powder, sea chests and cannon." Darren led the way out of the cabin, glad to have a chance to show his new lieutenant their new ship. Based on his experience with *Jodpur's* rotten timbers and the Hillhouse Yards attempts to cut corners, he now believed that knowing the details of how a ship was constructed was essential knowledge for any naval officer.

Kittery, second week of February 1779

Walking around *Scorpion* and seeing many familiar faces, Jaco sensed the frigate was ready to plow through the waves of the Atlantic. The last 10 barrels of gunpowder would arrive today, and they would slip out to sea tomorrow.

The lull gave him time to read the most recent letter from Reyna. After reading it twice, Jaco walked around his cabin to dissipate his anger and sense of helplessness at being 1,000 miles away.

Jaco poured two fingers of a whiskey distilled on George Washington's plantation into a short glass. The bottle had been given to him by James Madison to celebrate prizes and victories. The fiery liquid burned all the way down to his stomach, and the heat matched the angry fire in his brain.

His long, jet-black hair was disheveled from an ascent to the crow's nest earlier in the day to test the range of his spyglass. Now he brushed his hair with a vengeance, trying to assuage his anger, before he tied his hair in a ponytail using a piece of rawhide. Still seething, he sat down at his desk to compose a reply.

My dearest Reyna,

The news about the loss of Savannah broke my heart. I suspect that Charleston is Lord Cornwallis' next target.

Please offer my condolences to Leah Fonseca on the loss of her son Adam. Bayard Templeton is beneath contempt. Shooting a defenseless boy who wanted to protect a cow he'd raised since birth is something only a coward would do. I am at a loss for words to express my sorrow and how to console you.

The month or so I spent in Charleston will have to suffice to carry me through the difficult times ahead. I miss you terribly. Every day, I remember the scent of your hair when it blew in my face aboard the sailboat.

Alas, I have a job to do, and that is to make it painful for the Royal Navy to sail its ships off our shores.

All my love,
Jaco

When *Scorpion* slipped away from the pier, the weather was, according to Jack Shelton, "brisk". Jaco just thought of it as unpleasantly cold. The temperature was well below zero, and the strong wind from the nor' west chilled everyone on board. It helped somewhat that their last breakfast in Kittery had been a warm and hearty one—eggs, bacon and oatmeal—served at two bells or 6:00 a.m. High tide was at seven a.m. and Jaco wanted to be headed out to sea as the tide began to ebb.

Once into the Atlantic, Jaco ordered a course of east so' east to let *Scorpion* run with the wind to get away from the coast and into the warmer waters of the Gulph Stream. But after hours of plowing through gray-blue water, the temperature had risen only two degrees, but the ship was well east of the tip of Cape Cod, and *Scorpion* was headed due south to warm its creaking timbers. The frigate's wake was a straight white line in the gray-black water.

Jaco ordered that only the officer of the watch, the quartermasters and the bosun's mate stay on the quarterdeck, wrapped in wool blankets. The sailors on watch could remain on the gun deck out of the wind, where it was distinctly warmer. If needed, they would be called up to handle the sails.

He'd known Jeffords since he was a brand new lieutenant on *Providence*. Quartermaster's mate Cooper had been one of the first recruits to sign on to *Scorpion*. Jaco thought the time was right for a private conversation.

"Mr. Jeffords, Mr. Cooper, may I ask a personal question?"

Jeffords answered, "Go ahead, Cap'n."

"I'm curious, what did you do with your prize money?"

Jeffords rubbed his head and smiled. "Sir, my share was a right good amount. Our family is now pretty kedge. We are all healthy, and we even have some of the prize money left after I bought my two brothers each a new boat, so the family now has a fleet. We also bought a nicer house and twenty acres of farmland near Manchester, New Hampshire. When I paid off the money lender, who charged my father an ungodly interest rate for money to buy his boat, I told him to go to hell. That Cap'n, beggin' your pardon, sir, was the best part. The man was a usurious devil. We had to pay him even when we didn't have money for food other than fish we caught. Now we've seen the last of him, and we still have a bit of money left over."

"Mr. Jeffords, I appreciate the feeling of relief. You spent the money well."

"Aye, Cap'n, but my father and my brothers want to save enough money so that their children don't have to make a living fishin'. It is a hard, dangerous life."

"And you, Mr. Cooper?"

The black man towered over him, and when he grinned his white teeth were visible in the moonlight. "Sir, I paid tuition for my two brothers to go to a private school until they are sixteen. When they finish, I hope I will have more prize money to pay for them to attend a college. The rest we're savin' for a rainy day."

"Well done. Mr. Cooper. This war will not last forever, and we need educated men and women to lead our country to a prosperous and peaceful future. That being said, while this damned war lasts, we will do our best to fill everyone's pockets with more prize money."

Cooper laughed. "Sir, I'd vote for that!"

* * *

Over the winter, the yard had installed two additional long twelves, giving *Scorpion* a main battery of 22. Jaco was concerned the additional weight would slow the ship and cause it to handle differently. Hackett had assured him that the diagonal cross members built into the ship would keep the hull from 'hogging' or sagging in the middle, but only the sea could tell Jaco how the extra weight affected *Scorpion*. During the day, with the topgallants unfurled, the wind over the frigate's starboard stern quarter moved the frigate along at a comfortable 10 knots. So far, the extra 8,000 pounds from the two guns and carriages had not affected the way *Scorpion* sailed.

Early in the morning of day three, 15-year-old Midshipman Morton Geiger, who'd replaced Wilson, was on his rounds to make sure nothing was amiss when he spotted a sea chest sliding back and forth on the berthing deck. Geiger addressed Colin Landry, one of the three leading topmen.

"Mr. Landry, please get that sea chest secured properly."

Landry, who was talking with Cato Cooper, said, "Aye, sir, I'll see to it."

As Landry walked toward the sea chest, a man lying in his hammock said, "Landry, you don't have to take orders from a Jew-boy."

Landry slipped a rope through the handles of the sea chest and knotted it to a ring on the bulwark to make sure the chest wouldn't move. Then he walked past the hammock and quietly said, "Grantham, if you ever say something like that again, I'll have you charged for insubordination. Geiger is a midshipman, and don't you forget it."

Brandon Grantham, a 22-year-old Bostonian with flaming red hair, had arrived in the Massachusetts Bay Colony from Ireland at the age of 10. He rolled out of his bunk and stood face to face with Colin Landry. "Them Jews are all bloody shylocks and you can't trust none of them. Our priests in Boston and back in Ireland call them Christ killers."

Landry heaved a deep breath, then spoke evenly. "Mr. Geiger is an officer on this ship, and from what I can see, he'll be a good one. What a man does is what matters, not his faith, and not the color of his hair. Where I come from, red-haired Irishmen are thought to be drunken, insolent bastards with bad tempers. But when I saw you, I didn't go around barking at the moon, spreading unpleasantness about broganeers to my fellow seamen, now did I? I suggest you keep yer opinions to yerself. If you don't, you might find yourself clapper-clawed, or worse, swimming with the sharks. On *Scorpion,* we don't put up with that kind of talk. Maybe if your priests emphasized the bit about being a good neighbor, you'd have grown up with better manners, but it is not too late to learn. So, if I or any of the mates hear you speak ill of our midshipman or our officers or our shipmates again, I'll make sure you are brought up on charges."

"Fuck off, Landry." Grantham shoved Landry in the chest, hard. "Get out of my bloody face."

Landry took a step forward, but Quartermaster's mate Cooper intervened. "Stop! I've heard enough from you, Grantham!"

"Enough of what?" The voice was the ship's new Third Lieutenant, Lewis Payne.

None of the three men spoke.

Payne stood with his hands on his hips. "Ah, the cat's got everyone's tongue, now. Well, it's too late for that. Now this can go one of two ways. As soon as I leave, you will settle the matter by fighting. So that means, when I come back, at least two of you will be charged. Or you can tell me what just happened, right now. You're the senior man, Cooper. Speak up!"

"Sir, Grantham made a very chuffy comment about Mr. Geiger. Landry responded that his words were unacceptable on *Scorpion*."

Payne pointed at the three seamen. "You, you and you, up on the gun deck by the bow chasers. Now."

Grantham put an arm in his hammock as if he was preparing to get in. "I'm supposed to be sleeping before I go on watch."

Payne replied sternly, “Sorry, Grantham, you’re going to forfeit some sleep. And the next time you want to avoid trouble, don’t start it. Up by the bow chasers, now, or I will charge you with disobeying an order.”

Grantham shuffled forward at a pace that verged on disobedience. Payne prodded him along with a firm shove in the back.

On the gun deck, Payne had the men face line up facing him. “Now, tell me exactly what happened, word for word. You first, Landry.” The Third Lieutenant’s poker face didn’t give away what he was thinking.

When Landry finished, Payne looked at Grantham. “Is that accurate?”

“Aye, as far as it goes. But no right-minded ship has Jew boys as officers, and I’ll be damned if I take orders from one.”

Payne looked at Cooper. “Is Landry’s version the truth?”

“Yes, sir.”

“Do you know if Mr. Geiger heard Grantham?”

They all shook their heads.

“Cooper and Landry, you are dismissed. Grantham, you come with me to the captain’s cabin and wait outside the door.”

“Sir, am I being charged?” For the first time, Grantham looked unsure of himself.

“Not yet, but you may be.”

A sharp rap on the captain’s cabin door brought an equally curt, “Enter.”

Payne and Grantham found their captain looking out the stern windows with his hands clasped behind his back. Jack Shelton was standing off to one side.

They'd already heard about the incident from Geiger, who had heard part of the exchange between Grantham and Landry and was embarrassed that he hadn't taken stronger action on the spot. Jaco did not turn around as he spoke.

"Mr. Grantham, why did you sign on to be a member of *Scorpion's* crew?" He wanted to use the word "my" but didn't.

"Because I hate the bloody British, sirrr. And to earn prize money." The more nervous Grantham felt, the stronger his accent became. "Me older brother and I arrrr supportin' thrrree younger sisters, and a bit o' prize money would go a long way to feedin' and clothin' 'em."

"Where were you born, Grantham?"

"Ireland, sirrr."

"I know that, lad. Where in Ireland?"

"Down south in Cork, sirrr."

Jaco turned around and put his hands on the back of one of the chairs. He was squeezing the back of the chair so hard his knuckles were turning white. "Were you raised a Catholic?"

"Aye."

"Aye, what?"

"Aye, sir."

"What do you think of Quartermaster Mate Cooper?"

Grantham's thick Irish accent again showed. "I doooon't knoo. He's no bad for a darkie."

Jaco's anger boiled even hotter. Cooper was one of six former slaves on the crew. Two others were gunner's mates and gun captains.

"So, before you joined *Scorpion's* crew, had you ever met a Jew before?"

"No, sir, can't say I have."

"Why don't you like Jews?"

"Because they're all shylocks wantin' to take yer money, sir. And they killed our savior Jesus Christ."

"Where'd you learn that?"

"I spent a year in what they called a hedge school because the bloody British won't allow Catholics to attend the regular schools. It was taught by a priest, but my parents couldn't afford the cost. That was one reason they packed all us onto a ship and came to Boston."

"How many Jews do you think are on board *Scorpion*?"

"Don't know, sir."

"Guess."

"One or two."

"There are six that I know about. So let's get to the reason why you are here: to fight the British. If, during an action with the Royal Navy, I gave you an order, would you obey me?"

"Of course I would, sir. You're the captain. We all have to obey your orders."

"So, if one of my orders were relayed to Midshipman Geiger and he ordered you to follow my direction, would you?"

Grantham's eyes widened when he realized where this conversation was about to go. Making a snide comment was one thing. But he'd shoved Gentry, a leading topman and gun captain, and in effect his superior. That alone could get him a half a dozen lashes. Disobedience of a direct order could get one dangling from the end of a rope.

"I guess I would."

Jaco's tone was edged. "You *guess*, Grantham?"

"I would obey him, sir."

"That's good to know." Jaco unbuttoned his shirt so that a gold six-pointed star was visible. "Just so you know, I am one of the six Jews on board *Scorpion*. So, here is what I am going to do. One, I will make a note in the log; and when I am finished, I will read the words to you and you can make your mark next to them. Two officers who can read who will act as witnesses. The note will document that I have elected not to charge you under Article 12 of the Articles of War, but to put you on probation. If you violate the Articles of War again, or make a derogatory comment about a member of *Scorpion's* crew, or a prisoner, or a guest because of the color of their skin, their background or their religion, you will be charged under Article 12 for striking Leading Topman Colin Gentry. In addition, I am having you switched to Midshipman Geiger's watch so you can get used to taking orders from a Jew. You'll find we are any different from Catholics or a Protestants. What matters is how competent a man is, as a sailor or as an officer. The log entry will note that any other disciplinary problem caused by you will, among other punishments, cause you to forfeit your share of prize money. Do you understand?

"Aye, sir, I do."

"Good. And just so you know, your priest didn't tell you the truth. The Romans killed Jesus, not his fellow Jews. Now get out of here."

Grantham hustled out of his captain's cabin, glad to get off with a warning and probation. When he'd entered, he'd been sure he would soon be feeling the lash on his back.

Payne stayed back to talk to his captain. "Sir, I think you handled that well. My father is a lawyer in Boston, and he has often pointed out to me how the colonies which practice religious freedom are the strongest. When I told my father I wanted a commission in the Continental Navy, he reached out to one of his clients, Moses Michael Days, and Mr. Days sent a letter of recommendation to the Marine Committee. A few weeks later, I was a midshipman on the *Cabot*. So I have every reason to appreciate respect and cooperation across religious lines."

Before Jaco could say anything, there was a sharp rap on the cabin door. Jack Shelton cracked it open to reveal one of the bosun's mates from the watch team. "Captain, lookouts have spotted two transports escorted by a sixth-rater."

* * *

Jaco studied the unknown ships from Perfecto Corner, snapped his Dollond spyglass shut and turned to the officer of the watch, Hedley Garrison. "Where are we?"

"Halfway between Bermuda and Savannah, sir. That convoy is heading west so' west, as close hauled as they can, headed straight for Savannah."

Midshipman Geiger was also studying the ship. "Sir, the frigate is signaling. How do you want *Scorpion* to respond?"

"Show them the Gadsden flag on the mainmast and our ensign on the stern. Once our colors are flying, beat to quarters. And now, Mr. Geiger, explain to your fellow officers how you would engage these three ships."

Geiger glanced at the transports, about three miles away. They were raising staysails between each of the masts. "Sir, the transports are crowding on more sail. Even so, we should be able to run them down before dark. Assuming the frigate is on an opposite tack, I would exchange broadsides at a range of between four to five hundred yards, which will favor our long guns, then reverse course. I expect the frigate will do as well, but we should have the edge when it comes to maneuvering. The Royal Navy captain will want to close and may be willing sacrifice his ship to buy time for the transports to get away. We'll keep our distance and let our long twelves do their work. The wind is from the northwest, which means neither frigate has an advantage, at least for the moment."

With the exception of Lewis Payne and the two midshipmen, all the officers had been through this drill before. The officer of the watch had to defend his plan to defeat the enemy in front of his fellow officers. Then Jaco let them execute their plan until he took command just before the firing began.

Hedley Garrison spoke first. "Mr. Geiger, how would you shorten the engagement with the frigate?"

"Sir, I don't know how, other than hoping our long guns rip the other frigate apart."

Jaco didn't want Geiger embarrassed, but this was time for a teaching moment. "Hoping for an outcome, Mr. Geiger, is not a plan. You need a course of action that keeps the ship you command one or more steps ahead of the enemy. Then you adjust based on what the enemy does. So, you're off to a good start. Instruct Mr. Jeffords as to the course you want to take so we know which side the enemy frigate will pass. I would adjust our course to so' by so' west to intercept the transports. Ball or chain shot?"

"Sir, at four hundred yards we use ball, sir."

"Then inform the second lieutenant and quartermaster here, so they know."

Geiger did so. Garrison smiled as he responded, "Consider it done." Jeffords put a hand to his head. "Aye, sir, new course so' so' west."

"Mr. Geiger, since this is your plan and your action, you will stay on the quarterdeck. Mr. Marshall, you have the maintop and the swivel guns. Gentlemen, I suggest we get ready because that frigate will try to make us pay dearly for the chance to capture two transports."

The Royal Navy captain did what he was trained to do—turn towards his enemy. Geiger studied the on-rushing frigate on a beam reach heading so' east. The English captain had shortened sail because, with his ship heeled over, he did not want his bottom exposed or his port battery forced to fire at maximum depression.

Scorpion had the opposite problem. Her guns were pointed at the water. So, "Captain, when we get close, I will give Bosun Preston the order to slacken sail to level the ship. Once we fire, we'll sheet the sails home, pick up some speed and then tack."

"Mr. Geiger, I would tack as soon as the last gun fires. That way we may be the first to turn, and if the Royal Navy frigate turns as well, we keep hammering away. If not, we get a shot at the frigate's stern."

The young midshipman nodded, then walked to the front railing of the quarterdeck and had a short conversation with *Scorpion's* bosun. He returned and said to Quartermaster Jeffords and Cooper, "Once our bow passes their stern, we will wear ship to port immediately. New course will be east so' east."

At less than a mile, Jaco could see the Royal Navy captain looking at *Scorpion* through a spyglass and wondered what he was thinking. Jaco knew that at 400 yards the British 12-pounders would do little more than dent the three layers of wood that made up *Scorpion's* hull. However, they could turn Scorpion's quarterdeck into a living hell. As for the two carronades on the quarterdeck and the forecastle, they would be even less effective—unless they were fired at short range. It was his responsibility to make sure that did not happen.

The British frigate started to angle toward *Scorpion,* and at about 600 yards the starboard bow chaser started spitting out cannon balls. The first skipped over the water, well short of *Scorpion*. The gunner adjusted the elevation and the next one thumped against *Scorpion's* hull and bounced off to fall into the water. The third ball punched a hole in the foremast's mainsail.

Although Jaco could have ordered his 9-pounders in the bow to fire, he held them back, knowing they were at the extreme end of their range.

Only two quartermasters, Midshipman Geiger, First Lieutenant Shelton and Jaco were on the quarterdeck. Bosun Preston and his Marine lieutenant Patrick Miller were on the main deck, crouched down behind the bulwarks along with the Marines and sailors who would help haul on lines when they wore the ship. "Mr. Geiger, your call when we open fire."

The midshipman nodded. "Sir, first I want to fall off to open the range."

Jaco's terse "Permission granted" sent Geiger to Jeffords and Cooper, and then to Preston to give them instructions. As the ship turned slightly to starboard, away from the onrushing Royal Navy frigate, Geiger went to the front rail and yelled, "Mr. Garrison, open fire as your guns bear."

Jaco heard a faint "Aye, aye!" and smiled. The young man was learning. He hoped Geiger would survive long enough to put the lessons to work.

Jeffords kept easing *Scorpion* windward to maintain at least 400 yards distance from the English ship. Geiger yelled, "Mr. Preston, slacken enough sail to level us out!"

Marines and sailors from the starboard battery let out enough line to reduce the pressure on the sails. *Scorpion* leveled noticeably and slowed. The British captain did the same, committed by doctrine to exchanging broadsides.

The number one cannon on *Scorpion's* port side boomed almost simultaneously with the those on the British frigate's starboard side. loud thump sounded on *Scorpion's* hull, and a huge chunk of the Royal Navy ship's upper deck bulwark flew upwards as a 12-pound ball plowed through the wood. The shot had been superbly lucky: the barrels of both carronades on the forecastle were now pointing at odd angles. Another ball from *Scorpion* ripped through the upper bulwark, exploding a rack of belaying pins. Sheets and braces tied to the iron rings near the rack suddenly went slack. Jaco wondered if the gun crew captains aimed specifically for such targets.

Then a section of *Scorpion's* bulwark went flying as a 12-pound British ball hammered into the port hatch. Another smashed into the middle boat of the three stacked between the fore and mainmast. Neither the top 16-foot-long cutter nor the 20-foot-long boat on the bottom were damaged, but the ball broke the middle cutter in two. Splinters sliced up several men who were helped below.

Jaco heard and felt the Royal Navy's 12-pound balls slamming into *Scorpion's* hull. One sent a gunport cover spinning wildly into the sea. Another took a chunk out of the top of the bulwark between the fore and mainmasts where the three layers of wood were the thinnest.

Scorpion's 12-pound balls stove in a 10-foot section of the British frigate's planking that protected the gun deck. The jagged hole let Jaco and those on the quarterdeck see the British sailors working to reload.

Suddenly the loudest sound was the wind through the sails. Geiger yelled, "Captain, am wearing ship to port. New course east so' east."

Scorpion now had the wind gauge, and the British frigate couldn't turn to the west to keep exchanging broadsides. Its captain had only one practical choice unless he wanted to get raked from the stern. He turned east in the hopes that he could exchange another broadside with *Scorpion*.

Jaco could tell Geiger was thinking ahead. He ordered Preston to have his men haul in the sheets as they pulled the yards around. "Sir, I want to gain some speed and then wear to port to cross the Britisher's stern. If he turns back to the north, we fall off and stay outside four hundred yards."

That is not what I would have done, but it is a great move. Jaco responded, "Good plan, Mr. Geiger. Gentlemen, I have the deck. Mr. Jeffords, execute Mr. Geiger's plan."

Shelton came forward. "Captain, if we close, remember to tell the men at the swivel guns in the masthead to fire."

"Aye." Jaco cupped his hands. "Mr. Marshall, if we get within two hundred yards, you know what to do." A green coated form started to climb the rigging of the foremast. It was Marine Lieutenant Miller. At 200 yards, the swivel guns were not going to be accurate, but each bag of canister sent 25 musket balls traveling fast enough to kill or maim a man.

The Royal Navy frigate was now heading north, sailing as close to the wind as possible. But *Scorpion* could sail closer. This kept the Continental Navy frigate upwind of the Royal Navy frigate's wake, which meant the English frigate could not cross *Scorpion's* bow. Those on the quarterdeck now saw they were battling *H.M.S. Jedburgh*.

Under his feet, Jaco could feel his ship accelerate. With the wind coming over the port beam, the faster *Scorpion* closed on the Royal Navy frigate. Jaco moved so he could stand on the port side of the wheel and next to Geiger. Timing when to wear off, get in a rear quarter shot and then change course to run parallel was critical. Jaco was still going to let Geiger make the call, but if the midshipman misjudged, he would step in.

Through his Dollond spyglass, Jaco studied the figures on *Jedburgh's* quarterdeck, trying to get a hint as to what their captain's next move might be. He doubted that the captain of a Royal Navy frigate would run from a fight with a ship smaller than his.

Scorpion's starboard bow chaser bellowed. Over the smoke that streamed back down the starboard side, Jaco saw the sparkle of shattering glass as the 9-pound ball went through the captain's cabin. The second ball went high and wide, sending up a geyser or water way out in front. The third cannon ball plowed into *Jedburgh's* stern hull. *We're going to cross your stern at inside 200 yards. What surprise do you have for us? Your best option is to veer suddenly to starboard and try to ram us. We cannot let that happen.*

"Captain, I think we should turn."

"Aye, Mr. Geiger, proceed."

The young man went to the forward railing and cupped his hands around his mouth. "Mr. Preston, we're going to fall off now. Mr. Garrison, fire as you bear with chain shot." Turning back to the men at the wheel, Geiger ordered, "Mr. Jeffords, fall off to starboard, course east."

Number one and two 12-pounders spit out flame and smoke almost simultaneously, followed by the sharp crack of the swivel gun on the foremast. Then there was the bellow of the number four and five cannons. A snapping sound, clearly audible even on *Scorpion,* carried over the water. Slowly, *Jedburgh's* mizzenmast fell to the starboard side, taking the Royal Navy ensign down into the Atlantic. Next, a round of chain shot slammed through the bulwark aft of the mizzenmast. Jaco felt suddenly sick as he saw dismembered arms and legs fly through the air.

He grabbed a speaking trumpet. "*Jedburgh,* strike and let us end this carnage." One of *Scorpion's* 12-pounders and two of *Jedburgh's* nines drowned out the answer.

Without the push of the sails on the mizzenmast, *Jedburgh* slowed noticeably. Jaco turned and ordered Bosun Preston to slack sails because he didn't want to give the British frigate a chance to ram.

"Mr. Geiger, pass the word to Mr. Garrison to cease fire. I think our British friend is done." He tried again. "*Jedburgh,* have you struck? Can we end this fight?"

"Aye. We'll wave a white flag. Our colors are in the water."

Jaco turned to Jeffords, "Get us within a hundred yards." Then to Geiger, "Pass the word to Mr. Garrison that if the British open fire, I want him to blow their ship out of the water." Geiger's eyes went wide; he'd never heard his captain speak like that.

Turning to the Royal Navy frigate, Jaco yelled. "Are you in danger of sinking?"

"No, but my ship is shot to hell."

Scorpion's captain and all those on the quarterdeck relaxed slightly. "Hang a light in the bow and stern. We'll be back after we take the transports and offer assistance."

Then, "Masthead, where away are the two transports?"

"Three points, about three miles aft of the starboard beam making a run for it."

"Mr. Geiger, go below to the gun and berthing decks and bring back an assessment of the damage, along with all the officers. Mr. Jeffords, fall off to a new course of so' so' west." Jaco leaned over the forward quarterdeck railing. "Mr. Preston, let's get the royals and the fore staysail out as fast as we can." *Scorpion's* bow swung round, pointing directly at the two sets of sails.

Jaco's first question, when the officers gathered at the aft end of the quarterdeck, was, "Wounded?"

Jack Shelton already had the answer. "Eight, sir. Splinter wounds, none deadly. All eight men should be fine, with scars to show their grandchildren."

"Damage?"

The port side hatch, the head on the same side, and we need two new gunports."

Not for the first time, Jaco silently blessed the designers and builders of Scorpion's three-layered hull. "First of all, Mr. Geiger is to be congratulated. He conned the ship through most of the fight. This was, as you know, his plan. So, Mr. Geiger, well done."

After the "Hear, hear!"s, the serious tone of the meeting returned. "Gentlemen, as we get closer, we'll make an assessment as to whether or not we think those two transports will resist. If they stay about a half-mile apart, we are going sail between the middle and ask them politely if they want to strike. If they don't, we'll convince them with our 12-pounders. If they surrender, then give some thought as to how we can take possession of all three ships. I'd prefer not to put 25-man prize crews on each ship. Mr. Marshall, go to my cabin and come up with a course to Charleston or Hampton, whichever is closer."

Thanks to the ship's ease of handling and sleek design, *Scorpion* slid easily between the two transport ships, named *Fort William* and *Fort Herkimer*. Neither had run out and both quickly agreed to heave too. Having seen what had happened to their escorting frigate, their captains didn't need convincing that any attempt to fight *Scorpion* would be both futile and bloody. Soldiers taken prisoner would live to fight another day; soldiers who were blown to pieces would not.

The two undamaged boats were lowered over the starboard side. While the boats were being readied, Jaco gathered his officers on the quarterdeck.

"Mr. Garrison, take a quartermaster's mate, ten sailors and ten Marines to *Fort William*. Mr. Payne, you do the same for *Fort Herkimer*. As soon as you get on board, send back someone with a report of what they are carrying. Do what you need to do to confine the crew and any soldiers below. Mr. Marshall informs me that Charleston is the closest port, two hundred and forty miles to the west. Show a bright green lantern on the stern so we can link up tonight. If you get to Charleston before *Scorpion*, go to Laredo Shipping and tell them I sent you; Max Laredo will probably buy these two transports right away."

Jaco sought out *Jedburgh's* two topsails on the horizon. "That leaves *Jedburgh*. Mr. Shelton, you and Mr. Miller are going to have the privilege of sailing *Jedburgh* back to Charleston. Take our carpenter, Mr. Gaskins. If the British frigate can't be repaired, we'll sink it. I'll keep Mr. Geiger and Mr. Marshall on board *Scorpion*. Any questions?"

Hedley Garrison spoke up. "Are we going to have a party in Charleston to celebrate?"

Jaco smiled. "Mr. Garrison, assuming that all four ships make it to Charleston, and if you can find time to organize one while we re-provision and ready *Scorpion* to depart in seventy-two hours, then yes, we can have a party."

Jaco forced himself to relax as he watched the transfer of sailors to both merchant ships. They were in the heart of the shipping lanes frequented by Royal Navy frigates. The longer they lingered, the more nervous he became.

Quartermaster's Mate Cooper, assigned to *Fort William*, crossed over to *Scorpion* in one of the cutters. Standing up in the small boat, legs spread for balance, he called up to the quarterdeck. "Captain, sir, Mr. Garrison said that both ships are transporting 200 soldiers from someplace in Germany called Waldeck, along with their horses, a battery of cannon, their weapons and ammunition. Their destination was Pensacola, Florida. Mr. Garrison said that since the weather is fine, he is going to confine the crew and the soldiers below by barring the hatches; it is only two days at five knots to Charleston."

"Good luck, Mr. Cooper."

Jaco watched the two transports surge ahead of *Scorpion* before he ordered the return to *Jedburgh,* whose sails were still visible. He had the cooks issue a ration of beer along with two biscuits soaked in rum and a handful of dried apples to each man. The food wasn't much, but until they secured from quarters, he wasn't going to allow the stove to be used to prepare a hot meal.

When only 200 feet separated *Jedburgh* and *Scorpion,* six rowers need only a few minutes to transport Lieutenants Shelton and Miller, Carpenter Leo Gaskins and his mate to the Royal Navy frigate. From the starboard Perfecto Corner, Jaco studied the battered *Jedburgh.* The ship's mizzenmast was broken 15 feet above the deck and the ship's boats were piles of torn-up wood useful only for firewood.

"Sir..." Jaco turned around to see Colin Gentry. "Mr. Shelton says that the hull of *Jedburgh* is sound. He thinks he can make five knots. *Jedburgh* only has about a week's worth of provisions left. There are thirty-one dead and sixty wounded; the British surgeon says thirteen of them won't live more than a few days. *Jedburgh's* captain gave Mr. Shelton his word that his crew will not attempt to retake the ship. They will start burying the dead as soon as the sails are hung."

"Thank you, Gentry. Anything else?"

"Yes, sir. The British captain wants to know what kind of cannon we have. And he thinks *Scorpion* has iron plates between layers of wood to protect the gun deck."

Jaco laughed. "Tell *Jedburgh*'s captain that he has to resign from the Royal Navy and join the Continental Navy to learn our secrets."

***

Even the arrival of three British prizes didn't improve the mood in Charleston. The people were certain the British were about to attack the city, and they were less than confident that the Continental Army would be able to again defeat the British as it had earlier in the war.

First off the transports were the Germans from Waldeck. They lined up on the pier guarded by Patrick Miller's Marines. Prince Friedrich Karl August of the German duchy of Waldeck kept three fully equipped regiments of 664 men each, ready for rental by any government who needed soldiers. The men on the ships were from the 3rd Waldeck Regiment and had already fought against the Continental Army in New York before they boarded the transports.

Their commander was not happy that his men would be confined to a small fort north of Charleston's defenses. General Moultrie had no other place to keep them and the surviving British sailors.

Miriam Bildesheim, along with her two oldest daughters, Chaya and Devorah, volunteered to act as interpreters. Hearing General Moultrie's plan, she offered an alternative, speaking in her heavy but understandable accent. "Herr General, I need carpenters, coopers und blacksmiths, and men to verk zee fieldz. Alzo, my inns and stores need verkers. Vith your permission, I vill ask if zay vould like to verk on a farm. I vill house, feed and pay zem. And if zey are gut zitizens, zay can stay after zee var and verk for me."

"How many men could you take?" General Moultrie sounded both relieved and astonished by this offer.

"As many as vant to kom. I vill tell zem if zay harm any of my other verkers or steal from me, I vill punish zem zee same vay zey are punished in Waldeck. Murderers vill be hung und zose zat steal vill find zemselves in chains and verked in zee fields. Zer life vill not be gut."

"Very well. Once they leave here, they are your responsibility."

"I understand. I vould like to pick zee men now."

"Please do."

Miriam Bildesheim rode up to the German officer. "Achtung, Herr Colonel." In rapid German she explained her offer, then directed him to form up the men in ranks and march them 100 yards up the road to where her daughters waited.

Miriam led the way, sitting erect on her horse. Once they were all assembled, she addressed the soldiers. Her voice carried easily. She said they could choose between becoming prisoners of war or working for her. Those who wished to leave the Waldeck regiment were asked what their skills were. Miriam listened attentively, occasionally asking questions.

When she was finished, Devorah, Chaya and Miriam led away 76 men, including two blacksmiths and six carpenters, northward toward her nearest farm 12 miles away. Eight more followed Chaya into Charleston, where they would be put to work in their dry goods stores and inns.

The happiest man in Charleston was Max Laredo. After inspecting *Fort William* and *Fort Henry*, he wrote out a draft on the Bank of South Carolina to purchase the two ships from the prize court. Within hours, the paperwork was signed, documenting that they were now owned by Laredo

Shipping AB and renamed *Gothenburg* and *Karlskrona*. Max also offered the seamen from the three British ships contracts to serve on his ships for two years. Within hours, he had enough to fully man both cargo ships because the pay was higher.

* * *

That night, when they were alone in the garden after dinner, Jaco wrapped his arms around Reyna's slim waist and pulled her close. "I don't care what people think, I just want to hold you."

Reyna rested her head on his shoulder. "I am afraid. Many of our fellow Charlestonians will die before this is all over. I don't want you or either of my brothers to be among them."

"What about you? You are one of the surgeons for the 2nd Carolina militia. That puts you on the battlefield."

"Aye, that it does. But I will be careful."

"My love, musket balls don't have eyes. They hit what they hit. On my ship I cannot tell if who gets hit is random or God's will. This is why every Yom Kippur, we ask God to put us in the book of life for the coming year. My point is, don't tempt God."

"Wise words, my love. I will try to heed them."

"Don't just try, stay far from the battlefield."

"My duty to help the wounded, and I will do that. Just as you will go to sea again."

"I worry about you, my darling Reyna."

"I know, and I worry about you. Every time you leave, I wonder if I will ever see you again." They both sighed deeply, then rocked slowly back and forth together.

CHAPTER 13
RUNNIN' AND GUNNIN'

Portsmouth, third week of February 1779

Darren was struck by the coincidence that the three ships in his squadron were all named for Roman weapons. A gladius was the Roman Legion's short sword. Pilum—plural for pila—were long javelins whose sharp points penetrated wooden shields and impaled the shield holder—perhaps that name would prove apt in battle against the well-shielded hull of *Scorpion*. Hastas were six-foot long thrusting spears used by the Roman Legion's phalanx to keep attackers at bay; he hoped *Hasta*'s long guns would do likewise. *We are,* he thought, *the Royal Navy's phalanx sent to hunt the* Scorpion*!*

By holding this meeting off the Naval Base, Darren added an air of informality. However, his primary reason was to meet away from the prying ears and eyes of senior Naval officers who might want to add their "input" to the discussion and provide "guidance" to the young captains.

After much thought, Darren had decided that this would be a "captains only" meeting; he wanted to get to know the two other men and to learn how they thought. He reasoned they would speak more freely without their subordinates present.

First to arrive was Phineas Taylor, captain of *H.M.S. Pilum*. At 6-foot-1, blond and blue eyed, Taylor was the poster child of what Royal Navy captain should look like. He was quiet and soft spoken.

Like Smythe, Taylor came from a well-to-do family of merchants and wanted nothing to do with the family business in Leeds. Because his parents suggested the Army via the Royal Military Academy, he volunteered for the Royal Naval Academy instead, even though he knew nothing about ships or the Royal Navy. Taylor had graduated the year after Smythe started, and had made lieutenant in three years. He had been serving on a fifth rater when the war broke out, and had been given a prize to bring home. In wartime, the Royal Navy expanded rapidly and promotions were accelerated. Like Smythe, Taylor was a brand-new captain.

H.M.S. Hasta's captain, Hamilton Meegan, was the opposite of both Smythe and Taylor. He'd grown up on the streets of Norwich and, in 1765 at age 10, found himself on board a Royal Navy fifth rated frigate as a powder monkey. Two years later, the captain realized that the pugnacious, assertive Meegan was a natural leader and secured an appointment for him as midshipman. By then, Meegan had taught himself to read and write.

Meegan followed the captain to a fourth rater and made lieutenant. When the war began, he was promoted to commander and given a 12-gun brig. He, too, had been recently promoted to captain, but he was 31—seven years older than Taylor and nine older than Smythe.

The dining room in his parents' house was perfect for what Smythe wanted to accomplish. The 12-foot long table provided the surface area he needed to lay out charts, and there were the four toy ships he had bought to use as visual aids.

On a side table in the dining room, Olivia Smythe placed two pitchers of hot water for tea, as well as sweet rolls she'd baked early that morning to go along with a plate of cheese and ham chunks. She introduced herself to both officers, then retired to a back room she used as an office to work on Smythe & Sons' books.

After each man helped himself to tea and what food he desired, Darren opened the meeting. A blue-backed Royal Navy chart of the Atlantic coast of North America from Nova Scotia to the tip of Florida and the Bahamas was already spread out, held down by four glasses.

"Gentlemen, thank you for coming. I asked you here so we could fully discuss what we are about to undertake away from our peers and betters." Out of the corner of his eye, Darren saw Taylor smile at his reference to more senior captains and those with titles.

"Shortly, all three of our ships will have their full complement of twenty 12-pounders. As a new build, *Gladius* will go out for sea trials on the 26th of February and return March 3rd to take on a full load of provisions. Assuming there are no defects, *Gladius, Pilum* and *Hasta* will put to sea on March 5th. We will sail as a squadron to North America where our mission is to either sink or capture the American frigate *Scorpion*. Have either of you heard of this frigate?"

Meegan wasn't shy. "Aye, *Scorpion's* captain has made a bloody monkey out of every Royal Navy captain that's taken him on."

Taylor nodded, then spoke softly. "I have read some of the reports. *Scorpion* is fast and maneuverable. Its guns are longer ranged than ours, accurate, and they savage any ship they target. Some say its hull is impervious to our cannon balls."

"I assume both of you understand the challenge given to us by the lordships who run the Admiralty." Smythe picked up the toy ship whose hull he'd painted black. "Gentlemen, what I am about to share with you is considered most secret and only a few Admirals know. I've met *Scorpion's* captain, Jaco Jacinto."

Darren described the battle in which Jacinto on a lightly armed, three-masted schooner outfought *H.M.S. Sorcerer* despite the larger ship's advantage of surprise and heavier broadside. He summarized the conversations Jacinto and he had shared over the course of a week on the way to Brest. Then he told of the action off the Isle of Lewis in which *Scorpion* took on three Royal Navy frigates, put two out of action, and damaged *H.M.S. Puritan* before escaping into the Atlantic. He specifically emphasized Jacinto's unpredictability and his favorite tactics:

1. Fire from 400 to 600 yards;
2. Maneuver to get a stern shot rather than exchange broadsides inside 200 yards;
3. Use chain shot to tear up rigging and bring down a mast;
4. Use the swivel guns on the masthead to kill his opponent officers on the quarterdeck and main deck gun crews, and
5. Avoid a fight that ends in a boarding action.

Darren placed the four wooden boats on the chart. "Understanding what we are up against will help us defeat Captain Jacinto. Today we are going to discuss how we shall search for *Scorpion* and the tactics we will use if we find the rebel frigate. Individually, none of our ships, no matter how well-sailed or fought, will carry the day. But together, I believe we can overwhelm *Scorpion* and force Captain Jacinto to haul down his flag."

Charleston, Tuesday, 9 a.m. February 17th, 1779

When Shoshana Jacinto walked into the Charleston County Courthouse, she didn't feel like a pioneer. The business accomplishments of Abigail Minis in Savannah and Miriam Bildesheim in Charleston had paved the way for her. In many ways, she and her best friend Reyna were rebelling against societal norms that held women belonged in the home. She thought this was hypocritical; women on the frontier did men's work as well as raise children.

Both Edgar Burrows and Raphael Soriano had said she was ready, and a panel of three judges and two attorneys would focus on her knowledge of the law, not her sex or her age. Shoshana had just turned 19.

Her long, sandy brown hair was tied in a braid and hung down between her shoulder blades. She wore a simple light blue busk with white trim around the neck and sleeves. When Shoshana strode proudly into the room, the loudest sound was the tapping of the wooden heels on her leather shoes on the wood floor. She stood until she was invited to take a seat, and then folded her hands in her lap. *Let the inquisition begin.*

The senior member of the bar exam intoned the date, time, place and the purpose of the session. Shoshana was the first woman to "sit" for the admittance exam to the South

Carolina Bar. If she passed, Shoshana could represent clients in court in front of a judge and jury. If not, she would continue as a law clerk and take the exam next year.

The senior judge, Manning, was in his sixties and had a round face and red nose, and before speaking he cleared his throat loudly. "Miss Jacinto, you do realize that none of the members of the South Carolina Bar are women."

"I do, sir."

"Have you attended any of the classes at the Inns of Court in England?"

"No, sir. How could I? They do not allow women to attend."

"Then you do not have a formal legal education."

Shoshana knew where this was going and decided to put an end to this attempt to discredit her as a potential member of the bar. "Judge Manning, many would-be lawyers come to this exam without attending classes, having read law at home or as a clerk in a law office, as I have done. Neither my sex nor whether I studied law at a particular school has anything to do with this exam, which is supposed to test my knowledge of the law. Nothing else matters. So, shall we start with questions about the law itself, court filings and proceedings, or commercial contracts, including those that involve companies outside South Carolina? I already have negotiated contracts with stock corporations in England, the Netherlands and Sweden."

Shoshana made eye contact with each member of the panel, all of whom she knew, all of whom she had dealt with over legal matters, and all of whom knew, even if they would not admit, that she was more than qualified to be a member of the bar. Edgar Burrows at the far end of the panel was smiling. He was president of the bar association, and he had made the formal recommendation for Shoshana to appear.

Manning nodded. "I take your point, Ms. Jacinto. Let us start with an international transaction. Suppose you had to negotiate a contract with a firm in say, Spain. How would you go about that?"

Shoshana seemed to stand taller and resembled an eagle about to pounce on its prey. She said, "Recently, my work involved setting up a Swedish stock company for a client here in Charleston, so my answer is not hypothetical, but based on actual contracts, commercial transactions and licenses. Because my client trades in France and Spain as well as other countries, I researched the appropriate laws and incorporated what was required into the contracts." She presented a crisp, fact-filled summary of the work she'd done for Laredo Shipping to set up a stock company in Sweden, register their ships with Lloyd's insurance and shipping register, as well as with the Swedish government. The work included acquiring licenses for the ships to pick up and deliver cargos to Spain and France. When she finished speaking, two of the judges were open-mouthed.

The questioning went on and on before one judge asked, "Miss Jacinto, if you were defending a male client and facing an all-male jury, do you not think you would be at a disadvantage?"

"Judge Mahone, out of fairness to my client, I would hope the jury would carefully consider the *evidence* I present in my client's defense. If they dismiss my efforts in any way because I am a *woman*, then, sir, I suggest they have no right to sit on a jury and their prejudices would be cause for an appeal."

And if women were allowed to sit on a jury, the question would be moot. But saying so would be inflammatory, and the goal here is to be accepted to the bar, not anger the panel.

"That is an interesting position, Miss Jacinto."

"Sir, while my statement may be intellectually interesting, the law is on my side ..." Shoshana rattled off the section of South Carolina and British law that applied. "So, yes, diminishing my presentation of evidence because I am a woman is grounds for an appeal because my client was not given a fair hearing."

The judge responded. "But, if a man were representing your client, you would agree that such a risk, with the attendant delays and expenses, would not be a factor."

Shoshana forced herself not to rise to the implication that no woman could effectively represent a client in court so long as even one member of a jury objected to her presence. She chose her words carefully as she spoke in measured tones that conveyed her passion for her chosen profession but concealed her resentment against societal norms that held that women were not the equal of men. "Sir, the law uses the words *man, person,* and *individual* interchangeably. Of those, I qualify as a person and an individual; and if the writer of the law used the word *man* in the sense of *anthropos* or homo sapiens, as described in 1758 by the Swedish botanist and anthropologist Carl Linnaeus, then I qualify on all three counts. However, the real answer to your question is that you yourself gave the precise reason why I should be a member of the bar. As a woman, I will have to be superior at every turn in order to prove that I deserve to be there. I accept that as the first woman member of the bar, everything I do will be scrutinized and examined minutely. In court, I will be forced to present stronger cases, argue more forcibly and creatively, and look for ways the law can be used to ensure my client receives a fair trial—and wins."

Judge Manning waited until the silence mounted. "Any more questions for Ms. Jacinto?"

There were none. "Ms. Jacinto, thank you for appearing today. We will notify you as to whether or not you are admitted to the bar by Friday. Your answers showed a deep understanding of the law and the legal profession. They were also refreshing, sometimes unconventional, and delivered with a passion that we expect from members of the South Carolina bar who appear in court."

That night, Shoshana's closest friends, Reyna Laredo and Melody Winters, who wanted to be a professor of languages, came over for dinner. Reyna was happy for her friend, who might become the first woman in any of the colonies to be admitted to the bar. She was also careful to hide her jealousy. In the medical profession, to hold the title doctor one had to graduate from a medical school, and that door was closed to her. She knew of no board before which she could sit and demonstrate her knowledge of medicine, anatomy and diseases to bypass that requirement.

The three young women were in the sitting room drinking madeira with Perla Jacinto, talking about the bar exam. None heard the firm knock at the front door until several followed. Perla got to her feet, saying, "I wonder who has come calling at this time of night."

The opened door revealed Edgar Burrows and Raphael Soriano. Burrows spoke, struggling to preserve a solemn demeanor. "Good evening, Mrs. Jacinto. Is Miss Shoshana here? I apologize for the lateness of the hour, but I have important news."

As she made them welcome and ushered them into the parlor. Perla's heart pounded like a blacksmith beating a bar of iron on an anvil. *Are they going to break my daughter's heart, or are they going to let her fulfill her dream?*

Shoshana and the rest of the women stood. Reyna put her arm around her best friend's waist.

Burrows tried to look serious but couldn't. He smiled and held out his arms. "Shoshana, welcome to the bar!"

Shoshana screamed for joy and jumped up and down like a little girl. She ran to the two lawyers and hugged each of them.

"What happened? I was sure they didn't like me!"

"Two didn't," Burrows said, "for no other reason than because you're a woman. They couldn't quibble with your knowledge. In the end, Judge Manning said that when you appear in his court, there will be at least one very able lawyer present. He looks forward to hearing your arguments, which he expects will be, to use his words, spirited and refreshing. The official letter and certificate will be delivered to our offices on Friday." His eyes twinkled. "We'll have to start charging clients more for your legal services so we can pay you more!"

Celtic Sea, first week of March 1779

Right after *Gladius, Pilum* and *Hasta* entered the English Channel, the frigates encountered a storm with 10-foot seas that tossed them around as if they were large corks. Darren never left the quarterdeck until the storm abated, even though he was doused by 40-degree water driven by a strong wind and chilled to the bone.

Traditionally, Royal Navy captains don't open their official sailing orders until they out of sight of land. This time, Darren waited until after the storm passed and he warmed up.

As commander of a squadron, he had been issued not a single folded sheet of paper sealed with wax but a pouch in which there were three letters. One was his sailing orders.

The second letter designated him, for the purposes of hunting *Scorpion*, a commodore and the commander of the squadron of three ships. The third was addressed to Rear Admiral James Gambier, Commander of the North American Station. Smythe had been told the letter directed Gambier to provide whatever support Smythe requested, and not to assign the three frigates to other tasks until *Scorpion* was brought to heel.

The three ships had weathered the storm undamaged. At the end of the second day at sea, Darren signaled the other ships to close up for night sailing and show a red lantern. He then asked the Marine sentry by his door to tell the bo'sun on watch to ask all *Gladius'* officers to join him in his cabin for the opening of orders.

When four officers, two midshipmen, the ship's bosun and quartermaster had gathered around the table, Marine Captain Peter De Courcy raised his glass. "To the King!"

After toasting the Navy and comrades lost, Darren picked up his orders and popped off the seal with the imprint of the First Sea Lord. The paper crinkled loudly as Darren carefully unfolded the thick sheet. De Courcy held up a candle to provide better light. Captain Smythe began reading the precise penmanship out loud.

Captain Smythe,

You are to sail H.M.S. Gladius, accompanied by H.M.S. Hasta and H.M.S. Pilum by the most expeditious route to North America. There you will report to the Commander, North American Station and give him the separate letter accompanying your sailing orders. He will be asked to provide all reasonable assistance to you as long as that support does not interfere with his mission of defeating the

French Navy and supporting the British Army in its efforts to put down the rebellion. In addition, the shore establishments in Halifax, Bermuda, Nassau and Port Royal have been notified by separate letters that your ships will be given priority in terms of provisions, repairs and ammunition.

Once in North American waters, you will hunt down and destroy the rebel frigate Scorpion. Until that is accomplished, you have no other mission. However, you may take prizes as long as the action does not compromise your primary tasking.

When you have either sunk, captured or rendered Scorpion ineffective, you will then report to the Commander, North American Station for further orders.

Good luck and God speed.
Sir Hugh Palliser
First Sea Lord

The second letter Smythe opened authorized him to fly the flag of a commodore. Bosun Louttit said he would have the ship's sailmaker have a commodore's flag ready by first light.

The officers were quiet as Darren filled his glass and passed the bottle around. "Gentlemen, we have our work cut out for us. To our success."

Mid-Atlantic, second week of March 1779

The harsh weather of the English Channel and Celtic Sea moderated as the three ship squadron sailed so' so' west toward the Canary Islands and then west toward the Greater

Antilles, the island chain that separates the Atlantic from the Caribbean.

Pushed by the Trade Winds coming off the west coast of Africa, the frigates had been averaging eight knots. They were sailing in a scouting line with *Gladius* in the center, *Hasta* approximately 12 miles to the north and *Pilum* the same distance to the south. The line enabled the lookouts to "see" a swath of ocean 48 nautical miles wide.

The pleasant weather let Captain Smythe drill the crew at least twice a day in clearing for action, loading drills and other emergencies he invented to relieve the boredom. He was on the quarterdeck when a call from the lookout came. "Deck, *Hasta* is signaling." The lookout called out the sequence of flags, which sent Bart Jernigan scrambling for the code book. Darren heard Jernigan tell Lieutenant Tewksbury, "*Hasta* has a single merchantman in sight two points off its port bow."

If he added the ages of his two junior lieutenants, Enfield and Tewksbury, they wouldn't total 30; yet they are able to expertly conn a Royal Navy sixth rate ship-of-the-line. *I'll wait to see what they do. Our own lookout should see the unknown ship any minute.*

Jernigan approached his captain. "Sir, Lieutenant Tewksbury would like to know what instructions you have for *Hasta*."

"Mr. Jernigan, signal *Hasta* to investigate."

The words from his sailing orders were tattooed in his brain: "... by the most expeditious route to North America ... you will hunt down and destroy the rebel frigate *Scorpion*. Until that is accomplished you have no other mission..." *Yes, he could take a prize, but what if the delay caused him to miss an encounter with* Scorpion?

On board merchantman Stockholm

Through a spyglass, Eric Laredo studied the frigate bearing down on him. The sight of approaching sails filled him with dread; he was sure they were Royal Navy frigates on the prowl for prizes.

According to his ship's papers, *Stockholm* was a Swedish ship registered in Stockholm and therefore neutral, even though the ship was crewed by South Carolinians. He was carrying a cargo of cotton, rice and indigo to the Netherlands, which was not contraband and so not subject to seizure. He had no intention of stopping unless the Royal Navy ordered him to do so. Gazing up at the large Swedish flag streaming from the stay to the top of the mizzenmast, he hoped the Royal Navy would leave his ship alone.

On board H.M.S. Gladius

On the gently pitching and rolling quarterdeck, Darren struggled to keep the circular field of vision of Horrocks' Dollond spyglass trained on the merchant ship. He could make out three masts and the sails, but not much more detail. The ship was still five miles away.

"Sir..." The speaker was Midshipman Jernigan. "*Hasta* says the ship is a Swedish merchantman."

The signal begs the question of what does the captain of Hasta *do? The Swedish flag could be a ruse. On the other hand, if stopped and searched and there was no contraband, the action could cause an incident.*

"Signal *Hasta* to resume station."

Darren hoped Captain Meegan would make a note in his log of the name of the ship, position at time of sighting and flag. But the mystery of the Swedish ship would have to be solved at a later date, probably by another ship's captain. *We must find and bring* Scorpion *to heel before we go prize hunting.*

Off the coast of Virginia, second week of April 1779

Darren's route took the three-ship squadron almost to the islands on the eastern edge of the Caribbean, then on the Atlantic side of the Bahamas and north until they were 50 miles from the mouth of the Chesapeake Bay. There was no sign of *Scorpion*.

Lookouts on *Hasta* spotted ships assigned to the Royal Navy's North American Station early one afternoon. Recognition signals were exchanged, and the three frigates closed up.

The flagship, *H.M.S. Raissonable,* 64 guns, was moving at a stately three knots, which let *Gladius'* cutter easily come alongside. Smythe had the dispatch case slung over his shoulder as he shifted from the bobbing cutter to the iron rungs of the ladder that reached from the waterline to the hatch in *Raissonable's* lower gun deck. There the admiral's flag lieutenant awaited him and escorted him to the captain's spacious cabin.

Admiral James Gambier had been relieved by Admiral Sir George Collier while *Gladius* was en route. Gambier had the reputation of being rude and disagreeable, so Smythe was relieved to meet a different man. Collier approached with hand outstretched for a firm clasp and shake. "Welcome, Captain Smythe, to the North American Station. I am delighted to receive some additional ships. I see you are flying a commodore's flag; are you on some specific mission of which I am not aware?"

Smythe opened the dispatch case and handed Collier the letter he'd been told to deliver. "Sir, our squadron's orders are to capture or sink the rebel frigate *Scorpion*."

Collier grunted. "These damned colonials are a stubborn lot. I admit that frigate has been a bloody nuisance, but hardly worth dedicating three frigates. I could use your ships in a series of raids we are about to conduct up and down Chesapeake Bay."

"Sir, my orders are clear. We are not to assist the fleet until we either capture or sink *Scorpion*."

The admiral popped open the seal and began to read. His eyebrows raised noticeably. When he finished, he folded the letter and placed it on his desk. "I see.... This letter tells me to provide what support you need. I don't know what I can give you. We are stretched pretty thin with half the station in the Caribbean trying to stop the damned French from making mischief. They've already taken some of our islands and merchant ships. I'll bet those paying for insurance at Lloyds are swearing at the French when they see the new rates. Where are you going to search for this rebel frigate?"

"Sir, now that I have delivered the dispatches, we shall sail south to Nassau to re-provision. Then we will look for *Scorpion* around the Bahamas, Turks & Caicos. That's where I believe the rebel will be hunting for prizes, because he prefers warmer waters to the northern waters off Canada. If we don't find him there, we will move north."

Collier poured two glasses of madeira and held one out to Smythe. "Well, Captain, good luck. Here's to your success."

North of the Leeward Islands, second week of April 1779

Twice in the previous two weeks, *Scorpion's* lookouts had sighted groups of sails. Both times they were troopships headed south, heavily guarded by two Royal Navy frigates and a third or fourth rater. Both times the escorting frigates sailed close to the transports, like a militant mother goose guarding her chicks. By now, *Scorpion* was low on supplies;

if they could not seize a prize they would have to find a friendly, or at least neutral, port.

Jaco's choices of where to replenish supplies and bring prizes was limited. Havana was Spanish-controlled and had a good harbor but would probably be watched by the Royal Navy. Similarly, now that the French were in the war, Jaco assumed Royal Navy frigates would be patrolling both Guadeloupe and Martinique. But the elder Jacinto had given his son letters of introduction to Dutch East India Company agents on the Dutch-controlled islands in the Caribbean, and to Rodrique, Hortelez and Company, who clandestinely acquired gunpowder and weapons for the Continental Congress. In the Leeward Islands, the Dutch-owned St. Maarten and Sint Eustatius were in the heart of the routes for ships carrying rum, sugar and spices from British-held islands in the Caribbean. At the southern end, just north of South America, Bonaire and Aruba remained in Dutch hands. Aruba and Bonaire were the safest, followed by Havana. Jaco decided to take *Scorpion* past St. Maarten and Sin Eustatius to determine if they were being watched, and perhaps find a prize or two along the way.

There was not a Royal Navy ship in sight, but that could change. The weather was pleasant, with puffy clouds dotting a bright blue sky that, on the horizon, merged with the blue-green sea. Visibility was excellent, and the island of St. Barts was just barely visible to port from the masthead lookout platform. Jaco planned look for prizes around Antiqua. The area should be filled with merchant ships, unless all commerce now traveled in convoys.

My orders say Scorpion *is to disrupt British commerce, so should we raid ports? If so, which one? What's the risk? Once we do, the British will know we are here. But if we take a single ship, the British won't know for days or weeks.*

With the steady wind from the west nor' west, Jaco waited until *Scorpion* was eight miles west of British-held Barbuda before he ordered Lieutenant Payne to tack to starboard to a course of so' so' west. The frigate was turning through the wind when everyone on the main and quarterdeck heard a loud crack.

The distinctive, viscerally painful sound of a mast tearing itself apart lodges in the brain forever. Everyone's eyes went to the masts so they could judge which way to run if a section came down. But nothing happened. Bosun Preston's trained eye couldn't see anything amiss. Then Landry yelled down from the lookout's platform, "Deck ho! The mainmast split above us between the top sail and the top gallant."

Jaco yelled out, "Deck aye," before addressing Preston. "Bosun, keep just enough tension on the sheets and the braces for the mainmast's top and top gallant until we get steadied up on the new course. Loosen the sheets on the other mainmast sails to take pressure off the rigging."

"Aye, aye, Cap'n. Mr. Gaskins is already on his way."

Followed by one of his mates, the 50-year-old Gaskins scampered up the ratlines with the sure-footedness of an experienced topman. From the lookout platform, he shimmied up the mast as easily as if he climbed rough wood posts several times a day. Gaskins stopped momentarily on the top sail yardarm to study the mast above him, then continued his climb. He looped a wide leather belt around the mast and leaned back, confident that the friction would keep him from sliding down. His mate did the same on the opposite side of the mast. Both men studied the break, conferring, then came down.

Due to several missing front teeth, Gaskins hissed as he talked. "Sssir, the mainmast sssplit along the grain about a third of the way between the lower and top mast capsss. We can sssee a crack four feet long, but it doesssn't appear to have gone all the way through, which isss why the massst didn't topple. We don't have a log on board big enough to be a replaccccement but I can lash stripsss of planking to make a sssplint."

"Can we do the repairs while we are sailing, or should we be at anchor?"

"Sssir, we can work fasssster if we were anchored in calm water. We can do it sssailing or hove to, but will be more difficult."

"How long if we hove to?""

"A full day, sssir, maybe longer. We have to sssplit boardsss and lash the ssssplint in place. With the ship bobbing about, the work takesss longer."

"And if we were at anchor?"

"Half a day. I can have more men up in the rigging to do the lashing."

"Get cracking on cutting the planking while I find us a quiet place to anchor." Jaco spoke matter-of-factly, but inside he was thinking, *Damn!!! We are in the heart of British controlled waters and have just lost one of our greatest tactical advantages—speed. We've just gone from being the hunters to being prey.*

Jaco hurried to his cabin to check the chart of Barbuda. On the southwestern side, a small peninsula called Palmetto Point, which resembled a trigger installed backwards on a pistol, was at one end of a long, sheltered cove. His French chart didn't show the presence of any fort on the point, and Jaco did not know where the British garrison was on the island.

Back on the quarterdeck, he ordered Mr. Geiger to gently wear the ship to port and head for Barbuda, and to send the watch aloft to furl the all the sails on the mainmast.

Next, Midshipman Geiger made a quick sketch on a slate of the bay on the south side of Barbuda, then he and two sailors boarded a cutter to take soundings with a line marked with knots every six feet and a heavy piece of lead at the end. Meanwhile, Gaskins set up two sets of sawhorses on the main deck and supervised two teams of men sawing 10-foot long planks into three-inch wide strips. His plan was to lash the strips around the mast like a tight belt.

The sun was past the noon peak and was headed toward the western horizon before *Scorpion's* starboard anchor finally splashed into the water. Leaning over the railing, Jaco could see sandy bottom 50 feet below. He waited until the ship swung around into the wind before dropping the port anchor. Now only a very strong wind from the so' west could pin the ship in the bay and make escape difficult.

According to Jaco's chart, *Scorpion* had just anchored in Gravenor's Bay. Palmetto Point was the northern tip of a crescent of pink sand beach that stretched so' east two miles to another small peninsula labeled Coco Point. Scanning the island first with the naked eye and then his spyglass, Jaco didn't see any signs of human habitation or the British Army. Out in the bay, Midshipman Geiger was in the cutter recording more details to be noted on the ship's chart.

Scorpion gently rocked in the calm waters as the carpenter's mates started on the mast. As a precaution, Jaco ordered all the spars and masts be inspected, and Gaskins found the mizzenmast's royal yardarm and the mainmast's topsail yard were also cracked. These could be replaced with spares stored in the hold, but the additional repairs meant they would be at anchor until tomorrow evening.

So much for getting underway in a few hours, Jaco thought, ruefully.

Jaco was awakened just after dawn by the bosun's mate alerting him through the closed door that the lookouts had spotted men on the beach. Hastily, Jaco pulled on clothes and made his way to the quarterdeck. Through his spyglass he saw three red-coated men on horseback. They cantered back and forth along the shore to see as much of the strange ship as they could, then rode off.

Well, now the British Army knows we are here, but we are not flying any flags so they don't know who we are. The Royal Navy base on St. Kitts is a half a day's sail away, so if there are warships there, they are a day away.

Slowly, the blueness of the sky was dulled by thin gray clouds which over the course of the day began to billow skyward, suggesting rain was in the offing. Leo Gaskins was supervising men screwing the rings into the wood that would hold the footrope on the new topgallant yard. "How long, Mr. Gaskins?"

"Two hoursss at mossst. Thisss be the last piece. We've jussst got to hoissst the ssspar up and lash her and we'll be done."

Jaco heard a distant rumble of thunder. "You'd best hurry. The storm will be a good test for your repairs."

"Aye, Captain. We've been lissstening to the sssky growl for sssome time."

Curaçao, third week of April 1779

Scorpion left Barbuda and sailed over seas as empty of British patrols as they were of potential prize ships to Port de France on Martinique where Jaco learned the French had taken St. Vincent, St. Lucia and Grenada. He was very disappointed that the French wouldn't sell *Scorpion* a log to replace the damaged mainmast. Not willing to risk pursuit or combat with a mast he didn't fully trust, Jaco headed for the Dutch island of Curaçao.

His French *Dépôt des Cartes et Plans de la Marin* for Aruba, Bonaire and Curaçao showed the water to deepen quickly off the south shore of each island. The soundings numbers suggested that a mile from the beach, the water was already deeper than the length of *Scorpion's* anchor hawsers.

Rather than trying to navigate the narrow channel known as Santa Anna Bay to the large harbor named Schottegat, the spot Jaco chose was under the guns of Fort Amsterdam less than a quarter mile from a small landing. The fort protected Willemstad, the largest city on the island. With the frigate safely anchored, Jaco hoped the sheltered water and good weather would make it easy for lighters to transport the logs Gaskins needed. In addition to replacing the cracked section of the mainmast and the split spars, he wanted to add to the spares stored in the hold.

Once the canvas shades were lashed in place, Jaco had Bosun Preston assemble the crew on the main deck, just forward of the quarterdeck. He would have preferred to stand amongst his sailors, but on the quarterdeck, the crew could see him and he could see all of them. "Lads, we are here in Curaçao, a Dutch held island, to buy logs to repair a cracked section of our mainmast and several spars. We will also purchase provisions. We should be here for about a week."

"Mr. Gaskins, Mr. Geiger and I will go ashore to purchase what we need. Once that is done, those who want to go ashore for a few hours will be allowed to do so. So you don't have to go begging for beer and ale, each man will be paid the wages he has earned since we left Kittery."

Jaco waited for the buzz to die down. Even though he was smiling, his next words were serious and somber. "However, there are some rules which you must obey..." What followed was a listing of his expectations that work on repairing the ship be carried out by those who have not gone ashore that day. *Scorpion,* he emphasized, had to be ready to weigh anchor and sail if a British warship appeared. Any sailor who returned so mauled that he could not stand watch would be fined. Jaco deliberately used a term his older brothers used to describe someone really drunk. Any fines or bail would be deducted from the sailor's wages and future prize money. Curaçao, Jaco emphasized, was a small island with a small community. Any *Scorpion* crew member who stayed behind would be easily found. Anyone who deserted, would, if found guilty, dangle from the yardarm.

"Besides drink, you will find all sorts of temptations in Willemstad, but I beg of you, avoid the schools of Venus and their pintle merchants. We do not have medicines on board that will cure the sauce." Solemn faces broke into smiles and those who were smiling at the thought of shore leave laughed at Jaco's slang for brothels, prostitutes and venereal diseases, which, they all knew, often led to syphilis and a premature, terrible death.

A Dutch officer was waiting on the small pier on the east side of Fort Amsterdam. He wanted to know if *Scorpion* needed powder and shot and how long the ship was planning to stay. Satisfied with Jaco's answer of no and about a week, he offered to recommend husbanding agents. Jaco declined, saying that he had the names of several and showed him an address on the letter he'd brought ashore. The Dutch Army officer gave Jaco directions, saluted and headed toward the embrasure that led into Fort Amsterdam.

Now that they were going into Willemstad, Jeffords cast off the line he was holding that kept the long boat equipped with a mast, mainsail and jib loose, to let one of the quartermaster mates sail the boat back to *Scorpion. Then h*e rejoined the three officers and the ship's carpenter. "Cap'n, have you been here before?"

"No, Mr. Jeffords, I have not. However, my father has contacts here who will help us. We need to find 9 Heerenstraat."

The narrow cobblestone street that was their destination was one street farther inland from Handelskade, which paralleled Santa Anna Bay. Number 9 Heerenstraat was a stone house with an orange tile roof, a copy of the houses found in Amsterdam. The business offices and storerooms were on the main floor, with the living quarters above.

Seeing a *mezuzah* on the upper right corner of the door, Jaco knew he had found the right place. He rapped twice. A small, wiry man with hair bleached by the sun opened the heavy door, made from thick planks of oak. Jaco guessed the man was about his father's age.

"*Wer ben je?"* Who are you?

Jaco recognized the Dutch language but didn't speak it. Instead, he responded in Spanish. Since the island had formerly been a Spanish colony, and the Spanish colony of Venezuela was only about 50 miles to the south, most islanders were fluent in both languages. "I am Jaco Jacinto, captain of the frigate *Scorpion*. My father Javier and my uncle Gento send their greetings and best wishes."

With those words, Jaco bowed his head slightly and held out the letter so Amadeo Toledo could take it.

"Please come in." Amadeo said, switching to the same language. He nodded to the four men standing a respectful distance behind their captain and added, "If those men are with you, please ask them to come in as well."

The Americans stepped into the front room. On one side, there was a large table and chairs. On the other, a desk and smaller tables were cluttered with rolls of paper.

"I apologize, but I do not have any refreshments ready to serve you.

Jaco waited until Amadeo read his father's letter. "Sir, your apology is unnecessary because we did not expect any food or drink. We came because we need to buy provisions, but most importantly, we need logs to replace a section of a mast and several spars. My father said you could lead us to honest vendors for material and provisions."

Amadeo smiled at the Jaco's rapid Spanish. "Your Spanish is much better than my English. Yes, I can take you to those storehouses that have quality supplies. But wood for spars and masts, I must warn you, is hard to get and expensive. The island has only one sawmill, and we must import logs from Venezuela."

Toledo, whom Jaco guessed was about his father's age, set a brisk pace along the narrow cobblestone streets.

"So, Captain Jacinto, how do you propose to pay for the logs?"

"I have English gold sovereigns and silver crowns and shillings."

Amadeo nodded sharply, "*Bueno*. And the wood needs to be dry, no?"

"Yes, yes of course."

Amadeo changed the subject. "You are Jewish, no?"

"I am."

"Then, if you have some time, I would like to take you to our synagogue. It is something to see. Jews came from Portugal and Spain via Amsterdam way back in 1634. Our building was built in 1651 and one of our Torahs was brought here from Amsterdam in 1659. Our congregation is known as Mikvé Emanuel-Israel."

"*Perfecto. Scorpion* has several Jewish crew members besides Lieutenant Geiger and myself. I will ask if they want to join us."

"Then I insist. There are about two thousand of us here. If the island wasn't so small and so far from where Moses wandered in the desert, Curaçao could be called The Promised Land."

The six of them were walking along what Jaco remembered was labeled Waaigat on his French chart. There was no bridge over the half-mile long, narrow bay, even the sawmill, with stacks of logs and men working with saws, was little more than a stone's throw across the water. Still, they had to walk around the Waaigat.

"And you have boats to get the wood out to your ship?"

"We are hoping the yard has a lighter." Jaco didn't want to have to sail *Scorpion* up the narrow Santa Anna Bay channel. He was afraid of running *Scorpion* aground on either side or being trapped in the bay by marauding Royal Navy frigates.

"They will want to charge you for its use."

"Are the prices negotiable?"

Toledo nodded emphatically. "Of course, this is Curaçao!"

"Who will get a better price, you or me?"

Amadeo laughed. "It matters more that they know you are going to pay in gold and silver coins than what you are going to buy or how you are going to get the logs to your ship. But do not pay the first asking price. We follow the old custom of haggling!"

Discussions with the owner of the lumber yard went quickly once Gaskins marked the logs he wanted with a piece of chalk. The owner of the yard looked at Jaco and then at

Amadeo before he asked how Jaco was going to pay for the wood. When he replied he was paying in silver shillings and gold pounds, the sawmill owner said. "£142."

Jaco looked at the owner of the sawmill and simply shook his head as he jingled the coins in the purse made from soft, blue velvet. Despite the sawing going on in a shed 25 feet behind the mill owner, the sound of gold and silver coins was loud enough to hear. "£50 for the wood and another £10 if your men can have the logs alongside my ship before dark today."

"£100 for the lot, including delivery to your ship tomorrow before dark."

Amadeo was stone faced, but his eyes flickered. Jaco took it as a signal to go up in price. He put the purse on the sawhorse and the coins rang their valuable tones again. "£70 for the logs and £10. All in gold and silver coins. Logs delivered by noon tomorrow."

"No paper money."

Jaco held up the purse and shook it so the coins clinked loudly. He didn't want to show how much money he had with him. "Yes. The coins are in here. Half now and half when the logs are hoisted on my ship and inspected to make sure they are the same ones marked by my carpenter. I will send a working party here to help prepare and move the logs."

The owner rubbed his chin with scarred hands. Resin, dirt and sawdust had accumulated over the years, black accents along the tips of his fingers. "Agreed." He stuck out his hand.

Back on *Scorpion,* Jaco sent a working party led by Gaskins directly to the sawmill to start preparing the logs. He had Bosun Preston pass the word that once the logs were on board, shore leave would commence. The most vexing concern was how many men to let go ashore at one time, and for how long.

Not counting the ship's officers, *Scorpion's* crew consisted of 190 men. Over dinner the evening before the frigate arrived in Curaçao, the debate over how many had bounced between 25 and 50 men. Logistics—they had to be sailed ashore in *Scorpion's* boats—and risk—potential of desertion – dictated that the number be closer to 25.

Time in port to make the repairs were estimated at four days, which mean to give every man a chance to go ashore suggested the number be 48. Shuttling that many men ashore in the ships boats would require two trips by the 18-foot long boats, which could each carry 12 passengers and a crew of two. The smaller 14-foot cutter could make a single run, depositing two officers.

As for how long they would allow men to stay ashore, instinct warned Jaco that the more time the men were ashore, the greater the chance of trouble. Everyone in the wardroom assumed a percentage would return drunk. Jaco ran his hand through his thick, coarse hair on the top of his head as he listened to the discussion. The 19-year-old in him wanted to allow the men to stay out as long as possible. His duty as captain of the Continental Navy frigate *Scorpion* wanted to minimize the time ashore, maybe even not let the men go. But he had committed to allowing shore leave and was not going to go back on his word.

As captain, the final decision was his. "Gentlemen, the crew must be at the landing by two bells into the first watch. At that time, we will have the boats waiting to shuttle those men who are at the landing back to *Scorpion*. By four bells, we should have brought on board all who returned from leave. Anyone not there will be considered to have missed muster. If there are missing sailors, all further shore leave will be canceled until the missing sailors are found. To bring them back, we will send a shore party ashore led by Mr. Garrison with Bosun Preston and several other sailors. Their orders are to bring the missing sailors back to *Scorpion,* in irons or tied if necessary. Once they are back on board, we will charge them under the Articles of War."

Hedley Garrison leaned across the table so he could look directly at his captain. "Sir, canceling shore leave for one miscreant who may have had too many tankards of ale or beer is very harsh. If we have several who miss muster, I understand, but for just one, I suggest you reconsider."

"Mr. Garrison, I take your point. However, we are a ship of war and need every man jack we have. We as officers have a responsibility to make good decisions. So do the members of the crew. I want them to police their own behavior. This way, if they take care of their shipmates, we will not have any Articles of War hearings. My decision stands."

Brandon Grantham reached to get his hand into the wooden bucket containing 190 small squares of sail cloth, of which 48 had a number. Sailors who wanted to go ashore that day stood in line to pull out a square. If the canvas had a number, then he was one of the lucky ones. Grantham's had number 32 written in ink.

His next step was to line up in front of a table and exchange his piece of numbered sail cloth for a silver Dutch guilder. As a seaman, he was entitled to a pay of $6.66 a month in Continental dollars. No one on board knew how to convert a Continental dollar to a guilder, but Jaco suspected that the silver coin was worth a lot more than the dollars, which was nearly worthless even in the country where they were printed. In Curaçao, he suspected the dollar had no value at all.

With the lucky 48 lined up along the bulwark, Jaco reminded them of the rules, that there was a large clock on a tower on the fort they could see from almost anywhere in Willemstad, and that, if they do not return to the landing by 9 p.m., they would be considered deserters.

Once ashore, Grantham and one of his close friends, fellow Bostonian Samuel Riddell, were in a group of eight men looking for a tavern. Twice along the way, two women came out of buildings, showing their ample bosoms and raising their skirts. Grantham dragged Riddell, who was five years younger than he, away by the arm. “Lad, you don’t want that. Those women are draggle tails who will scald you. Within days, your spindle will hurt every time you pee.” It was common knowledge on board *Scorpion* that prostitutes tended to spread sexually transmitted diseases.

They stopped outside the door of a tavern called Windlass and looked at each other. Some shook their heads but the majority said, “Let’s try it.” The three-story building was made from flat stones and covered with a planked wood roof; inside, a smell of cooking, tobacco, body odor and stale beer and ale greeted the sailors.

Like most bars in seaports, the staff spoke a smattering of many languages, including English. Curaçao was a frequent stopping place for ships bringing slaves and supplies to plantations throughout the English, French and Spanish held islands of the Caribbean. The English word beer is *bier* in German and Dutch, *bière* in French and *cerveza* in Spanish, so extensive language skills weren’t needed. After delivering their tankards of Dutch ale and beer, a young woman with large breasts, the tops of which were visible over her blouse, plunked herself onto Grantham’s lap and started stroking his thigh. Other women who wanted to sell their sexual services pushed themselves into position amongst the men. The men tried to ignore the women, who were gliding their hands all over their bodies. Grantham put his wooden tankard down, wiped the froth from his mouth with the back of his hand, and pushed the woman away. She resisted, but Grantham was insistent and used two hand to shift her off, saying, "I'm here to drink, that's all." There was no way he was going to let this woman touch him.

Irritated, the young woman l made a face. She stood in front of him with her hands on her hips. In excellent if accented English, she said, "You must be from the Urinal of the Planets."

Curious, Grantham answered, "Where, pray tell, is that?"

"Ireland."

He thought the attempt at an insult was amusing. Laughing, he said, "Aye, lass, I was born there, but my parents were smart enough to leave before we all drowned in the piss. Now, do us all a favor. Tell all the other game pullets like you to bugger off. We're here to have a drink, that is all."

One tankard and one tavern down, Grantham and his fellow sailors moved on. Outside, the bright sunshine hurt their eyes as they walked down Keukenstraat looking for a place to have another draft of ale or beer. A painted sign depicting a familiar shape beckoned. The tavern called was *De Bierpul,* or in English, The Tankard.

Inside the great room, smoke from the fire as well as tobacco hung from the ceiling, making it hard to see at first. Riddell pointed to a table in the back that was empty. He led the other seven sailors toward it single file.

Part way there, a burly man missing several front teeth shoved Riddell into the laps of two men sitting at a table, causing their tankards to spill their contents. Laughing, a third man reached across the table and emptied his tankard over Riddell's head.

With loud belch that sent his foul breath of stale tobacco and ale into Grantham's face, the aggressor pointed a dirty, pudgy finger at Grantham, who was pulling Riddell to his feet. "Your busboy friend is clumsy. He needs to buy my friends here a round to replace their spilled drinks."

The man's accent suggested he was from Scotland, so Grantham retorted, "The only clumsy person I see is someone from louse-land. From where I stand, *you* owe *my* friend a drink."

The Scotsman was unstable on his feet. He blinked twice as his brain processed Grantham's defiance, giving time for Riddell and the others to make their way to the table.

Theo Nutt, the number two, port side gun captain, leaned over the table and spoke to his shipmates. "I'd bet a glass of ale that Scotsman wants a fight."

Grantham shook his head. "We're not going to give him one. I for one don't want to feel the bosun's lash, nor do I want my prize money account made smaller by fines."

The others nodded in agreement.

Two women brought over eight tankards of fresh beer. One of them said, "Sirs, our beer was brewed yesterday right here in Curaçao, so it is fresh."

Scorpion's sailors nodded their thanks, and Grantham slid two stuiver coins (20 stuivers equalled 1 guilder) across the table. This was more than enough for the eight beers and a tip for the women.

The evil smelling hulk reappeared at the end of the table. He leaned on his hands as he leered at each of the sailors. He belched loudly. The men closest to him leaned back to get away from the stench. The woman tugged at his sleeve and said something in a language none of them understood. The Scotsman didn't even turn his head as he pushed her away.

All of the sailors stood up, but it was Grantham who said what they were all thinking. "That is no way to treaty a lady."

A bug jumped from the man's clothing onto the rough wood of the table. The man scratched his head and another louse fell onto the table. His foul body odor was causing all of the Americans' noses to twitch. "Her? She nary a lady, she's just laced mutton who wants to sit on your spindle for a few stuivers. I'll do what I want and no one to stop me."

"Laddie, I think we're done."

The eight sailors stood up and started walking towards the door. The Scotsman tried to block Grantham's path. "And where are you going?" He extended a muscled arm thick as a hawser. When Grantham tried to push the arm away, the man resisted and put his other hand on Grantham's shoulder. Seeing Nutt's foot behind the man's heel, Grantham pushed the Scotsman in the chest. He staggered back, lost his balance, and crashed to the floor. The eight men from the *Scorpion* picked up their tankards from the table and dumped them on the man's head.

Grantham leaned over, and said deliberately, "Do not touch me again. Next time, I won't be so ruddy nice."

* * *

The bells on the clock tower on the square outside the entrance to Fort Amsterdam tower rang eight times, and then once, signaling that it was 8:30 in the evening. Midshipman Josiah Marshall, who had gone ashore with the first boats, counted noses. Forty-five men were standing on the pier. Preston walked up and down the line of men to determine who was missing and if any of their mates knew where they might be in the small town of Willemstad.

Thirty minutes later, Lieutenant Geiger waited until the bells rang for the ninth time before he started counting heads. Still only forty-five sailors were there. He ordered Preston to start ferrying the men back. Each trip to *Scorpion* required about 20 minutes. Add in unloading, and the last sailors had an extra hour to return to the dock. Geiger was facing the town, hoping the missing men would appear as if by magic, when Seaman Grantham spoke up. "Begging the Lieutenant's pardon, sir, but I think I know where the men may be. It is a place called *De Bierpul,* and there's a rustyguts fellow from louse land, I mean Scotland, a-spoiling for a fight, and he has three mates with him. He'd tried to pick a fight, but we up and left. Mayhap another group wasn't so diplomatic."

Geiger could smell beer on his breath and tobacco smoke emanating from Grantham's clothing. "Mr. Grantham, tell me what happened."

The lieutenant listened attentively to Grantham's story. Nutt giggled when the Irishman described pouring beer all over the Scotsman's head. Geiger was alarmed at first, then he realized the man had used good judgement and defended himself without a fight. But the next *Scorpion's* sailors who visited *De Bierpul* might have had a rough time.

Given the man's previous hostility, Gieger wondered for a second if Grantham was trying to set him up for a fall. But there was a genuineness to the way he was talking, and there was also the enthusiastic nodding of both Nutt's and Riddell's heads. He looked at the three sailors, then looked for Bosun Preston. *Scorpion's* bosun was holding onto a line while one of the frigate's longboats was taking on its load of men. "Mr. Preston, I need Grantham and three men who are sober right now. Mr. Grantham believes he knows where his missing mates are. Give them the belaying pins from the box we brought ashore."

"Aye, sir. And I'll have the quartermaster pass the word to the captain that you are looking for three missing men. You think they are in some house of Corinth, sir?"

"No, Mr. Preston, Mr. Grantham thinks that some surly-boots Scotsman may have picked a fight. He tried before, with Grantham and his messmates, but they left before they got into a scrap."

Preston looked at the Irishman. "And you walked away from a fight, Mr. Grantham?"

"Aye, Bosun, I did. Captain Jacinto said if I caused any trouble, I'd meet your cat."

The bosun nodded. "That he did. I'm proud of you."

Morton Geiger tried not to make a face when he opened the door to *De Bierpul a*nd smoke and a stench of unwashed bodies mixed with stale beer and ale wafted over him. He took two steps into the tavern and the three men with him—Grantham, Hiram Berry and Enos Slipper—fanned out, two on each side. Geiger held a belaying pin behind his back as he let his eyes adjust to the dimly lit great room. Two pistols primed and at half cock were stuffed into his waistband.

One of four men at a table pointed at the newcomers and all turned around. Out of the corner of his mouth Grantham said, "The Scotsman is the big man with the beard."

Out of the murkiness, a woman appeared. "Gentlemen, there are several tables, pick one. What's your preference, beer or ale?"

Geiger looked at the woman. "Thank you, ma'am, but we're not here to drink. I believe three of my men may held here against their will."

The woman's eyes flashed and she bit her lip, but she didn't say anything.

Morton Geiger held the belaying pin behind his back, as did the other *Scorpion* seamen. "Ma'am, I want no trouble, just my three shipmates. Where are they?"

The woman stared at Geiger. She was about to say something when the big Scotsman pushed himself to his feet and lumbered over. The woman glared at him, "Silas Wallace, go sit down. I don't want no more trouble."

The Scotsman pushed the woman aside and poked Geiger hard with his index finger before looking over at Grantham. "So yer back, eh."

Grantham said nothing. Morton Geiger, who was probably outweighed by 70 pounds and considerably shorter, grabbed the man's index finger and bent it up and back. At the same time, he brought up the shaft of the belaying pin, made from good Maine oak, underneath Silas' chin. Then he pressed his hand down, keeping back pressure on the finger. His movement caused Silas Wallace to bend to his side to try to alleviate the pain and pressure. "Sir," the lieutenant said, "I am not here to fight, I am here to retrieve my men. Where are they?"

"Go bugger off before I make mice-feet of you."

Forcing himself not to react to the man's putrid breath, Geiger pushed up more with the belaying pin and pushed back on the finger; a little more back pressure would pop it out of joint. Wallace yelped. Geiger continued exerting pressure in opposite directions, jaw and finger joint. "Don't make me search this place or bring more men. If I do, it will end badly for you, Mr. Wallace. So again, where are my men?"

The woman tossed her head in the direction of the back of the tavern. "Out back."

"Show them, ma'am." Morton Geiger sent Hiram Berry and Enos Slipper to follow her. With two of Geiger's men gone, the men at the table started forward. All three had drawn long knives.

Grantham grabbed both of Lieutenant Geiger's pistols and aimed them. "Don't. Or two of you die."

The three men stopped and raised their hands. In a calm, cool voice, as if he'd done this a thousand times, Grantham said, "Be good lads and put the knives on the floor."

The three men did as they were told just as the door opened behind Grantham and Geiger. In walked Bosun Preston with more four sailors. "Sir," Preston called out, "do you need any help? I have another six outside."

Geiger bent Silas Wallace's finger back a bit more. The Scotsman gasped from the pain. "No, Mr. Preston, I have everything under control. Our missing men are out back."

Scorpion's bosun started to walk toward the doorway at the back of the tavern, but the woman appeared, helping along one of the missing sailors. His face was covered with dried blood. He was followed by the other two sailors, who also had blood on their torn clothes. Even in the dimly lit room, the bruises on the men's faces showed that they had been beaten badly.

Lieutenant Geiger waited until the injured sailors were helped out the door and only Grantham, Preston and he were still in the tavern. "Ma'am, we shall take our leave now. Thank you for your assistance."

With his free hand, he touched his fore and index fingers to his forehead. Then he bent back Wallace's finger until he felt it snap out of joint. Wallace jerked, wailing with pain. Morton Geiger grabbed a handful of Wallace's dirty hair and pulled his head back.

"Here's something to help a stupid mopus like you remember not to jack with the Continental Navy." Geiger brought his knee up sharply into Wallace's groin. The

Scotsman doubled over, gasping for breath as lighting bolts of pain jabbed into his brain from two places as it tried to figure out what hurt more, his hand or his crotch. Morton Gieger pushed him backwards and he fell, sprawling on the floor, holding his groin.

Shore leave resumed the next day, and no one in any of the taverns threatened a *Scorpion* crew member.

* * *

After four days anchored off Curaçao, *Scorpion,* with a new mast section and several new spars, headed northwest toward Jamaica, looking for prizes. Finding none, Jaco sailed nor' east by east through the Windward Passage, then nor' nor' west towards the Bahamas.

Rain, thunderstorms, low clouds and mist, along with variable but light winds, slowed *Scorpion's* progress. Under Jaco's bare feet, the oak deck, despite its grain, was cool and slippery. Everything—yards, rigging and sails—dripped water. *Scorpion* was barely making three knots.

Not being able to see the stars to take a sighting during the night meant that Jaco didn't know whether *Scorpion* was closer to Mayaguana, the southernmost island in the Bahamas, or North Caicos. Or, were they already in the Atlantic? If not, were they close to a reef? The only sounds were the water hissing by the hull, occasional groans from the rigging and masts, and the clacking of blocks as they swung loosely under slack sails.

Coupled with the lack of visibility, not knowing the ship's position made Jaco very nervous. They were navigating by dead reckoning, using their speed, course and time to estimate their location. However, currents and tides could have put them miles from where they thought they were. In the open ocean, this wasn't a problem. But not knowing where they were while working through an area with reefs and shoals, along with small islands that were only a few feet above the water, put a knot in Jaco's stomach.

He consoled himself with the thought that any other captain in the area was enduring the same weather. Still, rationalizing that other captains were in the same 'boat' didn't help. The fear of what he didn't know gnawed at his insides.

"It is as quiet as an empty church midweek." The voice was Jack Shelton's.

"Aye, Jack, but I am uneasy."

"We passed the word to the morning watch not to ring any bells, yell, or use the bosun's whistle. All the gun crews are by their cannon, and we have our best lookout up top—"

The distinct sound of a ship's bell ringing twice, a pause, and then twice more interrupted Jack Shelton's report. The mist absorbed the sound like a sponge, making it hard to discern anything more than the general direction of the sound's origin.

A lookout scampered down the foremast's ratlines and ran towards the officers. "Sir, Landry says a ship is two points off the starboard bow. He can't see the bloody thing, but he's been hearing noises and the bells gave him a rough bearing."

"Aye. Tell Landry to—"

A ship loomed out of the mist 100 yards off the starboard side, angling to cross *Scorpion's* bow at a 45-degree angle. If both ships continued on their present courses, they would collide. A strange voice, amplified buy a speaking trumpet, called out, "Ahoy there! This is *His Majesty's Frigate Jason*. What ship are you?"

Jaco spoke softly. "Have the starboard battery load ball and run out, quietly and quickly." His next command was to the quartermaster on duty. "Mr. Cooper, use what momentum we have to fall off to starboard. I want to pass behind this ship."

Jaco wanted to buy time and keep the Royal Navy frigate from raking the *Scorpion*. Using his own trumpet, he called out, "Say again, what ship are you?"

"*His Majesty's Ship Jason*, 32 guns. And you are?"

Scorpion began a slow turn to the right. The other ship's shape was grayed out by the mist and her off-white canvas sails were almost invisible, but the band with the gunports was a lighter shade than the hull. Jaco waited a few seconds until the first of the port battery's guns could target *Jason,* then he raised hand well above his head bellowed, "Continental Navy Frigate *Scorpion*, 22 guns."

He dropped his arm, which was the signal for Hedley Garrison, standing half out of the companion way, to give the order to fire. The first of *Scorpion's* long 12-pounders belched fire and smoke. *Jason* was less than 100 feet away.

The British captain had anticipated trouble. Flames from *Jason's* answering 12-pounders shone through the mist and light rain, but half its port battery no longer pointed at *Scorpion,* which was passing its stern quarter. The rest sent 12-pound balls thumping into *Scorpion's* hull at point blank range. Even so, the layers of oak, pine and oak did their job: none of the balls penetrated the gun deck.

On the main deck, however, one ball ripped through a rack of belaying pins mounted just aft of the mizzenmast, sending splinters all around. Another ball cut the ratlines leading up the foremast. A third ripped a chunk out the upper deck bulwark. And, because they were firing at an angle, one went through the pantry forward of the captain's cabin, destroying Jaco's bunk before shattering one of his cabin's windows as it exited.

Meanwhile, the higher velocity 12-pound balls of *Scorpion's* long twelves smashed into *Jason's* hull. Where they didn't penetrate, they sent spear-long splinters from the interior side of the planking hissing through the gun deck. As they reloaded their guns, *Scorpion's* sailors could hear the screams from *Jason's* wounded. Garrison came on deck briefly to get a better view and judge the range. "Sir," he said, "we're double-shotting the next round with ball and chain."

Jaco turned to his quartermaster. "Mr. Cooper, start coming to port so we can rake this fellow from the stern." Jaco didn't care if the men on *Jason* heard him; even if the Royal Navy ship turned, *Scorpion* would follow.

With the light winds and slow speed, the turn seemed to take forever. The fog, gun smoke and mist created a milky white curtain that occluded the larger ship, but there was only so far it could travel. As visibility slowly improved, it seemed that either *Jason* was rudderless or leaderless or both, because the ship had not attempted to turn. Jaco suddenly felt uneasy. *Why? What does* Jason*'s captain know that I don't?*"

Flame and smoke erupted from the number one port side cannon, then the number two. Before number three fired, Landry yelled down from the foremast. "Deck! There's a two-decker half a mile ahead, starboard side!"

That answers my question. Jaco turned to his First Lieutenant and quartermaster. "As soon as the last cannon fires, fall off to starboard and run south."

Suddenly, a large grey-black hulk loomed directly ahead. Its two rows of cannon were considerably heavier than those on *Scorpion*.

"Mr. Cooper, fall off to starboard, now!"

Bosun Preston had his sail handling crews ready on the main deck. *Scorpion* began to turn just as the two-decker started firing. Even at 500 yards, the ship's 24-pounders found their mark. One ball slammed through the beak. *Scorpion* shuddered and the figurehead dissolved into a cloud of splinters.

As *Scorpion* continued to turn, 18- and 24-pound balls from the two-decker pounded the frigate like giant sledgehammers. Those on the quarterdeck could feel the ship stagger from the impact of each ball. Not even the layered hull could withstand this punishment for very long. Splinters began to fly off the interior planking. Some of these shredded the hammocks hung in netting along the bulwarks; others found softer targets. Badly gored men were taken below by their crew mates.

The quarterdeck planking was also ripped apart, and Jaco felt an oak dagger embed itself in his arm and another stab his thigh. By the wheel, Morton Geiger was pulling shards of wood from his arm and side. There was a two-foot wide furrow in the planking where a 24-pound cannon ball had acted like a plow in a field. Splinters protruded from the little shelter where Cooper stood, making it resemble a hedgehog. Cooper was calmly steering *Scorpion* as if nothing were amiss. Frantically, Jaco looked around for Jack Shelton. Neither he nor a large section of the quarterdeck railing were to be seen. "Mr. Geiger! Find Mr. Shelton, if you will. If he is wounded, take him to the ship's surgeon." He pushed out of his mind the thought that the sailors might only find parts of his first lieutenant.

Scorpion's cannon on the port side kept firing. The loading drills and the practice were paying off. But *Scorpion* had only 11 guns on the port side that could bear. The two-decker had at least 20. Side by side, if the battle continued for any length of time, *Scorpion* would be reduced to matchsticks.

Then *Scorpion* was clear and aft of the two-decker. Jaco had the option of fleeing or.... "Mr. Cooper, bosun, bring us to port and across the stern!"

Bosun Preston raised an arm in acknowledgement, never interrupting the stream of orders he issued to get specific braces and sheets spliced and secured. One could tell the urgency of his commands by the amount of profanity that laced his orders.

Hedley Garrison came onto the main deck. "Sir, we're down to ten cannons on the port side. Number four gun was struck as it fired. The gun is a mess and so are at least a dozen men."

"Mr. Garrison, we are going to pass astern of this two-decker; you may fire as the cannon bear. We are going to give this two-decker a bloody nose and then fall off to starboard and put as much distance between ourselves and these ships as the wind and our sails allow in this damned weather."

Then....

"Deck! A third frigate astern of us, five hundred yards away!"

Jaco looked aft and saw nothing. "Where away?"

"Two points aft of the starboard quarter."

Jaco peered through the light rain and mist. The ghostly shape of another frigate, about the same size as *Jason,* was barely visible. Five hundred yards was close to the maximum effective range of a British 12-pounder. *I'll take that risk and hope we can escape. I do not want to continue to trade broadsides with a two decker on our tail!*

Scorpion's guns fired in turn, each of the ten balls went through the stern cabin of *H.M.S. Stirling Cross* in passing, and then *Scorpion* was past the two-decker. The mystery frigate started firing. Most of its balls either hit the water, skipping past *Scorpion,* or popped through its sails. Jaco heard one crash into his cabin below his feet.

And then there was quiet, deathly quiet, with only the sounds of *Scorpion* hissing through the water and the wind through the rigging. The Western Atlantic was ahead of *Scorpion,* and Jaco was desperate to find out what had happened to Jack Shelton.

14
LICKING WOUNDS

Western Atlantic, fourth week of April 1789

Jaco went down to the surgeon's cockpit to see if Shelton had been brought below to what was known as "the surgeon's cockpit". Jaco saw a bucket of sea water next to Dr. Ferguson's table, used to clean his instruments. Between patients, the bucket was dumped over the side and refilled. The fresh sea water was then laced with rum Jaco had authorized the surgeon to keep in his compartment, in keeping with Reyna's recommendations. Dr. Alden Ferguson, a graduate of the University of Edinburgh's School of Medicine, agreed with Reyna's suggestions and said he would do his best to follow her research. Dr. Ferguson was open to Reyna's ideas about cleanliness, but what he could do in the confines of the orlop deck was limited. Still, he had additional bottles of rum for use in cleaning wounds before stitching and after. Very few of the splinter wounds Ferguson had treated on *Scorpion* had become infected.

So far, the butcher's bill was seven killed, five seriously wounded, and 13 more with splinter wounds that might mend. One man, Jack Shelton, was missing.

The only conclusion Jaco could reach was that his friend and first lieutenant had been blown over the side. If Jack had been wounded and bleeding when he landed in the water, either sharks would make a meal of him, or he was slowly dying of thirst as he floated. Both were terrible ways to die.

Losing Jack—close friend, confidant, and his second in command—was a blow to Jaco's confidence and psyche. His loss was a terrible price to pay for escaping the three Royal Navy ships.

There was, he reminded himself, an outside chance that Jack might have been picked up by the British, or come ashore on the North Caicos Island, just south of the battle. But much as he wanted to go back and search, Jaco knew that if he did, *Scorpion* would run into *Stirling Cross* and its two escorts. His priority and duty to his crew were clear. Grimly, deep inside, Jaco knew if he had been blown overboard, he would expect his first lieutenant to assume command and get *Scorpion* safely away —even if it meant leaving him to drown.

The last seriously wounded man succumbed two days after the skirmish. The sails set so *Scorpion* was barely moving, Jaco read the burial service. The only other sound was the wind whispering through the rigging, as if the ship was paying respect to the dead. The weighted, canvass burial shroud was sent on its way to the bottom. There was a somberness to the men as they slowly went back to duties that reflected Jaco's own mood. This last funeral was the event that finally forced Jaco to accept Jack's death.

His friend was gone and was not coming back. Jack's death hammered the cost of the war home. Jaco would remember the good times they had together, but for the rest of his life there would be an empty place.

Jaco followed Hedley Garrison's suggestions on how the diminished gun crews should be reorganized, and who should be promoted. Once these changes were noted in the ship's log, he wrote that Hedley Garrison was now *Scorpion's* First Lieutenant and Morton Geiger was promoted to Second Lieutenant. The log entry stated that until Josiah Marshall passed his lieutenant's exam, Jaco could only make him the ship's acting third lieutenant.

North Caicos Island, fourth week of April 1789

Jack Shelton watched *Scorpion* sail out of sight, leaving him alone in the sea. One minute he had been standing at the aft end of *Scorpion's* quarterdeck, and the next he'd been flying through the air. He'd had a few brief seconds to be terrified before he smacked into the water awkwardly on his back. The impact took his breath away, but he stayed on the surface. He struggled to unbuckle his sword belt and let the pistols sink to the bottom. He felt like a pin cushion with all the splinters that had pierced his body, and the salty water stung.

A large plank, which he could tell by its paint was from *Scorpion,* floated by. Once he managed to get upon the board without being dumped back into the ocean, Jack pulled the splinters out one by one.

There was nothing Jack could do until the mist cleared. Based on what he remembered from looking at the chart before the battle began, the North Caicos Island was about a mile to the south. Until he could see the sun, he had no idea in which direction to paddle.

Jack alternated between sitting on the board with his legs dangling into the water and laying on his stomach. When the mist cleared, he found himself less than a half a mile from the shore of an island. With measured strokes, Jack paddled into the surf and then, when the water was only up to his waist, waded ashore. Less than 100 feet inland, Shelton found a small shack made from planks of driftwood at the edge of a cleared area shaded by a mix of pine and palm trees. Inside, he found a machete, several wooden bowls and plates, and an iron pot. More driftwood planks served as bed, table and workbench.

Late in the evening the rain returned and poured down. Parch-throated, Jack laid out the bowls to collect water and drank from them as fast as they filled up. The sweet water had a slightly salty taste but it quenched his thirst. Before he stretched out on the plank bed, he knelt and prayed, thanking God that he had been spared and asking that *Scorpion* and its crew be kept safe.

Jack awoke to the sound of heavy rain. Hungry, he walked out of the shack and a few yards away, he found coconuts on the ground. Using the machete, he cracked them open and drank the sweet liquid, then hacked them into chunks to eat.

Day three brought sunshine and a chance to explore. Following the white sand beach to the west, Jack found a small inlet across which was another island. In the afternoon, after another meal of raw coconut, he headed east and came across a shallow pond of very, very salty water. On the far side, Jack saw several donkeys. The shore at the far end of the pond was encrusted with salt.

"And who may you be?"

Jack spun around. A black-skinned man stood with hands near his weapons, a pistol stuffed in his sword belt and a cutlass.

"Jack, Jack Shelton." He was keenly aware of the machete held at his own side.

"You speak like an Englishman. Where be you from? Bermuda or the Bahamas?"

"Neither. I'm from Connecticut."

"Where be Connecticut?"

"Connecticut is a British colony in North America."

"One of them that's rebelling?"

"Aye, 'tis."

"How did you come here?"

"I was blown overboard."

"During that battle I heard a few days back."

Jack nodded.

"You want to leave this island."

Jack took the statement as a question. "I do."

"Do you know where you are?"

"North Caicos, I think."

The man nodded slightly and started forward. "The name's Ezra. I rake and bag the salt here. When I have enough, I take the bags to a town on another island called Providenciales. There I sell the salt to ships' captains. If you'll help me load my boat, I'll take you over. Perhaps you'll find a ship that can take you north."

"It would be my pleasure to help."

They shook hands.

Central Caribbean, first week of May 1789

Smythe's squadron swept south from Virginia, past Charleston, Savannah and into the Straits of Florida. Still no *Scorpion.* As they headed east, paralleling the north coast of Hispaniola, the clouds become thicker and darker. At the south end of the strait that separated Puerto Rico and Hispaniola, Smythe had Ned Jernigan run up the signals for "Remain within one mile, reduce sail as flagship does for the night." In the back of his mind was Drew Rathburn's tale of when *H.M.S. Temptress* was caught in a hurricane. Drew had been one of only five survivors.

That night, the edge of a spring storm was enough to pelt them with rain, buffet them with gusty winds and pound them with high seas. Lightning lit up the sky and thunder cracked like cannon. The rain was so heavy that at times the water on deck was ankle-deep.

When day broke, Smythe was relieved he still had a squadron of three ships, bobbling like corks in the 12-foot seas. Overhead and to the north, the sky was dark gray. They could see the lighting and hear the faint rumble of thunder. Gusty winds caused masts and yards to groan and strain. As much as Darren wanted to go faster, adding more sail increased the risk of losing a mast, or worse, losing sailors over the side.

The ship's stove had been doused, and the men only had hardtack dipped in rum, along with dried meat the rebels called jerky to go with their ration of beer. They'd picked up several barrels of the dried, smoked meat for each ship when they re-provisioned in Nassau.

Darren started a crew working the pumps to empty the bilges of a foot-and-a-half of water. He was exhausted. Now that the weather was abating, he wanted to go to his cabin to dry off and get some sleep.

That plan sank when the three ships were hit by a strong gust that broke *Gladius's* mizzenmast. One minute the mast was there; then a loud crack and the popping of stays, and it hung for a few seconds until the yardarm for the royal sail crashed onto the quarterdeck, narrowly missing the helmsman. The top section of the mainmast followed.

Bosun Louttit appeared, axe in hand, along with five other sailors. They began hacking away at the sheets, lines and braces that covered the deck. The soggy mizzen mainsail was rolled and lashed to a bulwark.

Worried that *Gladius* was not the only ship damaged by the sudden gust, Darren used his spyglass to check the others. *Hasta* was down to parts of its fore and mainmasts, but its mizzen appeared to be intact. He looked at *Pilum* just in time to see the frigate's foremast come crashing down. A steady exchange of signals informed him that no lives had been lost, but all needed to make port for repairs. Sailing at a cautious four knots, Darren estimated they could reach Port Royal in six days.

When the sun came out, Louttit rigged lines for the crew to dry their clothes. Exhausted, Darren relinquished the quarterdeck. "Mr. Soames, signal the squadron that new course is west nor' west. Destination Port Royal. Maintain V formation."

Western Atlantic, second week of May 1779

Jaco stood on the quarterdeck, looking aft. The new, unpainted planks under his feet were a daily reminder of the loss of one of his closest friends. Each time he turned away from the repaired railing, he would say softly, "Jack, wherever you are, God bless. I miss you."

The action with *Jason* and *Stirling Cross* had cost *Scorpion* Jack and members of its crew, the first to die under his command. Their losses weighed heavily on his mind. The good news was that the remaining injured men were recovering and would be fit for duty in a week or two.

Despite their best efforts at repairs, *Scorpion* was wounded, not mortally, but his best course of action was to get her to the shipyard where she'd been born and where she could be rebuilt. Large dents on the outside of the hull, made by 18- and 24-pound cannon balls, were easy to see by leaning over the gunwales. On the inside, in the berthing and gun decks, the ship's planking was split in many places. He could see cracks in several ribs that Gaskins said would hold until the returned to Kittery, but he'd not trust to weather any storm. Jaco levered one potential splinter out of a plank on the gun deck that was over a foot long and took it to his cabin as a reminder of what large cannon balls could do, even to *Scorpion*. Two of the large balls had hit just outside a gunport and had smashed two supporting ribs. Gaskins pegged a splice in place, but Jaco doubted the repair would survive another hit by an 18- or 24- pounder. The most visible damage was to the beak, most of which had been carried away. They were lucky the bowsprit hadn't collapsed, breaking the stays for the foremast's royal, topgallant and topsails. Had that happened, *Scorpion* would not have gotten away.

Jaco ordered a course toward Kittery, 1,000 nautical miles to the nor' nor' west and into the prevailing wind. At seven knots, the zig-zag course *Scorpion* would take meant the trip would take 14 or 15 days. That night, he wrote in his journal.

> *This has not been the cruise I thought we would have. We have taken no prizes, and while we inflicted damage to* <u>Stirling Cross</u> *and one escort, we lost men in the exchange of fire. Worse, I lost Jack, my confidant and good friend, and I miss him. And, I believe, the crew will miss him too. On the quarterdeck, I keep wanting to say something to him, and then realize, he is gone. I can't help feeling foolish, but I guess that shows how much I miss him. I feel terrible that I often took Jack's wise counsel and cheerful demeanor for granted.*
>
> *Nonetheless, I take heart in that the Royal Navy knew* <u>Scorpion</u> *was about and felt her sting.*

Port Royal, first week of June 1779

When *Gladius, Pilum* and *Hasta* glided up the channel, the only ships in the harbor were a two-decker named *Stirling Cross* and the frigate *Jason*. Both were missing masts, and their damage showed they'd been in a fight. Once his squadron was riding at anchor, Darren signaled, "Captains ashore."

Darren was hot, itchy and uncomfortable as he waited for the two other captains' cutters. This was the first time since his meeting with Admiral Collier that he'd worn a uniform. Since the two other officers had never been to Port Royal, Smythe led the way toward the brick building that was base headquarters. The sun, still low in the sky, exaggerated their shadows: small—Meegan; medium—Smythe; and tall—Taylor.

The three were ushered into Captain Owen Bewley's office on the third floor. The port captain was a sprightly man despite the injuries he'd suffered during a naval battle in the Bay of Biscay in April 1758. The most visible were the splinter scars on his face. After Smythe introduced his captains, Bewley addressed Smythe. "So, Commodore, what can Port Royal do for you?"

"Sir, my squadron needs priority in getting back to sea. That means men to repair our ships, provisions, and logs for masts."

Bewley pursed his lips and rocked on his toes. "Given there's a two-decker and a frigate in the harbor, both of whose captains are senior to you, that's a tall order."

"Sir, did you not receive the letter from the First Sea Lord instructing you to give my squadron priority?"

"Ahhhh, *that* letter. Yes. Still you're going to have to wait. The base is a bloody shambles. We're short on everything:

planking, logs for masts and spars, cordage. You name the item and we don't have enough. Bloody supply ships have been diverted or are late. All the bases at this end of the world are short. What's all this urgency of yours about, anyway?"

"We're pursuing a rebel ship called *Scorpion* that has been especially troublesome. My mission is to sink or capture the frigate."

"Aha! *Stirling Cross* and *Jason* ran across *Scorpion* off North Caicos just two weeks ago. You might want to talk to their captains. However, my best guess is that a month will pass before we have the necessary wood to fix your ships. Sorry, but that's the ruddy truth."

Off the east coast of North America,
second week of June 1779

In the small port on Providenciales, Ezra introduced Jack Shelton to Captain Lucius Brandon, the owner of the British merchant ship *Dori Anne* whose hold was now filled with bags of salt. Brandon was glad to welcome aboard anyone who could use a sextant to navigate, and he didn't ask questions about Shelton's background other than what he knew about sailing and navigating. The deal they struck was that when *Dori Anne* reached New York, Captain Brandon would pay him £25 and Jack Shelton would walk ashore. Brandon let Shelton go through the ship's slop chest and take what clothes he wanted. After some cutting and sewing, Jack had two pairs of pants and two shirts that fit.

Every day when Jack Shelton stood on the deck of the *Dori Anne*, his stomach tightened as he studied the three Royal Navy ships—two frigates and a sloop of war—escorting their convoy of 11 merchant ships. To pass the time, he imagined that he was still on *Scorpion* and what he or Jaco would do to capture the merchant ships and harry their escorts. The sobering thought was that if any of the Royal Navy captains discovered that a Continental Navy lieutenant was on the *Dori Anne*, Jack would be pulled off and imprisoned.

Kittery, fourth week of June 1779

As much as he wanted to take leave and sail immediately to Charleston, Jaco stayed in Kittery until *Scorpion* was hauled out of the water. Hackett and several of his shipwrights had already conducted a thorough inspection of the inside; now was the time to check the outside.

The scaffolding built alongside *Scorpion* allowed Jaco a different view of the damage, which was more extensive than he had realized. The dents from the 18- and 24-pound balls were much deeper than those left by 12- and 9-pounders. Where the heavier balls hit, the outer planks were loose and would, over time, break off.

There was, in Hackett's words, much work to be done. The yard needed at least a month before the ship would be ready for sea. After Hackett finished, Jaco wrote in his log and then his journal that *Scorpion* would not be ready for sea until mid-July.

Chapter 15
DUEL ASHORE

Boston, fourth week of June 1779

The first evening Jaco was in Kittery, he penned a letter to Jack Shelton's parents, explaining how Jack had been blown overboard and lost, and saying how sorry he was. Frustrated because the words didn't seem right, he balled up several sheets before he had something that he hoped conveyed the right message.

A letter from the Continental Congress solved Jaco's problem as to where to house the crew. The note, signed by John Adams, the chairman of the Marine Committee, ordered Jaco to pay off the crew and tell them to return the first week of January 1780 because the Continental Congress simply didn't have enough money to pay for the repairs, re-provision the ship and send the crew to sea. Money in hand, the crew dispersed to homes, packets, or inns. Jaco accepted Morton Geiger's invitation to spend the weekend with his family in Boston before he took the packet to Philadelphia.

Abraham Geiger had arrived from Vienna in 1750 when he was 23 years old, after working in the court of the Holy Roman Empire, where generations of his family had helped finance the monarchy headquartered in Vienna. In the new world, he lent money for crops, ships, and new buildings at lower rates than the Boston banks. He was now loaning money to the Continental Congress to pay for the war.

The sun was out and the temperature was in the seventies, so after lunch Abraham Geiger suggested the family take a walk along the Charles River. They were not the only Bostonians out on Sunday in the nice June weather. A breeze from the west was blowing the pungent smell of drying, salted fish out to sea, so all that was in the air was the distinctive odor of a fresh-water river turning brackish before emptying into the sea. The Charles River was far more agreeable to the senses than the stench that emanated from Philadelphia's Delaware River.

Jaco was in the midst of a discussion with the head of the Geiger family when four young men blocked their path. One of them was Edmund Radcliffe, who pointed his cane at Jaco and announced, "Jacinto! I see you are now in bed with Boston's most infamous moneylender. Is he borrowing from you, or are you borrowing from him?"

Surprised by the sarcastic and disrespectful tone of Radcliffe's voice, Abraham Geiger turned to Jaco. "Do you know this man?"

"Aye, I do. Edmund Radcliffe. He was cashiered out of the navy for planning a mutiny."

Geiger addressed the man confronting his guest. "Mr. Radcliffe, I know your father and your family. He would not approve of your disrespectful behavior."

Radcliffe ignored the older man and tapped the tip of his cane against Jaco' chest. "Still unnecessarily risking your sailor's lives and taking their prize money, I see."

Jaco pushed the cane to the side and stepped closer. The smell of whiskey on Radcliffe's breath was strong. "Radcliffe, don't be chuffy. Go back to the tavern whence you came."

Radcliffe sneered. He hated his former commanding officer with a passion. "Are your sea-going decisions still driven by that hussy in Charleston named Reyna?"

Eyes narrowing and his pulse racing, Jaco ignored the chortles of Radcliffe's friends. He wanted to hit Radcliffe but controlled his growing anger. His tone was cold when he spoke. "What did you call Reyna?"

"I believe I used the word *hussy*, but...." Radcliffe turned to his friends, who were enjoying the repartee. "I think *game pullet* would be more appropriate. But then, what hold does a woman have over a captain who chooses Charleston as his port of choice when it is threatened by the British? Maybe *witch* would be the right word. Or maybe you run a hen-frigate."

Radcliff was obviously trying to provoke Jaco with another slur about his judgement and his relationship with Reyna, whom he had just called a whore. The Bostonian was a head taller, but Jaco got close to Radcliffe so he could whisper, "Don't provoke me, Edmund. The fact that you were not tried doesn't mean the charges have gone away."

Abraham Geiger put his hand on Jaco's shoulder. "Let us go. This man is not worth our time."

"You are correct, sir. He is not worth anything as a naval officer or as a man or even as a son. Even his father won't hire him."

Those last words stung harder than anything else Jaco had said. Edmund grabbed Jaco's shoulder. "What do you mean by that, Jacinto?" he snarled.

"Exactly what I said. You are not worth anything and you have no one to blame but yourself for your reprehensible reputation and lost prize money."

"*Your* testimony ruined my reputation!"

"Rot! You know that's a lie laid on with a trowel. I gave a factual account of your actions. You are not worth the powder to blow you to your Christian hell, which is where you belong. Now leave us alone."

The cane swept up to bar Jaco's path. "Jacinto! I demand satisfaction. You just called me a liar!"

"Mr. Radscliffe, are you challenging me to a duel?"

"Aye, that I am."

"Are you sure? You could lose more than you already have."

"I thought you Soooutherners loved duels," Radcliffe drawled the word, turning it into an insult. His face, formerly flushed, had gone white with rage.

"I hate duels and have never fought one, but for you, Edmund Radcliffe, I will make an exception. Since you are challenging me, the rules say I pick the weapon, time, place and results that determine the winner. So, I choose swords, tomorrow, noon, first blood. There's a stand of woods that surround a small field on the Newberry Pike about three miles north of Boston on the way to Portsmouth, New Hampshire. The field is just south of a tavern on the edge John Pike's farm. Bring your second and a doctor."

Radcliffe and his friends hurried off leaving a stunned Geiger family. Abraham Geiger spoke first. "Jaco, you don't have to do this. We can just pay him some money and he will go away."

"No, Mr. Geiger, money won't satisfy him. Edmund Radcliffe tried to take over my ship. He went so far as telling the swivel gun crews on the mizzenmast that in an action with a Royal Navy ship to fire at *Scorpion's* quarterdeck to kill Jack Shelton and me. So this is very, very personal. If you are interested, tonight I will tell you the whole sordid story. The sad part is that no one in Congress wanted to try him because they were afraid hanging Radcliffe would alienate powerful supporters of our rebellion here in Boston."

The elder Geiger persisted. "Jaco, I cannot let him kill you."

"He won't, but he'll try. I will find a way to win."

Abraham Geiger put his hand on Jaco's shoulder. "My sons and I will be there as your seconds and to prevent any mischief by Mr. Radcliffe's friends. I don't like the looks of them and, I suspect, neither do you."

* * *

Jaco and Morton left the Geiger's house shortly after sunrise to arrive early, to make sure that Radcliffe didn't position a sharpshooter in the woods that bordered the field on two sides. Jaco told Morton, as they were walking the field, that he believed Radcliffe meant to kill him. Jaco was sweating in the humid air and guessed the temperature had already risen into the upper 70s. The Geigers and several of their friends arrived ahead of Radcliffe's party, which included a physician. The formalities were observed, and the duelists positioned themselves.

As a young man, Jaco had learned how to use a sword, knife and a tomahawk from his father who emphasized three rules:

1. Start by being defensive to keep from getting killed and to gauge your opponent's skill.

2. Feign or make attacks, or your opponent will think you are scared.

3. Force your opponent to take risks that give you openings to strike.

Those words ran through his mind as he stood with the tip of his sword resting gently on the ground by his right foot. The well-balanced 81-year-old sword, made in Germany in 1698, had sharp edges on both sides and a sharp tip for thrusting. His grandfather had brought the weapon to South Carolina and his father had carried it during the French and Indian War. When he'd become a midshipman, his father had given the sword to him, and it had served him well during the boarding action that took *H.M.S. Coburg*.

Five paces away, Edmund Radcliffe slashed a long rapier back and forth, its tip hissing in the humid air. Off to the side of the field, the horses that pulled the carriages snorted nervously, sensing the tension in the air. Radcliffe's friends stood in a group, making bets on how long the duel would last, and whether or not their friend, a skilled swordsman, would strike a deadly blow. One man held an expensive Josiah Emery pocket watch, imported from London, to time the duel.

The Geigers and their friends stood apart from Radcliffe's noisy minions. They were far more sober and quiet. Abraham Geiger's gaze shifted back and forth from those who came to support Radcliffe and the duelers.

Radcliffe's second stood halfway between the two principals, holding a handkerchief in the air. He looked at both men and cried aloud, "First blood and both stop. Mr. Jacinto, if you draw first blood, you declare if you are satisfied or if you wish to continue. Mr. Radcliffe, if you draw first blood, the duel is over. Please confirm."

Both said they understood. Opposite Radcliffe's second, Morton Geiger also stated his understanding of the terms. The cloth was released, signaling the duel was to begin.

Jaco let his center of gravity settle and kept his left hand out to the side for balance. Radcliffe grinned as he strode forward, swinging the rapier so the tip made a menacing circle. He wanted Jaco to focus on the sword tip rather than his moves. A flick of Jaco's right wrist and his sword clanged against the rapier, batting the long, thin blade to the side. Radcliffe smiled confidently and brought the sword up, writing an 's' before he made small circle in the air between the two men.

Again, Jacinto batted the rapier away, this time with more force as if to say, *Show me what you have.* Jaco stepped to his left to force Radcliffe to move and possibly frustrate his planned move. Radcliffe kept his left hand behind his back in traditional fencing position as he tracked Jaco. *Radcliffe, this is not a fencing match, this is a sword fight in which one of us could get killed.*

The smile on Edmund Radcliffe's face changed to a snarl as he lunged forward. Their swords clanged as the thrusting and parrying went on for what, to Morton Geiger, seemed an eternity.

Both men stepped back and studied each other. Their chests were heaving. Sweat flowed down Jaco's back, causing his linen shirt to cling. Several times, Jaco had deliberately allowed an opening where Radcliffe could have scored a minor blow; each time, Radcliffe had tried instead for a killing thrust and Jaco had parried the deadly strike. The hate that filled Radcliffe's eyes meant that Radcliffe wanted to run his rapier through his body, not cut him. Just as deliberately, Radcliffe had blocked every attempt Jaco made to strike a superficial cut that would give him grounds to call satisfaction. This was, Jaco realized, not a duel of honor, but a fight to the death. Fear gnawed in his gut.

Radcliffe lunged forward with the tip of his rapier targeted at Jaco's right side. Jaco parried the thrust, forcing the rapier wide, opening up Radcliffe to a thrust at his mid-section. Sensing his vulnerability, the Bostonian retreated before Jaco could strike.

Sensing he might have the initiative, Jaco took several steps forward with the sword pointed at Radcliffe, who retreated. Jaco feinted a lunge at Radcliffe's torso and then, at the last second, flicked the tip of his sword up. Jaco didn't feel the resistance of blade on flesh, but he saw the result. Radcliffe's white sleeve was split and bloody.

As per the rules, he stepped back and lowered his sword, waiting for Radcliffe to do the same according to the agreed upon terms. He'd drawn first blood. He faced Radcliffe's second. "I'm satisfied. There is no need to continue. The duel is over."

Radcliffe glared at Jaco as a doctor examined the minor laceration. "The duel is over when I say it is over, you bloody Jew bastard." He drew a short sword from a scabbard on his second's sword belt and, a blade in each hand, charged at Jaco.

Stepping back, Jaco's eyes darted from one blade to the other and then to Radcliffe's face, contorted with anger and hate. In a furious exchange of thrusts, parries, and counter thrusts, Jaco managed to avoid being cut. With only one weapon to Radcliffe's two, he was at a disadvantage.

"Morton! get my tomahawk from my saddlebag!" he managed to shout.

Jaco retreated each time Radcliffe came at him, careful to stay away from Radcliffe's cheering friends because he suspected they would trip or hold him so that Radcliffe could deliver a killing strike. Radcliffe tried to box him in so that his back was to his bloodthirsty friends. Jaco ducked under several thrusts by the rapier and moved back into the field.

Then Morton Geiger reappeared, holding not only Jaco's tomahawk but a pistol, which he pointed at Radcliffe's chest. The young man said, "The duel is over. My principal has said he is satisfied."

Radcliffe sneered at the young naval officer. "This duel is over when I say it is, and that is when this jackanapes is dead!" He started to move toward Jaco, but Geiger got between the two men and pressed pistol against Radcliffe's chest, stopped him in his tracks.

Geiger held out the tomahawk so that his captain could seize it. "Now you both have two weapons. That should even up the fight." Morton stepped back and to the side.

Jaco now had a weapon he could throw as well as use to parry, strike and slash. The break had also given Jaco a chance to size up Radcliffe's friends. He was sure they wanted to see him lying on the grass, mortally wounded; if they sensed Radcliffe was losing, they might take matters into their own hands.

What Jaco didn't see was that Abraham Geiger and his two other sons had drawn pistols. They'd come armed, suspecting treachery. And treachery is what they now saw. One of the bravos, the one who had bet his friend would kill the South Carolinian captain, started to moved towards Jaco from behind. Seeing this, the three Geigers aimed their pistols at Radcliffe's friends. The bravo halted, then retreated, rejoining the others.

Another clash of swords and Jaco felt the tip of the rapier cut his left side. He ignored the pain and the blood leaking onto his shirt. *So, now we are even.*

Sensing an opening, Radcliffe charged again. When Jaco parried with his sword, he lunged forward, trying to stab Jaco with the short sword. Radcliffe didn't anticipate Jaco's slash with the tomahawk that hit Radcliffe's left arm halfway between his elbow and wrist. The sharp wide blade slid down Radcliffe's ulna bone, slicing muscle and tendon until the steel reached the scaphoid bone. When Jaco yanked the tomahawk back, Radcliffe's hand was hanging by a few tendons. Radcliffe stared at the blood gushing from what was left of his arm and then looked at Jaco. His face was a mix of rage, pain and shock.

The doctor rushed forward screaming, "Stop! *Stop!*" He tied a bandage around Radcliffe's left arm, just below the elbow, to stop him from bleeding to death.

Radcliffe's friends half led, half carried him to the steps of the doctor's carriage. He was given a shot of whiskey and some opium to drink before the doctor strapped a dowel in Radcliffe's mouth.

On the other side of the field, Jaco could hear Radcliffe's screams as the doctor finished what his tomahawk had started. It took nearly twenty minutes, not because the doctor worked slowly, but because Edmund kept thrashing about. When the work was done and the limb bandaged, Radcliffe's left arm ended six inches below the elbow.

But while this was going on, Radcliffe's second walked over to where Jaco and the Geigers were standing. "Captain Jacinto," he said quietly, "thank you for not killing my friend. You had every right to do so, when he attacked after you declared yourself satisfied. As far as my side is concerned, the matter is closed, and I will insist that Mr. Radcliffe respects the results."

Abraham Geiger nodded approval, and his sons relaxed.

"Sir," Jaco replied, "I, too, consider the matter closed. Mr. Radcliffe will now have to live with the consequences of his anger and pride for the rest of his life. I wish him a speedy recovery and hope this is the last of his mistakes in judgement."

Back in the Geiger's home, Jaco asked for a glass of whiskey. This he used, as Reyna had taught him, to wash the cut on his side. The wound was not deep enough to require stitches, so he tied a clean bandage that had been boiled in water, again as Reyna had taught him, around his waist. That night he could not sleep; his brain kept replaying his moves and countermoves of the afternoon.

* * *

Two days later, when he was waiting to board the packet that would take him to Philadelphia, *Alacrity's* captain handed him two letters. One was from Reyna. The handwriting on the other looked familiar, but he couldn't think whose it might be. He decided to read the letter from the unknown person first. Later, he would devour the one from Reyna. He popped open the beeswax seal and unfolded the paper.

My dear friend,

I hope you have not been to distraught on my behalf. After I was blown over the side and Scorpion escaped into the Atlantic,_I made an escape of my own. By the grace of God, I reached the shore of North Caicos. There I met a man who helped me sign on board a ship bound for New York—a British ship, mind you—and one that joined a convoy escorted by the Royal Navy. As you can imagine, I gave no indication of my rank while on board.

In New York, I bought a horse and rode to Philadelphia, where I knocked on your father's door. To make a long story short, I now am an employee, albeit a poorly paid one, of the Continental Congress' Marine Committee. I help the committee select and promote officers while Mr. Adams and Mr. Hopkins specify what types of ships we need.

You, sir, will remain captain of Scorpion as long as you choose to take the frigate to sea. There is no better man to do that. God speed, my good friend, and good luck.

When we are free from the British yoke, you and I can grow old together and tell stories about the history we made.

Very respectfully, your friend and former 1LT,
Jack Shelton

Jaco let the letter drop and jumped up, whooping "Hooray!" For a little longer Reyna's letter would have to wait. He wanted to down a celebratory drink.

CHAPTER 16
DUELS AT SEA

Philadelphia, first week of August 1779

With *Scorpion* in the hands of the builder, there was the question of cost. Hackett wanted assurance that the Continental Congress would pay him for the work, which would consume time and resources, in English pounds. Jaco promised Hackett he would get the money from Congress, and if they wouldn't pay promptly, he would take the funds out of his own pocket. With that in mind, he booked a trip to Philadelphia to meet with the Marine Committee—and find Jack Shelton. Hedley Garrison and the other frigate officers remained to oversee the repairs to *Scorpion* while Jaco was gone.

Jaco was still angry at himself for allowing himself to be sucked into a duel. As the schooner rounded the tip of Cape Cod, Jaco rested his elbows on *Alacrity's* main deck bulwark and stared at the gray-blue water. He had posted a letter to his father describing the incident. Writing about the fight had been cathartic, but he still believed he should have walked away and never have fought Radcliffe.

But what if he had refused the duel? Would Edmund Radcliffe spread rumors around Boston that he was a coward? And how would that affect his command?

The packet arrived in Philadelphia early in the morning on the incoming tide, and the smells of the city assaulted his senses. Whenever he was in Philadelphia, Jaco felt dirty. He didn't know if it was the stench of the river or the politics. He often wondered how his father stood the odor or the political intrigues that went along with trying to manage a war.

After a brief meeting with his father, he eagerly set out for where Shelton was visiting Joshua Humphrey's shipyard.

When the two friends met, they shared a manly bear hug. Neither one said anything for a few moments, then they both began to laugh. For the rest of the morning they walked about together, catching up on each other's adventures.

Word about the duel had reached Philadelphia. In the hallway between sessions of the Continental Congress, Adams had privately told Javier that he wished Radcliffe would mind his P's and Q's. From this Javier had concluded that Edmund Radcliffe was causing problems for his family in Boston.

In a private moment with the Jacintos, after they'd read an article in the *Boston Gazette* describing the duel, Shelton shook his head. "We should have hung the bastard when we had a chance. Mark my words, Radcliffe will be a bane to us all until the day he dies."

With a pouch full of English pound notes and half the money needed to pay Hackett, Jaco boarded the schooner *Doylestown* for the trip back to Boston. The three-masted schooner had been built in the same yard as *Cutlass* but was about 20 percent bigger. Designed from the ground up by Joshua Humphreys to carry passengers, mail and cargo, *Doylestown* had a long, narrow hull and a pointed bow. In open water the schooner showed her speed when she easily left a Royal Navy frigate in her wake. Three days after leaving Philadelphia, the schooner coasted to a stop at a pier in Boston.

Coosawatchie, SC, fourth week of September 1779

From where Amos Laredo crouched, he could watch the ford of the slow moving Pocotaglio River. He was in South Carolina's wetlands, and the smell of decomposing vegetation surrounded him. The swamp-like aroma was different from the "upland" smell in the nor' west part of the colony. There the only odors came from cooking fires, fresh grass and the pleasant smell of fresh earth when crops were turned over for the winter.

Here, the river was straight and shallow for several hundred yards before beginning a series of bends through swampy lowlands. A firm sandy bottom two feet below the surface made the ford an ideal place to cross.

Seventy-five yards behind where Amos knelt, five men held the reins to the horses of his small detachment of 25 men. His mission was to watch for British reconnaissance patrols and, if warranted, ambush them and withdraw. Amos' orders said he was not allowed to be drawn into a firefight with a superior force.

His plan was simple. Wait until half of the British cavalry patrol was either on his side of the river or crossing before opening fire. Each man in his unit carried two rifled muskets and was an experienced hunter who could drop small game at 200 yards and kill a deer at 300. All were in a position with their rifles supported by a log or tree branch to maximize accuracy. At 100 yards from the crossing, his men were well out of the accurate range of the smooth bore, short-barreled carbines the British dragoons carried.

Bayard Templeton was familiar with the area. Coosawatchie was a small town surrounded by a mix of large plantations with slaves and small family farms, and two of the plantation owners were former clients. He did not, however, intend to look them up. Templeton's current mission was to encourage slaves to escape and fight for the British, and to defeat any militia units he encountered.

Common sense suggested that the ford was a perfect place for an ambush. Templeton held up his arm to stop his column of 48 men. His horse seemed restless as he studied the woods on the far side with a spyglass. He didn't see any movement, but he knew how silent men could be when the least noise would scare off game—and then you had no supper. But if the troop did not ford here, they would have to turn northwest and follow the Pocotaglio a dozen or so miles to another crossing, which was just as likely to be guarded.

Templeton gestured to his second in command. "Lieutenant Duffords, take sixteen men, cross the river, dismount and set up a skirmish line fifty yards on the other side. We will cross in three groups. I will cross with the second section of sixteen and Sergeant Buford will cross with the rear guard. Be prepared for a fight."

Amos watched 16 Green Dragoons cross the river, dismount, and kneel in the grassy field. A second group of 16 started into the river; when half were across, Amos squeezed his trigger. A flash and the musket went off, and one of the green-coated dragoons grabbed his stomach as he fell from his horse into the water.

Amos had assigned his best shots to shoot at officers and sergeants. Twelve of the men crossing the river were hit by the first volley before Amos' men shifted their focus to those kneeling in the grass. Lieutenant Duffords fell from a ball that ripped out his throat. The man next to him spun awkwardly around as his right shoulder dissolved into a mass of torn tissue and bone fragments.

Bayard started yelling at his men to get across the river when two balls ripped through his clothing. One grazed his hip, the other cut his right bicep, tearing and burning his flesh as it passed through his sleeve.

Just as suddenly as it had started, the firing stopped, leaving Templeton and his troop in control of the ford. He was tempted to chase the rebels but decided that would be foolhardy. Away from the clearing and the road, the rebels would have every advantage of cover and initiative. Now the loudest sounds were the groans of the wounded. Twelve men, including one sergeant and his second in command, were dead. Eight more were wounded and might not survive the ride back to Savannah. He ordered his men to make horse drawn stretchers.

Clearly, the rebellion was far from over in South Carolina. Looking down at the corpses of what had been his men, Templeton decided then and there that the only way to win was by destroying everything dear to the rebels. Even if that meant killing their wives and children.

Beaufort Precinct, SC, second week of October 1779

Templeton's greatest weapon, he had discovered, was not muskets but a single piece of paper. Armed with General Sir George Clinton's June 30th, 1779 proclamation that stated any slave who joins the British cause will be given his freedom, he stopped at each plantation. Before a gathering of all the slaves, Templeton would read the document aloud while the unhappy owners looked on. The proclamation was not well received by any plantation owners, Loyalists or those who supported the rebellion. At any sign of resistance to allowing those slaves who wanted their freedom leave, the plantation owners were shot and their houses burned, even when they were women and children.

The Maybank plantation was the second stop this day. His men sat on their horses in a row behind the slaves. Templeton stood on the porch; the family and supervisors were under guard off to one side. When they departed the Maybanks plantation, his column was followed by 72 men—former slaves—and their families. When they reached Savannah, the new recruits would join British Army pioneer units to build fortifications, bridges and other structures needed by the regular units of the British Army, and act as scouts.

Templeton's Dragoons were met at Monck's Corner by four riders. The sergeant of the group was carrying revised orders from Clinton to no longer shoot the women and children, and to take prisoner all military-age men. Templeton signed the acknowledgement and turned the new recruiters over to the riders so he could continue his march northward to Orangeburg, SC unimpeded. The intelligence given to Templeton said that a gunpowder mill owned by Ezekiel Adams and Miriam Bildesheim was hidden in the woods near Orangeburg. But where? No one was talking, at least not yet.

100 miles east of Wilmington,NC,
fourth week of October 1779

After a fruitless eight-week patrol through the Leeward Islands and up the North American coast, Smythe brought his squadron into Nassau to re-provision. There was no word of *Scorpion,* and Smythe wondered where the rebel frigate could be.

The port captain in Nassau had given him two useful tidbits of intelligence. One, the rebels and their French allies had tried and failed to take back Savannah. Two, Sir Henry Clinton had ordered Newport, Rhode Island evacuated. Those troops, along with some from New York, were headed for Savannah.

Just before his squadron left Nassau, the three captains had settled on a patrol line, from 10 miles east of Wilmington, North Carolina stretching 150 miles due east. Smythe's hypothesis was Jacinto would attack a convoy headed to Charleston. And, if they didn't catch him in the act or escorting prizes to rebel-held Hampton, Virginia, they would intercept him as he searched for prizes.

Kittery, fourth week of October 1779

Jaco was incredibly frustrated. In Philadelphia, Adams had promised he would send sailing orders and the balance of the money for fixing *Scorpion,* but so far, neither had arrived.

Hackett would not allow more than two days of provisions to be brought on board, because he was afraid Jaco would sneak a small crew aboard *Scorpion* and sail into the night, leaving him with a bill that would be paid in next to worthless Continental dollars.

On the last Friday of the month, *Alacrity* sailed into Kittery harbor and docked on the other side of the pier from *Scorpion*. Jack Shelton hopped onto the pier before the schooner had ceased moving. His first stop was the gangway of *Scorpion*.

"Jaco! Help me bring the locked chest from *Alacrity* to your cabin. I need to go see Mr. Hackett. If all goes well, you can start recruiting a crew you can set sail as soon as the work is finished. The officers know where most of the crew live, so we can start seeing who wants to come back. Let me conclude my business with Mr. Hackett. ”

“I don’t think he has more than a week of supplies.”

“Then we will sail to Boston where you can get everything you need and finish recruiting a crew. There I will give you your sailing orders.”

“To use your favorite expression, from your mouth to God’s ears. We will get to sea as fast as we can.”

“Aye, but first we have to meet with Mr. Hackett.”

The shipyard owner had a bill waiting. After Jack scrutinized the receipt for the work done on *Scorpion,* and the estimate on what still needed to be done, as well as for the provisions he could supply, he handed it to Jaco, “Is this what was done and what needs to be finished?”

“Aye, Jack, ‘Tis that.”

“Excellent.” Jack counted the pound notes so settle the bill under Hackett’s watchful eye. When he was done, Hackett said, “Thank you,” before scribbling his name, the date and the words “Paid in full” on the last page of the bill.

“Captain, would you please excuse Mr. Hackett and me for a moment?”

His friend’s formal tone indicated Jack was about to deliver a message from the Marine Committee that he was not supposed to hear. Jack waited until Jaco was out of earshot before speaking.

“Mr. Hackett, the Marine Committee is very disappointed in that you held *Scorpion* hostage over a bill that the Continental Congress committed to paying.” He started to say, “We are at war for our independence and need *Scorpion* to help us win,” but didn’t.

Hackett held his tongue for a few seconds and then spoke in very measured terms. “Please convey to Mr. Adams that while I am an ardent supporter of the rebellion, I also have a shipyard to run. Logs for trees, pitch, tar, rolled copper and hemp are not free and do not come cheap. In addition, my workers have to be paid so they can eat. So while I sympathize with the Continental Congress’ desire for generous discounts and payment in Continental dollars, my terms still stand for repairs. Half when we understand the work that needs to be done, half when have finished, and payment in viable currencies, that is to say, Spanish dollars, Dutch guilders or English pounds—of which, thanks to the ship which I designed and built, the Congress has a substantial sum. Allow me to point out there is no virtue in exchanging one form of tyranny for another. Whether it is king’s men or congressional dilettantes, theft is theft.”

Jack rubbed his mouth to hide a grin. “Sir, I will so inform Mr. Adams and the rest of the Marine Committee.”

Walking back to *Scorpion,* Javier’s words “Scratch a patriot and you’ll find a businessman” ran through Jack’s head.

Jack had another mission in Kittery. The Continental Congress wanted the Continental Navy enlistments to match those of the Continental Army, which was from January 1st to December 31st; therefore, those who came on board would have to serve until December 31st, 1780. As the men trickled inn, they were offered the deal Jack had negotiated with the Marine Committee: a 15% bonus on their salary, to be paid in English pounds to them or their heirs.

When *Scorpion* set sail from Kittery and then Boston, it had a full crew, signed to the new enlistment term. On board were 150 from the prior crew and 45 new members recruited in Boston.

The new sailing orders were for *Scorpion* to capture British ships in the Caribbean and off the east coast of the colonies. After a fruitless search of the waters north of the Bahamas, *Scorpion* pulled into Charleston for provisions in early January 1780. The port captain had a letter from the Marine Committee ordering *Scorpion* to sail back to Philadelphia as fast as it could. The frigate made the 600-mile Charleston to Philadelphia trip in three days thanks to favoring winds.

In a meeting room on the second floor of Independence Hall a week later, Jaco was re-introduced to Benjamin Harrison, a Virginian, and a Marylander by the name of Thomas Johnson. Johnson complimented him on his past successes, then inquired, "Captain Jacinto, we understand *Scorpion* is seaworthy, is that correct?"

"Yes, sir."

"Good!" Johnson gestured to Benjamin Harrison, who said, "The Committee of Foreign Affairs wants *Scorpion* to sail to Brest as fast as possible and bring the Swedish Count Axel von Fersen and three of his aides to Boston. He will be an advisor to General Washington."

"Yes, sir, but you do realize that the accommodations on *Scorpion* are sparse. My cabin is small, and it serves as meeting room, wardroom, ship's office and my bedroom. We can give Count von Fersen one of the lieutenant's compartments, but his aides will have to sleep in hammocks with the crew."

"Well, Captain, you will have to work those details out with the Count. What is important is that he arrives safely in Boston as soon as possible. This means that *Scorpion* neither looks for prizes nor engages with Royal Navy ships unless absolutely compelled to do so. Even then your priority should be to disengage and escape without allowing the Count to be captured. Von Fersen is coming with the blessing of the Swedish king, who supports our cause."

"I understand, sir. We will sail as soon as we have a full load of provisions, which should be in less than two days."

"Good. Remember, Captain, time is of the essence. I will have your orders, dispatches and some other documents for you, as well as money for re-provisioning in France, delivered to your ship today."

Rather than chance the North Atlantic in winter, which from Philadelphia was the shortest route, Jaco sailed southeast until he was sure the ship was in the winds known as the Westerlies. The detour to the south added 600 nautical miles to the 3,160 nautical mile trip, but then steady winds pushed the frigate along at an average of nine knots, and *Scorpion* anchored in the French port 22 days after leaving Philadelphia.

With a full load of provisions and extra powder and shot, there wasn't much room for baggage in *Scorpion's* hold. Thankfully, the count and his staff brought a mere half a dozen chests, which could be stored at the aft end of the berthing deck. The count refused to displace Jaco from his cabin and the officers from their small compartments. Instead, he and his aides slept in hammocks at the aft end of the crew's compartment. The fourth man, the Count von Fersen's servant, ate and slept with the crew.

The return trip from Brest took much longer because *Scorpion* had to sail south to pick up the Trade Winds. Five weeks after leaving Brest, *Scorpion* slipped into Boston. Freed of passengers and resupplied, the frigate headed south along the North Atlantic coast, looking for prizes.

Charleston, first week of April 1780

Amos Laredo slipped into Charleston by rowing a boat across the Cooper River to avoid the British units besieging the city. At the Continental Army headquarters, he was escorted to General Benjamin Lincoln's office just before 10 p.m.

He could hear a heated discussion when he rapped on the door. The conversation stopped and General Lincoln, who had been appointed by the Continental Congress to take over the defense of Charleston, opened the door. The other man in the room was General Moultrie. A map lay on the table of the candle-lit room.

Moultrie introduced Laredo to Lincoln, and after a few polite words the 24-year-old heir apparent to Laredo Shipping got right to the point. "General Lincoln, we've heard that you are talking to the British about surrendering. The men in my company are ***not*** going to surrender, sir. We are going to continue our raids and ambushes as long as we are alive."

Lincoln looked at Moultrie, who nodded mutely.

"Sir," Eric continued, "We are not on the list of units that surrender. Even as we speak, one of my officers is with the rest of 2nd Carolina, asking if any of them want to join us rather than surrender. We will accept only those who know how to live off the land and who can ride and shoot. We have sufficient weapons and powder, and we will resupply from what we take from the British."

"How soon do you need an answer?" The general asked.

"I will come by tomorrow at your convenience."

"How many men do you command?"

"My company has one hundred and twenty-six."

"And how many do you think will join you?"

"Faced with the choice of being British prisoners or continuing the fight, I think many will join."

"Captain, come back at ten in the morning. I will have your orders."

At lunch the next day, Amos was quietly eating with his family. His lieutenant reported another 100 men were ready to join the new 4th Carolina Dragoons. All were returning home to get their bullet molds and clothes suitable for hunting.

Reyna waited until they were almost finished eating when she asked, "Amos, who is going to tend your wounded?"

"I guess we'll find a doctor." Amos' tone suggested he hadn't thought much about the topic.

There was fire in Reyna's eyes. "That's poppycock. There aren't any doctors outside Charleston and Columbia. I will be your doctor."

"No, you won't. Fighting is not for... for...."

"What? Say it, Amos. Go ahead, you want to say little girls and women!"

Frustrated, Amos just stared at his baby sister.

"I can ride and shoot better than most of your soldiers, and I am one of the best doctors in Charleston. I just don't have the title. So don't argue with me. I will have my saddle bags packed along with my musket. And I'll have a case with medical supplies we can carry on a horse so I can take care of those who get shot. As far as medicines go, we'll use many of the Indian treatments I know work, and we'll make alcohol in your camp."

Amos looked at his mother and father. Neither said anything for a minute, then Adah Laredo spoke softly. "That pig Templeton shot my ten-year-old nephew in cold blood. If Reyna wants to join you, let her. If not, she will sneak out and find you, and that is much more dangerous. And if Charleston falls, she can ride in and out much easier than you can."

Amos knew an order when he heard one. "Yes, *Mamá*."

Adah looked at her son with coldness in her eyes. "Promise me that you will kill Templeton."

East of Hampton, VA, fourth week of April 1780

When *Scorpion* was a week out of Boston, clear skies revealed a formation of four Royal Navy ships—a frigate about *Scorpion's* size, a sloop of war and two large transports—three miles off. Theoretically, the wind from the nor' west gave the British the advantage.

Jaco studied the four ships through his spyglass before turning to his officer of the deck, Lieutenant Morton Geiger. "Mr. Geiger, tack us through the wind to port and take up a course of so' west by west. That will put us on a course to intercept the convoy and give us a chance to see what His Majesty's Navy is about."

When he felt the ship begin to change course, First Lieutenant Hedley Garrison came up on deck. "What do we have here?"

Jaco handed him his spyglass. "Take a look."

Garrison resembled a falcon sighting its prey as he peered through the Dollond. "If the sloop comes to see who we are, we put it out of action and take on the frigate. Then the transports are ours."

"My thinking exactly. No colors until we are challenged. Go ahead and quietly clear for action, but don't run out or send anyone extra up the rigging." *When I was on the sloop* Providence, *John Paul Jones drummed into my head that a good captain always had a strategy supported by the right tactics to win. Surprise is one such tactic.*

As Jaco watched, the frigate ran up a string of flags. The sloop, which had been trailing the convoy, fell off the wind and headed toward *Scorpion,* unfurling its royals.

Scorpion's main deck was heeled over in a beam reach, with the wind over her port side, so lookouts on the Royal Navy sloop could not see the Marines and sailors positioned on the gun deck at the fore and aft companion ways.

Each of *Scorpion's* lookout platforms already had six canvas sleeves with a thin wooden disk at each end, containing powder and 25 musket balls. Called canister, this ammunition turned the three-inch bore of a swivel gun into a shotgun. One of the competitions Jaco ran was to see how fast a man could climb the ratlines with a sling containing two bags weighted to simulate the sleeves of shot and powder. The fastest man to the lookout platform earned an extra ration of rum.

When the distance between the ships was down to two miles, Jaco studied the enemy ship's armament. Twelve gunports meant the frigate carried 24 cannons, probably 9-pounders in her main battery and 6-pounders on her quarterdeck. The sloop had eight gunports and was probably armed with 6-pounders. *Scorpion* had a slight edge in the weight of a full broadside, even though the frigate had the numerical advantage in cannon.

"Sir, the sloop is changing course and signaling. How do you want to respond?" Morton Geiger tried to keep the excitement out of his voice but failed. His pitch was higher than usual.

"Mr. Geiger, we're going to wait as if we are consulting our signal books for the appropriate answer. When I give the word, raise the Gadsden flag on the mainmast, and then our ensign in the stern."

"Aye, Captain."

"Mr. Jeffords and Mr. Preston, stand by to come about to port. We are going to pass alongside the sloop. Let her feel our sting to give them pause to continue the action. Mr. Payne, once we are out of the turn, run out and fire as you bear. The sloop may turn with us or away, so be ready to change the targeting. Mr. Miller, except for the swivel gun crews, your Marines will help Mr. Preston with the sails. I expect the frigate will want to engage, and if so, we will be happy to oblige. To your stations, gentlemen. I have the quarterdeck!"

The captain of the sloop had lowered the signal flags and then raised them again as if to say, "I'm waiting for your answer."

"Mr. Jeffords, Mr. Preston, stand by to come about to port. New course, so' west by west, but we may adjust. Mr. Geiger, show them our colors, if you please."

Jaco waited until he heard the snap of the flags in the wind and glanced up to make sure they were both streaming. In a loud voice, he commanded, "Mr. Jeffords, ready about to port. New course so' west by west."

Almost instantly, *Scorpion's* bow started to turn through the wind. With the tack underway, Jaco addressed his Second Lieutenant. "Mr. Payne, we'll pass the sloop at about four hundred yards. Plan on only one shot per cannon, but if the sloop turns away, we may get more. I want to put her out of action quickly, so stay with ball unless we are inside two hundred yards."

Payne put the back of his hand to his forehead as an acknowledgement.

"Deck ho!" The lookout called. "The frigate is turning our way and the transports are changing course to west so' west."

Jaco looked up and cupped his hands. "Deck, aye." He studied the frigate through his spyglass and saw its cannon were already poking out from both sides. *Scorpion's* tack to pass behind the sloop and her ship's flags were signals enough to the Royal Navy captain that they were facing a rebel ship. Jaco returned his attention to the sloop, which was trying to wear downwind to a course nearly opposite to that of *Scorpion* to sail out of danger, but their turn slowed their speed. Jaco ordered his crew to fall off to port to allow *Scorpion* to close to inside 300 yards. From that angle, Jaco could read the sloop's name: *H.M.S. Crater*. "Mr. Preston, slack the sails!"

The frigate's bosun must have anticipated the order because the sailors handling the sheets for the sails on all three masts were already letting them out. *I must be getting predictable. No, your crew is thinking like you are!*

Their junior midshipman, a stocky 16-year-old from Portsmouth named Josiah Marshall, came up the companion way. He swallowed hard and in his most adult voice reported, "Captain, Mr. Payne is double-shotting the cannon."

Jaco nodded. "Tell Mr. Payne to fire as his guns bear."

Marshall disappeared, and seconds later the number one cannon on the port side boomed. The impact of the ball sent chunks of wood flying off from *H.M.S. Crater's* bulwarks just forward of the captain's cabin, and the ratlines for the mizzenmast fell to the deck.

In rapid succession, the next three port side cannons fired. Jaco could imagine the carnage the 12-pound balls were creating on the sloop. When the number five gun bellowed smoke and flame, *Crater's* mainmast jumped, hung in the air above the jagged stump, broken off six feet above the main deck, then fell. Part of the upper section landed on the main deck and seemed to settle, until the next two 12-pound balls slammed into *Crater*'s hull, ripping large holes in the side. The sloop shuddered and the mast toppled to port, dragging down the upper section of the fore and mizzenmasts.

Before he could yell cease fire, the number ten cannon fired and carried away the starboard railing on *Crater's* quarterdeck. For a moment, Jaco couldn't help imagining what it must be like on the sloop, then he turned his attention to the onrushing Royal Navy frigate.

Jaco figured that the Royal Navy's captain's orders were to protect the convoy at all costs, even if the tactic sacrificed his own ship. By sending *Crater* out to investigate he'd lost his advantage in numbers; now what? If both ships continued to head toward each other, they would exchange broadside inside 200 yards. Or... to *protect the transports,* Jaco reasoned, *he will fall off to starboard and attempt to cross Scorpion's bow.* That move would give Jaco the choice to either match the Royal Navy frigate's turn and exchange broadsides, or tack west and work toward the transports.

Or, or, or... If I were the Royal Navy frigate captain and my orders were to protect the convoy at all costs, *I would force a boarding fight. I might win or I might lose, but in either case the enemy frigate can't chase the transports.*

The last thought created a knot of fear in Jaco's stomach. Boarding actions were unpredictable and ugly, and being rammed would damage *Scorpion's* hull. Jaco studied the onrushing frigate, only 1,000 yards ahead, bearing down with mass and momentum. "Mr. Jeffords, Mr. Preston, stand by to fall off to port on my command. New course will be so' so' west. Mr. Geiger, tell Mr. Payne his starboard battery may fire when their guns bear." *This new course will let us exchange broadsides at a range favorable to* Scorpion. *If the English captain tries to close, we continue to fall off to the south, maintain our distance and keep pounding away.*

The British frigate started to turn to stay parallel with *Scorpion*. The range, with both ships headed roughly so' west, was now 400 yards. The Royal Navy frigate fired first. The first balls skipped and sank and never reached *Scorpion*. The British gunners adjusted their aim. Jaco heard a pop as the next ball went through the mizzen mainsail, and he yelled at his bosun, "Slacken all sails to level out the ship."

Then 11 of *Scorpion's* cannon fired as if they were a string of large firecrackers. The sound was painful to Jaco's ears even on the quarterdeck. Instinctively, he grabbed the railing as he felt the ripples of concussion from each muzzle blast push him back. Two balls went high, evidenced by holes in the British ship's foremast mainsail. Others struck lower, creating a brief storm of flying wood.

There was a ripple of flashes followed by clouds of smoke as the Royal Navy frigate returned a full broadside. Chunks of wood flew from *Scorpion's* main deck bulwark. Several cannon balls popped through sails. One cut the sheet to the foremast's topsail, which started flapping. Another took a two inch deep chunk out of the mainmast that would have to be splinted later.

Acrid, choking, gray-white smoke temporarily obscured Jaco's view and set him coughing. Jaco recoiled as a cannonball passed between himself and Garrison. The noise from *Scorpion's* long 12-pounders drowned out the thumps from the British frigate's nine-pound balls hitting *Scorpion's* hull, but he felt the impacts as the ship shuddered beneath his feet. A 9-pound ball carried away two rows of the quarterdeck companion way steps. Another went through the bottom of the middle cutter in the stack between the fore and main masts. With its keel broken, the boat settled awkwardly onto the one below. Another 9-pound ball shattered the side windows of his cabin. The last ball carried away the railing just behind the quartermaster, sending splinters into the bosun's mate manning the starboard swivel gun. Jaco helped carry the man to the edge of the quarterdeck, and two other men carried him below.

But the damage was not one-sided. Jaco could see jagged holes in the Royal Navy frigate's bulwarks, and he could imagine the carnage on its smoke-filled gun deck. By now, the English ship's red painted gun deck was probably slippery with blood from men ripped apart by iron and splinters. Jaco forced his mind back to studying the Royal Navy ship and commanding his ship. Not all the enemy frigate's guns were still capable of firing, but the ship stayed doggedly between *Scorpion* and the transports.

Enough of this. With each enemy cannon fired, more of my sailors get hurt. "Mr. Preston, Mr. Jeffords! Stand by to come about to starboard. New course nor' by west or as close to the wind as *Scorpion* will sail! Pass the word to Mr. Payne to keep firing as long as his guns bear." To no one in particular, he said out loud, "We need to finish this madness as quickly as we can."

The Royal Navy frigate turned with *Scorpion;* battered as she was, the ship could still maneuver. He waited until just before the two ships were parallel, the moment when the British ship would fire all the guns that could bear, then ordered his crew to let *Scorpion* fall off the wind. Soon their bow was on a course to pass astern of *H.M.S. Hayden*. He could see the crew of the British frigate scramble to turn to port.

"Mr. Jeffords, come to port so your course keeps us twenty yards off to *Hayden's* starboard side as we run her down. If the captain tries to cross our bow, don't wait for a command. Just turn the wheel opposite and keep us from a collision. I'll let Mr. Preston know; I am going to the bow to see if *Hayden's* captain is ready to strike."

As Jaco started to clamber up on to the beak with a speaking trumpet, he heard someone bellow "Get down, sir!" And felt a shoulder ram into his midsection. He landed with a painful thump on the main deck just as he heard the bark of a swivel gun. Musket balls sang over the two men, smacking into the inside of the starboard bulwark, the deck, beak, and figurehead.

Overhead, the foremast swivel gun barked a reply. One Marine in the maintop yelled down, "All clear! We got the gunner."

Jaco looked at Grantham, the seaman who'd tackled him. He was grinning. "Sorry, sir, but that jackheen wanted to kill you."

"Grantham, thank you, but what is a jackheen?"

"'Tis not a word one uses in polite company, sir, but jackass is close enough."

Jaco laughed. A sailor chased down the speaking trumpet that had rolled away and handed it to him. He pulled himself to his feet, trumpet in hand, and approached the side. A blue coated figure was at the starboard aft corner of *Hayden's* quarterdeck.

"*Hayden,* are you ready to strike?"

The man answered, "Aye. I was about to haul down our flag. I apologize for my sailor's rude behavior. That was ungentlemanly."

Jaco ignored the apology for a tactic he himself had used. He had transports to catch. "Haul down your flag and raise a white one. I am going after your transports. When I come back, we will discuss what we will do next. Any resistance will be dealt with harshly. Are you in danger of sinking?"

"No. Our hull is still sound. We will tend to our wounded while we wait."

"Please signal *Crater* to come alongside *Hayden* and also raise a white flag. I want to avoid any further bloodshed."

"Understood."

Jaco waved and returned to the quarterdeck There he ordered Geiger to watch and record signals from *Hayden*. "Mr. Jeffords, fall off to port and then head straight for those transports. Tell Mr. Preston how you want the sails trimmed."

Through his spyglass, Jaco estimated that the two transports were two miles off, moving slowly. Now *Scorpion* had a problem. "Mr. Geiger, please have all the officers join me in my drafty and shot up cabin at once."

Midshipman Patterson and Hedley Garrison were the last to enter, their faces darkened with grime from the smoke and gunpowder residue. Patrick Miller closed the door, which was the cue for Jaco to start.

"Gentlemen, so far we have bested the escort, but we must take the two troopships. Once we have convinced them to haul down their flags we will then have four prizes, and we don't have enough sailors to put a prize crew aboard each one. We are about seventy-five miles from Hampton, Virginia. Any suggestions?"

"Aye, sir, let's march them into Chesapeake Bay like a column of bloody Marines." The speaker was Captain Miller, who rarely spoke, but when he did he usually made sense.

"Explain, Mr. Miller."

"Sir, by the time we take these two transports and get everyone gathered up, the sun will have set. Tonight we should have a full moon and will be able to see all four ships. We don't put a soul on board any one of them except to make a brief inspection and tell their captains what we expect, and explain that if there is any mischief we will finish what we started."

"And we make sure our guns are at the ready with their frigate in the range of our long twelves," Garrison added. Geiger nodded at this. Jaco looked around the room. "As Captain Miller says, if any of the English captains is addle-pated enough to attempt to flee, then we use our cannon to show them the error of his ways."

The two troopships were less than a mile ahead of *Scorpion,* sailing line astern with one slightly to starboard of the other. The setting sun was silhouetting their sails, making the ships easy to see. Scorpion was fast overtaking *Cochin.* Jaco planned to pass the large ship, ask the captain to surrender, then do the same for the leading ship, *H.M.S. Northport.*

Inside a half mile, just as Jeffords was easing the wheel to enable *Scorpion* to slide to *Cochin's* port side, two hatches opened in the stern and the black snouts of 9-pounders slid out. One fired, and then the other. The first 9-pound ball slammed into *Scorpion's* figurehead, which burst apart. The second ball went through the mainsails on all three masts.

Jaco screamed, "You stupid bastard! Mr. Garrison, run out the bow chasers and ...." His last words were drowned as *Scorpion*'s port and starboard bow chasers fired. The 9-pound ball from the starboard bow chaser ripped through the wood just to the right of the rudder post and into the aft hold, where it splintered the first barrel of gunpowder it struck, then disintegrated in a shower of sparks after it hit the iron staves of a second barrel, creating a cloud of loose gunpowder amidst glowing chunks of hot metal.

The aft part of *Cochin* disappeared in a series of large flashes and gray-white smoke. The blast collapsed all three of *Cochin's* masts. The concussion rolled over *Scorpion,* causing those on the main and quarterdeck to reach for something to steady themselves. The change in pressure caused the yardarms to rattle and the masts to groan in mourning for those which were shattered on *Cochin*. Flashes and explosions continued for about three seconds, and debris flew several hundred feet into the air. Pieces of jagged wood ripped through *Scorpion's* topsails and top gallants. Chunks of wood and body parts landed on its main deck. When the smoke cleared, all that was left was a section of *Cochin's* bow slowly settling the Atlantic.

Jaco yelled. "Slack all sails! Mr. Jeffords, steer clear of the wreckage if you can. Mr. Marshall, if we have a seaworthy boat, go search for survivors."

Ahead, *Northport* had hove two and was already launching boats.

Scorpion came to a stop in the middle of the wreckage. All around the ship were corpses, few of them whole. When a potential survivor was found, the boat rowed to the man, a sailor lifted the head up and, if he was alive, pulled him into the boat. If not, his body was gently lowered back into the water.

Marshall's boat brought six men back to *Scorpion*, Quartermaster Mate Cooper's had a similar number. As *Scorpion* drifted, a long boat rowed over to within hailing distance. In the stern was a Royal Navy lieutenant who called out, "May I speak to your captain?"

Jaco leaned over the bulwark. The cutter was less than 20 feet from the side of his ship. "I am *Scorpion*'s captain. Are you prepared to strike?"

"Aye, I'm *Northport's* first lieutenant. My captain will haul down his colors. He is not as stupid as the hothead who captained *Cochin*. What are your orders?"

"Recover as many survivors as you can. Fly a white flag. Remain with the other ships I have captured. We are all sailing into Hampton, Virginia and should arrive tomorrow. If you follow my orders, no further harm will come to you."

"Aye, we can do that."

"What is your cargo?"

"We have 200 German mercenaries from Ansbach-Bayreuth on board, plus their weapons and ammunition. *Cochin* had the same number."

Scorpion's captain nodded numbly, wondering what the captain of the *Cochin* had been thinking when he'd ordered his crew to fire.

Once the boats were back on board *Scorpion,* the frigate set sail toward *Hayden* and *Crater*.

CHAPTER 17
FORMER ENEMIES, NOW FRIENDS

Off Cape Hatteras, first week of May 1780

The series of Royal Navy raids in Chesapeake Bay between May 10th and May 24th, 1779, had laid waste to many of the shipyards and docks up and down the bay. Now, a year later, they were back in business but not fully stocked, and the charred bricks were a grim reminder of the Royal Navy's visitation.

Jaco ordered the three prize ships to anchor and directed *Scorpion* to a pier. Then, one by one, the captured ships were brought to a dock and the prisoners marched away. The Royal Navy ships were stripped for supplies, after *Scorpion's* supply of gunpowder was replenished. But there were no 12-pound cannon balls at the base; they had to be cast at a nearby foundry.

The wait gave Jaco time to meet with the Court of Appeals in the Case of Capture, recently created by an act passed by the Second Continental Congress to replace the British Admiralty Courts. It had taken Congress four years after General George Washington formerly requested them to be created.

Jaco was told that the troopship *Northport* would bring around £4,000 at auction; however, the court's surveyor didn't think *Crater* and *Hayden* were economically repairable and would only bring a total of £800 pounds for their fittings. The bells from the warships were sealed in a wooden box and brought to *Scorpion* to be added to Jaco's collection.

Once the new cannonballs were delivered and stowed, *Scorpion* sailed into the Western Atlantic. Jaco grimly told his officers that they would head south and see what type of mischief the frigate could create to help Charleston from falling to the British.

Charleston, Friday, May 12th, 1780

Perla Jacinto stood next to Adah Laredo on the porch of the Jacinto's house, watching the British Army and Loyalist units march down Meeting House Street into Charleston. Now the Loyalists and their British allies would be in charge, and hard times were coming. Nevertheless, the Jacintos and Laredos, along with many other families, had vowed they would continue to support the rebellion. They were determined to find ways to resist and make the lives of the British Army soldiers miserable.

* * *

Lord Cornwallis sent a combined force of infantry and dragoons under Bayard Templeton to defeat any militia units they encountered and to commandeer or destroy shops that manufactured weapons or gunpowder for the rebels. At the top of Major Templeton's list was the Bildesheim gun shop. He looked forward to confiscating the property and arresting everyone he found inside.

As soon as Templeton walked into the door, however, he found it was now a shop that made iron fittings. None of the gun molds or tooling that he remembered were there. Hastily, he strode over to the separate building that housed the mills used for grinding equipment, but the mills too were gone; all he found was an empty building.

Briefly, he wondered if Miriam Bildesheim had finally had the good sense to die. Butupon being questioned, one of the local Loyalists assured him she was still very much alive. That meant she was probably still fomenting trouble.

If there was one person in the world Templeton hated, it was that proud old woman with her German accent. He thought her progressive ideas of shared profits, based on the writings of her fellow Prussian Immanuel Kant and Scotsman David Hume, would create false hopes amongst the poor who might think they could actually run businesses and prosper.

Two Loyalists told him that they were sure there was still a gunpowder mill, and it was probably northwest of Dorchester, hidden in the forests along the Santee River among the land owned by Bildesheim and members of her wretched community of farmers. Templeton asked for and received orders to destroy the mill. He set out at the front of 100 Green Dragoons on horses, followed by 100 members of the South Carolina Royalists on foot, clad in the red coats of the British Army. The unit had been formed in Florida, mostly from men of the Ninety-Six District of South Carolina.

Downwind and a mile from the first cluster of farms and homes, Templeton took in a deep breath, enjoying the pleasant aroma of meat being smoked; soon his unit would be enjoying whatever was being cured. Ahead, he could see smoke curling from the smoke house's chimney. The wood and brick structure was at the end of a row of houses and paddocks where horses were kept.

Establishing his presence in the center of the town, Templeton ordered his infantry to search each house in teams of four, with weapons at the ready. Women and children were corralled into the open, grassy common area. A dozen men of military age were rounded up from the barns and nearby fields, then poked and prodded to join their families. Templeton already despised them; it was a man's duty to pick a side and fight, just as he did.

He eased his horse over so that, in the saddle, he towered over one man, his wife and three young children. Templeton's leather saddle creaked as he drew himself up to emphasize his superior position as the leader of the Green Dragoons. He spoke in a loud, imperious tone. "You there, where is Bildesheim's gunpowder mill?"

The man answered steadily. "I don't know."

"Did you sign a contract with Miriam Bildesheim for the land and agree to till hers?"

"That I did. But I have nothing to do with gunpowder mills, and no knowing where it is, for it is not my concern."

"But you support the rebels!"

"No, sir. We just want to be left alone. Some of us are loyal to the king, some of us think otherwise, but whoever we pay taxes to, we wish to live in peace."

At this, there were nods and murmurs of agreement from the other families.

"Miriam Bildesheim is a rebel. Helping the rebels is treason. The king can seize your land, hang you, and throw your family into prison. So, sir, I ask you again, *where is the gunpowder mill*?"

"I cannot tell you what I do not know."

The man's wife looked at the faces of the soldiers. Alarmed, she gathered the children closer as if to shield them.

Templeton gestured angrily to one of his infantry lieutenants, who said to a sergeant, "You know what to do." Banister Tarleton, the commander of the British Legion, had told his officers, "Do what you have to do to find the gunpowder mill. Our Lord Cornwallis will justify the means by the results."

Ten men raised their muskets and fired. The man and his wife folded from the impact; the three children were knocked off their feet. Mortally wounded, the man looked up and croaked out, "God damn you, Templeton..." He was about to say something more when one of the Loyalists shoved his bayonet through the man's throat. The dead family's blood stained the dirt and grass.

Templeton looked around at the rest of the families gathered before him. Some children were crying. Mothers, white-faced with fear, were trying to comfort them. Others stood, stoical, staring angrily at the Green Dragoons.

"Now, I will ask all of you once again. Where is the Bildesheim powder mill?"

No one moved. After a few seconds of uncomfortable silence, a man spoke out from the end. "None of us know where it is. We are simply farmers."

Another group of soldiers faced the man's family, raised their muskets and fired. Another family lay dead or dying. Horses in their paddocks, startled by the gunfire and alarmed by the smell of blood, whinnied frantically. An ugly silence hung over the assembled families.

Another man spoke out, his wife trying to pull him back. "Templeton! You can kill us all but you won't learn where the mill is because none of us know! If you kill us all, there will be no one to till the fields or harvest the crops. You will have no food for your soldiers! Your search around here is akin to a rabbit hunting with a dead ferret. So be off and leave us alone."

Templeton stood up in his stirrups. "I will be back with an order from the King to seize these lands. All of Miriam Bildesheim's property will be forfeit!"

With a jerk of the reins he pulled his mount's head around and spurred it into a canter.

Two days later, Templeton was leading his troops to another cluster of farms in what he referred to as Bildesheim's empire. This one was the farthest north on his list. He had skirmisher's 100 hundred yards out on either side of the road, and in the back of the column were two wagons filled with smoked meat taken from the last group of farms.

According to his scouts, the road ahead went into the forest for about a quarter mile before the trees ended and fields of indigo began again. Templeton ordered four horsemen and four infantrymen forward to flush out any ambush; he waited until they were halfway through the wooded section before motioning his column forward. The normal noise of birds calling out when they find food, or woodpeckers hammering a tree trunk, had stopped. The loudest sound was the clopping of the Green Dragoons horses on the hard dirt. His stomach wambled in uneasiness.

Templeton and his lieutenant emerged from the woods and blinked and then squinted as their eyes adjusted to the bright sunlight. There was no sign of his advance riders or infantry. Frantically he looked around and saw only the tall grass swaying in the light wind. He ordered the first section of 24 infantrymen to fan out through the indigo field, but they found nothing other than a few rabbits. The eight soldiers and four horses were gone as if they had evaporated.

When all the Dragoons had advanced from the woods and were out in the open, Templeton heard a bird call. The notes were dying in the wind when the woods behind erupted in ripples of musket fire. Templeton yanked a pistol out of a saddle holster as he wheeled his horse and charged back down the column, past Dragoons, looking for someone to shoot.

He never caught so much as a glimpse of the enemy, but 23 of his men were dead and six more were wounded. The foot soldiers cautiously moved into the forest and found the bodies of their eight missing comrades lying in a neat row, stripped of their weapons and ammunition. All had been killed with knives.

Dorchester, second week of May 1780

The Sayer/Bennett map, printed in London in 1775, designated the area along the Cypress River where the 4th Carolina Dragoons made their camp as "swampy." Locals, however, knew that the river basin had many places that stayed dry all year.

Their chosen place, like any wetland, had its own unique smell that came from the stagnant water and decaying vegetation. The boggy, frequently water-filled area around their camp acted as a moat and hid their tracks. The little "islands," many of which were only a few hundred square feet, became listening outposts so men could warn the camp with a bird call or, if needed, by firing a weapon.

Cypress, gum and tupelo trees in the wetter areas mixed with ash and oak in those that stayed dry, providing shelter for deer and other game. The closeness of the trees meant one had to dismount and lead one's horse through the forest, splashing through the shallow water that teemed with fish.

Each time Amos Laredo rode into the area, the smell from the water and decaying vegetation, which they called swamp gas, reminded him of where he was. Their base was a good place to hide, but not one where he wanted to live for any length of time.

The route to the camp was marked with signs known only to members of the 4th Carolina. For those who were not familiar with its terrain the swampy, boggy forest was an intimidating barrier.

To make their base more habitable long term, the 4th Carolina built small shelters that kept the land underneath dry, and raised beds with canvas hammocks to keep the occupant off the ground.

Three foot deep pits kept the flames from their cooking fires hidden. The only giveaway of human habitation was when their small smokehouse was turning raw meat into the jerky which they carried in their saddlebags. The fragrant smoke wafted through the forest, and if one was downwind, one could follow the pleasant, hunger-inspiring odor right to the camp.

Yet with all the creature comforts they had built into their camp, morale in the 4th Carolina was low. Despite dozens of successful ambushes against British Army units, the members of the unit sensed the war was far from over. Most of the men came from Charleston and now that the city was in British hands, they worried about their families. No one knew what the British would do to civilians if they found out that a family member was a member of the 4th Carolina.

Amos Laredo needed to ensure that the men would not go home to their families. They, just like he was, were all volunteers. When Amos recruited them before the fall of

Charleston, he made a point that when they joined the 4th Carolina, they were in the unit for the "duration." In other words, until they were wounded and unfit to ride, or until the war was won.

Evening was about to fall. In the forest, one minute it was light and the next, dark. Amos decided to hold a meeting in the last few minutes of daylight, before the men and women drifted off to their hammocks.

For this meeting, all the 228 men of the 4th Carolina Dragoons were gathered around him. Most were sitting; the dozen who were about to ride to their two outposts were standing off to one side, eager to use as much light as they could to navigate.

"Gentlemen, our cause has now become even more personal. Every man..." and because his sister and eight other women were sitting amongst the officers. "... and woman of the 4th Carolina has family in Charleston. Our duty is to make sure they do not suffer under the British any longer than necessary. We will kill as many British soldiers and Loyalists as we can, using our hit and run tactics that we know work."

Amos looked around at the members of the 4th Carolina. "As many of you already know, the British have sent one of our neighbors, Bayard Templeton, to hunt us."

Seeing many nodding heads, he went on. "Reyna and I going to slip into Charleston to spread the word that we—the 4th Carolina Dragoons—are continuing the fight. Reyna and my mother are establishing a network so we can communicate regularly with our families. We have a muster in a safe place, and mother will be contacting your families. We will not be told how this system works so if we are captured, the chain will not be compromised. If one your families feels threatened, we will bring them either to this base or to one of my grandmother's farms so they will be safe. So, gentlemen, get some sleep. Our counterattacks will be relentless. We won't stop until we wipe that murdering bastard Bayard Templeton and his Green Dragoons off the face of the earth and push the damned British out of South Carolina!"

Rather than cheers, many of the men said loud amens. Others called out, "Hear, hear!" Some went up to Amos and assured him they were Dragoons until the end, whenever it proved to be. Amos Laredo was now confident that the 4th Carolina would make the British Army wish it had never landed in South Carolina.

* * *

Miriam's three story house was built around a central stack of chimneys on either side of the central staircase. The arrangement allowed each living space on each floor to have its own fireplace. On the main floor, the largest rooms were in the front of the house. One was a formal dining room with seating for 22 that opened onto the central entranceway. On the other side, she had a parlor with two large rocking chairs and four padded armchairs arranged around a table. A doorway at the far end of the room led to a separate room where she had a writing table and a chest filled with documents. This small room also opened to the kitchen in the back of the house.

It was in the parlor that Miriam Bildesheim received guests, and tonight her guest was Captain Graf Heinz von Korbach of the Waldeck Regiment. His unit had been on its way to help the British defend western Florida from the Spanish, French and rebels when their ship was captured by *Scorpion*. His regiment was one of three 664-man units that Fredrich Karl August, Prince of Waldeck and Permeant, kept ready for "foreign service." Revenue from these contracts supported the prince's effort to build roads throughout his kingdom.

Von Korbach stood with his heels together and his hands clasped behind his back until Miriam handed him a glass of whiskey and eased herself into a rocking chair.

Before the captured Germans had become part of the Charleston community, Miriam had only spoken German with her family members, because she thought it was important that they be fluent in more than one language. Here was a chance to speak the language of her childhood with a fellow native speaker, and she relished the opportunity. She spoke the precise, hard sounding dialect of German known as "hoch Deutsche" or high German, which was the preferred language of the Prussians.

"This whiskey is made on one of our farms from corn. It has a unique taste and is stronger than schnapps."

The German officer held up his glass, "*Für ihre Gesundheit, Frau Bildesheim.*" To your health, Mrs. Bildesheim. Von Korbach's German was softer and his accent was known as "platte Deutsche." Instead of the harsh sounding "icht" for "I", he used a softer pronunciation that sounded as if the word was spelled "isht."

"*Danke, Herr Hauptmann. Zu unsere Freundshaft.*" Thank you, Captain. To our friendship!

Both native Germans tossed down the whiskey. Miriam motioned to one of the other chairs in the room. "Please, sit."

"No, Frau Bildesheim, what I have to say should said standing." Von Korbach put his glass down on a table. "The men from my regiment want to help you defend your farms. You have been kind to us, and very generous. After the war, we want to stay and become part of this community. We have seen the fear in the women and children caused by this

Major Templeton and his Green Dragoons. If you let us, we can help."

Miriam rose to refill both their glasses. She was thinking furiously. "How many of your men wish to fight on our side? You know if they are captured, they will be treated as deserters."

"All seventy-six of us. And yes, we know what the British and our fellow Germans would say of us and do to us. But if we don't take a stand, we ourselves will never be free. We have seen the people who have been kind to us put to death and their farms burned. Tarleton and Templeton are evil. One doesn't make war on women and children, only soldiers."

"What about your title? And what do you mean that you yourselves will never be free?"

"My title is just words on a piece of paper that gives me status in Waldeck and authority over the soldiers I command. Our blood, the taxes we pay, and the money Prince August receives for hiring out his three regiments pay for his castles and his court. The soldiers themselves get nothing. We are just cannon fodder for whomever pays Prince August. He doesn't care if we come home or not, as long as he is paid. My men believe, as do I, that fighting for freedom from princes and kings is a noble cause."

"What do you want in return?"

"We will swear allegiance to this new country because we want to stay, to work, to marry and raise families, free from a ruler who can come into our village and conscript every male over the age of eighteen, as Prince August does."

These were motives Miriam understood and heartily approved of, but practicalities must first be addressed. "How many of your men would you consider marksmen? Men who grew up hunting and can hit a moving target with a rifled musket at 200 yards."

"We have a few. Those who cannot can be taught."

"Herr von Korbach, please wait here." Miriam pushed herself to her feet and left the room. A few minutes later, she returned, leading by the hand a tall, broad shouldered, powerfully built young man whose dark hair and skin contrasted sharply with the blond-haired, fair-skinned German officer. Switching to English, she made the introduction. "Hauptman Graf Heinz von Korbach, zis ist my grandson, Major Amos Laredo, commander of zee 4th Carolina Dragoons. You two should talk."

By the end of an hour-long discussion, the two men had formed a bond based on respect for each other and had come up with a plan. Starting the very next day, the 10 worst marksmen would ride north and meet up with Laredo's men to receive training. A few days later, they would return and the process would repeat with another 10 until all the men were competent marksmen. It was a very good thing, Amos realized, that his grandmother had insisted he learn German. He would be able to translate for the marksmen.

"If your men perform well," Amos said, "they will be invited to join us on ambushes so we can show you in a battle how we fight. Lord knows, we can use more men. Between the war and Templeton's raids, there are very few men left to till the land."

Von Korbach nodded decisively. "I know some of my men would be happier as farmers. It is the life they know. They would rather feed men than kill them. But so long as there are marauders and men like your Templeton, there will also be a need for guardians and warriors."

Orangeburg, third week of May 1780

Two days after General Lincoln surrendered to Lord Cornwallis, the South Carolina General Assembly, which was staunchly anti-British, dissolved. Some went to North Carolina. Others stayed in Charleston only to be arrested and sent to St. Augustine. A small group hid in a church southeast of Orangeburg and re-convened.

Lord Sir Charles Cornwallis dispatched a 300-man force to bring them back to Charleston to face trial. Led by British Army Lieutenant Colonel Cornelius Akers, the force consisted of 50 soldiers from the 82nd Light Infantry Regiment under a lieutenant and a sergeant, 50 Hessians soldiers under Captain Dieter von Ditwurth, and 150 Loyalists—100 from Georgia and South Carolina and 50 from New York, along with a borrowed squadron Green Dragoons to act as scouts.

Twenty-five yards on either side of the main body, Akers deployed Loyalists familiar with the terrain to act as skirmishers. The British Army soldiers were in the lead, followed by the Hessians and the rest of the Loyalists. The heat and humidity soaked their uniforms and dulled their senses as they trudged along, four abreast.

Reyna, who was one of nine women with the 4th Carolina, lay in the dry grass for most of the morning, covered by strands of grass to camouflage her position. All nine of them had insisted that they be allowed to fight because either their husbands had been killed or their homes had been seized by Loyalists. Before they were allowed to join, Amos had them demonstrate their skill on horseback as well as with a rifled musket. Between skirmishes, they performed double duty as cooks or, under Reyna's supervision, nurses.

Like the other men and women in the firing line, Reyna rested the long barrels of her rifled muskets on logs stacked in front of her. Through the sights, she tracked a Green Dragoon lieutenant on horseback. Amos Laredo's soft voice carried amongst the camouflaged 4th South Carolinians. "Those of you who don't have assigned targets, remember, first in line, first row of the enemy. Ready.... Fire."

There was a flash just forward of the right side of Reyna's face as the sparks from the flint ignited the powder in the pan. A fraction of a second later, the musket fired. As she lay the musket down and picked up the second one, she saw the lieutenant topple from his saddle. Lying on the ground, the man thrashed as he screamed in pain, and then went silent.

Reyna sought out another officer or sergeant. Another flash by her cheek and her musket barked. The man looked at his chest and then in her direction before he fell over. She rolled over on her side and made sure the muskets were in easy reach. On Amos's command, they would, after the enemy fired, run toward the woods. Once she was under cover, she would find a tree to use as protection and reload both muskets.

A dozen Green Dragoons pulled out their pistols and charged the line of smoke rising from the grass. None got more than 20 yards before they were cut down by musket fire from the concealed marksmen. Well drilled, the British and Hessian soldiers formed two lines and fired two volleys. While they reloaded, Amos yelled for the first row to move back. Reyna crouched over and, with a musket in each hand, clammy from the humidity, made the dash for cover in the woods. She looked over her shoulder and saw the Germans and British soldiers fixing their bayonets.

Heart pounding, she leaned against a tree, ripped open a paper cartridge and poured the powder down the barrel, keeping a small amount for the pan. She rammed a ball in a waxed patch of deerskin down the 50-inch, rifled barrel. Next she emptied the remaining powder in the pan and closed the cover. Reyna leaned one loaded musket against the pine tree and peered around the sheltering trunk as she started to load the second. She cringed when a musket ball smacked into a nearby tree and another zipped by her, just a few feet away. The Germans and British soldiers were spread out and advancing.

Suddenly, the second row of 4th Carolinians, still hidden prone in the grass, fired at point blank range. Many of the British and German soldiers were struck down by the first volley, and nearly all the rest left standing were felled by the second. The Loyalists fired a ragged volley from the road. Their musket balls either kicked up dirt after cutting some grass or went singing through the trees. The 4th Carolinians had clear targets and fired from prepared positions; the British and their allies did not. Amos' second row of 4th Carolinians ran back to the woods and took up positions along the edge of the woods to reload. Reyna was now kneeling with the barrel resting on a branch, looking for an advancing target.

The Loyalist South Carolinians and Georgians on the road reloaded, then started yelling and running at the woods and the 4th Carolina's position. Some stopped to fire, but the majority kept charging. To Reyna, they all seemed to be coming directly at her.

Amos called out, "First row, ready! Fire!" Reyna swallowed her fear and aimed at a figure who was at most 50 yards away. As she pulled the trigger, she recognized the young man from one of her biology classes at the College of Charleston. He crumpled to the ground with a musket ball in his belly. She picked up the second musket, aimed, and her second shot hit another man in the chest.

Suddenly the field was quiet, except for the groans and moans of wounded men lying on the road and the field. Her training as a doctor urged her to run out and try to help the wounded. The warrior in her said, *stay put and reload.* Her stomach reminded her that she should be afraid.

Amos put his thumb and finger into the corner of his mouth and blew. His high-pitched whistle was the signal for all the members of the 4th Carolina to pick up their muskets and retreat to where their horses waited. Other than bug bites, no one in the 4th Carolina was wounded.

Two miles away, Bayard Templeton was leading 250 of his men on another raid when he heard the gunfire. He led his unit at a fast canter until they reached Vickers' shot-up column. He found a leaderless, demoralized group of 100 men sheltering by their supply wagons. Overhead, vultures were circling, and in the grass he stumbled over what interested the birds.

* * *

The 21-mile ride back to the 4th Carolina's base camp in the cypress swamp took three hours. Those that had not taken part in the ambush spread out to concealed positions that guarded the base, so the raiders could clean up in the river and eat.

After wiping her face and washing her arms and legs, Reyna sat alone on a large log that served as a makeshift bench. She held her head in her hands and rested her elbows on her thighs as she relived the skirmish. Seeing his sister sitting alone, Amos sat down beside her and put his arms around her shoulders. Reyna was on the verge of tears. "I hate this godforsaken war," she murmured.

Amos pulled her close. "I do too. But this is a war we must fight if we are to have our independence."

"I know. But Eric, today I violated the Hippocratic oath that says a doctor will do no harm. I want to save lives, not take them. I just shot Jeremy Hendricks, who was in my chemistry class at the college. His father runs an apothecary where my patients get their medicines and I buy supplies. How can I look his father in the eyes knowing I—a person who wants to be a doctor—killed his son?"

"Reyna, consider yourself lucky. There are men in the unit who have fathers and brothers and cousins serving in the British Army. Imagine how they feel every time they pull the trigger."

"That doesn't make killing Hendricks any easier." Reyna wiped her cheek, then she composed herself and stood up. She walked over to where the other women who of the 4th Carolinas were gathered. All had husbands or brothers who had been killed by Bayard Templeton and other Loyalists. They'd given their children to their grandparents to raise until the war was over. Quietly she sat down beside them and listened to their conversation.

Heinz von Korbach, who'd also participated in the raid, sat down with Amos and handed him a barbecued chicken leg. "Herr Laredo, in Europe your tactics would be considered ungentlemanly. You do not stand and face your enemy, and you shoot the officers first. That is not the way we are trained to fight."

Amos sighed. "This is not a gentleman's war. We're fighting an army that has the advantage of training, experience, artillery, ammunition and numbers. So we use tactics that take advantage of our marksmanship and our ability to move through the forest. And, to your point, killing their officers causes confusion and uncertainty, which is to our advantage."

"And you include women. Why?"

"They grew up hunting for food, so they can shoot. And every one of them has a reason to fight."

"For freedom, yes?"

"Freedom, and vengeance for their husbands and brothers killed in this war. Both are powerful motivators."

Von Korbach was silent for a moment. "And your sister, she is a doctor, no?"

"Reyna knows more about medicine than most doctors, but medical schools will not allow women to earn medical degrees, so she cannot say she is a doctor."

"I understand. In Germany, we don't allow our women to be educated at the universities, which is a shame. Many of them are smarter than we men are."

Amos, who knew his sister and her friends, smiled in full agreement. He hoped the freedom they fought for would include freedom for women to attend universities and work according to their hearts' desires.

Chapter 18
3 vs. 1 and Still Can't Get It Done

50 miles east of Georgetown, SC, third week of May 1780

At four bells, or halfway through the morning watch, *Hasta* and *Pilum* took up station on either side of *Gladius* on the edge of the visual horizon. The squadron's formation let them sweep a swath of ocean just over 40 miles wide as the three frigates sailed abreast and due east.

The small squadron had spent much of March, all of April and now the first three quarters of May patrolling line from 10 miles east of Wilmington, North Carolina out 150 miles into the Atlantic. All the captains agreed that this would be the best place to find their prey as it came down from its hiding place someplace near Boston. However, the effort was both boring and frustrating and did nothing but consume time and food. Now, for the second time, they were on their way to Nassau to replenish their supplies.

Late on the first afternoon on the way to Nassau, lookouts on *Hasta* and *Gladius* spotted a small ship under full sail. At about two miles, Smythe was able to verify that sloop flew the British ensign. As part of their plan, Captains Meegan and Smythe each fired a green flare, signaling *Pilum* that a friendly ship was sighted and to join on *Gladius*. Darren hoped the ship's captain would have some news.

Gladius and the new ship slowed to sail alongside each other, with 50 feet of water separating the two hulls. Smith stood at the railing with a trumpet and called over, "Do you have any news?"

"Aye! Charleston has been taken, which is a great victory! I am to tell Royal Navy ships to resupply there; the port has large stocks of ammunition and provisions."

"And where are you headed?"

"I carry dispatches to New York, then Halifax and home."

Smythe waved a salute, signaling he had no further questions. As he watched the sloop's sails catch the wind and it surge ahead, he wondered where Jaco Jacinto was, and whether he knew that his home city was now in the hands of the British. Would he come home? Could he be intercepted?

90 miles east of Charleston, fourth week of May 1780

Scorpion's initial approach to Charleston was from the south. Jaco intended to swing east and then approach Charleston from the southeast, and so avoid the Royal Navy. He aimed to arrive at a point 50 miles east of Charleston around noon, then work his way toward the harbor mouth. If they spotted any Royal Navy warships bigger than a 36-gun frigate, *Scorpion* could escape to the Atlantic in the growing darkness. In a grim, tense meeting with his officers, Jaco had reiterated, "We are not on a suicide mission."

Just after noon the lookout called down, "Deck, sail ho! Three points aft the starboard beam, distance about six miles. By the cut of her sails, she's a Royal Navy frigate."

Jaco and Hedley Garrison, the officer on watch, went to the starboard railing. Through his spyglass Jaco could barely make out the ship's top gallants.

"Mr. Garrison, we will investigate. Let us get our royals out, since we have the sun and wind at our back."

The normally cheerful Garrison's tone was flat, almost grim as he replied, "Aye, sir." The night before at dinner, he had reminded Jaco that they might wake up in the morning surrounded by the Royal Navy. This could very well prove to be the first encounter with a Royal Navy squadron that, no matter how tactically brilliant they were or how much courage they showed, could overwhelm *Scorpion.*

On board H.M.S. Hasta

The glare off the water from the late afternoon sun hurt everyone's eyes. By the time the lookouts spotted *Scorpion* to the west, the rebel frigate was less than three miles away, directly astern and closing. Captain Meegan's first words, after he identified the ship, were, "Bloody hell. We didn't find *Scorpion*, the bastard found us." Turning to his first lieutenant, he said, "Fire a red flare, then call the watch and get our royals out. Once this girl is going as fast as she can, beat to quarters."

Hopefully, Smythe's plan would work and we'll give this rebel a thorough clapper-clawing. An image of what a de-masted *Scorpion* might look like flashed through his mind.

On board Gladius

At the call, "Red flare from *Hasta*!" Smythe dropped the quill pen he was using to write in the ship's log onto a soft cloth on his desk and headed to the quarterdeck, forcing himself not to run. He arrived just in time to see the burned-out flare fall into the ocean. Then he began issuing commands. "Mr. Soames, fire a red flare to signal *Pilum*. Mr. Stanhope, ease your helm to starboard so we can join *Hasta*. Mr. Louttit, if this ship is *Scorpion,* we bring the frigate to heel this afternoon. Issue an extra tot of rum to the crew after we beat to quarters."

From his quarterdeck, Smythe couldn't see the ship that had prompted the red flare. Was it *Scorpion?* He decided to go aloft to have a look. As he climbed the ratlines, Darren's excitement didn't diminish the sobering realization that his squadron was about to engage a man he regarded as a friend, and the chances were high that one or both of them would be killed or maimed. He let himself hope they would both survive the encounter. The wind ruffled his hair and the sunlight glinted on the waves. It was a beautiful day. *Will I be alive to see the sunset? How many of my crew will live to see tomorrow?*

On board Scorpion

Over the beat of the snare drum, everyone on the quarterdeck and main deck heard the lookout call, "Flare from a second ship! Three points broad on the beam right on the horizon."

"Mr. Garrison, have all the officers gather on the quarterdeck once we are cleared for action. The second flare could be an acknowledgement of the first one or a signal to a third frigate. Once we know more, we can decide whether we engage them one at a time or run like hell."

On board Hasta

Hamilton Meegan studied the ship first with a naked eye, then through a spyglass. Eleven gunports, lean looks, sharp bow and small size all confirmed that *Scorpion* was the ship behind them. *Damn, that ship is fast.* Scorpion *is gaining on* Hasta *by at least two knots. Jacinto has picked a course to force me to turn to starboard. What will he do when he spots* Gladius *and* Pilum? Scenarios raced through Meegan's mind.

On board Scorpion

Through a spyglass, the officers on *Scorpion's* quarterdeck could read the name *H.M.S. Hasta* on the frigate they were chasing. As yet, no other ship was in sight. As soon as they were inside five hundred yards, Jaco ordered the starboard bow chaser to fire. The gun boomed and the officers with spyglasses saw glass shatter as the 9-pound ball struck *Hasta's* stern. Less than a minute later, a second shot hammered into *Hasta's* stern. A third ball missed wide to starboard. Jaco yelled out, "Mr. Jeffords, Mr. Preston, are you ready?"

Both men responded with a loud "Aye!"

On board Hasta

On the quarterdeck, Hamilton Meegan felt the first ball hit his ship and cursed the reach of Scorpion's fore chasers. He had cursed even more if he'd known that the first ball smashed through his pantry, destroying his bottles of whiskey, port and madeira before expending its energy by splintering six sea chests on the berthing deck. Ball two went down the middle of the berthing deck before slamming into *Hasta*'s stove, breaking the oven doors and shoving the heavy cast iron stove off the slate mount. The shock was enough to cause the cast iron to crack and the stove to spray gray-white ashes as it fell in large pieces on the wooden deck. Hearing the clanging, one of the ship's powder monkeys stopped to see if any of the warm coals that remained in the stove had fallen on the deck. None had, so there was nothing to report, other than the ship would need a new stove and they would be eating cold meals until something could be cobbled together.

Meegan focused on the relative position of *Scorpion's* bowsprit to where he was standing. When the relationship moved to either left or right, he would know that the rebel frigate was turning and he would counter to keep *Scorpion* occupied until *Gladius* and *Pilum* arrived. He couldn't see *Pilum* from his ship's quarterdeck, nor could his lookouts, but *Gladius* was only five miles away and closing.

Scorpion's forestaysail, jib and flying jib suddenly went slack; the sheets had been released and *Scorpion* was about to turn. Meegan waited until he was sure the direction the rebel frigate was turning before ordering, "Stand by to come about to port." As the men on the main deck hauled the braces around and secured the sheets, Meegan confidently addressed his helmsman. "Helm a-lee, new course is west by north."

On board *Scorpion*

Jaco waited until *Hasta* committed to the turn, then said, "Mr. Jeffords, hard to starboard back to our original course. Mr. Preston, get those yards back around so we don't lose much speed." *Scorpion's* rigging groaned in protest, but the ship responded and surged ahead as the sails were sheeted home. It was all handled so neatly that Jaco exclaimed, "*Perfecto*!" His outburst turned a few heads and set the men who heard him smiling.

Now *Hasta* was slower in the water, and *Scorpion* was in perfect position to rake *Hasta* from the port rear quarter. If needed, Jaco could then turn his ship to the west and exchange a broadside or two at 400 to 500 yards. "Mr. Patterson, fire as your cannon bear!"

On board *Hasta*

Captain Meegan saw the rebel frigate alter course and screamed, “You treacherous son of a bitch!” He ran forward, yelling at his quartermaster, “Stop the turn! Turn starboard, back to our original course—” His command was drowned out by a boom and the almost simultaneous crash of a 12-pound cannon ball ripping up planking. *Hasta* shuddered in acknowledgement of the blow.

A second ball took out a section of the port main deck bulwark and crashed through the forward stack of boats before punching through the starboard bulwark. Each ball that hit caused *Hasta* to shudder in pain. Meegan heard an ominous creaking. He looked up at the foremast and saw the top was swaying back and forth; the lookouts and marines were scampering down the rigging.

Most of *Scorpion's* balls screamed through the gun deck, upending cannon and sending shards of cast iron and oak stabbing indiscriminately into men and wood. Meegan felt every hit and they rattled his bones. He was both afraid and angry that his ship was taking a pounding. The worst of it was that his crew could not return fire.

Hasta's mizzenmast gave up trying to remain vertical and came down. At the same time, the ship's wheel disappeared in a haze of splinters, leaving his quartermaster staring at two bloody stumps where his hands had been. Meegan felt a piece of wood enter his side and looked down to see a handle from the wheel protruding from his midriff. He'd been stabbed before by a French bayonet in the other side; in a lunatic moment he thought, *I will have matching scars*.

Without a quartermaster or wheel to keep *Hasta* on course, the frigate began to fall off starboard to run with the wind, parallel to its tormentor. Meegan didn't have to give the order to fire: the remaining gun crews knew what to do.

One of *Hasta's* 12-pound balls struck *Scorpion's* side, but rebounded and dropped into the water. When a second ball did the same, he realized that the only way their squadron would take *Scorpion* was by boarding. Weak from pain and loss of blood, Meegan watched helplessly as *Scorpion* sailed away to the east—toward *Gladius* and *Pilum*. He looked at the mess of rigging and yards that covered the forward part of his ship, knowing that if *Scorpion* returned, he would have no choice but to surrender.

"Sir, we need to get you to the surgeon." It was his first lieutenant.

Meegan nodded weakly. "Aye. If *Scorpion* returns, you may haul down the colors."

On board Scorpion

From his quarterdeck, Jaco studied the damaged *Hasta* and watched a man in a blue coat being helped down the companionway to the main deck. *Hasta's* wheel was gone and the foremast was tilted at an odd angle. The top third of mizzenmast was lying in the netting above the main deck. *Hasta* was out of action. During the fight, however, the lookouts had spotted a third frigate whose royals now were visible on the horizon. The closer Royal Navy frigate was less than three miles away, and cannon sticking out of the gunports meant that the ship was cleared for action. *Scorpion* was running with the wind, headed nor' east; the two remaining British frigates were running at roughly right angles to intercept.

"Mr. Garrison, my compliments to the port battery. They got off two shots in a very short order."

"I will let Mr. Patterson know."

"While we have some time, hand out hardtack dipped in rum, some dried apples and a ration of beer. What's the butcher's bill?"

"No major injuries. A couple of splinters, but no one is with the surgeon. The three layers of planking did their job."

"Aye, the repairs were sound, but we're about to test our bulwarks again. Based on the bearing and the closure rates, I think we can get past the nearest frigate; but the far one will try to force us to turn so the closer one can get alongside. What say you?"

"I'd say they want to box us in so we can't maneuver or run."

"So, Mr. Garrison, let us muck up their strategy."

Jaco looked up at the seaman working his way out the mainmast's topsail yardarm. He had a coil of rope around his shoulders that would be used to replace a line connecting the end of the spar to the deck.

On board Gladius

Through his spyglass, Darren Smythe he could see *Hasta* was out of action. The sight reminded him of what *Griffin* looked like after exchanging broadsides with *Scorpion* back in January, '78.

Scorpion's pronounced sloping bow and 11 gunports made recognizing the rebel frigate easy. He had to admit that the ship had a graceful line that made it look fast and agile. If this ship was not *Scorpion,* then the ship was its sister.

Between the ship's speed and his position, *Gladius* was not going to be able to intercept the rebel frigate except at long range. To cut the angle in case *Scorpion* turned north to engage *Pilum,* Darren ordered a more easterly course. Captain Taylor was doing exactly what they had planned:

getting one ship in front and one behind *Scorpion* to force the rebel to fight both at the same time.

On board Scorpion

From the starboard Perfecto Corner, Jaco studied the two undamaged frigates. They appeared to be sister ships to *Hasta,* which meant they were armed with 12-pounders. And from the way they were moving it was clear they had a plan to force *Scorpion* to fight *both* at once. One on one, *Scorpion* would almost surely win. Two on one at the same time was a different story. While he was confident his crew would give a good account of themselves, the risk was too high. Looking back and forth between the two Royal Navy frigates and the geometry of the engagement, Jaco's mind raced. "Mr. Garrison, tell me what you think of this plan..."

After listening to his captain, Garrison smiled. "For a few moments there, I thought you wanted take both those frigates on at once."

"No, Mr. Garrison. Too many of us would be hurt. I prefer one on one matches against His Majesty's frigates because, unless something unforeseen happens, I am confident we will win."

"Good."

"Mr. Garrison, you've got the deck while I take a quick tour of the gun deck. When I come back, we'll work out the details."

On the quarterdeck the breeze kept things cool; below, gun smoke still hung between the buttresses that supported the main deck. The enclosed area reeked of sweat, spent gunpowder, and, to Jaco's nose, a bit a fear. He watched the crews haul the 4,000-pound cannons and carriages back into battery. Once in position to be fired, the gun captains pricked the canvas cartridges that had been shoved down the barrel before the ball was rammed home. Several stabs of the long, steel needle made sure there were holes in the canvas. Next, they poured fine grain powder from a flask into the touch hole until there was a small pile in the hollowed out area. After the gun captains closed their flasks, the only thing left to do was aim the cannon and touch the gun powder with the glowing end of a piece of hemp.

Captain Jacinto waited until all the cannons were loaded, primed and run out before he waved Patterson over to join him by the mainmast, where the three-foot diameter mast went through the gun deck. Then he addressed the gun crews.

"We have disabled one Royal Navy frigate, but there are two more who mean to do us harm. Both batteries must be ready to fire, and you need to make every ball count. Not because we are low on ammunition, but because we will have very small windows to hit the enemy so they cannot follow *Scorpion* and do us damage us in return. None of us want to be taken prisoner. We have trained to fire faster and more accurately than what the Royal Navy anticipates. If you do your work well, we will add three more frigates to our tally. *Scorpion* is undefeated and we want to make sure no Royal Navy ship takes us."

Jaco looked at the grimy faces. "In a few minutes, the cooks will be passing out rations again. I won't send you into battle hungry and thirsty!" A few men cheered at this. "I suspect we will be in action again in an hour. Good luck."

A voice rang out. "Three cheers for Captain *Perfecto*!"

Jaco grinned and waved. After the third cheer as he headed toward the forward companionway. On the main deck, he stopped to talk to Bosun Preston and Patrick Miller, whose Marines would make up half the deck crew that would handle the sails and yards. Miller said, "Sir, my Marines would like to show you what they can do with one of the cannons. They know the gun drill, and based on your plan you're going to need both bow chasers manned as well as both main batteries."

"Talk to Mr. Patterson, he owns the gun deck. That sounds fine, but understand that Mr. Preston has priority. Sails before guns, Mr. Miller!"

"Aye, aye, sir."

Why didn't I think of that? It's a good idea. Maybe giving the Marines a cannon on either side will foster more competition amongst the gun crews and make them all better.

On Board Gladius

Anyone looking at Darren Smythe would have thought he was studying *Scorpion* to discern what the rebel ships' next move would be. Instead, his Dollond spyglass was fixed on the man in the aft port corner of *Scorpion's* quarterdeck. *So, Jaco, the moment we talked about on* Cutlass *and feared is upon us. You and I again face each other in battle. God protect us both, so someday we can talk about this day.*

Darren expected Jaco to turn his ship, because otherwise *Pilum* would cross *Scorpion's* bow and rake the rebel frigate. A turn to port and to the north towards *Gladius* would allow *Scorpion to* engage *Gladius* at long range first, and then *Pilum*. Turning to starboard and the south would indicate an attempt to outrun his ships. *Which are you going to choose? And how do I counter?*

On board Pilum

The more Phineas Taylor looked the relative positions of the rebel ship and his own, the more he became convinced that *Scorpion* would pass ahead of *Gladius*. He asked himself, would the rebel captain engage *Pilum* this close to another Royal Navy frigate? Smythe was convinced that the rebel Jacinto was a risk taker and unpredictable, but also prudent. On the surface, the analysis was a contradiction but also was probably what made Jacinto difficult to fight.

With the wind from the so' east, none of the ships had the wind gauge. The clear skies and warm weather, coupled with the long, rolling swells, gave those on *Hasta* the feeling that their frigate was loping along. To Taylor's way of thinking, it was a perfect day for a naval action.

So, what is the prudent choice? He had turned *Pilum* so his ship and *Scorpion* would, if neither turned, pass within a few hundred yards of each other. Taylor believed he had to force *Scorpion* to turn to port, to force the rebel frigate closer to *Gladius* and so get the rebel ship into a vise, then pound it into submission. To accomplish that goal, Taylor decided to sail more easterly and block *Scorpion's* path. This gave *Pilum* the option to engage if *Scorpion* turned so' east.

On board Scorpion

Jaco was confident that the Royal Navy frigate to port would fall behind, given Scorpion's superior speed and navigability. The one a mile ahead was off *Scorpion*'s bow at about a 90-degree angle. He debated turning to starboard and running away, or turning to port. His instinct said tack to port; that would force the closer ship to reverse course, which would open the gap, thus allowing *Scorpion* to escape. Continuing on his current course of nor' east until the last possible minute would give him the advantage; he could delay his next move until the last minute and so flummox his opponent. Timing was everything, because he wanted to make sure that the ship to port couldn't cross his stern.

His gut said the time was now. “Mr. Preston, Mr. Jeffords, stand by to come about to port. New course, nor' west. Once we pass the frigate to our port, we keep going no matter what this ship does so we keep the wind gauge.”

Feeling *Scorpion* begin to turn, Second Lieutenant Patterson came onto the main deck to look at the situation. Seeing him, Jaco ordered, “Mr. Patterson, have both batteries ready to fire. With a little luck, we may have a chance to test your gun captain's long range shooting skills as we rake one of His Majesty's frigates from eight hundred yards. If your gun captains think they can hit the enemy frigate to port, they may open fire when their guns bear.”

Patterson waved an acknowledgement, paused to look at both the Royal Navy frigates and then disappeared down the aft companionway to the gun deck. Jaco walked to where Geiger was standing. “Mr. Geiger, pass the word to Mr. Marshall on the mainmast to fire the swivel guns at the quarterdeck at any distance inside three hundred yards. Make sure you have at least six sets of cartridges and powder for each gun. We may not have time to resupply.”

Jaco gave Geiger time to cross the main deck and yell up at Marshall. Bosun Preston bellowed something through the hatch, and within seconds, powder monkeys started up the ratlines on each mast with the cloth slings that had powder on one side and a bag of canister for the swivel guns on the other.

“Mr. Jeffords, helm a-lee.”

The flying jib, fore staysail and jib zipped through the stays as *Scorpion's* bow turned to port. Once steady on the new course, the frigate leapt ahead as if it were a racehorse galloping home. Jaco's eye estimated the ship to port was 800 yards away, a long shot even for his guns. The number one cannon on the port side boomed. He didn't see a splash.

On Board Gladius

Darren looked at *Scorpion* thinking, *That's the same move I would have made!* There was a thump from the 12-pound cannon ball striking the bow, but it did little damage. He ordered the 9-pounder bow chasers to fire as the ship came about to port, knowing they were at close to their maximum range. The 12-pounders would fire as they came to bear, but Darren had little hope that any of their balls would slow, much less stop *Scorpion* at this range. *We've already lost the three to one advantage we were counting on.*

Once the ship completed its tack, he ordered his quartermaster to angle for *Scorpion's* wake to follow the rebel frigate. His seaman's eye told him that when the finished the turn, *Gladius* would be at least a mile behind *Scorpion* and would lose ground every minute to the faster rebel frigate unless *Pilum* was successful in slowing *Scorpion.* If nothing else, *Gladius'* position took away some of his opponent's options.

Darren went to the forward edge of the quarterdeck. Seeing his second lieutenant standing in the companionway, he said, "Mr. Enfield, fire as your bow chasers bear and keep firing as long as you are in range."

Frustrated, Darren didn't add that their 9-pounders, assuming they hit *Scorpion at all,* would only annoy Jacinto.

On board Pilum

Phineas Taylor tried to stand calmly on his quarterdeck despite the fear that urged him to run below. He'd taken Smythe's advice and had only a minimum number of men dispersed on the quarterdeck. The only two standing close to each other were the quartermasters at the wheel. He'd ordered his first lieutenant to move opposite whatever direction he walked.

Pilum was sailing as close to the wind as possible without risking luffing its sails. This course would enable *Pilum* to fire a broadside, albeit at an angle, and not take return fire.

Taylor figured that *Scorpion,* heeled well over to starboard and sailing nor' west, would have to level the ship to fire its cannon, which meant the enemy frigate would slow. The courses of the two ships were converging and if *Scorpion* tacked to parallel *Pilum,* the move would allow *Gladius* to cut the corner and put the rebel frigate in a vise, just as Smythe had envisioned. Taylor assumed that Jacinto could see this as well, and he wondered why *Scorpion* continued on its present northwesterly course.

An easterly turn by *Scorpion,* Taylor reasoned, would be foolhardy, for that would allow his own ship to rake the rebel frigate from the bow, albeit at long range. As Taylor assessed the distance, his brows contracted and his forehead furrowed. *The rebel frigate's cannons protrude much farther than those on my ship. Those must be the long guns Smythe warned us about!* Taylor walked to the forward end of *Pilum's* quarterdeck. "Fire."

They were at 600 yards when the port side battery began firing, sending ripples of concussion down the ship. The wind from the southwest pushed the gunsmoke back against *Pilum's* hull, and the acrid, grey-white cloud partially obscured Taylor's view from the quarterdeck.

On board Scorpion

Jaco had deliberately put his ship in this risky position, but he had faith in the hull and the stoutness of *Scorpion's* masts. Twelve-pound Royal Navy's balls were hitting home, but so far the hull was performing as designed. From the portside "Perfecto corner", he yelled so both Bosun Preston and Quartermaster Jeffords could hear. "Stand by to wear ship to starboard. New course, nor' east."

Once the orders were acknowledged, he ordered. "Mr. Geiger, tell Mr. Payne to open fire with the bow chasers and then the port battery as soon as his guns bear."

A cannon ball popped through the bottom of mainmast's mainsail. Another thumped into the hull beneath his feet, just aft of the #11 gun on the starboard side. For the next two or three minutes, while *Scorpion* turned to starboard, the balls from the enemy ship could mow down the men handling the sheets and braces on the main deck. With its bow toward the enemy, the ship was defenseless except for its two 9-pounder bow chasers.

On Board Gladius

Darren studied the two ships ahead of his frigate with both the naked eye and his spyglass. So far, his tactics were working. Soon *Gladius* would come up on the port side of *Scorpion* they would have the rebel frigate in a vise. From where he stood, his friend and enemy had apparently decided to trade broadsides with *Pilum* at long range and then keep running to the east. That seemed very unlike Jacinto. Unless the rebel captain had gotten arrogant and overconfident.

On board Pilum

The gunsmoke quickly dissipated and Taylor saw the spacing between the masts change as *Scorpion* began to turn east. The distance between the ships was now down to 400 yards, and he had already sent his first lieutenant down to the gun deck to encourage the gun captains, figuring they'd get one more aimed shot as they crossed the enemy frigate's bow. If they could take down one of *Scorpion's* masts, capturing the rebel ship was possible.

Once they passed, *Pilum* would wear to starboard to sail parallel to *Scorpion* so his enemy could not cross his stern. Tacking through the wind to port was out of the question; *Pilum* would lose ground the frigate could never make up.

With his plan set in his mind, Phineas Taylor went back to watching *Scorpion*. *Gladius* had already started to turn to cut the corner. Smythe's tactics were working! By nightfall, he believed, *Scorpion's* captain will have had to haul down its flag.

On board Scorpion

On the quarterdeck, Jaco could hear thumps as the Royal Navy balls hammered his ship. There was a loud clang, which sounded odd, and Jaco was wondering what had caused it when another ball plowed through a line of men pulling the mizzen topgallant to port. The sickening, sucking sound of men being pulverized by a cast iron sounded over the quarterdeck.

Bosun Preston was yelling at a group of Marines and sailors to ignore the carnage and get the braces tied. Other sailors carried the wounded men, some of them missing limbs, below.

Jaco felt a ball hit below his feet. What he wouldn't learn until later was that the ball went through the bulkhead separating the main deck from the captain's pantry and then into his cabin, tearing up his bunk.

Jaco heard lines pop, and then there was a crack. The topsail yard on the mainmast had given way. Jaco felt *Scorpion* slow slightly.

Jaco heard a shout and saw Geiger and Marshall scampering up the yards to the royals' yardarms on the fore and mainmast. More shouts and three more men went up the mizzenmast to the royal yardarm and started untying the gaskets.

Another seaman he recognized as Colin Landry was hacking away at several lines. Below, Bosun Preston was directing men to pull on the yard to keep the topsail spar someplace close to its proper position.

The damage was significant, but not enough to change his plan. The Royal Navy frigate was 300 yards on his port side. Time to turn.

The royals popped as they were sheeted home, and there was a gap where the main topsail used to be. The sail and the yardarm were now lying on the netting above the main deck, stretched there to protect the men from falling debris.

"Mr. Jeffords and Mr. Preston, stand by to come to port. New course due north."

"Nor' it is, Cap'n."

Jeffords no sooner got the words out of his mouth when there was a shriek and the enclosure behind the quartermaster flew into pieces as a 12-pound ball went through the railing and cut through the back like a knife. The concussion of the ball's passing knocked the quartermaster's mate to the deck and slammed Jeffords against the wheel.

Both men looked like porcupines with small splinters sticking out of their bodies. Jaco leapt forward. "Mr. Jeffords, I've got the wheel. Both of you go below!"

"No, sir. I'll manage. The pain will keep me paying attention."

Scorpion's bow was now past the stern of the Royal Navy frigate, and Jaco thought the worst of the maneuver was done. *Scorpion*'s port battery began firing. He could see the balls hitting home by the wood erupting into the air.

Time to make his next move. "Mr. Jeffords, Mr. Preston, come about to port, NOW!"

Preston and several others had splashed buckets of sea water on the deck to clear away the gore. Now men formed up in teams along the bulwark to haul the braces and handle the sheets.

Morton Geiger came up from the gun deck.

"Chain shot, sir?"

"Aye, we're going to be inside one hundred yards, so double shot would be my choice."

Geiger nodded once, then looked at the Royal Navy frigate ahead and the one behind before going down to the gun deck.

On board Pilum

Taylor considered *Pilum* to be a handy ship, but he was both astonished and envious at how easily and quickly *Scorpion* turned. He'd already given the orders to fall off the wind to port, but his bluff-bowed frigate didn't turn as fast as the adversary's. He searched for the man Darren had described and found him on the forward port corner of his quarterdeck. The short, stocky man with his black hair in a short ponytail was clearly the man in charge. The only other men on the quarterdeck were two officers and the men at the wheel. *Pilum,* Taylor realized, was now in for a pounding. His ship had already been hit several times but was still fit to fight.

Taylor yelled at his bosun to get the sails around faster. Then came the sound of chain shot whistling through the air, accompanied by the sound of very large cannons being fired. Stays and braces snapped and one of the ratlines floated down onto the nets rigged above the gun deck. He was not sure which was worse—the sound of wind hissing through the links of chain zipping through the air at several hundred feet per second, or the sound of wood being smashed by cannon balls.

Despite the broadsides *Pilum had* fired at *Scorpion,* there was little visible damage other than the missing mainmast top sail and a few lines streaming in the wind. The rebel ship's hull looked unscathed. He now understood why Smythe said that *Scorpion's* hull seemed to be made of iron. His 12-pounders were having almost no effect. *And that's why he told us to aim at sails and masts.*

Taylor was ordering his quartermaster to adjust the new course when there was a sharp report. The quartermaster never heard his captain's order, because a ball decapitated him. His torso fell to the quarterdeck with blood pouring from the ruptured veins. A sudden rain of musket balls tattooed the quarterdeck. Two struck the quartermaster's assistant, who fell bleeding from mortal wounds.

Taylor looked for his first lieutenant; he was sprawled face down, with blood pouring from holes in his chest. *My God, I am the only one alive on the quarterdeck!*

Scorpion was about to angle past *Pilum's* stern and head out into the Atlantic. There was nothing anyone on his ship could do to stop the rebel frigate from escaping. He and the rest of this crew were now in survival mode.

Pilum's captain grabbed the wheel. He heard again the distinctive bark of a swivel gun, and his right hand pulling down on a spoke of the wheel to turn his ship to starboard dissolved into a bloody mess. At the same time, he fell awkwardly onto the deck, his right foot shattered. Taylor used his left hand to wrap the kerchief he wore on his neck around his calf and pulled the knot tight with his teeth to stop the bleeding. Then he reached over and pulled the cloth headband off the dead quartermaster's severed head and tied it around his right forearm. Just after he pulled the knot tight, he passed out from loss of blood.

He didn't see his bosun take the wheel. Nor did Taylor see *Pilum's* mizzenmast come down, broken just above the lookout platform and the lower mast cap. As it fell, the mizzen dragged the top gallant section of the mainmast with it, crashing into the netting.

On Board Gladius

Smythe turned his ship to follow *Scorpion* and quickly realized that, even missing a main sail, the rebel ship was still faster than *Gladius*. Through his spyglass, he saw the face of the stocky, dark-haired man on the quarterdeck. *One of these days, I'll find out what* Scorpion's *hull is made from, and why its cannons hit harder than what we have in the Royal Navy.*

He ordered Bosun Louttit to luff *Gladius's* sails so his ship could render assistance to the severely battered *Pilum,* which was lucky to have one of its masts still standing.

Chapter 19
The Matron Speaks

Charleston, fourth week of May 1780

In one of her concessions to being a septuagenarian, Miriam Bildesheim used a small step to make lifting her foot into a stirrup easier. Reyna buckled the strap holding the folding step to her grandmother's saddle bag, then mounted her own horse. She was looking forward to the trip into Charleston with the grandmother she respected and adored.

When she was young, Miriam had been six feet tall; now she was 76, and she'd shrunk to 5-foot-10. But seventy-plus years of life hadn't slowed her down. Those who knew her would say she was spry, active, and very much in control of Shayna Enterprises, Ltd. Four decades after she and her husband started their businesses, Miriam Bildesheim was one of the wealthiest individuals in South Carolina, possibly even the Thirteen Colonies.

Once Reyna was settled in her saddle, Miriam nodded to the men sitting in the four wagons, patiently waiting in the growing light. Each wagon carried twelve 100-pound crates containing bricks of processed indigo that would be delivered to South Carolina Import and Export, Ltd. which had letters of credit from customers in Europe.

Before the revolution began, English looms took about 70 percent of Shayna's production, which was well known for its quality. With shipments to England shut down, South Carolina Import and Export's agents in Europe had found willing new customers in Denmark, Prussia, Sweden and Russia who paid higher prices than the English mills for all the indigo her farms could produce.

The two women were riding side by side far enough in front of the procession so their conversations could not be overheard. Miriam spoke softly. "Reyna, are you vorried zat zee British may take you prisoner?"

"Yes. However, I can prove I was in Dorchester to examine four pregnant women and treat five others. If asked, I am going into to Charleston to pick up medicines I ordered and make some more alcohol. Even the Loyalists know I travel out to farms to treat the sick and deliver babies."

"Vell, you should stay in Charleston for zee ball zat Lord Cornwallis ist having on June 17th to celebrate zee British victory. He sent invitations to *Tantes* Devorah and Yael. Zee British vould like all zee eligible young vomen of Charleston to attend and meet vat zay call 'eligible English gentlemen from gut families'. By zat, I think zee British are saying zat some come mit titles."

"But, Baba, I am engaged to Jaco."

"I know zat, your family knows zat, and the Jacintos know zat, but I do not think zee British know. Zee ball vill be a place you can get to know your enemy better."

Reyna rode in silence. She wondered if the British major she'd shot would have been one of those with a title. Then she was struck by an appalling realization. “Baba, I have nothing to wear!”

“Talk to Tante Devorah. She vill find something in zee store for you.”

Tante Devorah was Miriam’s daughter who ran one of the larger dry goods stores in Charleston. Tante Yael ran The Dockside Inn, a three-story, 22-room inn overlooking the Cooper River. The inn was often booked by wealthy Charlestonians for special events. Yael’s twin sister Rivkah ran the 11 room Charleston in and Tavern. Miriam was planning to stay at the larger inn; her house had been taken over by the British Army and given to the officers from the Hessian-Kassel regiment.

“Baba, do you really wish me to go?”

“*Ja*, I do.”

“Then I will.”

Miriam turned and smiled at her granddaughter. “Gut.”

75 miles east of Grand Turk Island,
second week of June 1780

Jaco had climbed the ratlines, and now he scanned the empty sea around him as *Scorpion* drifted, wallowing gently in the Atlantic. Freed from the tension of the sheets that tied them down, the frigate’s sails flapped noisily. The yardarms, loose from the pull of their braces, groaned as the long three-foot swells moved the frigate up and down.

The broken topsail yardarm had been replaced, but in his daily inspection Gaskins had found something more sinister. Small amounts of seawater were leaking into the hull, and Gaskins needed to examine the hull from the outside.

The diminutive carpenter was sitting on a small plank hung from two poles with ropes slipped through pulleys at each end. The poles were lashed to the bulwark and a rack of belaying pins. The object of his interest was *Scorpion's* planking just aft of the first thwart ship bulkhead in the bow known as the knighthead plate. He swung left and right, examining the planks with his eyes as well as his hands.

Back on deck, the hissing of the letter 's' caused by Gaskins missing front teeth was more pronounced than usual. "Sssir, she took a number of hitsss on the port ssside where the layering of the planking is much thinner than around the bow chassser gunportsss. A number of planksss are loossse and I sssuspect ssseveral of the ribsss are cracked or broken."

"And what is your recommendation?"

"The cracked planksss of the hull should be replaccced. When we open her up, we can sssee the ribsss better and sssplice them asss needed."

"Can you do the work?"

"Aye, me and my matesss can, but not while we are mucking about at sssea. We need quiet anchorage and enough good oak and pine to do the job right. Methinksss I'll need about a week, maybe more."

"How bad are we leaking?"

"A wee bit, sssir, nothing ssseriousss. My fear is if a bloody British cannon ball hitsss the sssame area again, the wood will give way, and then we'll have a real messs on our handsss."

Jaco nodded. This was not news he wanted to hear. There was the question of what port would be the best equipped with wood and tools. Sint Eustatius or any of the other Dutch islands in the Leeward Islands were out. If *Scorpion* was there for more than a day or two, there would be a line of Royal Navy ships waiting for *Scorpion* to come out. Havana, about 700 miles or four days away by the most direct route, seemed the best answer, unless he wanted to again sail down to Aruba, Bonaire or Curaçao.

"Mr. Gaskins, make a list of everything, I mean *everything*, you need to fix the hull. When you finish, bring the list to me."

"Aye, Captain."

Jaco walked aft. "Mr. Geiger, get us under way again. I'll take the deck while you and Mr. Marshall go to my cabin and use the chart to plot a course to Havana."

Nassau, Bahamas, first week of June 1780

Right after the battle with *Scorpion*, Smythe sailed *Gladius* back and forth between *Hasta* and *Pilum* to render what assistance his ship could. Twice before, on *Deer* and *Puritan*, he'd brought seriously damaged ships to port; he knew what the captains or their surviving officers faced. At noon each day the squadron stopped to bury its dead.

Thankfully, the squadron made Nassau in four days. There the wounded were brought ashore and *Pilum* and *Hasta* could be sufficiently repaired so they could safely sail to either Halifax or Port Royal or even England, where they could be hauled out of the water, fully inspected and repaired or broken up.

Smythe felt guilty. His squadron had engaged *Scorpion* and come off second best. Nearly 60 Royal Navy sailors and Marines had died, and as many were wounded. Even if he survived the inevitable infection and fever, now that Phineas Taylor was a double amputee, his career in the Royal Navy was probably over.

Smythe was convinced the real problem and threat to the Royal Navy were *Scorpion's* cannon and how her hull was built. If the rebels, or worse, the French built ships like *Scorpion*, the Royal Navy's dominance would be severely tested, possibly eclipsed. But as a very junior captain, Smythe realized that few if any admirals would listen to him.

There was one, however, and that was Admiral Davidson, the Duke of Somerset, to whom he wrote a long, detailed report describing their plans, the events leading up to the fight, and the action itself. He then made three fair copies, and each of the four documents was co-signed by Meegan and Taylor.

Without a squadron, Smythe was just another frigate captain. He was ordered to report to the North American Station in Charleston.

Charleston, second week of June 1780

As there was no Royal Governor in residence, Lord Cornwallis and his staff took over the Royal Governor's mansion as his headquarters. He used the sitting room, emptied of furniture except for a table and four chairs, to hold "court" for those he summoned or who requested a meeting with him.

When Cornwallis summoned the most influential Charlestonians after the British captured the city, one person —Miriam Bildesheim—did not attend. She was away at one of the farms of her *kollectiv*. When informed of the meeting that had transpired, Miriam said, "If Lord Cornwallis vants to meet vit me and if he ist a lord und a gentleman, he should send a proper invitation."

Based on the input from three men—Bayard Templeton, Cornelius Vickers, and Curtis Armstrong, who had promoted and presented himself as the Royal Governor's first secretary —that Lord Cornwallis should meet Ms. Bildesheim, a written invitation signed by Lord Cornwallis was hand-delivered by messenger. In proper form, she responded in writing that she would be happy to meet with the British General and suggested a time and date, which was accepted.

Miriam's network had told her that Vickers was now amongst the Cornwallis' inner circle. For years, Vickers had been offering her inducements—money, lucrative proposals, property, stock—to stop using Laredo Shipping and the Jacinto's import-export business. Each time she politely but firmly rejected his offer.

When Miriam walked into the sitting room of the former Royal Governor's mansion, she was accompanied on her right by Shoshana, whose grace, height, intelligence and beauty could dominate a room. Now that she was a member of the South Carolina bar, Shoshana was officially Shayna Enterprise's attorney. Reyna was to Miriam's left. She would, if needed, serves as a witness to what was said.

The British Army lieutenant who escorted the three women to the door gave the two younger women the once over before asking politely, "Are you ladies coming to Lord Cornwallis' ball on Saturday?"

Shoshana, who was a head taller than the British Army officer, smiled and blinked her green eyes. "Of course, both Miss Laredo and I are attending. We wouldn't miss the ball of the year!"

"I am delighted to hear that! I am Lieutenant Francis Petre, of the Barony Petre, and I look forward to seeing both of you."

Both young women smiled in acknowledgement, then followed Miriam into the room. Miriam stood in the middle and listened to the sound of the heavy door closing behind the trio. None of the women said a word.

Vickers, who was leaning against the window, stepped forward with an admonishing frown on his face. "Mrs.

Bildesheim, it is customary to curtsey when one enters into a room graced by a member of the nobility."

Miriam smiled at the portly Vickers, whom she regarded as a pompous *schwein* (pig), then used her eyes to shoot daggers at Bayard Templeton, resplendent in his Green Dragoons uniform. Then her face softened as she addressed Cornwallis. "Herr General, neither I nor anyvon in my family bows to anyvon other than Gott."

Cornwallis, who was standing in front of his desk, clasped his hands behind his back. "Well then, we know where your loyalties lie."

"No, Herr General, you do not. My loyalty ist to my family, und to vat is best for Shayna Enterprises and my employees. If zat means zee end to British rule of Zouth Carolina, zen zee British Army should leave."

Cornwallis ignored the two other women standing next to her. "Mrs. Bildesheim, do you know why I invited you here?"

"No, Herr General, I do not. However, before vee begin, may I introduce my granddaughter, Reyna Laredo, who cares for many of Charleston's sick, including your vounded soldiers, und my attorney, Shoshana Jacinto."

Cornwallis looked at Templeton and Vickers, both of whom had surprised looks on their faces. He then spoke. "Mrs. Bildesheim, I did not know that women were allowed to practice law or be doctors in the King's province of South Carolina."

Miriam lifted her chin. "Herr General, I zuspect there ist much you don't know about Zouth Carolina. Reyna ist a very good doctor. If she vas allowed to attend medical school, Reyna vould have the title. At zee moment, zat is not possible. But ven zis var ist over, I vill zee to it zat South Carolina has a medical school und a law school that accepts vomen. Miss Jacinto recently passed zee bar exam. And yes, she ist the first of what I hope vill be many lawyers who are vomen."

Cornwallis softened. "That is very enlightened thinking."

"Zank you. So, Herr General, vy am I standing here?"

"I'll be direct. I understand your farms supply much of the food to Charleston, and I would like for these farms to supply the British Army as well."

Miriam kept her hands clasped in front of her waist. "My customers here in Charleston pay a fair price. Vill zee British Army?"

"We would like to negotiate more favorable pricing. We are, after all the British Army."

Shoshana looked at Templeton, who was off to her right, standing against the wall behind Cornwallis. Raphael Soriano had warned her that Templeton was an arrogant buffoon. If they ever met in court, she looked forward to challenging him—and winning.

Reyna was watching Vickers intently. Her father didn't think much of the man. He was known in Charleston for his underhanded dealings with farmers and shipping companies. He would quote one price, but when it came time to pay, he would find a reason to pay less.

"Vy should I sell my produce and meat at less zan zee market price? And if ve zell vat ve have to zee British Army, many in Charleston vill not have enough to eat. Vat good ist zat?"

"Because if you don't, I have the authority from King George to seize your crops and put you out of business."

Miriam nodded emphatically three times before she spoke. "I zought zo." She let the three words hang in the air for several seconds. "Zo, I vas invited here zo you could threaten me if I did not give in to your demands for lower prices for food for zee men who kill my employees and burn zer homes. Vell, Herr General, your threats do not scare me. If you think you can vin zis var by threatening old vomen and murdering farmers, vomen und children as Herr Templeton here hast done, zen you haf already lost."

Cornwallis' face reddened. He wasn't used to be challenged by anyone, much less a commoner of Prussian background. "Are you accusing Major Templeton of murder?"

"*Nein*, I am stating a fact. Ven you shoot an innocent ten-year-old boy, zat ist murder. Ven you shoot two families because zey can't tell you vat zay don't know, zat ist also murder. Templeton vill say vat he did vas var. Zee people who vitnessed vat happened know better."

"Your people rebelled against their King, not Major Templeton. We are trying to put down this rebellion."

"Zee boy vas my grandson Michael, vich makes zis var very, very personal. Venn zis var ist over, I vill see zat Herr Templeton pays for his crimes."

"That day, Mrs. Bildesheim, will not come. The British Army and England will put down this rebellion, and it is your rebels who will pay the price for your treason."

Miriam's shook her head and spoke in a soft but firm voice. "Vee vill zee. Right now, zee British Army ist only safe in zee three cities it controls—Charleston, New York and Savannah. To vin, you must control zee countryside. In ze meanwhile, Herr General, if zee British Army vishes to buy from Shayna Enterprises, I vill be happy to zell vat I have for a vair price—after zee people of Charleston buy vat zay need."

Cornwallis flushed, trying to contain his anger. "That is not acceptable. You shall pay for your impertinence and lack of respect for the King and his army. I will have you arrested."

Miriam smiled so her white teeth showed. Her voice turned to steel as she stepped toward Cornwallis until her face was a scant ten inches from his. Her voice was soft and gentle as she spoke. "Just like you did vit Abigail Minis in Savannah? Zen you found out zee food stopped, zo you released her. No, Herr General, you need me. God villing und if I am not murdered, I vill be vatching ven you surrender your army. Zat may not happen tomorrow or zee next day or even zis year, but in zee end, you British vill be defeated. You simply do not understand zee vill of zee people in zee Thirteen Colonies. Vee don't vant you here, und zee zooner you leave, zee better."

Cornwallis didn't move as Miriam gently brushed off a piece of imaginary lint from Lord Cornwallis coat, knowing full well that a commoner is not supposed to touch a person of nobility. "Zink about zat, Herr General. Vee vill meet again."

Reyna and Shoshana saw appalled expressions on the faces of nearly everyone in the room.

The septuagenarian whirled around as easily as if she were in her twenties. "Come, Reyna und Shoshana, vee are done here."

The two younger women turned gracefully and followed. As they walked to the door, the smiles on their faces could not be seen by the British general.

Charleston, Saturday, June 17th, 1780

Thunderstorms brought rain during the day, and the cold front that pushed them cooled the evening air. By the evening the temperature was supposed to be in the sixties, which would, despite the humidity, make being dressed up comfortable.

Reyna and Shoshana sat patiently in Perla Jacinto's dressing room while their mothers braided their long hair. An open window let in the cooler air. Shoshana said, without turning her head, "I wonder if the colder air will cool the ardor of the British officers who want to impress us South Carolina girls."

Reyna giggled. "I don't think so. These men probably haven't met an eligible woman since they left New York."

Shoshana looked straight out the window. "We're going to be a whole new experience for them."

"In more ways than one. I wonder if any of them realize that several of us want to kill them as soon as they venture out into the countryside."

The closed carriage stopped under the portico of the Royal Governor's mansion and a Hessian soldier opened the carriage door, clicked his heels and bowed. From the gaggle of young officers at the top of the steps, two—one British Army and one Hessian—walked down the stairs and held out their arms. The Hessian lieutenant greeted Reyna by saying "Good evening" in English.

Reyna responded in German. "*Guten Abend, Herr Leutnant, Ich bin Reyna Laredo.*" Good evening, Lieutenant, I am Reyna Laredo.

Looking into her dark eyes, the lieutenant used the German syntax normally reserved for friends and family members. "*Sprichst du Deutsch*?" Do you speak German?

"*Ja, ich sprecht ein venig, meine großmutter war aus Preußian.*" Yes, I speak a little. My grandmother is from Prussia.

The young officer smiled and bowed slightly. "*Wunderbar, ein Landsmann. Ich bin Ludwig Reinhard aus*

Wiesbaden." Wonderful, a fellow countryman. I am Ludwig Reinhard from Wiesbaden.

At the top of the stairs, Reyna heard the music playing in the ballroom. A British captain came up Reyna. "Your name, miss?"

"Reyna Laredo."

The captain found her name on his list. "Miss Laredo, welcome to Lord Cornwallis' Victory Ball. Refreshments are in the dining room on the left. Dancing in the ballroom on the right. Please step into the foyer, where I will announce you. After I do, count slowly to three and walk forward, and I will introduce the lovely ladies behind you."

Reyna's and Shoshana's friend, Melody Winters, had been in the carriage right behind theirs. They waited off to the side at the bottom of the stairs until Melody was announced, then the three women made their way to the left. They walked past the length of the buffet table, teasing each other that they wouldn't be able to eat much with the tight corsets they were wearing.

Melody's father was a rice broker, and she had been Reyna's and Shoshana's friend ever since they'd started school together. The war had torn Melody's family apart. Her father was a staunch Loyalist, while her older brother was an artillery officer in the Continental Army under General Washington in New York. Her younger brother Dennis had just turned 15 and wanted to join Templeton's Green Dragoons. This was a choice that Melody and both her parents, even her Loyalist father, strongly opposed.

Reyna didn't want her brother's unit to kill a family friend. She hadn't told Melody that she was the 4th Carolina's doctor. She continued to be haunted by the face of her fellow student registering the shock of being torn apart by a musket ball and the realization he would soon be dead.

The three young women sampled delicacies, then strolled into the room where couples were already performing the cotillon. In the background was an announcement that went unheard by all three. Captain Darren Smythe, captain of His Majesty's Ship *Gladius,* had just arrived.

Smythe asked the captain making the announcements if Miss Reyna Laredo or Shoshana Jacinto had arrived or were expected. The British infantry officer eyed Smythe, flipped through the list and saw the check marks. "Sir, both Miss Jacinto and Miss Laredo are here." Then he indicated a man in a Green Dragoon uniform trying to look important. To Darren, he merely looked pompous. "That chap over there by the name of Bayard Templeton is a local and would know the particulars."

Smythe walked straight up to Templeton as if he were approaching a junior officer. "Sir, excuse me, are you Major Templeton?"

"That I am, and who might you be?"

"Darren Smythe." He assumed that Templeton knew the uniform of a captain in the Royal Navy. "Sir, would you be so kind as to point out either Miss Reyna Laredo or Miss Shoshana Jacinto?"

Templeton's raised eyebrows and look of disdain sent off an alarm bell in Darren's brain. "The two *Jewesses* are over there, halfway down the wall. The wench towering over the others is Miss Jacinto and the short hussy with dark hair is Miss Laredo. Why would you want to talk to a couple of Jews, and traitors to boot? You could do much better, Captain. If you wish, I could introduce you to some of Charleston's better and more *loyal* families."

As Templeton spoke, Darren's dislike of him grew exponentially. The less said, the better. He uttered a curt, "I appreciate the offer, Major, but no thank you." He started weaving through the guests, thinking that if Templeton represented the king's support in South Carolina, the British Army was in trouble.

Darren circulated around the room to make sure Templeton wasn't watching him. As he moved, he kept glancing at Shoshana, whose height made her easy to spot. Through breaks in the crowd, he found himself examining Reyna and Shoshana as he would a ship at sea, from royal to the waterline and from stem to stern. Both, he concluded, were far more attractive than any women he'd met in Portsmouth or Halifax.

Summoning his courage and thinking, *This is worse than facing Jaco Jacinto in battle*, Darren approached the two women and bowed slightly. "Ladies, please excuse me for being very forward. Allow me to introduce myself. I am Captain Darren Smythe." Addressing Shoshana he said, "I know your brother Jaco Jacinto," and nodding to Reyna, "who is your fiancé. I know we wear different uniforms, but I consider Jaco a good friend."

Both girl's mouths dropped. When Jaco was in Charleston, he often talked about Darren in the most positive terms. Reyna was the first to speak, and she put her hand on Darren's arm. "Oh, my word! This is most unexpected. Good heavens, I never thought we would ever meet."

"Neither did I, but here I am.

"And who is this?"

Melody Winters, who had stepped away to talk to another friend, had returned, and now she stood beside Shoshana, facing Darren. Their eyes met and Reyna was sure she saw sparks of interest fly.

Reyna made the introductions. "This is another of my childhood friends, Miss Melody Winters. Miss Winters, this is Captain Darren Smythe of the Royal Navy. Believe it or not, Captain Smythe and Jaco are friends."

Melody looked at Reyna and then at Darren, her eyes wide. "I am astonished. Are officers in the Royal and Continental navies in the habit of forming friendships? Do you exchange uniforms the way the Greek and Trojan warriors exchanged armor, as described by Homer in *The Illiad*?"

Darren laughed, delighted by her wit and knowledge of the classics. "Two years ago, his ship took the one I was on. Afterwards, we spent many hours talking, even though I was his prisoner...." He stopped. He did not want to inquire after Eric Laredo, whom he still believed was a prisoner of war. Darren wanted to change the subject because he was looking at the most beautiful women he'd ever met and did not wish to offend them. "Miss Winters, I am delighted to meet you." He took her offered hand, lifted it and kissed the back.

"Captain Smythe, that gallant move just bought you several dances. Do you?"

"Do what?"

"Dance! Do you know the cotillion, or what we call the contredanse? Sounds rebellious, doesn't it?"

"Unhappily, I do not. Dancing is not something I learned at the naval academy."

Melody grasped his hand. "Then this is a good time to learn a step or too. Don't worry, there are more than a few of your countrymen who are making a fool of themselves on the dance floor. Your mistakes will not be remarked upon, and I forgive them in advance. Come with me."

Someplace in Melody's words, Darren heard an order and meekly followed the 22-year-old blonde out to the dance floor. Reyna looked at Shoshana and both started laughing at the same time. Shoshana said, "He's smitten."

A tall, angular man walked up to the two women. He was one of the few men taller than Shoshana. "Good evening, ladies, I apologize to you, Ms. Laredo, for depriving you of your friend's companionship, but I would like to dance with Miss Jacinto. I am George Boscawen, Third Viscount of Falmouth." He was wearing the uniform of a captain in the British Army and held out his hand "May I have that honor?

Reyna gave a subtle nod and said, "Shoshana, enjoy yourself. I need something to drink."

Reyna was halfway to the dining room when the young Hessian officer who'd escorted her up the steps stepped in front of her and bowed. "*Fraulein Laredo, wilst du mit mir tanzen*?" Miss Laredo, will you dance with me?

She smiled brightly. "*Natürlich.*" Of course.

At a break in the music, Reyna and Shoshana managed to slip away from ball and the line of young officers who asking to be added to their dance cards. They both wanted to breathe fresh air; they were feeling the tension of being amongst enemies.

Walking through the garden, they passed a small alcove where they unexpectedly found Darren and Melody sitting on a wooden bench. Darren stood up and motioned to the empty place, made larger when Melody slid to the end. "Please, do join us."

Neither Reyna nor Shoshana sat down. Reyna asked, "How was the dancing?"

Darren quickly answered, "Melody was beautiful and graceful. I, on the other hand, was clumsy."

Melody laughed. "Captain Smythe wasn't the worst dancer out there. With practice, I think he could become a passable partner."

"Miss Winters is being polite. Inept is the correct word for my performance." The Royal Navy officer's face turned serious. "Miss Laredo, might we talk privately someplace? I need only a few minutes."

"Captain Smythe, if you are going to talk about Miss Jacinto's brother and my fiancé, then we can all hear what you have to say. I trust Miss Winters with my life. So, are you the bearer of bad news?"

Darren cast a glance around before replying. "I am relieved to say I am not. Captain Jacinto was, as of two weeks ago, alive and well. My squadron engaged *Scorpion,* yet he managed to get away."

Reyna couldn't help laughing. "You meant to say that once again my future husband and *Scorpion* bested the Royal Navy."

"Aye, I do. I can't share the details here, but if there were someplace private we could meet, then I could be, within limits, a bit more open."

"Are you going to try to pry out from me where I think Jaco is?"

"No, not at all. That would be ungentlemanly and I wouldn't do that."

Shoshana put her hand on Darren's arm. "Captain, how long are you going to be in Charleston?"

"A few more days. Why?"

"My family would be delighted to have you come to dinner at our house. I'll invite Miss Winters, that is if she wishes to come, and we can all talk in privacy." She stressed the last word.

"Splendid! I'll hire a carriage. And if is permitted, I will pick Miss Winters up and escort her home afterwards."

Shoshana smiled. "You won't need a carriage. Her house is only a block from ours."

Darren looked at Melody, whose eyes sparkled as she spoke. “I was hoping to see you again.”

CHAPTER 20
LETTERS TO SWEETHEARTS

Charleston, third week of June 1780

Each night since the ball, Smythe had been a guest of either the Jacintos, the Laredos or the Winters. He was surprised by the gracious hospitality and how warmly he was welcomed, as if he were a member of their families. This was very different from the stiff formality he'd encountered in Gosport, particularly when his parents introduced him to families with eligible women.

He found the openness and genuine friendship confusing, because the Laredos and Jacintos were the enemy. But now, he could call them friends.

And then there was Melody.

She was all he could think about. She knew how to cut right through his barriers, put him at ease and make him laugh. When the war broke out, Melody had been hoping to become a professor of languages at the College of Charleston. At present, she was teaching French, Latin, Greek and Spanish in a local school, and she was in the process of learning German. His heart was firmly telling his brain to figure out when and how he could return to Charleston.

Gladius was leaving on the afternoon tide, and he needed to finish the third of four letters he intended to post. The first two would go into the locked box where the Royal Mail was kept on the packet ship leaving tomorrow for England. The latter two would be delivered tomorrow by couriers after *Gladius* set sail.

In the letter to his father and brother, he described the research Reyna was doing and included a drawing she had made of a design for a surgical instrument that was not in the Smythe & Sons kit her parents had bought her. The design was, at least to his eyes, new.

Reyna had several ideas for other surgical instruments, and had told Darren there was no firm in Charleston capable of making them to standards of quality and precision. His questions for his father and brother were: Would Smythe & Sons be interested in licensing her designs? And if so, how should they proceed?

His second letter was addressed to his mother and father to assure them he was well, and at the moment in Charleston. In the last sentence, he wrote that he had met a Miss Melody Winters and hoped, when the war was over, to court her.

Letter three was a thank-you note addressed to Reyna and Shoshana. The note was brief, informal; a genuine expression of his thanks for their hospitality and friendship. This one was the easiest of all four to write.

The last note vexed him. He stared at the paper, at a loss for words. In all his life, he'd never met a woman who spoke four languages as well as the King's English. Melody, like Reyna and Shoshana, was determined to be educated and have a professional career of her own. This was a concept he welcomed!

Melody's smile and easy laugh had captivated him when she blamed the Laredos and Jacintos for compelling her to learn foreign languages. In the Jacinto household, there were days when only Spanish or French was spoken, and if she wanted to speak to her friend on those days, she had to communicate in that language. The Laredos did the same thing, only the languages were German and Spanish.

Melody had candidly told him how the war had split her family. She'd confessed that her sympathies were with the rebels, and she did would not move with her father and mother to Halifax or Nassau or whatever colony was offered if the British lost. Charleston was her home and where her friends lived.

Those words, spoken with conviction, had scared him. Was he falling in love with a woman who wouldn't marry him because she would have to move to England? Would he give up his career in the Royal Navy to marry Melody?

Desperately, Darren wanted to pursue her hand in marriage, thinking, *These things will sort themselves out in time*. He had enough money to live anywhere they chose. He was, by almost any definition, "very well off". Later he would tell Melody about his wealth, but he wanted her to love him for who he was, not his money.

Several sheets of Royal Navy letterhead were crumpled up on the floor. Writing her name was easy. The sentences that followed were hard to compose.

Determined to finish, Darren dipped his quill pen in the bottle of blue ink, which he had purchased locally and which he surmised had started as a South Carolina indigo plant, and tried again.

Miss Winters,

I must confess that writing this letter is one of the most difficult tasks I have ever attempted. Words simply cannot describe how I feel about you. Every time I close my eyes, I can see your beautiful face and imagine your soft voice with, as you say, your South Carolina accent.

The past few days have been the happiest in my life. From the bottom of my heart, I thank you, your friends and your family for opening up your homes to me and for your hospitality in what must be, no, what are very trying times.

Today my first visit to Charleston comes to an end and I must do my duty. My fear is that you will forget about me and move on with your life. There are plenty of eligible men in Charleston, and if you decide to marry one, it will be hard, but I understand.

However, if you are agreeable, I very much wish to see you again. I will not and I beg you will not allow this damned war to drive a wedge between us. Do not let distance or that I am a Royal Navy officer colour your thinking. All can be dealt with.

Again, as I said to you last night, I want to see you again. Hopefully, you feel the same about me. Please, and I am smiling broadly as my pen scratches across the paper, write in English for my French is terrible, my Spanish, German, Italian and Latin non-existent. English is, unfortunately, the only language I speak.

God willing, we will see each other again soon.

Darren Smythe

Havana, fourth week of June 1780

Scorpion rode at anchor in the inner harbor opposite the Spanish Navy's base in Havana. The incoming tide flowed past the ship, leaving a small wake. Above the quarter and main decks, the crew had hung a canvas awning that stretched from bow to stern; that along with the cool sea breeze from the Florida Straits kept the temperature pleasant. Nonetheless, by mid-afternoon, the deck was hot underfoot, and to cool it Jaco ordered the deck hosed down with sea water.

The berthing deck was hot and stuffy despite the open hatches. Jaco allowed the sailors to sling their hammocks on the noticeably cooler gun deck to sleep at night.

Every day, Lieutenant Patterson and Midshipman Geiger went to the local market and brought back fresh produce and meat. They bought several cast-iron grills and pieces of slate that were placed on the quarterdeck under the feet of the grills. At night, the cooks treated the crew to grilled meat, fresh vegetables and baked bread made in the ship's stove.

Jaco also allowed small groups of his sailors go ashore. Each contingent was reminded that Spanish jails were not very pleasant places, and any sailor who created a disturbance would be dealt with harshly. Worse, fines would come out of their pay and prize money.

As he did in each port, Jaco stayed out of the local bars and taverns. He had promised Reyna he would do so, and he saw no value in drinking in a bar what he could drink in the privacy of his cabin or at meals with his officers.

His biggest fear about shore leave was not desertion, although that was always a real possibility, but disease. Reyna, as well as *Scorpion's* surgeon Dr. Ferguson, were quite graphic in their explanations of some of the diseases his men could catch from the local prostitutes, whom the good doctor called Piper's wives. Ferguson's favorite term to describe a sailor who has contracted a sexually transmitted disease was "Frenchified".

Nonetheless, Jaco struggled to control his impatience as *Scorpion* rode at anchor, unable to hunt for prizes. Yes,

Spain was at war with England. Yes, Spain was an ally. Yes, they had all the supplies Gaskins needed, but this was Cuba and things moved slowly. Ten whole days after the order was placed, the first boat pulled away from the naval base's pier loaded with planks of wood.

While he waited, Gaskins and the sailmaker constructed a shroud that hung down over the side so prying eyes from the shore wouldn't see how the hull was built. Havana had been occupied by the British during the Seven Years War and Jaco suspected details of *Scorpion's* frame and construction could be sold to the British.

Jaco did not want to begin repairs until the ship had everything on board in case they had to sortie quickly. Now, with the supplies to hand, Gaskins and his mate could begin. First to come off was the external planking that would let them examine the ribs.

Gaskins climbed out of the narrow confines of the bow and stretched, pressing a hand on the small of his back. "Captain, there'sss much more damage than I thought. We're going to have to sssplint the first sssix ribsss and to do ssso, take off more planking."

"How long?"

"Two, maybe three weeksss. We'll sssplint the ribs firssst. Then re-plank. Remember, sssir, we have to measure, cut and fit each piece and then peg the planksss in place."

"Can you finish any faster?"

"No, sssir. Not if you want the work done right. If we run into a problem, I may need more time."

Gaskins never sugar coated his estimates. If he said two or three weeks, that's how long he needed. Jaco nodded several times. "Well, Mr. Gaskins, I suggest you get started!"

Jaco was resigned to not leaving Havana until the end of July. Staying longer also meant that he would have to attend more formal dinners with the Spanish Navy. Hopefully, a hurricane wouldn't come along before the repairs are completed.

Jaco retired to his cabin to update his journal and ship's log, as well as write letters to his father and Reyna. The words in the ship's log were clinical, describing the cracks in the ribs and what the repairs would be. In his journal, he bared his soul because the words were cathartic. His father said that keeping a journal would help him later in life when he could, with the luxury of time and more experience, read them again.

He could not confide in Hedley Garrison; his relationship with his First Lieutenant was simply not as strong or as deep as with Jack Shelton. Garrison was more than competent and should have his own ship, but since Shelton, who was a friend to both, had been blown over the side their relationship had changed. They started keeping their distance from each other. Jaco believed the reason was the fear that he might lose another close friend.

Friday, June 30th, 1780, in port Havana

Finally, we were able to start the repairs. By lunchtime this afternoon, Gaskins had pulled enough planks for us to see the damage and that was far more extensive than we thought. The cracked ribs may not have failed under normal sailing, but if hit with another cannon ball or worked in a heavy sea, they would have come loose and Scorpion would have taken on water.

While the damage would not have put Scorpion out of action, the thought certainly gives me pause. We have been very lucky so far in that enemy balls have not been able to penetrate either the gun or berthing deck except when they hit a gunport. As a result, our casualties have been very low, but what is more important, the ship's design protects our gun crews and enables them to operate at peak efficiency.

I have not timed how fast we are shooting, but from the results I believe Scorpion is shooting at the rate of one ball per minute and a half. Our cannons are more accurate and our long twelves hit much harder.

We will remain in Havana until the repairs are finished near the end of July. The Spanish are having a party for my sailors at the naval base to celebrate our Fourth of July.

The event will be good for my crew, but frankly, I would rather be at sea, hunting the enemy. Looking back on the fight a few weeks ago, I believe Scorpion may be the subject of a determined hunt by the Royal Navy. I do not think it was a coincidence that three fifth-rate frigates were acting in concert to try force Scorpion to fight two or all three at once. While I think we would have given a good account of ourselves, three against one in a close action is not one I want to fight. Such a battle could cost me my ship and, most likely, my life.

As I sit here writing, I wonder if I will ever see Reyna or Charleston again. Luck has been on the side of Scorpion and it is only by the grace of God that I have, so far, *escaped unscathed. Every day I ask myself, should I give up my command?*

Every day, I tell myself, no, I must not. I pray that God has written me in the Book of Life for this year and hopefully for many more. The day I will stop asking this question is when the British grant us independence. But then I ask, will I live to see that day? Lately, I fear I may not. If we win our freedom, then giving my life to our cause will be worth my sacrifice. Freedom is that important.

Satisfied with his entry, he closed his journal and wrote a letter to Reyna, which he delivered to a Danish ship captain headed to Charleston to pick up a load of indigo bricks before sailing to Copenhagen. The captain agreed to carry letters from the crew, and Jaco hoped Reyna would figure out a way to get the northbound letters to Boston, where they could be sent to the men's homes.

Near Dorchester, SC, third week of July 1780

There was a lot to smile about in the camp of the 4th Carolina Dragoons. While they had not participated in the Battle at Mobley's Meeting House on June 10th, 11th and 12th, they could cheer about the results. Continental Army and men from South Carolina militia units had defeated Loyalist troops decisively and stopped Cornwallis' campaign to burn and loot farms in Mobley Settlement, 75 miles east of their encampment.

The following week, another group of South Carolinians stopped Loyalist troops who were planning to hang South and North Carolina militia men they'd captured. The fighting was brutal, pitting family members against each other. In the end, the Loyalists were forced from the field, leaving their dead and wounded behind.

Both battles, albeit small ones, buoyed the men of the 4th Carolina. Amos' command now numbered almost 300 men, 70 of whom were Waldeck Germans who readily adapted to their way of fighting.

Templeton was now venturing out of Charleston with his entire force of dragoons, supported by infantry. The British Army held Charleston and four forts along the Santee River—Watson, Motte, Granby and Ninety-Six.

With the fall of Charleston, the Continental Army in Georgia, North and South Carolina had evaporated. However, groups led by Francis Marion, Thomas Sumter, William Davie, Andrew Pickens and Elijah Clarke harassed British units by ambushing their supply columns. And they had begun to loosely coordinate their operations and to refer to themselves as Patriots.

Charleston, third week of July 1780

In order to maintain her cover, Reyna spent most of the summer in Charleston, venturing out to Dorchester only for a few days at a time. Staying at home let her continue her research as well as keep an eye on the British. On Sundays, weather permitting, she sailed with her father and mother on Cooper River.

South of the city, they would come alongside another sailboat and exchange picnic baskets. The one Reyna passed over contained information on ships that came into Charleston, the British Army and Loyalist units in the city, and letters to the men of the 4th Carolina. In the basket passed to her were letters from the 4th Carolina to distribute to their families.

Today, late in the afternoon on Sunday, Reyna was walking up the steps to her house after delivering the letters when a young man with blond hair asked with a heavy accent, "Are you Miss Reyna Laredo?"

Reyna stopped and looked at the suntanned young man; he was about her brother Eric's age. "Yes, I am."

The man bowed slightly and held out a letter. "My name is Christian Thagaard, the second lieutenant on the Danish Merchant Ship *Odense*. I was asked to deliver this by your fiancée, Jaco. His ship is in Havana undergoing repairs."

"Is he well?"

"Oh, yes."

"When did you leave Havana?"

"Six days ago. We are loading our cargo now and should leave for Copenhagen tomorrow."

"Thank you."

The man bowed. "My pleasure, and you are as lovely as Captain Jacinto described."

"Why thank you, Mr. Thagaard. You are so kind."

She hadn't seen Jaco since January and had been sending letters to his father, not knowing when Jaco would get them. Her last one had described Darren Smythe's visit to Charleston.

Reyna held the letter to her chest and went straight to her bedroom. Carefully, she peeled the wax seal back and unfolded the letter, which contained a second sheet.

My dearest Reyna,

This letter should be hand delivered to you by Christian Thagaard, an officer on the Danish merchant ship Odense that will be stopping in Charleston. I posted my last letter from Hampton, Virginia on May 12th, 1780 which was, as I sadly learned, the day Charleston surrendered. Since then, I have been worried about your safety, knowing the British and their Loyalist friends like to hang those who want independence.

The fall of Charleston brought the war to our doorstep and makes everything more difficult for all of us. No longer can Scorpion bring prizes to Charleston; nor can I, when I am not at sea, come visit you. But we will endure and win if we do not lose faith in our cause. We are at war with the most powerful country in the world. At sea, we are outgunned and outnumbered. However, we on board Scorpion believe that our desire for freedom and independence will carry the day.

We brought three prizes into Hampton: a sloop-of-war, a frigate and a troopship. Neither of the warships will bring much in the way of prize money because they were badly battered by Scorpion's cannons. Since then, we searched for prizes in the Caribbean and the Bahamas without success. The British have started using frigates to escort convoys of merchant ships to keep them away from privateers and the likes of Scorpion.

When we learned that Charleston fell, we came south to cause the British some pain and ran into three British frigates. After a difficult battle during which we put two—H.M.S. Pilum and H.M.S. Hasta—out of action, we ran away from the third ship, which name I do not know.

Without Jack Shelton we don't have anyone on board who speaks Latin, so we have no idea what Hasta and Pilum mean. Would you ask Melody? If anyone knows, she will.

Scorpion took some damage which we didn't discover until a week after the battle when we sailed to Havana to make repairs. You know the Spanish, they take their time and we probably won't leave until sometime in the last week in July. Hopefully, the Royal Navy won't be waiting for us, tho' surely by now, their spies know we are here.

Words cannot express how much I miss you. Every day, I look at the likeness I have of you and pray that I will come home safe. So far, Scorpion and I have been very lucky, for we have suffered very few casualties. Yet, when I am on the quarterdeck, I know that splinters, musket and cannon balls do not respect anyone and I could fall at any time. If I die, my last mortal thought will be of you.

I apologize for my morbid thoughts. Despite them, I am confident that we will prevail. After our victory, I will return to Charleston so we can spend the rest of our lives together.

Reyna, I love you with all my heart and my soul. You bring light to my days. Soon, we will be together again!

Your fiancé and soon to be husband,
Jaco

To be continued in the next Jaco Jacinto Age of Sail novel:

Death of a Lady.

Prize Money Formulas

To sailors on warships and privateers in the 17th and 18th Centuries, prize money was a big deal. For a ship's captain, capturing a prize could bring generational wealth. To an ordinary seaman, his share could be a year or more of his wages.

Prize law became relatively well defined during the Seven Years War and by the end of the American Civil War, prize law, as we know it today, was fully developed. A discussion of the legal issues is well beyond the scope of this section of *Carronade* that is intended to help the reader understand the amount of money at stake.

Prizes taken by the Royal Navy were usually turned over to a British Admiralty Court either in England or in a colony (Vice Admiralty Court) which then handled the disposition of the ship. Royal Navy captains were then free to go back to sea knowing the process that will pay them and their crews was well-defined.

Privateer captains were faced with a different set of choices. One, they had the option of waiting in the port where they brought the prize until the sale of the prize and its cargo was complete. Two, they could take payment in "cash" or a draft. Or three, they could accept an IOU in which the court would collect the sale price, deduct its fee, and the write a draft which would be sent to the owner of the privateer. These IOUs were negotiable instruments.

The Thirteen Colonies and the Continental Navy followed roughly the same process as the Royal Navy except if the colony did not have an Admiralty Court, either an auction house or a local court supervised the transaction. On January 15th, 1780, after repeated urging by General Washington, the Continental Congress passed the law that created the Court of Appeals in the Case of Capture to specifically handle sale of ships taken as prizes.

Once the captured ship was in port, a surveyor appointed by the court evaluated the ship and its cargo. This assessment became the basis of the IOUs as well as the auction value of the ship. Repairing battle damage were usually paid for by the buyer.

The Continental Navy used a variation of the Royal Navy's prize money formula. And, within the Continental Navy, captains used the promise of prize money as a recruiting tool by changing the allocation based on rank.

When he was captain of *Providence* and later on *Ranger,* John Paul Jones reduced his share and increased the percentage given to the crew. What follows is a comparison of the formulas used by the Royal and Continental Navies and what I am calling the 'John Paul Jones Formula'. All of these are net of court fees.

Category	Royal Navy Formula	Continental Navy Formula	Typical American Privateer Formula	John Paul Jones Formula
Admiral, Congress, Consortium owner	one eighth	one eighth	two fifths	one eighth
Ship's Captain	one quarter	one quarter	one fifth	one eighth
Lieutenants, Marine Officers, Surgeon	one eighth	one eighth	one tenth	one eighth
Warrants - Bosun, Carpenter, Gunner, Purser, Quartermaster	one eighth	one eighth	one tenth	one eighth
Midhipmen, Marine Sergeants, Mates	one eighth	one eighth	one tenth	one eighth
Remainder of the Crew	one quarter	one quarter	one tenth	three eighths

Privateers had crew sizes that were all over the map and their pay scales varied from consortium to consortium

Throughout the rebellion, sellers of goods and services preferred to be paid in silver Spanish dollars, English pound notes or coins or Dutch guilders. Why? Because each of the Thirteen Colonies issued their own script and the Continental Congress did the same. Without any established value or basis for the currencies, the 14 different currencies quickly became worthless. Conversion rates for Continental dollars to British pounds or guilders or Spanish dollars or French lives are difficult to determine because there was no standard, and the value of the Continental dollar plummeted like a rock.

Pay in the Continental Navy was based on the skill of the individual. The Royal Navy was a bit more specific; captains were compensated based on the rating of the ship, i.e., a captain of a first-rate ship of the line made more than the captain of a fifth-rate frigate shown in this chart.

Ship's Crews and List of Major Characters

Scorpion

Captain—Jaco Jacinto (all cruises)

First Lieutenant—Jack Shelton (until he is blown over the side in April 1779)

Second Lieutenant—Hedley Garrison (1778 and 1789 cruises), replacesJack Shelton as First Lieutenant

Third Lieutenant—Philip Patterson (1778 cruise)

Third Lieutenant—Lewis Payne (1779, 1780 cruise), promoted to Second Lieutenant 1780

Midshipman—Earl Wilson (1778 cruise)

Midshipman—Morton Geiger (1779, 1780 cruise), promoted to Third Lieutenant for 1780 cruise

Midshipman—Josiah Marshall (1779, 1780 cruise)

Marine Captain—Patrick Miller

Surgeon—Dr. Alden Ferguson (1779, 1780 cruise)

Bosun—Bradley Preston

Quartermaster—Abner Jeffords

Quartermaster First Mate—Cato Cooper

Carpenter—Leo Gaskins

Seamen—Colin Landry

Seaman—Brandon Grantham

Seaman—Samuel Riddell

Seaman—Theo Nutt

Seaman—Hiram Berry

Seaman—Enos Slippers

Marine Private—Elias Marchais

H.M.S. Liber

Captain—Darren Smythe

First Lieutenant—Drew Rathburn

Second Lieutenant—Noah Soames

Midshipman—Cyrus Tewksbury

Midshipman—Chauncey Enfield

Captain of Marines—Peter de Courcy

Bosun—Agnes Louttit

Quartermaster—Elijah Stanhope

Gunner's Mate—Gavin Dawson

Carpenter—Derwyn Evans

Carpenter mate—Hugh Marlee

Seaman—Ian Flagg

Seaman—Garth Vanders

Seaman—Jonathan Williams

Seaman—Garret Benson

Seaman—Tim Herring

H.M.S Gladius

Captain—Darren Smythe

First Lieutenant—Nathaniel Watson

Second Lieutenant—Chauncey Enfield

Third Lieutenant—Cyrus Tewksbury

Quartermaster—Hiram Spivey

Bosun—Agnes Louttit

Quartermaster's mate—Wiley Darby

Gunner's mate—Jonathan Williams

Gun Captain—Gavin Dawson

Family Trees and Other Major Characters

The Bildesheims

Miriam Bildesheim, married to Leo

(Children are listed in order of age)

Chaya Bildesheim, daughter, married to Armando Delgado and manage several large farms

Devorah Bildesheim, daughter, never married, runs the dry goods store in Charleston

Yael Bildesheim, daughter, married to Ricardo Delgado, runs the Charleston Inn

Adah Bildesheim, daughter, married to Max Laredo

Eve Bildesheim, daughter, farmer

Leah Bildesheim, daughter, Rivkah's twin, married to Emory Fonseca

Rivkah Bildesheim, daughter, Leah's twin, married to Levi Navarro

The Jacintos

Javier Jacinto married to Perla Todros

Javier's brother is Gento. Together, the brothers manage South Carolina Import and Export, Ltd.

Sister Yona died in 1771

(Children are listed in order of age)

Isaac Jacinto, heir apparent to the business

Jaco Jacinto, Continental Naval Officer

Shoshana Jacinto, attorney

Saul Jacinto, crippled by polio at 8, student

The Laredos

Max Laredo is married to Adah Bildesheim

Children are listed in order of age with the oldest listed first

Amos Laredo, Captain, 4th Carolina Dragoons

Eric Laredo, privateer officer, POW, and now Laredo Shipping's agent in Amsterdam

Reyna Laredo, Jaco's fiancée and medical practitioner

The Winters

Theodore (Ted) and Amelia Grayson Winters, runs a firm that provides supplies for ships

(Children are listed in order of age)

Asa Winters, Captain of Artillery and Engineers, Continental Army

Melody Winters, teacher of languages

Ezekiel Winters, student

The Smythes

Lester and Olivia Stowe Smythe,

(Children are listed in order of age)

Bradley Smythe, engineer and designer or many of the surgical instruments manufactured by Smythe & Sons

Gerald Smythe, medical doctor and chemist who compounds medicines sold by Smythe & Sons

Emily Smythe Burdette, married to Francis Burdette, solicitor, helps her mother with Smythe & Sons accounting

Darren Smythe, Royal Navy Captain

Other major characters

Stacey Davidson, Rear Admiral, Royal Navy, mentor to Darren Smythe

Greg Struthers, former Continental Navy officer, now president of the Bank of South Carolina

Henry York, solicitor and partner at Scoons & Partners

Bayard Templeton, Loyalist Charlestonian attorney who joined the British Army

Darren Smythe's and Jaco Jacinto's Ships

<u>Continental Ships Commanded by Jaco Jacinto</u>

	Scorpion (fictional)
Type	Frigate
Rigging	Square rigged with 3 masts
Displacement	600 tons
Length	155
Beam	28
Max Speed	14 knots
Crew (officers and men)	200
Main Armament	Twenty 12-pounders on 1778 cruise Twenty-two long 12-pounders on its 1779, 1780, and 1781 cruises 4 long 9-pounders 10 swivel guns

Royal Navy Ships Commanded by Darren Smythe

	***Liber* (Fictional)**	***Gladius* (Fictional)**
Type	Sloop	Frigate
Class Based On	*Swan*	*Enterprise*
Rigging	Square rigged with 3 masts	Square rigged with 3 masts
Displacement	220 tons	593 tons
Length	96’	120.5’
Beam	26’	33.5’
Speed	12 knots	11 knots
Crew	125	200
Armament	Fourteen 6-pounders	

About the Author

Marc Liebman

Marc retired as a Captain after twenty-four years in the Navy and is a combat veteran of Vietnam, the Tanker Wars of the 1980s and Desert Shield/Storm. He is a Naval Aviator with just under 6,000 hours of flight time in helicopters and fixed wing aircraft. Captain Liebman has worked with the armed forces of Australia, Canada, Japan, Thailand, Republic of Korea, the Philippines and the U.K.

He has been a partner in two different consulting firms advising clients on business and operational strategy, business process re-engineering, sales and marketing; the CEO of an aerospace and defense manufacturing company; an associate editor of a national magazine and a copywriter for an advertising agency.

He is an award winning author and four of his books have become Amazon #1 Best Sellers while another won three national awards. All of his novels have been rated 5 Star by Readers' Favorite.

The Liebmans live near Aubrey, Texas. Marc is married to Betty, his lovely wife of 52+ years. They spend a lot of time visiting their seven grandchildren.

The Captain's Nephew

by

Philip K.Allan

After a century of war, revolutions, and Imperial conquests, 1790s Europe is still embroiled in a battle for control of the sea and colonies. Tall ships navigate familiar and foreign waters, and ambitious young men without rank or status seek their futures in Naval commands. First Lieutenant Alexander Clay of HMS Agrius is self-made, clever, and ready for the new age. But the old world, dominated by patronage, retains a tight hold on advancement. Though Clay has proven himself many times over, Captain Percy Follett is determined to promote his own nephew.

Before Clay finds a way to receive due credit for his exploits, he'll first need to survive them. Ill-conceived expeditions ashore, hunts for privateers in treacherous fog, and a desperate chase across the Atlantic are only some of the challenges he faces. He must endeavor to bring his ship and crew through a series of adventures stretching from the bleak coast of Flanders to the warm waters of the Caribbean. Only then might high society recognize his achievements —and allow him to ask for the hand of Lydia Browning, the woman who loves him regardless of his station.

A Sloop of War

by
Philip K.Allan

This second novel in the series of Lieutenant Alexander Clay novels takes us to the island of Barbados, where the temperature of the politics, prejudices and amorous ambitions within society are only matched by the sweltering heat of the climate. After limping into the harbor of Barbados with his crippled frigate *Agrius* and accompanied by his French prize, Clay meets with Admiral Caldwell, the Commander in Chief of the island. The admiral is impressed enough by Clay's engagement with the French man of war to give him his own command.

The *Rush* is sent first to blockade the French island of St Lucia, then to support a landing by British troops in an attempt to take the island from the French garrison. The crew and officers of the *Rush* are repeatedly threatened along the way by a singular Spanish ship, in a contest that can only end with destruction or capture. And all this time, hanging over Clay is an accusation of murder leveled against him by the nephew of his previous captain.

Philip K Allan has all the ingredients here for a gripping tale of danger, heroism, greed, and sea battles, in a story that is well researched and full of excitement from beginning to end.

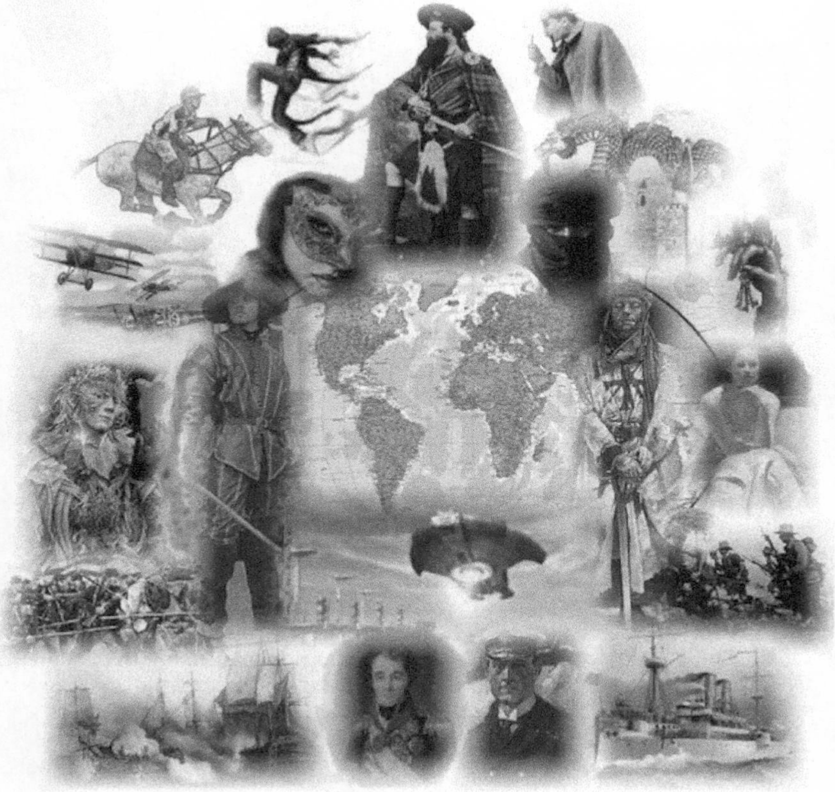

Penmore Press

Challenging, Intriguing, Adventurous, Historical and Imaginative

www.penmorepress.com

Lightning Source UK Ltd.
Milton Keynes UK
UKHW011119260821
389520UK00001B/7

9 781950 586899